A SPECIAL 2-IN-1 EDITION

A BRIDE FOR DONNIGAN

♥

HEART OF THE WILDERNESS

BY JANETTE OKE

BETHANY HOUSE PUBLISHERS
MINNEAPOLIS, MINNESOTA 55438

Cover by Dan Thornberg,
Bethany House Publishers staff artist.

Published by Bethany House Publishers
A Ministry of Bethany Fellowship, Inc.
6820 Auto Club Road, Minneapolis, Minnesota 55438

Printed in the United States of America
First Combined Hardcover Edition for Christian Herald Family Bookshelf: 1993

Library of Congress Cataloging-in-Publication Data

Oke, Janette, 1935-
   A bride for Donnigan / Janette Oke.
       p. cm.
   1. Women pioneers—Fiction. I. Title.
PR9199.3.O38B73   1993
813'.54,dc20
ISBN 1-55661-327-X   92-46297
ISBN 1-55661-328-8 (Large Print)   CIP

JANETTE OKE
A BRIDE FOR DONNIGAN

BETHANY HOUSE PUBLISHERS
MINNEAPOLIS, MINNESOTA 55438

Cover by Dan Thornberg,
Bethany House Publishers staff artist.

Published by Bethany House Publishers
A Ministry of Bethany Fellowship, Inc.
6820 Auto Club Road, Minneapolis, Minnesota 55438

Printed in the United States of America

Library of Congress Cataloging-in-Publication Data

Oke, Janette, 1935–
   A bride for Donnigan / Janette Oke.
     p. cm.

   1. Women pioneers—Fiction. I. Title.
PR9199.3.O38B73   1993
813'.54—dc20   92–46297
ISBN 1–55661–327–X   CIP
ISBN 1–55661–328–8 (Large Print)

To the special cousins
I grew up with—
Bob, Don, Richard, Tom, Kenneth Archie
And Eva

JANETTE OKE was born in Champion, Alberta, during the depression years, to a Canadian prairie farmer and his wife. She is a graduate of Mountain View Bible College in Didsbury, Alberta, where she met her husband, Edward. They were married in May of 1957, and went on to pastor churches in Indiana as well as Calgary and Edmonton, Canada.

The Okes have three sons and one daughter and are enjoying the addition of grandchildren to the family. Edward and Janette have both been active in their local church, serving in various capacities as Sunday school teachers and board members. They make their home in Calgary, Alberta.

Contents

1. Kathleen 11
2. Donnigan 20
3. Decided 30
4. Settled 40
5. No Turning Back 50
6. Preparations 59
7. Passage 67
8. Meeting 73
9. Adjustments Begin 83
10. Confused Beginnings............................. 93
11. A Start 100
12. Settling In 110
13. The Tempest 120
14. A Long Talk....................................... 130
15. Erma 139
16. Sean 147
17. Understanding 157
18. Fiona 167
19. Brenna 176
20. The Continued Search........................... 185
21. Family 195
22. Eamon 203
23. The Discovery 211

Prologue

This series of WOMEN OF THE WEST has presented a number of different personalities in various circumstances that women of the past faced, and it seems right that a little attention be given to those who came, "sight unseen," to the Americas to be brides of frontier men.

We know from history that these marriages did occur. But what do we really know about them? What would move a man to seek a complete stranger to be his lifelong mate? What kind of woman would respond to such a request? How might she feel as she traveled over oceans and frontiers to get to her unknown destination? Did the marriages indeed *work*?

I don't pretend to have all the answers—but from a little research and with a little imagination, we can journey with one such couple to that significant first meeting and experience some of the emotions they must have felt on the way to that moment—and afterward.

Chapter One

Kathleen

She stood for a long time staring through the dark of the morning mist at the posted notice. Her lips moved ever so slightly as she read again the strange words by the aid of the flickering streetlamp beside them—then read them once more to make sure she understood their meaning.

"Ladies!" The word seemed to shout off the printed paper. "The Opportunity of a Lifetime in the New American Frontier! Well-Secured Ranchers, Farmers, and Businessmen Desire Wedded Partners to Share Their Life and Prosperity. INQUIRE WITHIN."

"Surely it doesn't mean . . ." She mentally began an argument with the words. But she didn't even finish the unspoken statement. Her eyes were locked on the notice, and she read it through for the fourth time.

"Would a girl—a woman really think of. . . ?" Her argument picked up again. "No, surely not. I never could even—even *think* of such a thing."

But a few of the phrases still clung to her mind. "Well-secured." "Prosperity." And then the strange little phrase "wedded partners." Did it really mean what she thought it did? She could only imagine one possibility. But she had never heard the phrase "wedded partners" before. Was the sign really saying that men—somewhere—were *advertising for wives*?

Her slight shoulders gave just a hint of a shrug. The thin

11

coat, much too small even for her tiny frame, was reluctant to allow even that much room. She seemed to shrink back within its strained seams. The chill of the early morning made her shiver slightly in spite of her resolve to endure the cold.

"Sure now, and I'd best be on or I'll be late for my hawking," she scolded herself and was about to leave when two other young women approached quickly—excitedly.

"There—ya see it for your own eyes. I wasn't yarnin'. Look—right there."

Kathleen did not have time to move away from the notice on the wall. The girls seemed not to see her, so intent were they on their mission. They shoved right past her, and the taller of the two read the notice aloud for the shorter, more sturdy one. Kathleen took a step backward and hoped she was hidden in the shadows.

"Ladies. The opportunity of a lifetime in the new American frontier. Well-secured ranchers, farmers, and businessmen desire wedded partners to share their life and prosperity. Inquire within." There could be no mistake—the now-familiar words had been confirmed by another.

"Well, I never—!" exclaimed the shorter girl, and the two clutched each other and hooted and squealed. Kathleen found her cheeks staining red. For a reason she couldn't quite understand, she felt embarrassed.

"And you're thinking to apply?" demanded the shorter girl.

"Aye, Erma," answered the taller, a bit of Scottish brogue tinting her words. "And I've already done."

"No! Go on with ya, lass!"

Another squeal. Another shriek of laughter.

"And why not? There's no *prosperity* to be had here in London. Not for the likes of me."

"But to leave home—"

"*Home?* Home has been little more than the streets for me—"

She broke off, but her words trembled in the cold, early morning air. Both girls became instantly serious, and Kathleen again shivered in her thin coat.

"Do you think—? I mean, do you really think that a body—well, might. . . ?" The one called Erma was unable to finish the sentence.

"What's to lose?" said her companion with an obvious shrug of her broad shoulders. "We have nothing here."

Erma nodded. "And you've already signed up? What do you have to do? I mean, do you need to have a dowry? Make promises?"

"Just give your name and promise to be there on the day of sailin', that's all."

"It can't be that easy."

"But it is, I tell you. They're already holdin' a passage ticket with my name on it. I saw it for myself."

Kathleen stirred in the shadows. She had to get to work. She would lose her job if she didn't; and though it wasn't much, it was all she had, and it did bring in a few pence each week.

It was the first time the two girls seemed to notice her. Their heads jerked around in quick attention, but when they saw the slight girl move into the light they visibly relaxed.

"You gave me a start, dearie," said the bigger, taller girl.

"Sure, and I'm sorry," apologized Kathleen, her Irish accent becoming thicker with her discomfort.

"No need to fret," said the shorter Erma. "No harm done." Her voice was soft and friendly, and Kathleen felt herself drawn to her immediately. She wished—but she quickly chided herself and shook her shoulders as though to also shake off her desire for the unattainable. Yet it would be so nice—so nice to have a real friend.

"Are you thinkin' of signing up?" Erma continued, her eyes still on Kathleen.

Kathleen was about to make quick denial but Erma went on.

"Peg here has already signed. Says there's nothing to it. I . . ." The girl hesitated, then lifted her chin as though suddenly coming to her own resolve. "I'm thinkin' on signing myself."

The bigger girl, Peg, gave a squeal and reached to impetuously give her friend a hug.

"I need to get to my work," apologized Kathleen, moving to leave. "I'll be losing me job and that's the truth."

Peg cut in quickly. "When we get to America, we won't need to worry none about hawkin' posies in the street or sweepin' out the city gutters." Then she stopped and seemed to look more closely at the slender girl before her. "You've a pretty face," she observed candidly. "They'd be right glad to have you sign."

Kathleen stopped mid-stride. She opened her mouth but no words came out. She felt her face flushing again.

"If you're thinkin' on signin'," the girl named Peg said in a confidential tone, "don't wait too long. They only have room on ship for about twenty, and the passages are being taken real fast."

"Where do you sign?" Erma asked Peg quickly.

"Right there—through that door. I'll take ya in," said Peg excitedly. The two girls turned toward the door and Kathleen stood and watched them go, feeling alone and forgotten.

"If you decide to join us, we'd be most happy to travel with ya," Erma flung back over her shoulder.

So she had not been forgotten, after all.

Kathleen stirred herself once more. She had to get to work. She pulled her thin coat more closely about her shoulders, took a deep breath and moved forward. She needed to make up for lost time. If only she could hurry. If only— She shook the thoughts from her head and hunched into the biting morning air. She couldn't hurry and that was that. She would do the best she could to make up for lost work time. And she started off down the dark, dirty streets, her body rocking slightly with each step she took. The decided limp had been with her for as long as she could remember.

———

The day did not go well. Kathleen had been a few minutes late in spite of her extra effort to get there on time. The old man who ran the bakery had been terribly upset with her. He scolded and swore and threatened to cut her pay. She knew and he knew that if he did, she'd never hear the end of it from Madam.

Madam! Kathleen inwardly hated the title, though she had never allowed herself the pleasure of hating the person. She was, after all, the only mum she had. She was, after all, the woman whom her father had married two years after the death of her own mother. Kathleen, who had been a child of three when her mother died, had few memories of her own mother, but what she had she cherished.

Madam was the woman who had taken over the home and the man who was Kathleen's father. The woman who had presented him with a daughter and two sons. Three children that Kathleen herself had tended more than their mother had. Three children who were more than a little spoiled and difficult. But regardless of their faults, three children that Kathleen had quickly learned to love.

The years had not been kind to Kathleen. At seven she had lost the grandmother who had tried in her own limited way to shield and protect her. Also at a very early age she was expected to take on a mammoth portion of the household duties in spite of her thin frame and the limp that had been there since she learned to walk.

"She needs to learn the care of a house," defended the woman who insisted that Kathleen address her as Madam because of her French heritage.

Kathleen's father had nodded slowly. He did not interfere with "matters of the household," but Kathleen thought she read concern in his eyes many times.

So Kathleen had learned to do all the housekeeping chores by the time she was ten. She had also been nursemaid to the little ones, which included getting up in the night, changing their nappies, and taking them to Madam for the nighttime feedings. The limp that had begun as slight became more and more pronounced as she carted heavy babies and full laundry baskets on her tiny hip.

"She'll never marry," Madam complained to Kathleen's

father, fretting about the limp.

"Nonsense." Kathleen was surprised to hear him dare to argue. "Look at her pretty face."

"But a pretty face won't be enough. It might turn heads—but they'll quickly turn away when they see her take a step."

"I won't hear such drivel," Kathleen was surprised to hear her father state, his voice firm with command. Apparently he *did* still feel he was master in his own home. "Kathleen is intelligent and pretty. One is not—not brushed aside and discredited for—for one small flaw. Such—such drivel. Sure now—I will hear nothing of it again."

As far as Kathleen knew, Madam never spoke to her father about the limp again, but she did speak to the girl. Over and over, when the two were alone and Kathleen hurried as best she could about the house scrubbing laundry, preparing supper, or tending babies, the woman clicked and pratted over the girl's "unfortunate condition." Kathleen burned with the humiliation and unfairness of it.

And then had come the most difficult event of her young life. Her father became sick and, in just two months' time, had been taken from them. Madam ranted and raved. The man had left her, alone, with five mouths to feed. Kathleen was no longer asked to stay at home and care for the household—though most of those same tasks were still awaiting her when she returned home at nights, tired from a long day in the streets. It was not easy to find the job that Madam sent her off to secure. She was thirteen and frail and basically unskilled except in household chores. She could read and do sums—her father had seen to that.

As Madam had warned again and again, her limp figured into her success in finding employment. Most shopkeepers did not want her as an apprentice. They feared the customers would be unnerved as she moved about to serve them. Nor was she to be accepted as a governess. Only the old man at the bakery had seen her limp as a possible asset. People, bless their souls, often responded to a handicap. With her small, sensitive, and pretty face, combined with the pathetic limp that wasn't even a carefully practiced put-on, Kathleen might prove to be a good source of income selling his penny rolls and tuppence meat pies.

He had been right. Kathleen sold more wares than any of his other hawkers—though he had never revealed that fact to her. Daily he lived in fear that Kathleen might find a job elsewhere or meet some young man who would wish to make her his wife. So when she arrived a few minutes late after stopping to read the posting, the man was beside himself with worry. What if he lost her? A good share of his daily profits would be lost as well.

When she did appear, he scolded and raged and piled her basket with a larger than usual load of his baked goods.

"And mind ya get right on with it," he fumed. "Ye've already lost half the mornin' crowd."

Kathleen struggled under the weight of the load. Silently she went back out into the cold to peddle the breads and pastries.

As she called out to passersby and collected the pennies for the sale, her mind went back again and again to the words in the notice. "Well-secured. Prosperous. Wedded partners." Would a man from the American frontier be willing to accept a wife with a limp? No, it was unthinkable. But the words still stayed in her mind to haunt her throughout the entire day. She wished—she *almost* wished—that she were one of the other girls. Like Peg, tall and straight with broad shoulders and a strong back. Or the shorter one named Erma. She had such kind eyes. Such a soft voice. The girl was plump and solid, not scrawny and slight. She would have no trouble pleasing a frontier husband, with her robustness and friendly demeanor.

Then Peg's words returned to her thinking. "You have a pretty face. They'd be right glad to have you sign up."

But Peg had not known of her limp.

Just as quickly, the words of Madam came to mind. "But a pretty face won't be enough. They'll turn away when they see her take the first step."

It was true—even a frontier man would never accept the likes of her as a "wedded partner."

At the end of the long, difficult day, Kathleen made her way home through the gray streets, the gray buildings now enshrouded with gray fog. The gray gutters were almost hidden by the deeper gray shadows. Her shoulders drooped with weariness. Her steps dragged, accenting her limp.

Undoubtedly the week's washing was still to be rubbed out on the scrubboard. There was supper to prepare. She did hope that young Bridget had been sent to the shops for meat and vegetables. When the days were damp and chill with fog, the younger girl often refused to go.

Kathleen loved Bridget in spite of her willfulness. There was no way that she could have withheld her love. The girl looked like their father. Kathleen, he had told her over and over before his untimely death, was the picture of her mother. So Kathleen mothered Bridget, even as Madam spoiled her. Kathleen did so want the young girl to grow up to be a credit to their father. To that end, she pleaded and scolded and fussed at her young half sister, teaching her manners, letters, and sums. For the most part the girls got along well—unless Madam interfered and chided Kathleen for "demanding" too much of one "so young and delicate."

Kathleen reached the small cottage and pushed open the heavy iron gate with her shoulder. The gate growled and whined on its rusty hinges.

"And if Father were here, he would use some oil," Kathleen said to herself. "It won't be long until it'll refuse to budge."

A deep sigh escaped her as she moved toward the crumbling concrete step. She dreaded to enter the room and deposit her few small coins on the kitchen table. The house, always dark with gloom since her father had died, represented so much work to be done. She wished that she could just— What? She didn't really know. All she knew was that she wished she didn't have to lift the latch and cross the threshold into the dank kitchen chamber, the gloom, and Madam. But enter she must.

She put her hand on the door latch and dragged her reluctant foot up to the last step.

With a flurry that was totally unexpected, the door jerked inward out of her grasp. There stood Bridget, hair tossed, cheeks flushed, hands clapping to her breast. "Kathleen!" she shrieked. "You'll never guess what has just happened! Mama is marrying again!"

Chapter Two

Donnigan

"Whoa."

The man shifted slightly to draw back on the reins he held firmly in a large, calloused hand. The big black he was riding immediately responded to the command, though he tossed his head and champed on the bit. The man smiled and reached out his other hand to stroke the wind-swept mane. The horse's neck was warm and damp with sweat beneath his touch. They had both enjoyed the run.

He swung one long leg over the horse's back and stepped down from the saddle. As he moved away, the horse followed, still working on the bit and tossing his head.

"Don't be so impatient," the man said, but the tone was gentle and his voice was low and deep, touched softly with the drawl of the south.

His eyes swept the fields before him. It was his first crop—and the grain he had planted already stood tall on sturdy stocks. He couldn't hide the sparkle in his eyes, but the big stallion who rubbed his nose impatiently on his master's shirt sleeve did not seem to notice.

"Look at it, Black," he said to the horse, for he had to speak to someone. "Best crop I've ever seen."

The black just snorted.

He stood for several more minutes surveying his fields, then turned back to the horse. "Don't know why you're always in such a hurry," he scolded. "We've got all day."

But the black blew and lifted his head. As he felt the reins being gathered once again, he tossed his head at this signal that they were about to resume their journey.

The horse was big, but the man was in direct proportion. He was tall, being six foot two, his shoulders broad, his arms tight with muscles built by hard work on the land. Thick blond hair above a ruddy complexion and a pleasant expression completed the picture.

He swung up into the saddle easily and lifted the reins. The black jerked around eagerly and sprang to a gallop back across the ridge the moment he felt the touch of heel to his side.

When they reached the fork in the trail, the man turned the horse eastward instead of toward the building site, and the stallion did not hesitate. He knew every trail of the farm almost as well as his master, and this direction took them to the pastures where cattle and horses fed lazily on plentiful prairie grass.

They had to stop to open a gate. The horse stomped and snorted his impatience, but the man was slow and deliberate in each movement. "Easy, Black. Easy," he drawled softly as the large animal tugged on the reins.

They entered the pastures together, and the man turned back to lift into position the wooden post that supported the gate wires, slipping the loop of wire over the top to fasten it securely. Then he remounted and they were off again.

By now the sides of the black were shiny with sweat, but the man still had to hold the horse in check.

The man's closest neighbor, Wallis Tremont, had once observed, "I think thet horse'd run 'til he dropped." His voice had conveyed his admiration as he looked at the animal.

Donnigan smiled now at the thought and had to admit that Wallis likely was right. The black sure did love to run.

Man and horse crossed a small creek, wound their way up a hill, and topped the crest to look out over a sweeping valley. There beneath them grazed fifty-odd head of prime stock. The sparkle returned to Donnigan's eyes, and a slow smile turned up the corners of his mouth and crinkled the tanned skin around his eyes.

"Spring calves sure do look good," he told the horse.

The black pawed the ground.

"I know, I know," he said with a chuckle. "You want to see the horses."

But he did not give the horse permission to move on. Not just yet. He loved to look out at the herd as it grazed peacefully in the valley. He had long dreamed of just such a scene before him. His. Yet even now he could scarcely believe that the dream had actually come true.

Oh, not all of it. He still had a ways to go. Still had fences to build and buildings to raise. And there were the payments to make. His crops were still in the fields. His herds were not the size he hoped to make them. But the crops looked good. The herds would take care of their own growth. He had good stock. That was what counted. And time would take care of the line of annual payments that stretched out before him. He felt good. Blessed. Happy. He was right where he wanted to be—and still young enough to enjoy many years of being there.

Donnigan's body shifted as the big black beneath him pawed the ground again and snorted his annoyance at being kept in check.

"All right. All right," said the man, for the first time just a hint of impatience in his voice.

He lifted the reins and urged the horse forward. "So where do you think they'll be feeding?"

The black did not wait for a second invitation. With a toss of his head he headed south, taking the rise in long, powerful strides, the foam on his broad chest flecking the man who sat in the saddle.

"Easy. Easy," Donnigan chided gently, his hand slightly tightening the reins.

They topped the rise, and there they were—three geldings, seven mares, and six foals. At the sound of the approaching hooves all heads lifted and excited whinnies welcomed the black. One mare left the herd and trotted toward them, her head held high, her nostrils distended. Other mares joined her, trotting a few paces, stopping, snorting, tossing heads and swishing tails. The geldings shifted about, seeming uneasy at the appearance of the black stallion. Only the younger foals seemed unaffected. They fed or gambolled or chased after dams just as though the big black was not quickly covering the distance between them.

Donnigan rode right up to the shifting herd. They swirled and bolted around him, and though his demeanor seemed just as relaxed, his eyes were ever alert for the playful kick that could mean a bad bruise or even a broken leg should it strike a rider.

"Look at that young colt," he said to his black. "You ought to be plenty proud of him. He looks just like you."

The colt was playfully nipping another foal and dancing and kicking in mock battle.

The black paid no more attention to the colt than to the rest of the milling herd.

Donnigan studied each of his horses carefully. For the most part he was more than pleased with what he saw, but his eyes did narrow when he saw Sergeant, one of his work geldings, appear to move forward with a very slight limp. He seemed to be favoring his right front leg. Donnigan watched the horse take a few more steps, his eyes squinted against the harsh afternoon sun, and then he lifted his rope from the saddle horn and moved the black into closer proximity.

With one quick flick of his wrist the rope snaked out and encircled the neck of the surprised roan. He did not fight the noose about his neck, but his head lifted and he snorted his complaint.

Donnigan moved the black to a hold position and swung down from the saddle.

"Whoa, boy. Whoa, Sarg," he soothed as he moved along the rope to the gelding.

Gently his hands began to rub the nose, caress the neck, and then slide down toward the right front foot. The horse responded by lifting the foot when the hand reached the hoof. Donnigan was relieved at what he found. No serious problem, simply a small stone lodged against the frog.

Holding the hoof with one hand against his bent knee,

he reached into his pants pocket and withdrew his knife. After opening the blade with his teeth, he began to gently nudge the stone from its wedged position, all the while talking soothingly to the horse.

When the stone was gone, Donnigan ran a practiced finger over the entire area. There seemed to be no damage—no swelling. The horse should be fine.

Patting the gelding again, he released the leg and slipped the noose from the roan's neck. The horse did not step back but reached instead to rub his nose against the tall man's shoulder.

"Go on with you. Get outta here," said Donnigan affectionately with another slap on the animal's neck. "You won't be needed in the hay field for a few days yet."

The roan flung his head and moved slowly away, and Donnigan made his way back to the black, coiling his rope as he moved.

He replaced the rope on the saddle horn and reached for the reins. His eyes passed over the herd that had gradually stopped its shifting and returned to grazing.

"See that, Black. They're ignoring you already," Donnigan chuckled and rubbed the horse's nose. Then his eyes lifted to the sky. It was a clear, sunny day. A perfect day for— something. But Donnigan wasn't sure just what he would do with it.

It would be another week before the hay was ready. The crops were well on the way but far from harvest. The fences were mended, the barn cleaned and strawed. With plenty of water and feed, the cattle needed no care in the summer months. The horses had just been checked. The roan was now moving about with little trace of his former limp.

"Guess we aren't needed here," he said to the stallion. "Might as well head on home."

He gathered up the reins and stepped up into the saddle again. The black shifted and snorted. Donnigan knew that the horse would prefer staying with the herd. But it was almost two miles back to the house, and Donnigan had never enjoyed walking for no good reason. And he certainly had no intention of walking that afternoon in the hot sun with a saddle on his shoulder.

"Come on," he urged the black as he laid the rein against his neck to swing him around. "You'll be with the herd soon enough."

Then he added softly as though to himself, "At least you got a herd to go to. Me? I have to content myself with having conversations with critters."

And suddenly the joy seemed gone from the day. It was wonderful to have a dream fulfilled—but he sure was lonely.

———

By the time Donnigan had reached the farm buildings, the cloud of discontent had settled firmly about him. Not one to be given to brooding, he tried hard to shake the feeling. Surely, he reasoned, when he reached home and looked at the snug frame cabin that was his, the sturdy log buildings that were his barn and outbuildings, the strong, upright fences and corrals that he had spent days laboring over, the mood would leave him.

But even as he reined Black in before the corral gate and prepared to dismount, he realized he still felt discomfited.

He wanted to shake himself. To rid himself of his morose thoughts. To chide himself for feeling "down" when he had just surveyed so much that should make him feel "up."

"What's gone wrong?" he said aloud and realized that he was not talking to the black but to himself.

He had no answer. He just felt—yes, lonely. But surely a man who lived alone had a right to his lonely times. It seemed natural enough.

But as Donnigan moved to give the stallion his rubdown and return him to the corral, to the trough filled with clear spring water and to the manger filled with sweet hay, his thoughts were not easy to shake.

He was even more troubled when the black moved away from the water and hay and straight to the corral fence that was the closest he could get to the distant herd. He pushed his large body against the rails and lifted his head in a long, plaintive whinny.

The lonely call of the stallion seemed to shake Donnigan to his very soul. For a moment he regretted that he hadn't left the horse in the pasture with the herd and walked home through the heat. It seemed cruel to separate him from his kind.

In the next moment Donnigan lifted the saddle from the rail where he had placed it, then whistled to the horse. The black swung around, tossing his head and trotting obediently toward Donnigan.

"Don't get too excited," Donnigan warned him gently. "We're not going back to the herd. But I gotta talk with someone before I go stir crazy. We're gonna go see Wallis."

———

As expected, the stallion had wanted to take the trail back toward the pasture, but with a gentle nudge on the rein, Donnigan urged him toward the rough tract that was the country road. Black didn't argue, being too well trained to fight the command. Soon they were loping easily in the direction of the neighbor bachelor's place.

Donnigan wondered if they would find Wallis at home, but as they swung down the lane, Donnigan saw the man come to his door and peer out into the bright sun. Then the door swung fully open and Wallis squinted out at them.

"Tie yer horse and come in," he invited. "I was just gettin' myself some grub."

It seemed too late for dinner and too early for supper in Donnigan's thinking, but he only smiled. Wallis was not known to keep another man's time schedule.

He tied Black and followed the man into his shack, beating the road dust from his chaps with his Stetson as he walked.

The one room of the small cabin was in its usual disarray.

"Pull up a chair," invited Wallis.

Donnigan picked up a broken bridle and tossed it on the

floor in the corner as he took the chair Wallis indicated.

"I've had my dinner," Donnigan informed him as he moved toward the stove. "Just a cup of coffee."

Wallis lifted a coffee cup from the bit of cupboard and swished a dirty piece of dish towel around its interior. Then he reached for the heavy enamel pot and poured a cup of the black, steamy liquid. Without comment Donnigan accepted the cup and took a sip. It was strong as tar and as hot as shoeing tongs. He put it down on the table and licked his lips to cool them.

"So what brings you out?" said Wallis around a bite of bread and gravy. "You're usually too busy fer neighboring in broad daylight."

Donnigan smiled. "In between chores," he said without rancor. "Hay's not quite ready yet. Thought I might just get a little visit in."

Donnigan dared another guarded sip of coffee, looking at Wallis over the cup's rim. His eyes had taken on a certain knowing glint.

"Went to town the other day," Wallis said slowly, as though wanting to check his tongue but unable to keep his news to himself. "Got myself a paper."

Donnigan didn't see anything too extraordinary about that.

"Had me a talk with Lucas, too."

Donnigan knew Lucas well. He was the man who ran the local livery, stagecoach, and hotel. He had done right well for himself, folks said. In fact, he might be one who would become rich in the new West.

Donnigan sipped the coffee and nodded, waiting for Wallis to go on with his story about Lucas—or the paper—whatever it was that was making Wallis's eyes take on the shine.

But Wallis jumped right into the matter, his expression bright.

"Did ya know thet a man can order hisself a wife?" asked Wallis.

Donnigan suddenly swallowed more coffee than he had

intended. He sucked in air quickly to try to cool his scalded throat.

"Can what?" he exclaimed in disbelief.

"Can order a bride," declared Wallis.

Donnigan replaced the cup to the table slowly, frowning as he tried to comprehend the statement. "Go on!" he said at length. "You're funnin'."

"Ain't neither," declared Wallis, sounding just a bit put out. "Saw it with my own eyes. Right there in black and white."

Donnigan knew that Wallis could read nothing more than his name. He bought papers for show. A slow smile began to touch his lips. If Wallis wasn't joking, someone else was having fun at his expense.

"Who showed you?" he asked cautiously. He didn't want to offend Wallis, but he was sure now that someone had played a mean trick on the man.

"Lucas. Lucas hisself. He's sending fer one. Got her all signed up. They're bringing in a whole shipment of 'em. Be here by fall."

Donnigan could not believe his ears. The whole idea was preposterous. No. No, it was worse than that. It was degrading. Inhuman. What man would ever order a wife the same way he would buy an animal for his herd? A kettle for his kitchen? It was totally unacceptable. Unthinkable. Totally.

"I'm gettin' my money rounded up now. Almost got enough fer the ticket. You've been sayin' thet you'd like a few hogs—well, I got a couple I'll sell. Two young sows ready to farrow."

He stopped for a breath and Donnigan stared at him, still in disbelief.

"Well? Ya interested or not? If ya ain't, I'll load 'em up and take 'em into town. Someone'll want 'em."

This joke has gone too far, Donnigan was thinking. *The man is serious about this and—*

"Well?" prompted Wallis again, and Donnigan pulled his attention back to the query.

"Sure. Sure," he responded slowly. "I'm interested. I'll take 'em—the hogs, that is."

"Good," said Wallis, and Donnigan saw the light in the man's eyes again. Wallis rubbed his palms together as though he could not wait.

Donnigan felt sick. What could he say? At least until he had talked with the errant Lucas. But even the thought of Lucas made him shift uneasily. Lucas was not a man for joking around. If it had been Sam Cook or Pete Rawlings who had sold Wallis the bizarre story, Donnigan might have expected such nonsense. But Lucas!

Suddenly Donnigan knew he had to get to the bottom of the tale. He had to save Wallis from total embarrassment. He rose from his chair.

"I'd best be going," he said.

Wallis looked up from his gravied bread.

"What's yer hurry? Ya just got here."

"I—I need to ride on into town," Donnigan said lamely. Then quickly added, "When ya needin' the money?"

"By Friday," responded Wallis. "I want a wife from thet next shipment. They don't bring in another 'til spring, and I don't want to go through another long winter talkin' to myself."

Donnigan felt the loneliness of the man pierce his own soul. He understood about talking to oneself. He hadn't realized Wallis had felt that way, too.

"By Friday," he repeated, his mouth suddenly dry. "I'll have it for you by then."

He turned to go, noticing as he did that his coffee cup still held some of the black substance. Would Wallis be offended? Donnigan lifted the cup and drained it with one gulp. It was no longer scalding hot but was still just as bitter. He nodded at Wallis and reached for his Stetson.

He was about to duck his way out the creaking door when Wallis stopped him in his tracks. "Ya gonna sign up for one?" Wallis quizzed, the excitement in his voice again.

Donnigan did not even answer the question. He felt sick inside.

Chapter Three

Decided

Kathleen could not have been more shocked. She was aware that Madam had a social life outside the home. Madam kept company with a Mrs. Mercer, who introduced her to woman friends, and supposedly gentlemen as well, but Kathleen had never stopped to think of the possibility of another marriage. She stood now with her mouth open at the announcement from Bridget.

"Well, don't stand there letting in all the damp and cold," Madam scolded, entering the small room from the living area.

Kathleen moved forward and closed the door. Her eyes studied the face of the woman and she saw a flush in her cheeks. She longed to ask if Bridget had spoken the truth, but her tongue didn't seem to work.

"Why do you stand at the door when there is so much to be done? The supper isn't even—"

"I just told her about your coming marriage," interrupted Bridget.

The older woman stopped and flushed deeper, her eyes beginning to glow by the lamplight. Her hand fluttered nervously to tuck a stray wisp of hair under her day bonnet. But she gave no other response.

"I—I—" Kathleen did not know what to say. What was she expected to say? "I had no idea," she finally managed lamely.

"You are never here to inform," snipped the woman. "Mr. Withers does his calling by day, and you are always gone."

Kathleen was well aware of how her days were spent.

"He's a jolly fine old boy," cut in Edmund, Kathleen's eight-year-old half brother, as he held out the candy stick that the gentleman had obviously brought him.

"Watch your tongue," countered Madam. "You will show more respect."

The boy quickly sidestepped the hand that would have cuffed his ear. His eyes danced merrily as he laughed at his mother's failed, weak effort toward correction, and he left the room, still licking his candy treat.

"He *is* pleasant," Bridget assured her older half sister. "He has even promised that I may go away to the Academy."

The thought of Bridget leaving brought an unexpected stab to Kathleen's heart.

"Charles is to go off to school, too," went on Bridget.

"Oh, dear!" exclaimed Kathleen. It seemed that there had been a whole host of changes in her life in a few brief hours.

"And we will even be moving," broke in Charles, who had just entered the room. "To the countryside. I can hardly wait. I do hope I can have my own pony."

"Moving?" Kathleen cast a quick glance in the direction of her stepmother.

The woman just nodded as she began smoothing the lapel of Charles's jacket. She was always fussing over Charles. Kathleen had long observed that he was his mother's pet.

"Moving where?" Kathleen dared to ask.

"Now you needn't bother your head none about it," said the woman, as though all the changes would not affect Kathleen in the least. "Right now we are in need of our supper. We will have plenty of time to discuss the future after we have eaten. Put it on to cook, and while you are waiting you can start the scrubbing. I'll need my blue dress for tomorrow. It needs freshening. Mind you watch that the color does not run into the white collar."

With those words she turned and left the room, shooing her offspring ahead of her.

Bridget looked back over her shoulder. "I put the meat in the back cupboard," she called. Kathleen was relieved that the supper items had been purchased.

At the same time, she felt the anger within her burning her cheeks. Why was she always treated like a—like a common domestic? Quickly Kathleen pushed the anger aside. She should be thankful that she had a family, a home—just as Madam was always reminding her. Daily she saw girls her age who lived totally on the streets. Their lot was not a good one.

Suddenly her thin coat seemed heavy on her shoulders. She shrugged out of it and hung it on the peg by the back door. Marriage! She had never thought of the possibility. Though she didn't know why it had not occurred to her. Madam was still a young woman. And she was still appealing—in her own sort of way. Kathleen really should not be surprised to hear that a gentleman friend had proposed marriage to her stepmother.

Tired and chilled to the bone, she moved to the cupboard and began to prepare the supper vegetables and meat. She wished there was not laundry to do. It had been such a long and difficult day.

Then a thought came that lifted her spirits somewhat. With the marriage—and the move to the country—she would no longer need to tramp the dull back streets of London each day, calling out her wares. For that much she could be thankful.

She added coal to the kitchen stove. With the warmth of the fire cooking the evening meal and bending over heated scrub water, she was sure to feel warm again before long. She almost welcomed the thought of plunging her hands into the hot suds. She hastened to get the meat on to cook.

"I know that Mama said you didn't know Mr. Withers because you are never home when he calls," said Bridget after they had retired that night.

Kathleen nodded silently into the darkness.

"But do you know what I think?" went on the younger girl. "I think Mama doesn't want you to know him."

Kathleen stirred restlessly.

"Or—that Mama didn't want *him* to know you—I'm not sure which," went on the young girl candidly.

"What do you mean?" asked Kathleen.

"Well, either Mama was afraid that he'd think you pretty or—"

Kathleen couldn't believe the girl's ridiculous statement, but young Bridget hurried on. "Mama has always been jealous of you, you know. Papa often said that you looked like—like your mama, and—well, my mama didn't like it. She feared he preferred—"

"That's ridiculous!" Kathleen cut in quickly.

"You might say so—but it's true," Bridget insisted. And then she added, quite unknowing of how deeply her words hurt her older sister, "But of course she is also ashamed of your limp. She has always been afraid that someone will think you are her child, and she doesn't want a—a—cripple. She seems to fear that a man will think there is something wrong with *her*. That she might—might mother another child in—in even worse condition. I think that's the real reason she made sure that Mr. Withers has never had the opportunity to meet you. She keeps saying to him—oh, I've heard her myself, 'There are four of us. I have three children.' And she presents us just as though that's all there are."

There was silence.

"Kathleen? Have you fallen asleep while I'm talking?" Bridget asked into the darkness.

"No," came the soft reply.

"Why don't you answer?" prompted her half sister.

"What should I say?" responded Kathleen. Indeed, it seemed that the plans for the future had been made with no thought given to her.

"When we move—" began Bridget, but Kathleen interrupted.

"When *you* move," she corrected. "Sure now, can't you see,

Bridget? There are no plans for me to move with you."

Bridget stirred beside her in the darkness. Kathleen heard the sharp intake of breath and was sure the younger girl had not fully understood the situation before.

"I won't go without you," Bridget declared, her hand reaching out to grasp the arm of Kathleen's nightgown. "I won't." Her voice rose sharply, and Kathleen feared that her outburst would awaken the woman who slept just beyond the thin wall.

"Sh-h-h," she cautioned.

"Well, I won't."

"Sh-h-h," Kathleen said again, and her own hand went out to rest on the younger girl's flanneled shoulder.

"What will you do?" Bridget finally asked, a sob in her voice.

"I have my job," said Kathleen with more assurance than she felt.

"But where would you live?"

It was a question Kathleen could not answer, but she tried to keep her voice controlled as she responded with seemingly little concern. "There are places. Lots of places." But even as she said the words, she knew she could afford none of them on a hawker's pennies.

"When is the wedding—?" she began.

"Mama's? The end of the month. We will stay here until then. I heard Mr. Withers and Mama making their plans. He will send a carriage for our things and on the day of the wedding—"

But Kathleen wished to hear no more.

"We must get some sleep," she told the younger girl. "I was late for work this morning—and I don't want to be late again. I will need to be up early to get breakfast on."

The younger girl did not respond. Kathleen patted her arm in the darkness to let her know that she was not upset with her, then rolled over onto her side to try to get some much-needed sleep.

The minutes ticked slowly by.

In the darkness Bridget stirred.

"Kathleen," came a whisper at last. "I really meant it. I don't want to go without you."

"You may have no choice," Kathleen responded without turning over. "Madam gives the orders."

————

As Kathleen lay beneath the blankets, the even breathing of Bridget telling her that the younger girl was asleep, her troubled thoughts would not allow her the luxury. "What will I do? What will I do?" her brain kept repeating. The posting she had seen that morning suddenly intruded on her thinking.

"If I only had two good legs I wouldn't hesitate for a minute," she dared to think. "Surely my situation in the Americas couldn't become any worse than it is here."

But even as she entertained the thoughts, she wasn't sure of her bold statements. Maybe there were worse situations. At least she had Bridget and Charles and the spoiled young Edmund. At least she had a roof over her head and a warm bed at night. At last sleep claimed her in spite of her troubled thoughts.

Morning came all too soon, and Kathleen was reluctant to climb from the warm bed and stoke up the fire in order to make the breakfast porridge.

She was busy in the kitchen when the door opened and Madam herself appeared. She was enveloped in a warm, new-looking robe, her cheeks void of their usual rouge and her hair wrapped in bits of rag curlers.

"I know you must be wondering about your circumstance," the older woman began without preamble. "You have two choices. I don't wish to dictate your fate. After all, you are not my child." *Nor my responsibility* hung unspoken but unmistakable in the air between them. She hesitated ever so slightly.

"If you wish to come with us to the countryside," she continued, "I'm sure we will be able to find some position for you as household staff. You are quite useful in the kitchen.

Mr. Withers would be willing, I am quite sure, to accommodate a—a family serving girl."

The words stung Kathleen but she held her tongue.

"Or—if you wish to remain in London—you have your job. No doubt the baker will allow you to continue to work for him."

Kathleen still said nothing—just stirred the porridge round and round with the heavy wooden ladle.

The woman muffled a yawn. "There," she said, as if she had discharged all obligations. "It will be up to you." Then she turned and started from the room.

"I feel particularly weary this morning," she said as she left. "I won't be up for breakfast. Have Charles bring my tea and porridge to my room."

Kathleen continued to stir—looking deep into the porridge pot as though searching for an answer to her problem.

Her feet slowed as she walked by the posting, but she did not intend to stop. She knew the words by heart anyway. "Ladies! The opportunity of a lifetime."

Her eyes glanced at the words as she moved to pass by. Then she hesitated. Had it indicated anything about when one must decide? She stopped just long enough to glance over the words one more time to try to catch a date. She saw none.

Just as she moved away, a man stepped suddenly into her pathway. With a startled exclamation, Kathleen stopped.

"Are you joining our adventure?" he asked her in an accent Kathleen could not identify.

"Sure now, and what adventure are you speaking of?" Kathleen responded hesitantly, her voice lilting with her Irish tongue.

"Why, going to America, Miss—just like the sign says. Wonderful opportunity. Wonderful. And only a couple passage tickets left. If you want one you—"

"No," said Kathleen, shaking her head nervously. "No, I'll not be wanting one."

The man stepped forward and reached out a hand to tip her face toward the light from the lamppost. Kathleen felt a moment of panic.

"It's a shame," he said candidly. "A face as pretty as yours would be welcomed in America."

Kathleen angrily twisted away from his hand. He seemed to sense her annoyance.

"Pardon, Miss," he said, but his words and his tone contradicted each other. "I didn't mean to offend—just wished to see your face more closely."

Kathleen stepped back, her Irish temper quickly cooling.

"I thought you might be interested," the man went on as though to excuse himself. "That's all."

"And if I am?" The words had left Kathleen's mouth before she even knew she would say them.

"If you are—then come into my office and we'll talk about it."

"I'm lame!" Kathleen spat out, her anger flaring again. "I'm lame. No man—even in the Americas—would wish a lame bride, and that's the truth now."

But the man seemed not to notice her angry words. Instead, he studied her flushed face and sparkling eyes, and a smile crossed his features.

"Why don't you come in for a minute and we'll—"

"I'm a cripple!" she shouted at him again, and moved to pass the man. "See for yourself, sir," she flung back over her shoulder. And she began to clump her way, exaggerating her limp in order to convince the man.

"And what's a little limp?" the man called after her. "In America we allow people to be—different. We are all lame—in one fashion or another."

Kathleen wheeled to give him a piece of her mind, but she saw that he was not teasing her. His face looked serious. His hand was stretched out to her. Her rage subsided in spite of herself.

She stopped, swallowed, and took a deep breath.

"And when does this ship sail?" she asked almost in a whisper.

"In a fortnight" he answered.

Kathleen held her breath.

"I already have nineteen fine young women like you signed for the voyage. I need two more to fill the offers I have from America," the man continued in an encouraging voice.

"Nineteen?"

"Nineteen."

Kathleen could scarcely believe that nineteen young ladies had already laid their futures in this man's hands. Had the short, plump girl called Erma joined Peg in adding her name to the list?

"I'll think it over," she faltered. "Perhaps—"

"There's no time for thinking," replied the man. "I was just coming out to remove the poster. It takes some time to get all the proper papers in order. Anyone sailing on the ship will need to be signed up today."

"But I—" began Kathleen.

"What is it that gives you doubts?" asked the man.

"I know nothing about—"

He interrupted her, "If you are concerned about the gentleman that you will marry upon your arrival in America, let me assure you that they all have been carefully reviewed and selected. Each one is a law-abiding, proper citizen, well respected in his community and well able to provide, in fine fashion, for his—his bride."

Kathleen began to shake her head again.

"And if you fear that you would be rejected over a simple little limp, you do the men of America a grave injustice," he continued. "They are much more sensitive than that, Miss. The true person is found within. In America, we are quite willing to look past the—outer person."

Kathleen noticed his eyes remained on her face as he spoke. He seemed pleased with what he saw there. She wondered momentarily if his words carried truth. Was he really looking past the outer person—or just past the limp that carried the person along?

"I—I'm late for my work," she said simply.

"If you wish to sign—I'll hold the place for you until tomorrow morning. If you stop by tomorrow, I can get right on with the paper work and we should still be able to get you to America."

Confusion swirled about Kathleen. He was offering her a chance to go. He was saying that her handicap didn't matter. He was giving her passage away from the dark, cold streets of London. He was releasing her from being a servant to her own kin. She swallowed, then nodded mutely.

"Tomorrow morning?" asked the man.

"Tomorrow," agreed Kathleen, and she turned and hurried off down the street. She would be late two mornings in a row. The baker would be furious—and it would be all Kathleen could do to keep from responding to his temper. She would have to bite her lip and swallow back the words that she wished to use in response. Her job, her few pennies in wages, would depend upon it.

Chapter Four

Settled

Donnigan allowed Black his head on the trip to town. He felt strangely agitated by Wallis's report. The man really seemed to believe that he was able to order himself a wife. And from where? And who would she be when she arrived? Donnigan had never heard of anything so foolish. Wives came after the courting of lady acquaintances. You spotted one that was pleasing to you and went about wooing her. Donnigan didn't know too much about women, he conceded, but he knew that much. No self-respecting woman would allow herself to be purchased like a catalog item. And no self-respecting man would order one up like—like a new plow.

But Wallis was serious about it all. He was busy selling from his stock in order to raise the money. The prank had already gone too far in Donnigan's thinking. Didn't the fellas who started it, perhaps harmlessly enough, realize that a lonely man was often gullible and beyond reason?

Donnigan hoped he could keep his agitation well in check as he dealt with the situation. It was cruel to take advantage of a man in Wallis's position. Donnigan knew. Hadn't he too felt the pangs of deep loneliness? Didn't he know what it was like to have no one to share his dreams—his home? A man would do almost anything—within proper bounds—to fill the big, aching void in his life. And out here, miles from real civilization, there simply were not many women to be wooed.

Should one actually show up, she had her choice of the whole neighborhood of men and, most often, picked the one with the most coins in his pocket.

Donnigan knew that some of the young men around the area traveled to a city to find their mates. It was one thing if the man—or his pa—was a rancher with lots of hands around to see to the place while he was gone. For a farmer, it was different. Donnigan worked on his own—no hired hands to help with the farm chores or the planting. It wasn't possible to just pick up and head off to the city for the purpose of finding a wife. Wallis was in the same situation. Donnigan couldn't really blame the man for feeling desperate.

But surely *no* wife was a better situation than the *wrong* one, Donnigan reasoned, and if there was a smattering of truth to the rumor that one could just up and order one—wasn't it possible, even likely, that a person could end up with the wrong one?

Donnigan shook his head and put his heel lightly to the black's side. The horse responded gladly, whipping up dust as his hooves pounded the dirt roadway.

It was in this same dark mood that Donnigan confronted Lucas Stein. He had made inquiry and been told that the little man was busy in his office at the hotel. Donnigan shook the dust from his clothes the best he could and went in search of the man.

His knock on the heavy oak door brought a gruff growl, "Come in." But when the man lifted his head from the ledger and saw Donnigan before him, his scowl disappeared. "Harrison," he greeted. "Come in."

The change of tone was not lost on Donnigan. He did not regard the man as a friend in particular, but they got on well enough.

"Howdy, Lucas," he said, hoping that his tone held none of the agitation he was feeling.

"Sit down. Sit down," offered Lucas, indicating a dark leather chair. Donnigan did not have to cast aside broken bridles or other clutter. Lucas kept his office fastidiously.

Donnigan lowered himself slowly to the chair and wondered if he should spend time in small talk or just blurt out the reason for his trip to town. Lucas helped him decide.

"How're your crops doing?"

Donnigan's attention was easily diverted to his farm. He recalled the ride of the morning and his pleasure in seeing the crops grow taller and more mature by the day. He thought again of his herds and couldn't hide the glow in his eyes or lilt in his voice.

By the time Lucas had asked all the right questions and gotten Donnigan's enthusiastic responses, the men had conversed for some minutes.

"There are times I wish I had taken up farming," said Lucas, and Donnigan thought that he sounded sincere. "It would be so much more enjoyable to count calves and foals than spend my time adding up these miserable columns in this ledger." Lucas gave the ledger pages a disgusted flip of his hand.

"Well, a farmer—especially if he's on his own like me—has to keep a few ledgers, too, if he wants to keep things in order," Donnigan assured him and thought again of his reason for being there.

"Yeah—I reckon," Lucas responded. "Be a much better world if one wasn't so tied to balancing the books." He sighed.

There was a moment's pause and Donnigan judged it to be a good time to voice his concern.

"Stopped by to see Wallis," he said, and watched carefully for a response from Lucas. "He's in a big hurry to raise some money. Offered to sell me a couple of his young sows."

Lucas nodded, but the expression on his face did not change.

"Seems to have the notion that—that—well, he seems to have the misunderstanding that he can order himself a wife," Donnigan finished hurriedly and watched Lucas closely.

The man sat toying with the pencil he held in his hands. His head came up and he looked straight at Donnigan. "No misunderstanding," he said flatly, his expression still the same.

Donnigan felt his pulse beat faster. He willed his annoyance to stay in check.

"He thinks you told him that he'd just have to raise passage money and send off for one," he continued in an injured tone.

Lucas looked back down at the pencil. "Didn't he show

you the paper?" he asked calmly.

"What paper?"

"The newspaper with the advertisement."

Donnigan remembered then that Wallis had mentioned a newspaper, but in his excitement he had not produced it nor had he said anything about an advertisement.

"No." He shook his head.

"Well, it's right there in the paper," went on Lucas.

"Then someone has prepared a—an elaborate hoax," declared Donnigan hotly.

"No hoax. I checked it out thoroughly. It's all quite true and legal," said Lucas calmly, rolling the pencil back and forth in his hands.

"Now just one minute," declared Donnigan, leaning slightly forward. "Are you trying to tell me that the paper says you can send off for a wife just like Wallis told me and—and just order one in?"

Lucas nodded. "Something like that," he replied.

Donnigan's hand slapped down on his knee, making the dust lift and drift in a little cloud in the otherwise spotless room. He did not apologize, though he did feel a measure of regret.

"You order one? Like a—a piece of—of merchandise?" The thought was incredulous.

"Now just hold on, Harrison," said Lucas, and for the first time his eyes held some emotion. "It's not like you're making it sound."

"Then what is it like?" asked Donnigan, his face flushed.

Lucas laid aside his pencil and leaned forward. "It gets awfully lonely on the frontier," he explained as though he were talking to a child. Donnigan stirred restlessly in his chair, an expression of disgust and annoyance threatening to escape his lips.

"We need wives. We deserve a wife just as much as the next guy. But where do we get one? I don't know about you, but I'm not about to head off to the city to pick me up some painted dance-hall girl. I want a real wife. One who will be a fitting mother for my children. One who will be around to share life—not one who flirts a little bit and will run off with the next guy who comes along."

"And how do you know—?" began Donnigan.

"How do you ever know?" cut in Lucas.

Donnigan knew that Lucas had read his mind—was ready with the answer to his unasked question. How did one ever know if a marriage would be a good one? One that would bring happiness to both partners?

Donnigan took a deep breath and leaned back in his chair. For a moment the two men sat in silence, eyeing each other coolly. Then Donnigan asked his last question. "And the women—what about them?"

Lucas straightened in his chair, but his face did not flush as he again looked straight into Donnigan's eyes.

"They come out of need—mostly. For some, adventure. Or because they wish to better their circumstances. And we aren't fooling ourselves. Some of them come hoping to marry a rich man. But regardless of why they come, no one coerces them. They come voluntarily—of their own free will."

"You say 'they come' just as though—as though it has been done over and over," Donnigan observed.

"It isn't new, if that's what you're thinking. Many young women, and a few older ones, have already come to America as wives for—for the many men who would otherwise not—not have one."

"And it works?" Surprise edged his voice at this unheard-of method for finding a wife.

"Very well—in many circumstances. I checked it out myself."

Donnigan should not have been surprised. Lucas was not a man to plunge blindly into any new venture.

Donnigan straightened his broad shoulders and agitatedly tapped the fingers of his right hand on his leg. He shook his head slowly, but the fire was gone from his eyes, his voice.

"I don't know," he said at length. "It just doesn't seem right somehow."

"Don't judge too quickly—or too harshly," the man behind the desk said, reaching for his pencil again. "It is simply a matter of two people—both with needs—taking advantage of circumstances to meet the needs of both."

"You really see it—" began Donnigan.

"I really do," the older man assured him. "I could sit here and wait until I'm an old man—and never have a family of my own. Or—" He flicked the pencil in his fingers and let the sentence hang in midair.

Donnigan rose slowly to his full height. He lifted his hat from the floor where he had tossed it and turned it round and round in his hands.

"So you think Wallis is right to get himself a wife—?" began Donnigan.

Lucas nodded. "He has as much right to happiness as the next fellow," he answered evenly.

"But his place is—"

"I know," said Lucas. "Maybe she'll clean it up."

"But it's not fit—" Donnigan started.

Again the man interrupted. Donnigan wondered if he had been allowed to finish one sentence since he entered the room.

"They try their best to match the young woman with the man," Lucas said quickly. " 'Course, there are no foolproof ways of doing that. But they try. And if a man has special requests—he is free to express them when he applies."

Donnigan stood, hat still circling his hands. For one brief moment he was tempted to ask Lucas what kind of woman he had requested, but he swallowed the words. It really was none of his business. Instead, he nodded and placed his hat back on his head.

"Well," he said honestly. "I still don't like the feel of it all—but you've put my mind at ease all the same. If Wallis is—"

"Donnigan," cut in the other man and his voice was low and confidential. "You're still a young man with lots of years ahead to meet and marry—if the right girl happens to come along. But there aren't many girls in this town. I know that and you know that. On the other hand—you might just happen to get lucky."

He stopped and fiddled with the pencil, then looked straight at Donnigan. "Wallis and I are getting on. There won't be many more chances."

He stopped and tossed the pencil aside again, then shifted his position in his leather chair. "But there might not even be as many chances for you as you'd like to think." His voice lowered and Donnigan had to strain to hear. "I happen to know they aren't all spoken for—yet. If you were smart, you'd think about it. It only takes passage money and a small fee to the broker."

Broker? Was that what they called him? Donnigan winced.

"I don't think—" he began.

"Gonna be a long, cold winter," Lucas remarked, lifting his eyes from the ledger sheets and studying Donnigan coolly. "If you change your mind—come see me. Could be a real answer to some woman's prayer."

Donnigan turned and left the room. *Answer to some woman's prayer, indeed. What a self-righteous way of looking at peddling human life.*

He didn't even step into the hotel dining room to have himself a decent meal as he usually did when he was in town. He was too worked up. Too riled. Instead, he headed for the bank to withdraw the money to pay Wallis for the two sows, stuffed the money in his pocket, and went to get his horse.

As he mounted the black his thoughts were still dark and brooding. He turned the horse toward home and gave him his head. He knew the horse would want to run, and he figured a bit of wind in his face might serve to blow away a few cobwebs. Cool his agitation some.

At last he reined in the stallion and coaxed him to settle for a fast trot.

"We'll be home soon enough," he told the horse. "No use winding you."

He wished now that he'd stopped in town for a good meal. He was already feeling hungry, and he hated the thought of getting out the frying pan when he got back to the house. He was sick of salted pork and fried beans. He was sick of tough biscuits and stale coffee. Maybe he was just sick—he didn't know.

———

He stopped by Wallis's to leave off the money. The man grinned his pleasure as he reached for the coffee can stuck inside the fireplace chimney and added the dollars to his stash.

"Got it all now," he said, showing the gap in his front teeth. "I'll hustle it on into town first thing tomorrow."

Donnigan found himself wondering just what kind of woman Wallis had "ordered."

"When do you want me to pick up the sows?" he asked to shake his mind free of the nagging thought.

"I'll bring 'em on over. When ya wantin' 'em?" asked Wallis—but he was still smiling to himself.

Donnigan could hardly wait to leave, but he replied as evenly as he could, "I don't have a pen and farrowing sheds ready. I can work on them tomorrow. Should have them ready in a day or two."

"Friday? Ya be ready by Friday?" asked Wallis.

Donnigan nodded. He should be ready by Friday for sure.

"I'll bring 'em over on Friday, then. Seeing I can get into town tomorrow and take care of everything—I won't need to go Friday."

Donnigan had never seen the man so excited.

"Just think of it," Wallis said as he carefully recounted his money. "The ship will have her over here this fall. Fact is, it leaves next week, if I remember rightly."

"Do you—do you have any idea—who it is that you're—you're getting?" Donnigan didn't know if he had worded his question right, but he could tell Wallis wanted to talk about his plans.

"Sure do," said Wallis with another wide grin. "Sure do. Got her name and all the particulars right here."

He pulled a worn piece of folded paper from his shirt pocket and spread it out on the table.

"Name is Risa. Pretty name, don't ya think? Risa—can't say this next name."

For one moment Donnigan wondered how the man who could not read even knew that the name was Risa. Though perhaps he had been practicing the single name after being told what it was.

Wallis passed the paper to Donnigan. "See fer yerself," he said.

Donnigan turned his eyes to the sheet. Her name was Risa, all right. It gave her last name too, but Wallis had been right. It was a difficult one to figure. Donnigan made no attempt to pronounce it.

"Tall—five feet six inches. Blond hair, blue eyes. Pleasant disposition. Likes children. Good housekeeper. Excellent cook. Good seamstress. Likes to garden. Likes animals." The description ended, and as Donnigan read the last words he lifted his eyes to the shining face of the man before him.

"Pretty good, huh?" Wallis prompted.

Donnigan could only nod. She sounded too good to be true. *Perhaps,* he found himself thinking, perhaps she *was* too good to be true. Maybe all the descriptions of the new wives-to-be said the same positive things.

But Donnigan did not voice his questions. He did not want to dampen the spirits of the other man.

"Sounds real good," he said again, folding the paper and passing it back to Wallis.

Wallis was still smiling.

Donnigan cast one look of apprehension around the untidy small cabin. Risa sure had her work cut out for her. He shook his head and started for the door.

"See you Friday," he tossed over his shoulder.

He was about to step through the door when Wallis called out to him. He turned. The older man moved across the cabin floor and joined him in a few quick strides. "Iffen—" he began. "Iffen you'd like to get yer name on thet there list—I'd be glad to help ya out some iffen yer cash-short just now."

The words surprised Donnigan. Wallis had just sold him two sows to pay for his own "purchase," and here he was offering to help his neighbor so he wouldn't be left out.

"Thanks. Thanks, Wallis," he managed to stammer. "I think I could handle the passage money if—"

"Then ya really outta be thinkin' on it," said the other man. "Fella don't get hisself a chance like this every day."

Donnigan nodded and moved out the door.

He unsaddled his mount and gave him a good rubdown, made sure the trough had plenty of water, and measured out the oats before he turned to the house to fix his own supper.

He had never enjoyed the cooking chores at the best of times, but tonight they rankled him more than ever. He rattled pans and stomped around the kitchen. The fire was out and he was in no mood to rebuild it. He ended up eating some dry biscuits and cold beans. It all tasted like sawdust in his mouth.

He lit the lamp and picked up an old paper that lay on the floor by his chair. He wished he had remembered to purchase a more up-to-date version while in town, but he hadn't even thought of it. He'd already read this one over and over. There was nothing new or appealing on the inked pages. He ended up tossing it into the corner in exasperation.

He took a brief walk around the farm, hoping that the time under the clear sky and evening stars would help to settle him down.

It didn't work. The fact was, the more he thought about it, the more he realized how lonely his life had become. Maybe the other men were right. Maybe there was nothing wrong with getting a bride in such a fashion. Was it really that different from picking one out and going about trying to convince her that you were the man for her? Could you really know what people were like until you lived with them? Weren't even courted women full of little surprises—some good, some maybe not so good?

Donnigan went to his bed. He tossed and turned and fretted and stewed. It was almost morning before he swallowed his pride and made his resolve. Come daylight he would saddle Black and head for town. He would draw out the passage money, sign his name to the proper papers, and wait for the late September ship to arrive.

Chapter Five

No Turning Back

Kathleen stood on the deck of the *Barreth Lily* and watched the land she'd called home for more than a dozen years slip from her view. She had thought that she would be glad to see the last of it, but she was not. Her emotions were in turmoil, and her whole being yearned to slip from the ship and return to what she knew. Even though she had not been happy with her situation, it was all she had ever known.

But as Kathleen watched the shoreline fade into the morning mist, she went over for the umpteenth time the events of the last few days.

The baker, whom she had viewed as always angry and upset and berating her for not hurrying faster, selling more rolls and pies, being too frail to carry the proper-sized load, had suddenly become snivelling. "If it's more pennies ya be wantin', stay and I'll raise your take," he had declared, shocking Kathleen with his pronouncement.

She just shook her head slowly. "The arrangements are all made," she said firmly. "I can't change my mind now."

And Madam, whom Kathleen had expected to be relieved that the girl would no longer be her concern, had ranted and raved. It was apparent that the woman had really expected her stepdaughter to concede to being a member of the house staff at the new country home.

"What am I to do?" Madam had kept wailing. "Not one

50

staff member of my own to bring to the marriage. How do I
know if the others will properly receive me? How do I know
if they will carry out my orders the way I wish?"

Then she had turned on Kathleen.

"You are most ungrateful," she had accused, the tears
welling in her eyes. "After all these years of giving you a
home and shelter—and you reward me in this fashion. How
could you? You—you are a most—most unreasonable, un-
worthy *wench*!" She had spat out the last words, seeming to
strain to find something bad enough to say about the slight
girl who stood trembling before her.

Only Bridget had been genuinely sad to see Kathleen
leave her. "I shall miss you dreadfully," she had said through
unchecked tears.

"And I you," replied Kathleen, holding the young girl
close. And Kathleen's tears had trickled down her face and
fallen in the younger girl's tumbling hair.

"You will write?" Bridget had begged.

"As soon as I have an address to send you," Kathleen had
promised.

Bridget had pulled back and studied Kathleen's face, the
shock showing in her own. "You mean you don't even know
where you are going?" she asked in a whisper.

Kathleen had shaken her head. "I signed up too late," she
confessed. "There was no time to—to be matched—with an
American. But Mr. Jenks said not to worry. He will make all
those arrangements once we arrive."

Bridget's face had still reflected astonishment as Kathleen pulled her close one last time and patted her shoulder.

"Sure now, and take care of yourself," Kathleen had managed, her accent heavy with her concern.

Bridget had managed to nod her head as she wiped at
tears and then whispered conspiratorially, "When I get a bit
older, I'm coming to America too."

Kathleen had stepped back and looked at her sister.

"I am!" Bridget had declared vehemently.

Kathleen had given Bridget one more hug. "I'll be waiting for you and that's the truth of it," she had whispered against the girl's hair.

————

"There you are!"

It was Erma who interrupted Kathleen's thoughts. Reluctantly she turned from the rail to attempt a smile for her newfound friend.

"Are you still watching jolly ol' England?" asked Erma, teasing in her voice.

Kathleen shook her head. "There is nothing to see now but fog," she replied and had a hard time trying to disguise the tremor in her voice.

"Come. We are having a party," invited Erma.

"A party? What—"

"A celebration really. We have all gathered in a small room down below, and Mr. Jenks is serving wine and cheese."

Kathleen felt that she would rather stay where she was, the salty sea wind flecking her cheeks and tugging at her hair, but reluctantly she followed the other girl.

She had been more than pleased when they had gathered for boarding to find Peg and the robust Erma chatting and giggling in their excitement over the new venture on which they were about to embark. She and Erma seemed to respond to each other immediately, and Kathleen was glad to discover that she was to share a cabin with Peg, Erma, and two other girls by the names of Nona Paulsen and Beatrice Little.

It was crowded, for sure, but Kathleen was glad for the companionship, at least until she made some adjustments to leaving behind everything that was familiar.

Now she allowed Erma to take her hand and lead her hurriedly along the ship's polished, slippery planks. They went down a short flight of steps, took a turn down a narrow hallway, a right into another hall, a few more steps, another hall, up five steps, and again a right. Kathleen was beginning to feel dizzy.

"Wherever are we going?" she asked breathlessly.

"This is a special occasion," laughed Erma. "Mr. Jenks has reserved a special room. This is not where we normally will take our meals."

"I should hope not and that's for sure," responded Kathleen. "I would never find it a second time."

Erma laughed. "You'll get used to the ship," she promised. "They are all laid out generally the same."

Kathleen was surprised. "You've sailed before?" she asked the girl, who was still tugging her forward.

"My father was a captain," Erma responded. "He used to take us with him on some of his trips. I think he just couldn't bear to be away from Mum for that long."

"It must have been exciting," panted Kathleen.

"Aye. It was. I loved the sea when I was a girl." Then her voice lowered and her demeanor changed. "And then I hated it," she declared.

Kathleen stared at her wide-eyed.

"It took my father," said the girl, her voice flat—empty.

"I'm—I'm sorry," breathed Kathleen.

Laughter rippled out into the dark narrow hallway and led them the rest of the way to the celebration party.

The whole small room seemed to be filled with swirling skirts and raucous laughter. Mr. Jenks and a few waiters were the only gentlemen present. Kathleen looked about her in stunned silence. Here were the ladies addressed in the posting. Many ladies. Tall ones, short ones, plump ones, thin ones, dark ones, fair ones, young ones and, surprisingly, a few rather old ones.

They were not all pretty. They were not all well dressed. They were not even all well kept. But they all did appear to be celebrating.

As the two girls stood back, taking in the scene before them, Peg stepped from a cluster of laughing women, waved a hand that held a glass of sloshing liquid, and called rather loudly, "Over here. Join the party."

Kathleen held back but Erma pulled her forward. "Come. Let's join the fun."

Someone passed Kathleen a glass filled with—something. She took a tentative sip, didn't like it, so just held the glass in her hand and tried hard not to look too uncomfortable and conspicuous.

"I thought Mr. Jenks said about twenty girls," she managed to whisper to Erma.

"Twenty from England. The other twenty have joined us from the Continent."

"From the Continent? Mercy me!" exclaimed Kathleen.

"Many of the American men came from the Continent," Erma explained carefully. "They wish wives from their home countries. Only makes sense."

Kathleen nodded. She supposed it did make sense.

She hardly had time to think about it before a shout was heard over the din. "Here's to America," someone called, lifting her glass high in the air. More shouts followed. The party seemed to be getting more and more rowdy.

"Here's to the men," came another cry.

"Here's to their wealth," called a third girl with a hiccup and a giggle, and such a commotion followed her words that Kathleen could hardly think.

Mr. Jenks stepped forward then. Kathleen wondered if he intended to get control before things were entirely out of hand.

"Ladies!" he called. "Ladies!"

It took several cries before he made himself heard.

"Ladies. I wish I could ask you to take a seat," he smiled at them. "But as you can see, there are no chairs available."

"No problem!" shouted Peg, waving her glass in the air, and she plopped down on the carpeted floor, her skirts swirling out around her.

Giggles followed as one by one the women took her lead and settled themselves unceremoniously on the floor. Kathleen stood, her glass clutched in white-knuckled fingers, her eyes wide with shock at the scene. Never had she observed such unruly conduct.

"Ladies," said Mr. Jenks again. "I know you are all excited about this new adventure. And it *is* exciting. I wish you all the very best as you begin your new lives—in a new home—with a new—" He stopped and raised an eyebrow, then smiled at them all, "—husband," he finished, and was rewarded with loud cheers and lifted glasses.

Mr. Jenks had to wait further for the commotion to subside.

"We will be at sea for a number of days. I have a cabin located on the lower deck. It is easy to find, and I have posted my name on it in big letters. I will wish to see each one of you individually during the trip to make all the final arrangements.

"Many of you already have all of the particulars about the man you will be marrying, but a few—"

Mr. Jenks was forced to wait while the cheers filled the room again. Some girls pulled forth papers from hidden spots, like pockets, wrist purses, and bodices, and waved them in the air as they hooted. Kathleen even saw one girl raise her skirts and withdraw a paper from her stockings.

When the calls subsided, Mr. Jenks continued. "You will all need to see me. I will post a list with your name and the date and time that you are to appear. Please, try to keep the appointment. It will be most difficult to reschedule and could put your situation in jeopardy.

"You all have your room assignments. I know they are crowded but"—he stopped to smile—"you have good mates. We will do all we can to make the voyage as pleasant for you as possible.

"Now, I do have many duties to see to, so if you will excuse me. Please, feel free to stay and enjoy yourselves as long as you wish. The gentlemen here will be glad to serve you. And will show you back to your cabins, should you need assistance." He surveyed the group one more time and then added, "Good-day."

Mr. Jenks bowed and left the room to the cheers of the women.

Kathleen stood looking about her. Many of them were still on the floor. Some were even playfully rolling around, their skirts carelessly flying about them. Kathleen felt a little sick. Was this the kind of girl who "sold" herself to a man in America? *Whatever had she done?*

Her face blanched pale and she reached out to clutch Erma's hand.

"I—I'd like to go to the cabin," she managed to whisper. "Could—could you show me the way?"

Erma looked at her and her gray eyes widened. "Are you sick?" she asked anxiously.

"I—I think so," responded Kathleen. "I—I—"

But Erma waited no longer. She took the glass, still filled, from Kathleen's hand and set in on the table. It was promptly grabbed by another hand even before Kathleen could turn away.

Gently Erma led Kathleen toward the cabin. She did not rush. Kathleen had no trouble keeping up to the other girl as she limped along beside her.

"Here we are," said Erma as she opened the cabin door with the key she withdrew from her bodice. "Just you lie down, lovey, and get some rest. The feel of the sea is strange to some. I grew up with it—so I never give it a second thought."

"It's not the sea," responded Kathleen before she thought to check her tongue.

Erma's face showed concern. "Something else, then? Do you have a sickness that you didn't confess?"

All the girls had been grilled about their health.

"Oh no," quickly responded Kathleen. "I'm fine—truly. It was just—just—well I'm not used to such—such bawdy behavior. I—I—"

"Oh that," said Erma with a careless shrug.

"It was—was—oh, Erma, is that the kind of woman they expect us to be?"

"Now don't you go judging too harshly," said Erma firmly. "It's all—well, it's just a—a cover for their real feelings."

Kathleen could only stare.

Erma reached out a hand to give Kathleen a boost up on to her bunk. It was too close to the cabin ceiling. Kathleen felt as if she would soon be gasping for air, but she tried to calm her unsettled nerves. Erma sat down on the lowest bunk opposite and studied her hands in her lap before lifting her eyes to Kathleen again.

"We—we might not have come from the best—best circumstances," Erma began, "but at least we knew where we fit. Now—well, now everything will be different—new—rather—rather scary. For all of us. Oh, we know where we are going. The name of some unknown town. We know if we are to marry a farmer or a rancher or a hotel owner or—" She stopped and shrugged.

"We have been given a piece of paper with a name on it. Maybe a little information. Height, weight, age, coloring. Maybe not even that. But what do we really know? Does he have a temper? Is he quite sane? Will he make unheard-of demands? Use his fists? Drink too much?"

Kathleen drew in her breath. She had not thought of all those horrible possibilities.

"But Mr. Jenks said—" she began.

"Mr. Jenks is a man out to make a profit," Erma reminded her.

Silence hung heavy in the room as Kathleen absorbed that observation. If she had felt sick before, she felt doubly so now. She rolled to her side on the narrow bed and put her hands over her face.

"I'm not out to scare you, lovey," went on Erma quickly, "but we've all had to face the facts."

Kathleen began to sob quietly, her thin shoulders trembling against the worn gray blanket of the bunk.

Erma stood to her feet and crossed to the younger girl.

"Why did you sign on?" she asked quietly.

"Because—because Madam, my stepmother, was marrying again. She didn't want me—or so I thought. Turned out she did. Would have taken me as a housemaid. Oh, I should have gone. I should have," sobbed Kathleen.

"But you didn't have it so good, did you now?"

"No-o. No, it wasn't good," admitted Kathleen.

"Then you did the right thing. The man you wed might be—might be just the man you've dreamed of."

"I haven't dreamed of any man," sobbed Kathleen.

"Then you are a strange lass for sure," responded Erma with a shake of her head.

"Madam always said no man would want me with my limp," said Kathleen, wiping at her tears.

"Such utter nonsense!" exploded Erma. "Why, your limp is hardly more than a little tip. And with your pretty face. Why—I've already seen the deckhands givin' you the eye."

Kathleen could not believe the report. She waved the words aside with a slender hand and tried to sit up, bumping her head on the overhead planks of the cabin.

"Why did *you* sign up?" Kathleen asked, her hand rubbing her head.

"Told you—lost the captain at sea. There was a mix-up over money. We found we'd lost all else too. Between the two grieves, Mum couldn't—well, she just gave up. I lost her, too. I was alone—and well—Peg—I met her at work. She sort of took me in. Talked me into joining—and here I am." She shrugged her shoulders.

"But Peg—" began Kathleen and quickly checked her tongue. She didn't wish to criticize Erma's friend.

"She's drunk," said Erma flatly. "Don't think she's used to drink and she's just overdone it a bit. She'll come round."

Kathleen nodded.

"Truth is, it's all a means of bracing themselves a bit," went on Erma.

"Bracing?" asked Kathleen.

"Oh, I know they talk big—wave their glasses and cheer—but there's not a one of them that isn't just a bit nervous over what she's doing, and that's the way it really is."

Kathleen nodded slowly. She was beginning to understand.

Chapter Six

Preparations

In the days that followed his signing up and turning over the passage money, Donnigan had many moments of extreme doubt. There were times when he sharply berated himself and declared himself to be a silly fool to have fallen for such a ridiculous scheme.

But always when he returned to his cabin at the end of a long, tiring day, he found himself thinking of how nice it would be to be met by a warm smile, a few cheery words, and a plate filled with something hot and palatable for his supper.

It was at those moments that he could not keep himself from whispering under his breath the count of days until the ship should anchor in Boston Harbor.

He got through the haying season. He was glad for the heavy labor that sent him home so tired at the end of the day that he scarcely thought at all before he succumbed to sleep.

He had a few days of rainy weather and restless pacing. And then finally he was into the harvest season. He hoped with all his heart that nothing would happen to slow him down. But it did. More rain showers. Donnigan found them hard to endure and was almost jubilant when he heard a horse approaching and looked out his kitchen window to see Wallis tying up at the hitching rail.

Donnigan was at the door before the older man had a

chance to take a step toward the house.

"C'mon in," he called eagerly. "C'mon in."

Wallis advanced on the house, talking as he came. The man's usual chatter sounded good to Donnigan.

"This foul weather. Ain't good fer man nor beast. Here I was fixin' to have my harvest all in before thet there ship brings my lady—and then this here."

Wallis had turned from saying "Risa" and had begun to refer to the woman as "my lady." Donnigan smiled to himself. He hadn't even dared to think of his ordered bride so possessively as yet. For one thing, he still didn't know one thing about her. Not even her name. It would have been nice to have a name.

"I just got me going good—cut the west field and was hopin' fer sun—" kept on Wallis. Donnigan paid little attention. He pushed the door shut and turned to the stove as soon as the man entered the kitchen.

"Sit yerself," he interrupted. "I'll put on a fresh pot."

While they waited for the coffee to brew, they talked of farm matters.

"Thet second sow farrowed yet?" asked Wallis.

"She sure did. Got a nice litter. Six—plus a born dead. Got one runt in the bunch, but he's doing okay," replied Donnigan.

"Not a big litter—but a fair start," observed Wallis.

"Yeah. It's okay for a first one. She should do better next time."

Wallis knew the first sow had presented a litter of seven piglets—all healthy and of good size.

"They should be good sows," Wallis commented. "Came from good stock."

Donnigan nodded as he poured the coffee and took the two mugs to the table.

They sipped in silence for a few minutes and then Wallis spoke again. "Heard who yer gettin' yet?"

Donnigan shook his head.

Another silent spell.

"Must be kinda hard to wait," observed Wallis.

Donnigan nodded. "Yeah," he admitted at last. "A little."

"I been doin' a bit of fixin'," went on Wallis to Donnigan's surprise. "Ya know—when ya look at a place as a woman might—ya see it a little different."

Donnigan nodded. He hadn't even thought to look at his place through a woman's eyes. It looked just fine to him.

"So what're you doin'?" Donnigan asked his friend.

"Well, I put glass in thet there winda in place of the oiled paper."

Donnigan nodded. He had always wondered why a body would bother to have a window you couldn't see out of.

"An' I patched the roof. Rain ain't comin' in at all now."

Wallis stopped to take another long draft from the coffee cup.

"I figured how I might put up a few hooks on the wall," went on Wallis. "Ain't a place to hang bridles or nothin'."

Donnigan nodded. His bridles all hung on pegs in the barn.

"Might even put up a shelf or two," went on Wallis. "Kinda stack up the dishes and food stuff so thet they don't need to sit on the floor."

"Sounds good," said Donnigan with another nod.

"Figure I'll have it all fixed up fer her," Wallis concluded, looking real pleased with himself.

They played a game of checkers to help pass away the long hours of the rainy day, and Donnigan fixed pancakes and pork gravy for their supper. It was dark by the time Wallis retrieved his old Willie from the barn where he had been taken out of the cold rain and fed his supper.

Donnigan hated to see his friend go. He sure hoped the sun would be shining again on the morrow.

Donnigan began to take stock of his own cabin. Though it was sturdy and basically neat for a bachelor, he soon realized that it wasn't exactly the kind of home that would bring pleasure to a woman. He felt panicky. He didn't know where to start or what to do to make it more homey.

He did add a few more shelves and pegs. There would undoubtedly be more things that needed to be put away and hung up after there were two people occupying the premises. Then he went a step further and divided the one big room into two smaller ones. The smaller room at the east end became a bedroom with some privacy and the larger room was the living-kitchen space. Donnigan felt proud of himself for thinking of the idea. He even cut another window into the east end so that the bedroom would have a window all its own.

It was hard getting the job done. Donnigan was back at the harvest again with the weather cooperating quite nicely. His evenings, when he would have wished to put his feet up and rest his back a bit, were spent instead working on the changes to the house.

But even when he got the jobs completed, he still felt uneasy. The house still looked like just what it was: a bachelor's quarters. Donnigan finally gave up. When it came to frills and gingham, he was out of his element.

He did take a look at the yard. He had thought that he kept it fairly neat. Now he could see that what he thought of as neatness might also be seen as clutter. He went to work moving the woodpile a ways from the door, stacking it neatly in a long row against the back fence. He filled in a few holes that had been made by the sows when they had escaped their pens one day while Donnigan had worked the fields. He even thought of constructing a fence, but there wasn't time for that.

"It needs—it needs something," he admitted as he stood back and squinted to get a full look at the house and yard before him.

He wasn't sure what was missing, but he felt the picture he was getting was rather bleak and dull and desolate. He tried to go back in his mind to other houses he had seen in his younger years. His memory brought forth white picket fences and rose bushes in full bloom.

"Can't fix that," he said to himself, but, still dissatisfied, he shifted about to look at the house again.

At last he went to a shed and withdrew a spade. All along the path to the house and the wall by the door, he turned up the fresh soil and shook the grass roots from the dirt.

When he had finished his spading, he headed for the meadow behind the house. He had noticed many varieties of wild flowers there and considered some of them to be quite pretty.

He was disappointed to find that many of the prettier ones had finished their blooming season, but he went to work on what he found.

The transplanting was not easy. He had to trek back and forth, back and forth, one small plant after another held on the shovel surface so that its roots would not lose the dirt around them until it reached its new abode.

He was almost done with his task, gently patting another small plant in place while the sweat traced streaks down his dusty face, when a voice spoke directly behind him. Donnigan had heard no one approach and the voice startled him and brought him upright on his knees.

It was Lucas who stood beside him. Donnigan felt the color rise in his tanned cheeks. He opened his mouth to explain what he was doing, then closed it again. Lucas would have to be a fool not to see for himself.

Donnigan rose slowly to his full height and swatted the dust from his knees with the pair of work gloves he retrieved from the ground.

"Howdy, Lucas," he said, hoping that his voice held more warmth than he presently felt. "Didn't hear you arrive."

"You were busy," observed Lucas, and Donnigan wondered if he saw a glint of amusement in the other man's eyes.

"Thought the place looked rather bare," Donnigan offered in embarrassed excuse. "Don't want her shocked by the drabness of it all."

Lucas made no reply to Donnigan's remark. He was carefully studying one of the small plants that Donnigan had just placed along the walk. "Where'd you get that one?" he asked simply.

"Down by the crick," replied Donnigan, rather pleased that he had found such a pretty little cluster of flowers.

"What is it?" asked Lucas, bending down to get a closer look.

"I don't know—but it was blooming and I thought it— that a woman might think it rather pretty."

"Maybe it's a weed."

Donnigan straightened his shoulders and looked at the other man evenly. "I might not know the first thing about flowers—but I've made it my business to know weeds," he replied evenly.

Lucas rose to his feet again and nodded in concession.

"Come in," said Donnigan, moving toward the door. "I'll put on the coffee."

"Can't stay," said Lucas, and Donnigan hesitated.

"Wire came today," said Lucas. "The ship's in."

Donnigan whirled to face the other man. Suddenly he felt like a small boy waiting for the Christmas that finally arrived. It was all he could do to keep himself from tossing his hat in the air and giving a loud whoop. He restrained himself and gave a slight nod instead.

"Wallis know?" he asked as calmly as he could. He looked at Lucas and was surprised to see the undisguised glow in the other man's face.

"I'm stopping over there soon as I leave here," Lucas replied.

Donnigan swallowed hard. Never had his emotions played such havoc with his normally calm demeanor. He shifted his feet uneasily, feeling that he would surely burst at any minute.

"It'll take 'em a couple weeks to get here," Lucas continued. "They'll catch the train from Boston—then connect with the stagecoach the rest of the way. Jenks says he hopes to have them out here week from Saturday."

A week from Saturday! Donnigan's thoughts raced. After waiting for weeks—months—it suddenly seemed so soon and yet so long until he would actually be meeting—seeing for himself the one— He couldn't even think about it. It made his heart race.

He shifted again.

"Well, I'd better get on over and tell Wallis," Lucas went on. "He's right anxious."

Donnigan swallowed again and managed to nod his head.

Then Lucas reached into his inner coat pocket and withdrew a piece of folded paper.

"Here's the name of the lady you're to meet that Saturday," said Lucas casually, and Donnigan held his breath as he accepted the sheet. He felt a cold sweat encase his body, and he took a long, deep breath to steady the pounding of his heart.

He had to say something. Anything. Just so that Lucas wouldn't think him a complete fool.

"Suppose you've known your lady's name for weeks," he managed.

Lucas nodded his head. Took a step toward the team that waited where they had been tethered to a tree in the lane. Then paused and said simply, "It's Erma," and then walked away—but not before Donnigan had caught the excitement in his eyes.

Donnigan watched the man leave and then went in to put on the coffee. He knew that Wallis would be over just as soon as he got the word.

He was very conscious of the paper in his shirt pocket. He wanted to seize it quickly and pore over its contents— and yet could not bring himself to touch it. That little slip of paper—the name that it bore—was going to change his whole life.

He stoked the fire and filled the coffeepot with fresh water and poured in a handful of grounds before he allowed himself to sit down at the kitchen table and reach a trembling hand to the breast pocket.

"Name—Kathleen O'Malley," he read aloud and stopped to let the name roll over his tongue a few times before his eyes crinkled in a smile. He liked it.

"Twenty-one. Dark hair and brown eyes. Lots of experience in cooking and keeping house." That was all.

Donnigan read the paper again and again. He wished there were more—something to give him some—some indication of just what kind of person Kathleen O'Malley was. Was she tall? Short? Sullen? Cheerful? Did she like horses? Hogs? Would she want a garden spot? Hens? Was she—? Donnigan carefully folded the bit of paper and replaced it in his breast pocket. He sighed deeply. He guessed that he should be happy to have her name. At least he could step forward come the important Saturday and say, "Good-day, Miss O'Malley. I do hope your trip wasn't too exhausting."

The coffee began to fill the room with its steamy aroma, and Donnigan moved to shift it farther back on the stove.

"One thing for sure," he murmured, surprising even himself. "I hope she's not sulky and silent. I couldn't stand that. I don't want to have to still talk things over with Black once she gets here."

And Donnigan moved restlessly to the window to see if Wallis was making an appearance on the country road. He did wish the man would hurry.

His eyes dropped to the flowers he had just planted.

"Those are for you, Miss O'Malley," he said softly, and it gave him an odd sense of connection. He felt his cheeks warm. But he could not help himself from continuing—from changing his little statement. "For you—Kathleen."

The name felt new and strange on his tongue, but somehow, in the saying of it, Donnigan felt a stirring of sweet possession.

Chapter Seven

Passage

The troubles on the Atlantic crossing began on their second day out. After the raucous celebrating by the band of women on board, a time of illness followed. Kathleen could have felt that it served them right, but as she observed their intense suffering, she could feel only pity for them as they held their heads and groaned with each roll of the ship. It kept both Erma and Kathleen running to empty the chamber vessels and wipe the brows with cool wet rags.

By the time the women were once again on their feet and ready to take to the decks for walks in the open air, the winds became brisk and the ship began to toss and roll. Even Kathleen had to take to her bunk. Erma was the only one in the little band who did not become seasick.

At long last the storm subsided and the women began to stir and search for fresh air. The cabins were so small—so crowded—that even on the good days the air became stale and close. But on the days of the illnesses, Kathleen had often wondered if she would be able to endure. She longed, at times, for the cold, damp streets of London, where she could at least draw a breath of fresh air.

Though she became acquainted with many of the women heading for America, she really only learned to know well those who shared her own cabin and her own dinner table. She soon discovered that even though they shared the same future destiny, they were varied and different in their personality, background, and outlook. Some of the opinions expressed shocked and horrified the young Kathleen. She found that more and more she chose to walk alone about the decks or share the time with Erma rather than be a part of the chatter of the other women.

Many of the women from the Continent she did not get to know at all. The fact that some of them spoke very little English was of course one factor—but there were other differences, though Kathleen wouldn't have been able to put her finger on them.

"Some of them are farm women," Erma had explained, "and shy."

Kathleen had never lived in the country—at least since she had left Ireland at the age of two. Her father had spoken of the farm. To his dying day he did not cease to grieve that he had lost family property at the time he had fled his country. Always his dream had been to return—to reclaim; and though Kathleen knew nothing of the circumstances, she claimed his dream as her own after he had been taken from her.

"Sure now—and ye're an O'Malley," he used to tell her. "Ye've nothing to be ashamed of and plenty to be proud of, so hold yerself tall. And maybe someday—when God himself rights the wrongs in the world—ye'll get back what truly belongs to an O'Malley."

Kathleen wished later that she had asked more questions. Talked more to her father of his beloved homeland. Now, as the ship bore her to America, she reasoned that she would never have opportunity to see the land of her own roots again.

Perhaps other girls were grieving over lost homelands as well, for as the days passed, tempers became short and occasional disturbances erupted. One ended up in a hair-pulling duel, and two other girls were found rolling around on deck, skirts flying along with screams of obscenities. Kathleen had never seen anything like it—not even in the streets of London where such things were said to occur.

And then there was the girl from the Continent who

changed her mind about going to America after taking up
with one of the deckhands aboard ship. The whole incident
was rather scandalous, to say the least, and Mr. Jenks had
a good bit to say about it.

Kathleen waited impatiently for her appointment with
Mr. Jenks. She noted that she was the last name on his posted
list. It didn't surprise her. After all, she had signed up very
late.

However, she was not ignored. Several times during the
voyage the man sought her out. Once he even invited her to
his cabin to share his dinner. Kathleen was uneasy about
the invitation and sent word that she was not feeling well—
which, because of the tossing sea at the time, was no exag-
geration.

Still he continued to seek her. It began to be noticed by
the other women, and Kathleen found herself the butt of
crude jokes. From henceforth she tried her hardest to avoid
the man as much as possible.

As they neared the end of the journey, anticipation ran
at fever pitch. Kathleen walked about the deck, enjoying the
brisk wind that reddened her cheeks and whipped her hair.
But even as she wished solitude, she felt drawn to the others
as she heard their high-pitched, excited voices. She drew
near to a noisy group in time to catch a comment.

"The marriage ceremony comes first," a tall, bony-look-
ing girl was declaring. "I'm not putting one foot in the door
until I hear the words. No fallin' into *that* trap. I'm not leaving it so he can show me the door again if it suits his fancy."

"And I'm telling you, I won't stand for one minute of tom-
foolery," a big girl named Mary added. "I didn't come all this
way to be somebody's serving girl."

A few girls hooted in agreement.

"An' I don't plan to be slopping pigs—even if I marry a
farmer!" shouted another.

"No. Nor a milkmaid, either," called Peg.

"I'll cook—providing, of course, he gives me the makings," said a brassy older woman with a painted face and tinted hair.

"I'm hoping for a man rich enough to provide a young wench or two to help with the house chores," ventured a woman with blond hair piled haphazardly on the top of her head.

There was another shout of approval.

"Tell you one thing," a short, stout redhead said as she lifted her skirt to hike up her hose. "If I don't like what I find—I'll not be stayin' long."

A chorus of agreement followed the comment.

"And what will you do, lovey?" asked another.

"Aye—don't you worry none about Rosie. She can handle herself," replied the redhead with a wink of her eye and a toss of her skirts.

Kathleen moved away. "Marriage is a permanent thing," she argued to herself. "One doesn't pull out just because there are a few more household chores than one had hoped there would be." The whole conversation disturbed her.

Right then and there Kathleen made herself a pledge. She would stay with this arranged marriage no matter what it turned out to be. She would make it work. She would. She had agreed to it and would stick to her agreement.

She walked away from the shifting, chattering group and sought the stinging sea breezes to blow her discomfiture away.

She jumped at a touch on her arm, then saw that it was Erma who had joined her.

"Don't pay no attention to 'em," Erma said close to Kathleen's ear so that the wind wouldn't whip the words away. "It's all just nerves and bravado. We're all getting a little tight strung."

Kathleen nodded. She was certainly tight strung.

"Most of 'em are good, clean, hard-working girls who've never been away from home before. They're scared to death and that's the way it really is."

Erma moved closer to Kathleen and the smaller girl took comfort in her presence.

"Let's walk around to lee side so we can talk out of this wind," Erma suggested, and Kathleen followed with no hesitation.

They found a small bench sheltered from the wind and took refuge, wrapping their shawls tightly around their shoulders for warmth.

"There now," said Erma, giving Kathleen a forced smile, "this feels better."

Kathleen nodded, watching the rise of distant waves and feeling the pitch and roll of the sea.

"We'll be docking tomorrow," said Erma. "Have you seen Jenks yet?"

"In the morning," replied Kathleen.

"He sure has held you off," observed the other girl. "Yet at the same time, he's been almost courtin' you the whole passage."

"Courting?" echoed Kathleen. She had not felt courted— only harassed.

Erma nodded. "Why do you think the teasing from the others? They noticed all the attention. The 'How are you? Can I get anything for your comfort? Would you join me for dinner?' " Erma chuckled softly at Kathleen's shocked look.

"I don't think—" began Kathleen. Something about Mr. Jenks made her feel dreadfully uncomfortable. But she couldn't put it into words. Not even to Erma.

"Well, no matter," went on Erma briskly. "We're almost there now. Not much chance for courtin' from now on, is there?"

Then, to Kathleen's relief, Erma changed the topic. "See all the gulls? That means we're getting near land."

Kathleen lifted her face and studied the birds circling overhead. She could hear their cries and it awoke some deep, distant memory. Had their Irish farm been by the sea? Then her thoughts were interrupted as Erma spoke again.

"So you still don't know—?" she began, then stopped, knowing that Kathleen would be able to finish the question.

Kathleen shook her head. "Sure, and the suspense is givin' me goose bumps, and that's the truth," she answered with a shiver.

They sat in silence for a few minutes listening to the cry of the gulls and the swell of the seas.

"If you could wish—and have it come true—what would you wish for?" asked Erma softly.

"That he be Irish," responded Kathleen with no hesitation.

"And his trade?" asked Erma.

"I wouldn't care. He can be anything—just as long as he—" She didn't finish her statement.

"And what would he look like?" asked Erma, seeming to enjoy her little game.

Again Kathleen did not hesitate. "Dark wavy hair coming down at the sides with curling sideburns, with laughin', teasin' eyes, and a dimple in his chin." She had described her father just as she remembered him.

"I'd like a tall blond rancher with broad shoulders and a straight nose and even teeth with a—just a small, carefully trimmed mustache," laughed Erma.

"Oh, Erma!" cried Kathleen, laughing too, and then adding in sudden anguish, "And what do you think *they* are hoping for in us?"

Erma shrugged, then answered thoughtfully, "Companions. Cooks. Housekeepers. Someone to share laughs and—and trials. Someone who won't nag or chatter too much or complain over wet firewood or footprints across the kitchen."

Kathleen shivered.

"At least—I'm hoping that's what he'll want. I could be that, Kathleen. But if he wants more—then . . ." Erma let the sentence slide away to join the cry of the gulls and the sighing of the wind.

Kathleen reached for her friend's hand.

"The biggest wish of all"—her voice was a whisper—"is that you will be wherever I am, and that's the pure truth of it," she said with feeling.

Chapter Eight

Meeting

The next morning Kathleen went promptly for her appointment. Mr. Jenks rose to meet her as she entered the room and took the liberty of using her first name. "Kathleen," he beamed, taking her arm and steering her to a chair placed a little too close to where he himself had been seated. He reclaimed his chair, so close to Kathleen that she feared they would bump knees. She drew back in her seat as far as she could.

"And are you feeling quite well now, my dear?" he asked solicitously.

Kathleen assured him that she was fine.

"You are such a delicate little thing," he said smoothly, "that I feared for you on this arduous journey."

"I'm stronger than I look, sir," Kathleen responded a bit curtly.

He nodded and changed the subject. "We dock this afternoon."

Kathleen nodded her head.

"I was hoping that we would have some time to—to enjoy each other's company on the voyage, but the heavy seas—"

Kathleen shifted uncomfortably and broke in. "I'm anxious to hear where I'll be going, sir," she dared to say.

"Oh yes." He came back to attention and placed his hands on his knees. "Well—that, my dear, is still a matter of concern for me, as well."

Kathleen did wish that he would stop calling her his dear.

"As a matter of fact," he went on, "it has still not been decided."

Kathleen frowned.

"Oh, never fear," he said reaching to take her hand. "You will have a place, I can assure you. Even if I have to take care of you myself." He winked and grinned and Kathleen felt terribly annoyed.

"Why am I here?" she asked boldly. "Why make an appointment just to tell me that there have been no arrangements?"

"There *have* been arrangements," he said, and reached to give his mustache a twitch. "I would like you to take dinner with me tonight at my hotel. I'm staying at a rather elegant place downtown. I think you will like it. Perhaps without the tossing of the sea we will have better opportunity to—"

"That is unthinkable," said Kathleen, standing to her full five feet two inches. Her face flamed with her disgust. "I will stay with the others—wherever they are staying."

His face grew dark with anger. "You are a proud one, aren't you!" he spat at her. "And after all I've tried to do."

"Sure now, and I was of the impression that my passage was paid by an American gentleman," Kathleen reminded him heatedly.

"Yes, Miss," said the man, his anger now matching her own. "And he shall have you—pity him, whoever he is. I wouldn't want to deal with such a temper every day for the rest of my life."

Kathleen spun on her heel and left the room.

"Stay with the others," he called after her. "I want you around to take the orders of where you are to go."

Kathleen didn't answer. She needed to get into the wind to cool off her hot cheeks.

But she would be there when it was time to find out where she would be going. And she hoped with all her heart that it was a long, long way from Boston and Mr. Jenks.

———

There was much commotion when the ship finally pulled in and docked in Boston Harbor. The women milled around, squealing and shouting and clutching belongings. Kathleen crowded close to her cabin mates, her dark eyes big, her face pale. As crowded as the cabin had been, she wished for just a few more days of feeling secure there.

Their names were called out and they walked the gangway by groups of four. As her feet touched the firm dock, Kathleen nearly lost her balance. Erma, close beside her, giggled.

They were all placed into carriages and taken through the streets to a large hotel. It felt strange to be back in a city again. Kathleen noticed that it was much newer, much cleaner, than her familiar section of London. She wondered if it would be possible for her to stay on here. She felt a drawing to this new American city. A feeling that she might soon be able to "belong" here.

But the very next day they were called to a drawing room where Mr. Jenks presided.

"Ladies—we are about to the end of our journey together," he informed them as though this were a matter of deep sorrow to all. "You will be heading west—to one point or another. From here to Chicago you will share a train. There you will be met by a gentleman by the name of Mr. Henry Piedmont. He will give you your final tickets and send you on the last leg of your journeys. From Chicago on, you will be fanning out and heading in different directions—though still westward.

"I do wish each of you every happiness in your new land—and your new unions."

He bowed low and gave them one final grin, smoothed his mustache, and then said firmly, "Miss Kathleen O'Malley—you will need to see me for final instructions."

He turned on his heel and was gone.

All eyes seemed to fix on Kathleen. She straightened her shoulders, lifted her chin, and followed the man from the room.

He must have expected her to do just that, for he went

only a few steps beyond the door and turned to wait for her.

"This way," he said with a nod of his head, and Kathleen obediently followed him.

They crossed the hall and entered a small room, and he motioned toward a chair and turned to lift a sheet of paper from his pocket.

"Before I hand you this," he said, looking straight at her, "might I say that I am a tolerant man. I am staying on in Boston. I am quite willing to forget your outburst of last evening—should you have changed your mind."

For one moment Kathleen frowned, not understanding his words. When the truth finally dawned, she rose quickly from the chair, her face flushing, her eyes flashing anger. Without one word she reached out and snatched the paper from his fingers before he had a chance to react.

"You may be sorry, you know," he called after her as she moved from the room as quickly as her limp would allow.

Kathleen did not return to her room immediately. She had to find some privacy before she dared look at the paper she held. At last she found a chair tucked in a rather dark corner of a distant hall and dropped onto it, trying to still her anxiously beating heart.

Carefully she unfolded the bit of paper.

"Donnigan Harrison," said the paper. "He is a late signer like yourself. Not much is known of him. I hope you will not be sorry."

Kathleen crumpled the paper in her hand and then felt immediate remorse. Carefully she placed it on her lap and tried to smooth out the wrinkles. She would need that piece of paper. It was all she had.

"Donnigan Harrison," she repeated. Then her eyes lit up. She wasn't really familiar with the surname, but Donnigan did sound rather Irish. For the first time she felt some hope.

————

The train ride was long and stuffily hot. Kathleen had thought the boat trip had been difficult—but at least then they had enjoyed the crispness of the ocean winds. Not given the luxury of berths, they were crammed together in seats with hard straight-backs and no place to put their tired heads. The long nights were spent in restless shifting to try to find some way to relax tired bodies.

At last they reached Chicago. Kathleen may have been interested in studying the city had she not been so totally exhausted.

The man called Piedmont was on the platform when they arrived. As they stepped off the train, he rounded the women up and hustled them to a side room, much like herding cattle, and grinned at the group nervously as he called out names and passed out tickets. Kathleen had not felt particularly close to many of the women, but as she sat and watched group after group being hurried out to catch this coach or that train, she felt panic tighten her throat.

At last her own name was called along with a number of others, and she stood up and walked numbly past the man and accepted the ticket along with its instructions of where to go and how to get there.

She was more than a little relieved to look around her and find that Erma was also in the group.

But Peg was gone. As were Nona and Beatrice. There were just Erma and her and four other women whom she didn't know well. All four were from the Continent. She wondered if they spoke English. They seemed so shy and frightened. Kathleen moved closer to Erma, drawing some assurance from the presence of her friend.

Quickly they compared sheets and found to their relief and excitement that they shared a common destination. With excited cries they threw their arms around each other and wept unashamedly. It would be so wonderful—so *wonderful* to know someone, to have a friend in the new, strange land.

Soon they had boarded another train and were chugging their way out of the station. Though still not given a berth, they were not so crowded. By now they were so weary that Kathleen felt they could have slept almost anywhere.

She was right. The girls from the Continent fell asleep almost as soon as they boarded the train, the oldest of the group soon snoring loudly.

Kathleen did not stay awake to see if it annoyed other passengers. She rolled up her shawl against the coolness of the window, laid her head against it, and fell asleep.

She was stiff when she awoke in the morning, but at least she felt somewhat better.

"And how long are we to be on this train?" she asked Erma.

"I'm not sure. Someone said three days."

Kathleen winced. She was so tired of travel. Travel and heat and people and dust. It seemed that it all went together in America.

After the train came the stagecoach, which they met in a small, dusty frontier town of gray wooden buildings and gray wooden boardwalks. The sign at the post office indicated that it was Raeford. Kathleen felt that they must be going to the end of the world. She had given up craning her neck to look out the window. There were so many miles of the same thing. She did find the herds of deer and antelope and buffalo rather exciting. She had seen no such animals on the back streets of London.

But for the most part, they rode in silence. There was really very little to talk about.

When they reached a small station by the name of Sheep's Meadows, one of the girls from the Continent was separated from them and sent in another direction on another stage. Kathleen could sense the girl's panic. She felt her own hand go out to grasp Erma's. She was so thankful that she would not be going off all on her own.

Later, two of the other girls were sent off in another direction. Kathleen wondered how far they would travel before they were separated again.

There were still three of them when the stage pulled into

Aspen Valley. They all looked at their sheets of paper one last time. They were home.

Donnigan wished he had made arrangements for Wallis to ride along with him to town. He could have used some support. Never in his whole life had he felt so nervous—not even when he had been treed by a big grizzly or the time he had been thrown in the path of stampeding cattle. Somehow he had managed to escape those perils. It seemed there was no escaping this one.

He cast one last glance around his snug cabin. All the dishes had been washed. Even the pots. They were all stacked carefully on the shelf beside the stove. He had made his bed rather than just tossing the blankets up to cover the pillow. He had even used a scrub brush and hot soapy water on the floorboards. Things looked pretty good.

He moved from the room and closed the door firmly behind him. As he walked the dirt path toward the barn and corrals, he studied his makeshift flower garden. He had lost only one of the plants that he had brought from the meadow. But only three were still blooming. Still, it was better than nothing, he reasoned.

He would have loved to show up in town with the black. Everyone around admired the magnificent horse, and Donnigan couldn't help but feel that the big stallion would make some kind of favorable impression.

But the black hated the harness, and Donnigan knew that he could hardly ask his new wife to climb up behind him and be toted back to the farm cowboy fashion. Then there would be all the trunks and cases that she would have with her. No, it just wouldn't work to take the saddle horse. Donnigan hitched the team to the wagon and started off to town.

The stage was late. Most of the town didn't even notice, but the three men who paced back and forth waiting anxiously for its arrival and trying hard to hide their jitters certainly did.

Lucas, who felt in charge because of having collected the passage money from the other two men, pulled out his gold watch on the long gold chain over and over to study the time.

Donnigan simply checked the sky. The sun was moving on past where it should have been at the proper arrival time. Wallis stomped back and forth, back and forth, spitting chewing tobacco at the end of his boots. Then the three would shift positions slightly and begin all over again.

"Fool driver!" exclaimed Wallis angrily, letting go with another streak of brown stain. "Shouldn't be allowed to fritter away his time and keep workin' men waitin'."

Donnigan had to smile in spite of his own impatience.

"Do you want to come over to the hotel for coffee?" asked Lucas hospitably, but just as he asked the question a cloud of dust appeared in the distance.

With the sighting of the stage, Donnigan really felt his stomach begin to rile up. "This is it! This is it for sure," he said to himself. "There's no turning back now."

Then a new thought struck him. "What if she isn't even on the stage. Maybe she changed her mind or got sick or—"

He felt sudden exultation like he had when he had escaped the bear's long fangs. But only for a moment. He admitted to himself that even though he was terribly nervous about the whole doings, he would be dreadfully disappointed if she did not show up.

The stage rolled to a halt in a whirl of dust. As the three men held their breath, the stage master stepped forward and opened the door.

Out stepped a lady. She was not too tall, rather pleasingly plump and had a slightly nervous yet generous smile. She scanned the three men before her, then looked again at the tall blond man with the broad shoulders and wide Stetson and gave him a special smile. As Donnigan's heart leaped in response, Lucas stepped forward.

"Welcome, Miss—?" he said, lifting his hand to doff his hat.

"Kingsley," said the young woman; her voice was soft and husky with emotion. "Erma Kingsley."

Lucas suddenly looked as nervous as a schoolboy. "You're mine," he blurted, then flushed with embarrassment. "I mean—Lucas Stein here, ma'am." He reached out a hand and she accepted it.

Donnigan was momentarily disappointed, and then his attention jerked back to the stagecoach where another woman was making her appearance. She was tall and a little stiff, her eyes dark and piercing. She straightened to her full height and surveyed the men. Before any of them could make a move she spoke in broken but careful English, "Which of you is the gentleman Tremont?"

Wallis swallowed his chew of tobacco and his face turned deep red. Donnigan wasn't sure if it was the fault of the potent chew or his nervousness over meeting his Risa.

At length he seemed to get hold of himself, but not before the woman had given him a dark, stern look.

"Ma'am," he said and copied what he had seen Lucas do. Only in his great agitation, the hat that he had intended to doff flipped from his shaky fingers and went flying into the dust at his feet. He stammered and stuttered and bent to retrieve it, slapping it on his thigh and making a little puff of dust lift almost in the lady's face.

"Sorry, ma'am," he had the good sense to apologize. She did not look pleased.

Donnigan turned his attention back to the stagecoach door. So far two very different women had descended. If Donnigan could have had anything at all to say in the matter, he would have hoped the third one would be somewhat like the first one.

But as he lifted his head, a little wisp of a thing was descending the steps. Maybe his wife-to-be wasn't on that stage, after all.

The young girl moved slowly toward the little group, and Donnigan noticed that she walked with just the slightest limp. She was a pretty youngster. Donnigan wondered fleetingly if she was the daughter of a local farmer or rancher, but he hadn't seen her around before. Perhaps she was a visiting niece of someone.

Miss Erma Kingsley turned as the young girl neared them. She spoke again in a voice that didn't sound quite as strained now. "This is Miss Kathleen O'Malley," she said evenly, and Donnigan was glad he didn't have a chaw of tobacco in his lip. He surely would have swallowed it just as Wallis had.

Kathleen O'Malley? his thoughts ran quickly. *But she's a child. I—I ordered a—a woman.*

"I guess you must be Mr. Harrison," Miss Kingsley said to Donnigan, "as you are the only one left." She gave him a warm, candid smile and Donnigan found himself wishing again that the fates had been kinder to him. For a brief moment he envied Lucas. Then he turned to the approaching Miss O'Malley and carefully doffed his Stetson.

"Miss," he said and forced a smile. He could hardly address her as ma'am, now could he?

She returned his smile with a hesitant one of her own— and as Donnigan looked into the clear dark eyes, he felt his heart give a little flip.

Chapter Nine

Adjustments Begin

Kathleen had stopped to take a deep breath before disembarking from the stagecoach. Her heart was thumping and her hands felt sweaty. She straightened her bargain bonnet on her dark curls and smoothed the nearly new gloves over her small hands. Her whole outfit had been purchased in Boston as part of the "passage deal." It was simple and inexpensive, but it was new. Kathleen was grateful for that. Her own patched wardrobe had been painfully inadequate.

Now as she paused at the top of the steps and brushed the dust and wrinkles from her skirts, she took one more deep breath. *Please,* she begged whoever was "in charge," *Please let him be Irish.*

There was a little cluster before her when she stepped out. For a minute she stopped and squinted into the harsh afternoon sun, letting her eyes adjust from the dark interior of the stage.

There was Erma, already smiling confidently at a short, well-dressed, bespectacled gentleman who stood with his watch still in his hand as though he were timing something. "Surely he's not," Kathleen murmured under her breath, then quickly switched to, "He must be Mr. Stein." The gentleman was well into his forties, she guessed.

Kathleen's eyes shifted quickly to the other little man who was bustling about, thumping his hat against his leg and grinning rather ridiculously. The stern Risa stood frowning at him—and Kathleen judged that she was looking at another "match." The man was rather ill-kept, but his hair was slicked down and his face shining from a morning scrubbing. Kathleen judged him to be even a bit older than Mr. Stein.

"But I don't see Donnigan," she whispered to herself, and a stab of fear shot through her. Had there been a mistake? Had Mr. Jenks sent her all this long way out west with the name of a man who didn't really exist—just for spite?

Then her eyes looked beyond the two couples and she saw another man. Tall and broad and blond—and looking pained and worried. For a moment she thought she was looking at the very man Erma had described to her on board ship. Surely—surely this was Erma's intended. But no. Erma was already paired.

"Sure now, and he's a—a giant," Kathleen mused, her feet refusing to move farther. Just as she thought of turning and retreating to the safety of the stagecoach, the man looked up, seemed to realize who she was, and smiled. In that one warm, nervous smile, Kathleen saw a reflection of her own feelings. She managed a tentative smile in return— and then he was moving toward her with confidence and more grace than she would have expected from such a large man. Kathleen stepped forward to meet him. One thought was uppermost in her mind. *He's not Irish—and that's the truth of it.*

Lucas had made arrangements for them all to take tea together at his hotel. "We need to get acquainted," he'd said calmly to Wallis and Donnigan, and the two men had nodded in agreement. Donnigan had been glad to let Lucas take charge.

Now Lucas cleared his throat, nodded his head to Will, one of his hired hands, and offered his arm to Erma, who accepted it with a slight flushing of her round, dimpling cheeks.

"You must be weary. All of you," said Lucas, letting his glance take in the three women. "It's a long, tiring trip. We will take tea at the hotel."

Donnigan noticed that he didn't say "my hotel," though he could have. Lucas already owned half the little town.

Wallis, who still hadn't put his hat back on his head, self-consciously stuck an elbow out in the direction of Risa. She appeared not to notice.

Donnigan turned to Kathleen. She looked so tiny. So frail. So very young. His immediate instincts were to protect her. He reached to place his hand under her elbow to guide her across the roughness of the town's main street. *She shouldn't be in the West,* he found himself thinking. *It's too harsh. Too rugged. She'll—she'll—*

But she interrupted his thoughts. "Sure now, and I'm glad to be back on my own two feet." Then Kathleen bit her lip, remembering that men do not like chattering women.

He couldn't help but grin. Her accent was so thick that he had to concentrate to catch the words. She sure did talk cute.

He did have presence of mind enough to offer, "How long have you been traveling?"

It was Kathleen's turn to strain to untangle the strange-sounding words. My, he had an odd accent. She had never heard one speak in that manner before. He sure wasn't Irish.

She shook her head. She still felt nervous—almost to the point of being giddy, but she controlled her voice the best she could and replied softly, "I'm not sure." The "r" seemed to roll on her tongue. "It seems forever. The ship—then the train—then this here fancy cart." She nodded her head back in the direction of the stage, and Donnigan would have laughed except he saw the seriousness in her little face.

They reached the hotel and followed Lucas, who led the way with Erma. Donnigan could see the eyes of the three women carefully scanning the interior. It was really quite a nice hotel for such a small town. But then, Lucas did everything in splendid fashion.

The little side room was especially ornate. Donnigan

found himself wondering if Lucas had carefully redone it for just this occasion. He heard Erma exclaim "Oh, my!" as her eyes surveyed the room and a smile deepened the dimples.

Risa slyly took in the room in one quick glance, and Donnigan wondered if he hadn't seen her eyes light up briefly.

But it was Kathleen who captured his attention. He heard her quick intake of breath and saw her dark eyes widen as they quickly scanned the room. Pleasure and wonder seemed to eminate from her very being. Some word escaped her lips, though he wasn't able to catch it because of her heavy accent.

She likes pretty things, he observed, and it pleased him. Then he thought of his own plain cabin. Certainly there were no plush draperies, brocaded settees, ornate wallpapers, or thick carpets there. Stirrings of concern tightened his throat again.

But Lucas was inviting them to the linened table and nodding toward the side door to a waiter who stood ready to give the signal to the kitchen staff.

Donnigan was surprised by the whole affair. He had thought he knew Lucas. Now he realized that he really did not. It became clear that the man had class far more befitting an eastern city than their little town. He was refined, gentlemanly, almost suave. *He sure must have been studying his books or practicing somewhere,* Donnigan observed silently. *He sure didn't learn all this around here.*

The truth was, unknown to any of the town folk, Lucas had spent considerable time in careful research and preparation for the event. And he had practiced, night after night, in his own suite of rooms until he felt he would be totally comfortable in his new role.

Wallis, Donnigan's closest neighbor and friend, suddenly stood out as crude, cocky, and terribly unsophisticated. His lack of refinement had never bothered Donnigan before, but now as he watched him stumbling his way clumsily through a simple, rather feminine ritual like afternoon tea, Donnigan couldn't help but wonder what Wallis's Risa was thinking.

But to Donnigan's further surprise, the three ladies at the table seemed just a bit nervous and unsure as well.

Perhaps they are just tired out, he thought to himself.

"I'm sure our American customs are a bit primitive compared to your European ways," Lucas observed with a smile, "but for today, will you grant us the privilege of serving you? In the future, you may serve the tea."

That eased some of the tension around the table. Lucas took over the duties of both host and hostess, and the women seemed to relax.

Lucas tried to draw out his quests, addressing each of the women by turn. Donnigan noticed that Erma answered rather easily, dimpling with each reply. Kathleen spoke when spoken to, but her answers were brief and to the point and her words heavily accented. Donnigan observed Wallis frown and wondered if the man had understood one word of what Kathleen had said.

But it was Risa who had very little to say. Her brief replies were curt, choppy, and with no feeling. She, too, had an accent. Perhaps German—or Dutch—or Russian. Donnigan really had no idea. But every time the woman made even a small comment, Wallis grinned as though she had just made a standing-ovation public address.

It was a leisurely teatime, and Donnigan was thankful to Lucas for arranging it. It had helped to break the ice. Perhaps they would all feel just a bit more comfortable with one another. But Donnigan also knew—Lucas had made it clear—that once tea was over, the other two men were on their own.

Lucas had frowned when Donnigan informed him earlier that morning that he wanted two rooms in his hotel. Two rooms. One the best that he had.

Donnigan had flushed, then hurried on to explain. "I figure she—she has a right to one night to think it over—make sure she still—"

Lucas had nodded then. But he still seemed to feel that Donnigan was taking unnecessary precautions.

"I've arranged with the parson for a seven o'clock wedding," Lucas replied. "Then we'll take dinner in my rooms."

Yes, Donnigan thought, *I'm sure you have everything carefully and neatly arranged.*

Now as Donnigan glanced around the table, a strange idea occurred to him. *What if Lucas had been hitched with Risa?* The mental picture almost made Donnigan chuckle. He shifted his big booted feet under the table and tried with effort to wipe the grin from his face before anyone noticed it. But it sure would have been funny—Lucas trying to teach the straight-backed Risa to jump through his hoops.

Donnigan's glance slid back to Erma. Her round cheeks dimpled and her eyes sparkled with trust as she listened intently to whatever Lucas was saying to her. Yes. It appeared that Lucas would have no trouble with Erma.

But what was he doing thinking of the other two men? What would he do with Kathleen? Again Donnigan shifted uneasily. It was a perplexing consideration.

Kathleen was awed by the splendor of the town's one hotel. She had never been in a hotel before except for the one in Boston—and it had been rather old and stodgy and stale-smelling. And the girls had all been crowded on cots in a few airless rooms with single dingy windows that looked out on a dirty back alley. Kathleen had not been impressed—but she figured that's how hotels were.

But this hotel was like—was like a rich man's castle, a king's tara, Kathleen concluded—though she had never been in the likes of those either.

She was concerned by the white linen on the table. What if she spilled something? She was confused by the square of white linen near her plate. What was she to do with it? Unsettled by the fine china that looked as if it would break at her touch. Alarmed by the row of forks, knives, and spoons. Why would anyone ever need so many just to take tea?

And when the tea trays promptly arrived, Kathleen gasped. She had never seen so many dainty sandwiches, iced cakes, and fancy tidbits. She didn't know where to start—so she watched Lucas, who began the proceedings by passing the "proper" item to Erma and unobtrusively indicating the piece of silver that was needed. By following the flushed Erma, Kathleen felt that she could not go too far astray. She began to relax and enjoy the afternoon repast. Like the others, she was hungry. Their fare had been simple and scant for the entire journey.

As she savored the tasty food, Kathleen almost—almost but not quite—forgot the big man who sat beside her. Under other circumstances she would have been very aware of his presence. In fact, she marveled that the food took so much of her attention. In her need for nourishment, she even found herself thinking, *If this is America, I like it.*

But as her appetite was appeased, she found her thoughts returning to other things. Things like wedding vows. Strangers. Separation from Erma. Family back home. Suddenly Kathleen lost her appreciation for the food. Her stomach tied in knots. She pushed her plate back slightly as though she couldn't stand the thought of one more bite.

She cast a glance around the table. Lucas was still talking engagingly with Erma, who listened in rapt attention.

"—my living quarters are right here in the hotel," Kathleen heard him say, and then he quickly added, "I do hope that you don't find the arrangement disagreeable."

"Oh no," dimpled Erma. "It's most—most—pleasant." And her eyes scanned the room again as her cheeks flushed.

Kathleen found her eyes following Erma's. *Wouldn't it be a wonder to live in a place like this,* she found herself thinking.

Kathleen shifted her eyes to Wallis, who ate the sandwiches as though he'd been near starving. One patched elbow rested on the white tablecloth so the hand wouldn't have so far to go to reach the mouth. Kathleen noticed that he had pressed two of the dainty sandwiches together so they would make a more worthwhile mouthful.

Risa sat stiffly beside him. Even her tightly secured bun at the nape of her neck looked offended by the man beside her.

Donnigan sat too close to her for her to see his face. But she surprised herself by realizing that already she had it memorized. She could visualize the intense blue eyes, his most outstanding feature in her way of thinking, the straight nose, the tanned cheeks—one bearing a small scar that made her wonder what had happened—the firm chin with the slight cleft, the blond hair that wished to curl, especially at the nape of his neck.

But he was so big. So big and broad. Kathleen had been used to smaller men. Men more like Lucas in stature. For one brief minute she wished that she could change places with Erma. Erma was the one who had wanted the tall, blond rancher. Kathleen felt dwarfed beside him. Like a—like a small child looking up to her father. She didn't like the feeling. Didn't like it at all.

But Lucas was folding the square of linen that he had placed on his lap. Kathleen saw Erma reach for hers and fold it slowly as well. Kathleen followed suit.

"I'm sure we all have our own plans for the rest of the day," Lucas was saying.

"I have had your luggage taken to my—our rooms," Lucas said to Erma. "I'm sure you would like a bath and rest to refresh yourself."

Erma looked at him appreciatively—and then back to Kathleen. For one brief minute Kathleen saw panic in the gray eyes.

"The—the wedding—?" Erma began.

"Will be at seven," said Lucas evenly.

"I—I was wondering—since I know no one and—and Kathleen is my—my friend, could—could she attend me, sir?"

Kathleen's breath caught in her throat. She hadn't thought of attendants.

For one moment Lucas frowned slightly. He had already made all the arrangements. Then he looked back at Erma and nodded, if somewhat reluctantly. "Of course," he said. "That—that will be—fine."

Lucas turned to Kathleen; then his eyes lifted to Donnigan's. "At the church—at ten to seven," he said, and both Kathleen and Donnigan knew that Lucas meant for Donnigan to be sure to deliver her there promptly.

"I told the parson we'd be on over as soon as we et," Wallis was saying to Risa.

The woman raised no objection, just nodded her head and followed Wallis as he headed for the door, his grin still firmly in place.

————

"Are you tired—or would you like to walk?" Donnigan asked Kathleen solicitously, nervously fingering his broad-brimmed hat.

He really felt the need to get to know something more about this young girl, and the teatime had not really given them much opportunity to speak to each other.

Kathleen was weary, but she, too, felt the need to discuss their future plans.

"I'll walk," she replied evenly, wondering to herself if Donnigan had forgotten her limp. Would he be embarrassed to be seen on the streets with a lame partner?

They turned from the coolness of the day to the heat of the afternoon sun. Kathleen accepted Donnigan's offered arm. It seemed very strange to be on the arm of a man. She was used to scurrying through the streets of London on her own. Only the "ladies" were escorted.

They walked for a time in silence and then Donnigan spoke. "I have arranged for us to spend the night at the hotel," he informed her.

Kathleen lifted her eyes. She was waiting for him to say when they were to be at the church to stand before the parson.

"I thought you might be too tired to travel on out to the farm tonight—having traveled for so many days already," he went on to explain.

Kathleen nodded silently.

Her thoughts went on, tumbling over one another. *He said, "the farm." I'll be back on a farm. I wonder if one can see the sea?* Kathleen felt sure that they must be close to the sea. They had traveled so far. Surely the land couldn't stretch much farther. She lifted a hand to wipe her hot brow with the white hanky that had been purchased in Boston.

Donnigan stopped short.

"It's too warm for you, isn't it? I'm sorry. You really need to get out of the sun. You should rest."

Kathleen had never heard such concern in anyone's voice before. Certainly not concern over her well-being.

"I'm—I'm fine," she responded.

But he already was turning their steps toward the hotel.

"Your things have been taken to the room," he told her as they entered the cool lobby. He did not add that he had been totally surprised at the scarcity of luggage. The stage driver had needed to assure Donnigan over and over that the one little trunk was "all the luggage that the little lady had."

"I have the key—right here. I'll take you up."

With one hand under her elbow, he ushered her across the reception area and up the carpeted stairs. Kathleen felt woozy. Was it the heat—the events of the day—the man—or—or everything combined? So much was happening. So quickly.

They turned to the right at the top of the stairs and continued down a short hall. He presented the key and turned the lock in the door, opening it wide so she could enter. It was a pleasant room, with heavy blue and gold draperies, blue and gold carpet, and a soft bed that beckoned Kathleen.

"I'll send someone right up with hot water. You can bathe and rest," he assured her, then continued. "I'm sorry you won't have long. We need to be at the church right at ten to seven. If we don't, Lucas will have our hides."

He turned to leave, reaching for the doorknob to pull the door shut behind him.

"Wait!"

Kathleen's little cry stopped him.

"*Our* wedding?" asked Kathleen with more boldness than she thought she possessed.

"Tomorrow," he answered briefly. "Not 'til tomorrow."

He shut the door and was gone and Kathleen stared after him with wide, flashing eyes. Then she tugged a glove from her fingers and flung it on the bed beside her.

"Sure now—an' it's either you or me for the hall tonight, Mr. Donnigan Harrison, sir," she said angrily.

Chapter Ten

Confused Beginnings

As promised, there was a knock on Kathleen's door shortly before seven. She was ready and feeling somewhat refreshed, though she did wish she could have rested much longer.

But it was exciting to be off to Erma's wedding—even with the disappointment that Mr. Donnigan Harrison had chosen to stall concerning theirs. What if he continued to put it off? *What if he didn't plan to marry at all?* Kathleen felt her stomach churn.

He offered his arm, but because of the anger and confusion that still twisted her thoughts, she chose to refuse it. With head held high she limped along beside him, ignoring him as much as it was possible to do.

"Did you rest well?" he asked kindly, and she answered with a slight nod of her head and firmly pursed lips. If he thought it odd, he did not make comment.

He led her down the steps and through the lobby, out into the warmth of the evening and toward the end of the town's main street. Kathleen made no attempt at conversation, and he seemed to be sensitive to her mood.

She spotted the little church set back from the road before he lifted his hand to guide her down the wooden walk.

"Here we are—and on time. Lucas won't need to pace," said Donnigan with a hint of good-natured teasing in his voice.

They entered the church to find Lucas there ahead of
them. He was resplendent in a black formal suit with a small
rosebud tucked in his button hole.

The man whom Kathleen identified as the town parson
stood at the front of the room, book already spread open before him. *It appears that the preacher doesn't wish to keep
Lucas Stein waiting either,* thought Kathleen; and in spite of
herself, she felt a smile curving her lips.

Erma arrived promptly at seven. She came by carriage,
even though the hotel was only a few blocks down the street.
Kathleen could only stare. Erma was dressed in white with
a lacy veil covering her carefully coiffed blond hair. The dress
was a bit tight and Erma appeared to be holding her breath,
but Kathleen wondered how the man had managed to be that
close in his estimate of size for his new bride. The white-
gowned bride carried a bouquet of red roses and white car-
nations on her arm. Kathleen had never seen anything quite
so splendid.

"Your flowers," Lucas was saying, and Kathleen looked
from Erma to find Lucas offering her a small version of Erma's bouquet. She accepted it numbly.

A total stranger stepped forward and offered his arm to
lead her toward the man at the front. For one brief minute
she panicked, wondering if she was being led up to marry
this balding, stern-looking gentleman, and then she realized
she was simply being escorted up to be a witness to Erma's
wedding. She took the offered arm and walked forward, her
thoughts quickly scrambling to wonder what had become of
Donnigan.

But the parson was already speaking and Kathleen
forced her attention back to his words.

"Dearly beloved—" His voice was low and carefully mod-
ulated. Kathleen wondered if Lucas had brought him in just
for the event. He sounded so proper—so perfect. But she
quickly reminded herself that the man belonged to the whole
town. She knew Wallis and Risa had made use of his services
earlier that afternoon.

With that thought, Kathleen felt her face flush again. So

why hadn't Donnigan made arrangements? Or had he—and canceled them when he saw her lameness? Maybe she was a reject—just as her stepmother had warned.

Kathleen lost total concentration. Before she knew it the man with the book was saying, "May the God of heaven bless your union with His love, joy, and peace. Amen," and she knew that the short ceremony was over.

————

Donnigan was still struggling. He didn't feel any concern about the hotel dinner hour. That he had already arranged for, and it always seemed rather easy to chat over food if one felt that talk was necessary. And he knew that Kathleen was dreadfully tired and would wish to retire early—so that would take care of the evening. But what then? They had to talk seriously—sometime. They were due at the church at ten the next morning. But that hour seemed to be approaching awfully fast. He had a lot of thinking and sorting to do in a short time. He had thought himself prepared—and he would have been—had a girl like Erma stepped forward when the stage pulled into town. But a *child*? What was Jenks thinking of? Surely this—this—bit of a girl should still be at home in her family's care. So what was she doing here—ready to promise herself in marriage? Ready to take on the responsibilities of a grown woman? It didn't make a lick of sense to Donnigan.

He mulled over the problem all the time he waited for Lucas's ceremony to end, but he was no nearer a solution when the last Amen was spoken.

As the couple turned from the altar, Donnigan rose to his feet. He was the only one in the small church except for the parson and the wedding party. He wasn't sure if he should move forward with his congratulations or wait for the new bride and groom to come down the aisle. He waited.

The parson came first, with Lucas and Erma close behind him. With a bit of hesitation, Donnigan stepped forward and extended his hand.

"Congratulations," he said heartily to Lucas. The man, who was usually so composed, couldn't hide the merry twitching of his mustache. He had pulled the whole thing off—he was a married man, his twinkling eyes seemed to say.

Donnigan let his eyes shift back to his own bride of the morrow. She came slowly down the aisle on the arm of Grant Crayford, the town's officious banker. Donnigan had never been particularly fond of the man but had accepted him as a necessary part of the town. Now as the man placed his overly soft hand on the small hand that rested on his arm and leaned down to say something quietly to the young girl, Donnigan liked him even less. It was one thing for him to escort Kathleen, but quite another for him to be so solicitous—so possessive. Donnigan's starched collar suddenly felt too tight. He was a bit too quick in stepping forward and taking Kathleen's other elbow, gently easing her away from the dark-suited man.

"Our dinner is waiting," he said in explanation, and she allowed herself to be hurried away.

As she left the church, Kathleen saw Lucas assisting Erma back into the carriage for the short ride back to the hotel. Kathleen almost felt envy—and then Erma lifted her eyes and met Kathleen's for just one moment.

The gentle smile was still firmly in place, but the eyes shadowed briefly. *She's frightened,* thought Kathleen in that one quick exchange. *She's nervous and frightened.*

Kathleen wished to pull her hand free and go to the girl, but she managed a wobbly smile in return, hoping that it conveyed to Erma some measure of warmth and assurance, and then the carriage door was closed and Erma was gone.

———

Kathleen felt so weary she could scarcely keep herself alert to enjoy the tasty meal that was set before them. Donnigan kept talking and she hoped that she was giving sensible responses.

She was still angry and concerned about the hotel arrangements. She wasn't quite sure how she would handle it when the time came, but she had no intention whatever of sharing a room with a man who wasn't her wedded spouse.

I could sleep right here on this chair, she assured herself, feeling tired enough to do just that. *Or I could curl up on one of those settees in the lobby.*

But Donnigan was speaking again. "I know you are very tired," he was saying, "so rather than talk wedding plans tonight, we'll wait until morning."

Kathleen cast him a distant glance.

"I don't have special clothes," Kathleen admitted, her eyes held to her plate.

Donnigan shifted uneasily.

"Nor do I," he admitted. "Only Lucas would think of all those things."

"Do you mind?" asked Kathleen simply.

"No." His answer was curt. Almost sharp. Then his voice softened. "Do you?"

Kathleen shrugged her slim shoulders. Erma had looked awfully nice. But when it came to the truth, she had never even considered a wedding gown. "No," she said after a moment's hesitation.

"What you are wearing now looks real nice," Donnigan went on. It was the closest any man had ever come to complimenting her. Kathleen felt her cheeks warm.

The meal ended in silence. When they were finished, Donnigan rose to his feet and offered his arm to Kathleen.

"We'd better go up before you fall asleep at the table," he teased gently.

Kathleen longed for the soft bed in the room upstairs. Yet near panic gripped her. Now she would need to stand her ground. Now she—but how—and what would she say?

Donnigan led her up the steps and down the hall and again opened the door with the key. He held it for her to enter, but Kathleen stood rooted to the spot.

"This arrangement isn't much to my liking, sir," she said, her head lifting and her chin thrusting forward.

Donnigan looked puzzled. "Is something wrong with the room?" he asked innocently.

Kathleen's brogue was thick as she tipped her head and answered, "Sure, and the room is fine. It's the company that concerns me."

"The company?" It was clear that Donnigan was confused.

"On this journey I've shared a tiny closet-sized room with more women than I could count," went on Kathleen, "an' it didn't cause me one troubled moment—but sharing so large a room—with a man—now *that* I've no mind to do."

"A man?" Donnigan found himself peering around the door and into the room. His face still registered puzzlement.

"If you count yourself a man, sir," said Kathleen, her voice edged with anger.

"Me?" he asked incredulously.

Then Donnigan began to chuckle softly. "You thought— I mean, you thought that—that. . . ?" He couldn't finish the question.

"We won't be married until tomorrow," he reminded her.

Kathleen just stood and stared, her anger turning to confusion.

"My room is down the hall," explained Donnigan quickly, pointing his long arm with outstretched finger.

With the words he reached out and pressed the room key into Kathleen's hand. "Your key," he said and pulled another key from his pocket. Then he reached up and ran a hand through his blond hair. Kathleen could see the red gradually stain his tanned cheeks. Only the white scar stayed untouched. He licked his lips nervously and fingered the hat in his hand.

"I'm sorry," he muttered. "I didn't mean to cause you concern. I—I guess I didn't explain. I just didn't think. I'm—I'm sorry."

Kathleen felt the air leave her lungs—the anger leave her eyes. She stood for one brief moment trying to get back her control, and then a slow smile began to lighten her face.

"Sure now—and I did make a bit of a scene, didn't I?" she admitted.

He looked steadily into the dark eyes. Unexpectedly his hand lifted to touch the slim shoulder. "I—I'm glad," he whispered. "I'm glad you're that kind of girl."

Kathleen felt a stirring to her very soul. She swallowed hard, managed a nod, and moved into the room.

"I'll knock on your door in the morning," he called softly after her, and Kathleen heard her door close firmly.

Chapter Eleven

A Start

Kathleen had been fearful that once she fell asleep, she would not wake up until the afternoon of the next day. She was so weary from all the travel—all the emotional turmoil—but to her surprise she had a restless night.

First she had a difficult time getting to sleep. She thought of Erma and Risa and wondered how they would adjust to being wives of men they hardly new. She thought of Donnigan, her own man she did not know, and wondered if there were any secrets he was hiding. Indeed, she even wondered if his claiming another room was just a ruse so he might sneak off in the night, leaving her stranded and without means in this western town.

From there her thoughts turned to home. They quickly skipped over her stepmother and her plans for the marriage that would by now have taken place. She didn't even stop to wonder if the woman had found the happiness she had sought. Instead, Kathleen passed on to Bridget, and emptiness seemed to press in upon her. She missed Bridget. It was true that the girl was rather spoiled and undisciplined, but they held a fondness for each other.

Would Bridget be off to school? Yes. They were already into the fall of the year. The young girl would be in boarding school by now. Kathleen wondered how she was doing. Was the bit that Kathleen had been able to teach her standing her in good stead?

Kathleen even thought of Charles and young Edmund. Did they like the countryside? Had they been favored with ponies of their own?

Strangely enough, Kathleen even thought of the cranky old baker. Had he passed on her hawker's basket to another poor girl? Kathleen didn't even want to picture the girl in her mind. The back streets of London were really not a place for a young girl to be.

And over and over, Kathleen's mind went to Donnigan. Once again she said to herself, the disappointment still intense within her, "Sure—he's no Irishman, and that's the truth of it."

But what was he? And who was he? He was fine enough to look at—though his size disquieted her. He said he had a farm. Kathleen felt pleased about that. A farm would be a nice change from cluttered, dirty streets and dark, tall buildings.

He seemed a gentleman—though certainly not as polished and sure of himself as Erma's Lucas. But even as Kathleen had the thought, she stirred uneasily. She wasn't quite sure if she would have been pleased with a man like Lucas. He seemed so intense—so in control—so totally mechanical. Again Kathleen wondered if Erma would be happy.

"I must stop this," Kathleen scolded herself once again. "I will be a rag in the morning and not fit for a wedding and that's the truth of it." But even as she thought the words, Kathleen wondered again if there really would be a wedding.

———

Donnigan retired earlier than he should have. He just didn't know what else to do with his long evening. But he may as well have stayed up and paced the streets. He tossed and turned and thumped his pillow, then wadded it beneath his head and tossed again.

Never had his mind been in such a state. Never had he faced such a difficult decision.

"Twenty-one! That's ridiculous. She's more like—like—

I know what I should do," he told himself firmly. "I should bundle her up and put her right back on the stage and send her home to wherever she came from."

But Donnigan knew that he didn't have the money for a second passage aboard an ocean-sailing ship.

"Maybe someone would take her on as hired help—let her grow up a bit," he thought next. But he quickly dismissed that idea. How would he know if she was properly treated or whether she was taken advantage of?

"Well, I shouldn't marry her, and that's for sure," he told himself. But if he didn't marry her, what would he do with her?

It was quite obvious from the little luggage she carried that she wouldn't be able to financially care for herself.

"Well, I can't just take her to the farm without marrying her," fumed Donnigan. "Even if I slept in the barn."

There just didn't seem to be an answer. It wasn't that he was displeased with her. She was a pretty little thing—and she had spunk. He had seen that firsthand. In fact, when he really thought about it, if he'd had his pick of the three women who had disembarked the stage, he likely would have chosen her. The tall, prim Risa certainly would have made him quake in his boots. He wondered how Wallis was faring.

And Erma, though she appeared to be agreeable and cheery, made him wonder if such a constantly agreeing person might soon get on his nerves. But little Kathleen—when she smiled, her whole face brightened, and when her temper flared, those dark eyes shot sparks. He had a feeling that living with her would be a rather exciting adventure.

But she was so small—so young. He tossed again and in the stillness of the hotel room he softly cursed Wallis and Lucas for talking him into this crazy scheme and then the man Jenks who had no more sense than to send a child in the place of a woman.

He tried to push the disturbing thoughts from his mind so he could get some rest. "Twenty-one!" he snorted in disgust. "Why did she have to go and lie about her age?" He'd have to have a talk with her and sort it out in the morning.

And he did need to ask her to please stop referring to him as "sir." He much preferred Donnigan.

Kathleen was up and dressed, her belongings carefully packed, long before the rap came on her door. She knew, with the aid of the mirror, that she didn't look rested, but she figured that she could likely get through one more day on nerves.

Donnigan stood before her, silently fumbling with his hat. Kathleen felt relief in seeing him. At least he hadn't skipped town. She thought he looked as though he hadn't slept so well either.

He managed a smile. "Good morning," he greeted. Kathleen did hope he wouldn't ask if she had slept well.

"I don't know about you, but I sure am ready for some breakfast," he said in his easy manner, and Kathleen managed a smile and a nod. She had been feeling hungry for a couple of hours.

He led the way back to the dining room and placed their orders. Kathleen was glad for the strong, hot coffee. Not only did it taste good, but it gave her something to do with her hands.

"We need to talk," he surprised her by saying. He looked uneasy, but seemed determined to say what he had to say.

"Quite frankly," he began, shifting his big frame on the brocaded chair seat, "I had pictured a—an older woman. One a bit more—more mature. Bigger." He indicated a rough shape with his hands.

Kathleen felt the color draining from her face. It was her limp, she just knew it.

He stopped and Kathleen saw him struggle with what he should say next.

"Your—your—the piece of paper that I got said you are twenty-one." His eyes seemed to challenge her. He hated lies. It had bothered him all through the night that she might be a person that couldn't be trusted. How could you live with a person, sharing your life and your dreams, if you couldn't even trust her?

Kathleen met his gaze steadily. He saw her eyes widen with surprise—then darken with concern.

"It said that?" she asked almost under her breath.

He nodded.

Kathleen's eyes fell to her plate. She shook her head slowly. He thought he could see anger smoldering in the dark eyes when she raised them again.

"It's that Mr. Jenks," she said. "I—I told him my true age—but the man must have put down—I'm—I'm sorry."

The last words were spoken so softly that Donnigan had to strain to hear them. But her eyes spoke volumes. Donnigan was ready to believe that she was sorry, just as she had said.

"I—I don't think that Mr. Jenks is a man to be trusted," she finished lamely and her eyes registered anger once more.

Donnigan shifted his weight again. Suddenly he felt anger himself. Anger toward the man Jenks whom he had never met. He had to move on with the conversation or he would find himself asking questions that he might wish he had not asked.

"Why did you come to America?" he asked her simply. "I mean, at your age—why aren't you still home with your folks in Ireland?"

Kathleen took a deep breath. He had a right to some answers. She had a few questions of her own.

"I came from London," she said first and saw the surprise in his face.

"Sure, and I am Irish. But I have lived in London ever since—ever since my father had to give up his land. My mother died when I was a wee one. I hardly recall her face. My father married again—to a woman from France. Then my father died a few years back. We were left in—in rather—difficult—circumstances. I worked—if you call hawkin' rolls and pies on the streets of London work. And then—then Madam"—the name slipped out before Kathleen had time to change it—"my stepmum, decided to marry again." She

stopped and raised her eyes to his. "So I signed up and—"
She shrugged and looked down at her cup.

Donnigan sat silently digesting all that she had said.

"Why didn't you stay with your family?" he asked softly.

"They were moving to the country," she answered evenly.

"You don't like the country?" He thought of his farm and little cabin as he asked the question, and a strange fear accompanied the words.

"And I wouldn't know, would I now, not having memories of my own. But my father always said it's a fine place to be a livin'."

"So why didn't you move with them?"

Kathleen's eyes dropped again. Her fingers slipped to her lap where they clasped in agitation beneath the spread of tablecloth.

At last she raised her eyes again and Donnigan saw hurt and confusion there. "I wasn't wanted—except as household staff," she said honestly.

"Staff?"

She nodded, a bit braver now. Her chin came up and he saw the fire back in her eyes.

"Madam gave me two choices. A member of the household staff in the country—or a hawker on the London streets."

Donnigan had no comment. He lowered his own gaze and toyed with the cutlery by his plate. She'd really had no choice. And neither did he, he decided as he stirred restlessly. Child or not, there was really nothing for him to do but to marry her.

————

They arrived at the small church at ten o'clock. There was no fancy white gown or formal black suit. Lucas, dark suited, took his place beside Donnigan. Erma stood at Kathleen's side. They used their slightly wilted flowers of the day before. Only this time, Erma graciously offered Kathleen her bridal bouquet. The ceremony was short and direct, and in a few moments Kathleen looked shyly up at Donnigan. They were now husband and wife.

———

Donnigan did not really look at her again until they were traveling the dusty, rutted road to the farm on the high seat of the wagon. He wondered just how disappointed she was feeling, having visited Erma's posh hotel suite of rooms before leaving town so that they could bid each other goodbye.

But her face did not look dark and gloomy. She lifted her hand to remove her bonnet and brushed back her straying dark hair. Her face turned into the breeze that rustled the grasses by the roadside, and she took a deep, satisfied breath.

"I've longed for the country ever since I was a child," she admitted frankly, and Donnigan, relieved, took a deep gulp of the fresh warm air.

They rode in silence again, and then Kathleen tilted her head as though listening intently.

"What bird is that?" she asked, her voice expressing excitement.

"Just a wood thrush," he answered.

"You must teach me all the birds," she responded and then seemed to catch herself. She was not to be a chatterer. And she certainly was not to be giving orders. Her face flushed with her embarrassment.

But Donnigan seemed not to notice. "You like birds?" he asked, his voice deep and warm.

"Oh yes," she breathed and then fell silent.

"Would you fancy some hens?" asked Donnigan after a few moments.

"Oh yes," said Kathleen again. She would love hens— and geese—and ducks and—and maybe even— She checked herself again.

"We'll get some—come spring," said Donnigan, and the matter seemed settled.

Kathleen had so many questions she wished to ask. Where was his farm? What did he have there? If there were no chickens, were there sheep? Cattle? She wished he would talk about it. She longed to ask. But she would not make him angry by prattling on while he wished for solitude. She bit her tongue to keep the questions from pouring forth.

At the same time that Kathleen held herself in check, Donnigan was bemoaning the fact of her silence.

We'll never get to know each other at this rate, he thought dejectedly. There were many things he wanted to ask her. Wished to tell her. But she didn't seem interested in conversation. He didn't wish to make her uncomfortable by plying her with questions or to seem boastful by sharing with her about the farm he had carved for himself from prairie sod. But it was difficult to ride along for so many miles in complete silence. He would have been doing more talking if he were riding Black, he decided.

They drew near a small farm and Kathleen felt her heart quicken. Was it their farm? But no, Donnigan made no move to tug on the reins of the horses.

"That's Wallis's place," he said, and Kathleen looked at it with renewed interest. They were almost past when Kathleen spotted Risa. She was in the shade of the small building, bent over a tub of washing. Already a line was filled with clothing that fluttered in the afternoon breeze.

"I see Risa has gone right to work," observed Donnigan with a smile. Kathleen waved, but the busy woman did not look up from her scrubboard.

It wasn't long until Donnigan did turn the horse into a farmyard. Kathleen fell in love with it at once. It was so much better than the dark little cottage along the London street. And it was easy to see that it was much nicer than the farm Wallis and Risa occupied down the road.

But Kathleen bit her tongue and tried not to let her intense excitement show. He already thought her a child. He would be more than sure if she bounced up and down on the wagon seat and clapped her hands at the sight of her new home.

Donnigan stole a sideways look. He hoped to see a sparkle in her eyes—but he saw instead a stoical face and hands tightly clenched in her lap.

Donnigan helped Kathleen down from the high wagon seat and deposited her on the ground. He saw her eyes go to the flower beds that he had labored over on her behalf and for one moment they brightened, but she made no comment.

"I'll bring your things to the house after I care for the team," he told her. "You go ahead on in."

Kathleen hesitated.

"Would you like me to go with you—this first time?" asked Donnigan, almost shyly.

"Oh no. No, it's fine," replied Kathleen. But she did feel dreadfully strange about entering the home of the man, though she knew it must quickly become her home as well.

She lifted the latch on the unlocked door and stepped inside. The kitchen-living quarters were neat and roomy. Kathleen drew in her breath. It was more than she had dreamed of—her own country home. She wouldn't have traded places with Erma for anything in the world.

She moved slowly forward, taking in the small shelves that were stacked with dishes, the big black stove with its copper kettle, the table, chairs, the shelf with assorted books and manly items like belt buckles and a checker board.

At last she dared to venture farther and found the bedroom beyond. So much room for only two people. She and Bridget had been forced to share a room where they could scarcely stand up beside the bed.

Kathleen did clasp her hands. She wanted to dance around the little room, but she thought she heard Donnigan coming. She forced her face to become blank, placed her hands demurely at her sides, and returned to the kitchen just as he placed her small trunk beside the door.

"Is everything okay?" he asked soberly, hoping with all of his heart that she would respond with some enthusiasm.

"Fine," she said simply, with no emotion whatever.

He stood for one minute and then nodded his head. "I'll get some fresh water," he informed her and lifted the pail from its shelf.

After he had left the house, Kathleen did do a little jig around the table. It was perfect. Just perfect. She could be happy here. She knew she could.

She looked about again. "It will be so homey with curtains at the windows, hooked rugs on the floor, a throw over the big stuffed chair in the corner, a few bright—"

But Kathleen checked herself. He hadn't brought her here to totally disrupt his home. If she began to make all of those changes, he would think she wasn't happy with what she had. He would think her disgustingly demanding. No. Things were quite all right as they were. She would not risk his displeasure. She would ask for nothing.

Donnigan lowered the pail into the deep well, his thoughts on Kathleen's response to the farm and house. Or rather her lack of it. He hadn't realized how important it had been to him that she would like what she found. Now he looked at his place through different eyes. What was wrong with it? Did she want a place like Erma's? Well, if she did, she had the wrong man. Lucas Stein was the only man in the whole territory who could afford a place like that.

He knew his place was—plain. But with a little effort and the few dollars he could give her, she could fix all that. Women knew how to go about such things. He didn't. Had he known, he would have done it for her—like planting the flowers.

And then he thought of the many changes and the long miles of travel. "She's just played out," he reasoned. "Give her a few days and she'll get things in shape the way she wants them."

Donnigan forced himself to whistle as he headed for the cabin with the fresh pail of well water in his hand.

Chapter Twelve

Settling In

The next morning dawned warm and bright, and Donnigan asked rather shyly if Kathleen would care to see the rest of the farm. She could hardly hide her enthusiasm but kept her face straight while she answered him that she would.

"Do you ride?" he surprised her.

She shook her head slowly.

"I have a mare that I've been working on for you," he went on, "but I don't think she's quite ready if you're not used to riding."

Kathleen wished to protest, but she bit her tongue.

"How do *you* check the farm?" she asked him.

"I ride Black," he answered.

"Black?"

"My stallion." He waited, watching her face, but she was giving him no hints whatever. "He rides double," he said at last.

Kathleen's head came up and for one unguarded moment her eyes flashed excitement.

"Would you mind?" asked Donnigan.

"No. No, I wouldn't mind," she said simply, hanging the dishcloth over the pan on the wall.

Kathleen may have become an expert at hiding her feelings, but even she slipped when she saw the black. He was magnificent. He was also a bit scary. *Could they both really*

110

ride him? she wondered as the black horse raced around the corral, tossing his head and snorting.

At one whistle from Donnigan, the black dipped his head, snorted, and trotted obediently toward his owner. Kathleen longed to reach a hand out to the silky side of the animal, but she dared not do so without permission, and she refused to ask.

The black was soon bridled and saddled and Donnigan swung himself easily up. He reached down a hand for her. Black stomped impatiently, anxious to be off, but at a word from Donnigan he stopped his dancing.

"Give me your hand," said Donnigan. "Now, step up on my foot. When I lift, up you come behind me."

Kathleen reached up her hand, stepped on his foot and was lifted swiftly and easily from the ground to the back of the black horse. Never had she been up so high. It almost took her breath away.

"Put your arms around my waist and clasp your hands together," invited Donnigan.

Kathleen complied. She was glad that Donnigan could not see her flushed face.

"There's not much to see in the fields this time of year," Donnigan informed her. "The hay and crops are all in."

Donnigan held the black to a walk. The horse snorted his impatience and tossed his head, working the bit between his teeth. They traveled down a long lane, over the brow of a hill and past fields now empty of their summer's crops. The whole way the black sidestepped and danced and chomped at the bit.

"Does he always walk like this?" asked Kathleen innocently.

"He wants to run," said Donnigan.

Kathleen was silent for a few moments.

"Do you usually run?" she asked him.

"Usually," said Donnigan.

"Then—let him run," said Kathleen simply.

Donnigan half-turned in the saddle. "Are you sure?" he asked her. Kathleen nodded. Donnigan still looked doubtful.

"You'll have to hang on," he told her.

In answer she tightened her arms around him. He reached down with one hand to hold both of hers tightly and gave the black his head.

The horse answered immediately with a giant spring forward, and then they were rushing over the prairie grasses, the wind whipping at Kathleen's hair and fluttering her skirts. She had never experienced such an exhilarating sensation. On they went, covering the distance to the horse pasture in long strides, the muscles beneath her seeming to ripple with each forward lunge. Kathleen thought of the gentle roll of the sea.

They came to a fence and Donnigan pulled up the black with a soft "Whoa-a." Just on the other side of the fence a herd of horses was feeding. The black greeted them with an excited whinny, and many of the mares answered him. The herd began to stir, shifting, whirling, kicking up heels and playfully nipping one another.

The stallion stomped and pranced, eager to be back with his band.

"They're beautiful!" breathed Kathleen before she could check herself. "Whose are they?"

"Mine," replied Donnigan, pride coloring his voice. Then he blushed and corrected himself. "Ours." It was going to take some getting used to—this sharing of property, of their lives.

"Here, let me help you down," said Donnigan and reached his arm around to circle her waist. Kathleen felt herself being lifted up and out and lowered to the ground to stand beside the black. With one swift movement, Donnigan swung his leg over the black and joined her.

"We usually have to ride in to find them," Donnigan was explaining. "We were lucky today."

They stood for a moment watching the horses mill about. A few had approached the fence and extended their noses. The black moved eagerly forward to greet them. Others still ran and kicked and chased one another.

"Do they always act like that?" asked Kathleen.

"Only when the black comes around," replied Donnigan with a grin. "Then they show off a bit."

Kathleen would have liked to ask more questions but she held her tongue.

They watched the horses until the herd gradually settled. A few even went back to feeding.

"Ready?" asked Donnigan and Kathleen nodded. He gathered the reins and wheeled the reluctant stallion around, then mounted in one smooth motion and reached his hand for Kathleen. This time she did not need to be invited to place her arms around his waist. Firmly she clasped her hands together, hoping fervently that he would let the black run again. She could not hide her smile when he did. But Donnigan could not see it.

———

They surveyed the entire farm with its horses, cattle, fields, pastures, and woodlots before Donnigan turned the black toward home. They had been out for some hours. The day had grown hot, the hour past noon; still Kathleen was reluctant to relinquish the freedom she had felt when skimming across the prairie on the back of the big horse. She felt that she would just like to ride and ride—forever.

"I'll be in as soon as I take care of Black," Donnigan informed her as he eased her to the ground. Kathleen reached up a trembling hand to try to get her hair in order. The wind had wrenched the pins from their place.

She nodded her head slowly. She knew that Donnigan was saying that he would soon be in for his dinner.

Kathleen had never minded kitchen duties, so she washed her hands at the corner basin and began her search through the shelves. She found enough to fix them a proper dinner, but she realized that the American cupboard stock was different than what she had been used to.

Donnigan must have recognized the fact also, for as he washed at the basin later, he spoke without turning.

"We'll need to get into town soon and let you pick your

own fixin's. I haven't been in the habit of keeping much on hand."

Kathleen nodded, forgetting his back was to her.

He stood up straight to run the rough towel over his hands and face. "You can get the other things you'll want, too," he told her.

Her face must have registered her surprise. "What things?" she dared to ask.

"For the house. Whatever it is you need."

Kathleen let her gaze travel around the room. Oh, it was tempting. But she would not be demanding. Besides, Kathleen had never been given opportunity to "make a home" before. She didn't really know how one went about it—and she was afraid that she would make some terrible blunders if she attempted it. She did not want to risk the displeasure of the big man who stood opposite her in the cabin kitchen.

"The house is fine," she said, turning back to the stove. She missed seeing Donnigan's look of disappointment.

———

They were sitting on the porch enjoying the coolness of the fall evening. Kathleen had placed her shawl about her shoulders as the evenings could become chilly. They had shared this quiet time for almost four full weeks. It seemed a long time to Kathleen—and she still knew little more about Donnigan than she had the day she had entered his home. She longed to know—but remembered that he might resent her prodding. If there was one thing that Madam had stressed over and over, it was that a man didn't like being quizzed or nagged at.

Things had settled to a bit of a routine. Kathleen got the meals, did the laundry, kept the house clean. Donnigan cared for the animals, brought in the fresh pails of water and hauled the firewood. It seemed a good arrangement. In fact, Kathleen felt that she really should feel quite happy and contented. But she didn't. Deep down inside was a loneliness that hadn't been touched. In a way, she wondered if it really would have been that much different being a housemaid at Madam's new country home. She stole a glance at Donnigan, wondering if he could read her thoughts.

What bothered her the most was Donnigan's attitude. He still seemed to see her as a little girl. "Don't you lift that heavy pail." "Here, let me empty the wash water." "I'll build the fire." "I don't think the brown mare is ready for a young rider yet."

It galled Kathleen. She who had not just been independent but able to care for herself on the rough streets of London, and had also been responsible for others since she had been ten, was now being treated as if she were six.

At times it was all she could do to hold her temper in check. She was not a child. She was not without wits or ability. She was much stronger than he credited her with being. She was committed to this marriage—as strange as it was—but she longed to be an accepted partner, even if not an equal.

And she did long to ride the brown mare. The feeling that she had experienced on the black stallion with Donnigan holding the reins was only a taste of what it would be like to be in control of her own mount, she was sure. She couldn't wait to put her heels to the sides of the mare and sail over the brown hills and greened valleys.

————

Donnigan was sitting on the step whittling on a piece of wood. He couldn't have told why he had taken up whittling—except that it had helped to fill some of the lonely hours when he had been by himself in the house. He had rather hoped that he could put away his whittling knife with the coming of Kathleen. He knew that he would rather talk than whittle. But there didn't seem to be much talking done. He had looked forward to a winter of companionship—and here he was facing a winter of silence.

He had nothing against Kathleen—but she had not turned out to be what he had expected in a wife. He had wanted a woman who would come into his bare little cabin and fashion it into a home—warm and inviting and cozy. He had wanted a true companion—not just a maid in his kitchen. He had hoped for intimate chats about thoughts and feelings and dreams for the future. He had wanted someone to share every part of his life—and to let him be a part of hers. But Kathleen shut her thoughts and feelings away from him.

"It's her age," Donnigan told himself again. "When she matures—ages a bit—she'll open up more. I mustn't rush her. Give her time. Let her get the feeling that she belongs here."

Donnigan was pleased to see that the girl looked a bit healthier. She had been so pale, so weary, so frail, the first time he had set eyes on her. Already she seemed to be feeling much better, breathing in the fresh prairie air more deeply. Donnigan was glad for that. But he would be so glad when they were *really* partners. When Kathleen would look to him for companionship. For support. With all his heart he longed to give her more than a roof over her head, food at his table, the sharing of his bed at night.

His knife took a deeper cut than he had intended. His frustrations were showing in the work of his hands.

Donnigan hoped that his sigh did not reach the ears of Kathleen. Or if it did, that she wouldn't understand its meaning.

Kathleen sat on Erma's green and gold brocaded sofa and sipped tea. They had made it a habit to take tea together whenever Kathleen had a few extra minutes while in town.

"You are looking stronger, Kathleen—more—more robust," Erma observed.

Kathleen looked down at herself. Yes, she admitted, perhaps she was. Wasn't that one thing that had brought her to town? All her old dresses were getting too tight.

"I certainly feel better, I have to admit. I guess it's the fresh prairie air." She smiled at Erma.

"Or Donnigan," said Erma with a giggle.

Kathleen flushed. She had been Donnigan's wife for three months but she still blushed. For some strange reason she still felt like an imposter. A housekeeper.

"Do you ever get lonesome for home?" Erma surprised Kathleen by asking, and there was just the hint of sadness in her voice.

Kathleen thought about her answer. How much should she share? At last she nodded her head briefly. "Perhaps— just a bit—at times," she admitted, hoping that she wasn't giving anything away. Then she quickly added, "I guess that's natural enough."

"I guess," said Erma.

They both lifted their cups for another sip, then replaced them on the saucers.

"Do you?" asked Kathleen even though she felt she already knew the answer.

"A bit—at times," replied Erma.

Another sip of their tea.

"I suppose it's—it's because Lucas is so dreadfully busy," said Erma, then hastened as if to cover her confession. "I— mean—he is wonderful—just wonderful to me. I have everything—everything that I could possibly want. But he is so busy. He's such an important man. Why, he owns most of the town and he is so careful that everything be run—properly. I can't even imagine having so many things on my mind all at one time."

Kathleen nodded her head in support of Erma's claim. Everyone knew it for the truth.

"But he is so busy," Erma went on, her tone rather downcast. "He leaves long before I am up and doesn't come home some nights until I have fallen to sleep in my chair."

"What do you do with all your time?" asked Kathleen. Then quickly amended, "Not that you have spare time the way you keep things so spotlessly clean and—"

"Oh, I don't clean," explained Erma quickly. "The maid cleans—and the kitchen sends up our meals. If Lucas is too late, he sometimes stops at the dining room so he won't disturb me. He's very thoughtful, Lucas is." Erma gave Kathleen a forced smile.

"I would rather like to—to help out at the church or—or teach small children—or something—but Lucas says that wouldn't really be fitting," Erma went on thoughtfully.

She placed her cup and saucer on the delicate table by the sofa and smoothed imaginary wrinkles from her skirts. Then she looked up brightly. "Lucas says that my days will be more than full—once we have family," she said and color stained her cheeks.

"You are—are—?"

"I'm not sure—quite yet. But we do hope so. Lucas is so anxious for a son and I—well, I can hardly wait for a baby to—to help—" She stopped and toyed with the expensive looking rings on her fingers.

"I can hardly wait," she repeated with a little laugh, then rang for a maid to remove the tea things.

———

Donnigan hardly recognized Wallis when he met him on the street. The man was trimmed and pressed and polished until he shone.

"Well, aren't you looking fancy," Donnigan could not help but tease.

Wallis responded with a broad grin.

"And look at this," he invited showing his belt size. "I put on six pounds since she's been here."

"Must be a good cook," observed Donnigan. It was a known fact that Wallis hadn't been eating right for years.

"Good cook," said Wallis, nodding his head to emphasize the words. "Mighty good cook. Good at everything, that woman is. And can she work! Hey, I tell you that I never in my life seen anyone whip things into shape faster."

Donnigan reached out a hand and slapped his neighbor on the back. It was wonderful to see the man so happy.

"Haven't seen much of you lately," Donnigan observed. "Why don't you and Risa drop around for coffee?"

Wallis frowned slightly. "She ain't much for visitin'," he observed. "Oh, not thet she isn't friendly or all thet—it's just thet we got so much to do to catch up—to git the place in shape. We'll have time fer visitin' later on."

Donnigan nodded.

"You really outta stop by and see fer yerself how she's fixed up the place," said Wallis. "Ya wouldn't know it was the same cabin. Sure looks good. Sure does look good."

Again Donnigan nodded. He secretly wished that Kathleen had shown a bit more interest in fixing up their place; but if she was content with it as it was, why shouldn't he be?

A sharp whistle rent the air. Wallis spun on his heel and then turned back to Donnigan. "That's Risa. She's finished her shoppin'. She'll be wantin' to go." He turned, then said back over his shoulder, "That's the way she calls me." He grinned as though it was awfully cute to be summoned in such a way.

Chapter Thirteen

The Tempest

Kathleen lifted her head in surprise.

"I think I could put a lift on your shoe," Donnigan was saying.

The evenings were too cold now to sit out on the porch. Donnigan had brought his whittling indoors to the warm kitchen.

"A lift?" asked Kathleen.

"By building up the one shoe, the shorter leg would gain length. You wouldn't need to limp."

There, the truth was out. He was embarrassed about her limp.

"I worry about your spine," he went on simply. "I'm afraid the limp is hard on it."

Kathleen nodded mutely. Her back often ached so badly at night that she couldn't sleep. Could Donnigan be right?

"Do you mind if I try?" asked Donnigan.

Kathleen shook her head. She still wasn't sure if she should be thankful or offended.

Donnigan laid aside his whittling and crossed to where Kathleen sat near the stove.

"Let me see," said Donnigan. "Let me look at your boot."

Kathleen extended her legs, lifting her long skirts slightly as Donnigan knelt before her and carefully examined each foot.

"Now stand," said Donnigan. "Let's see how much—"

Kathleen obediently stood.

"Just as I thought," mused Donnigan as though to himself. "Not much at all—but it could make a real difference to your spine."

Donnigan worked many evenings before he was satisfied with the result. At last the boots were given to Kathleen for her to try.

At first the wooden lift made her foot feel clumsy and heavy, but Kathleen was surprised at how quickly she adjusted. Soon she was scurrying about the farm with scarcely a limp at all.

———

Kathleen stood at the kitchen window and stared balefully at the mounds of drifting snow. She had never heard such mournful wind, felt such bitter chill as with this early winter storm. Donnigan piled firewood almost to the ceiling of the cabin in his effort to keep her from shivering.

"You need warmer clothes," he told her, fussing over her again. "You're welcome to my flannel shirts, but I think you'd be swallowed up in them," he added, surveying her tiny form.

"As soon as the storm breaks, I'll head for town and look for some warm things for you," he told her. Kathleen shivered again, this time not just from the cold. Now he felt he had to dress her.

"At least put on a pair of my heavy wool socks," Donnigan invited as he stuffed more wood into the fire. "Helps a good deal if one's feet are warm."

Kathleen made a face behind his back, bit back her temper, and went to the bedroom to comply. She was committed to this marriage. She would not make a scene.

She hated to admit it, but the socks did help considerably. She even managed to stop her shivering.

What made her the most angry about the storm was that she was cooped up indoors after finally being given Donnigan's permission to ride. After many hours of gentling the brown mare, he had decided that she was ready for Kathleen—within reason. Kathleen was not to ride alone, not to ride the canyon trails south of the pasture, not to allow the mare her head. Kathleen inwardly chaffed over all the restrictions, but she did not argue. She did not wish the privilege to be retracted.

"I thought you might like to name her," Donnigan had said as he presented the reins to Kathleen for the first time.

"You haven't named her yet?" Kathleen asked in surprise.

Donnigan nodded. "I did," he replied, "but my names are never too fancy."

Kathleen had thought of the big black stallion. She certainly would have named him something different than Black had she been doing the choosing, so she nodded in silent agreement.

Kathleen ran her hand over the smooth nose of the mare and along the shiny neck. "Make friends with her," Donnigan advised, "but let her know who's boss."

It wouldn't be hard for Kathleen to make friends. She already loved the mare.

Kathleen had named her new mount Shee. "It means elf. My father used to tell me stories about them," she explained to Donnigan. If he had thought it a strange name for a horse, he had not said so.

They had gone for one ride. The day had been sunny but brisk. They both knew that winter was already rapping gently on Nature's door and would soon make entrance into their world. Kathleen longed to hold it back. She hated the thought of being confined to the cabin at the very time she had been given access to the trails of Donnigan's farmlands.

One ride together—one glorious ride, and then the storm had come and shut her in.

Kathleen turned her back to the window and winter. She didn't want to acknowledge the storm. Because of it she was stuck in the cabin being Donnigan's little girl again. She had hoped that the freedom she felt on the horse's back would help her to feel more like an adult, would help Donnigan see her as an adult.

When the storm's fury had broken, Donnigan went to town. It was still too cold for Kathleen to endure a trip on the cold wagon seat, he told her. Once she had warmer clothes they would go to town together.

In her agitation, Kathleen paced the kitchen, stopping occasionally to shove split logs into the fire with more force than necessary. It was a long day. She thought about going to the barn and saddling Shee for a ride but decided it would be better not to. Donnigan had handled the saddling chores. Kathleen wasn't quite sure if she could do it right.

"I need to watch what he does so I can do it for myself," she determined and paced the floor some more.

"I can at least go to the barn," she finally decided. The horses seemed pleased to see her. She stroked the brown neck of Shee and tried the curry a bit. She even dared to lean across the manger and rub the black's nose. He snorted and jerked his head, and Kathleen jumped back so quickly that she bumped her head on a support pole.

She decided to give the horses a treat of oats. Just then she heard the rumble of the wagon in the yard. Donnigan was home. She supposed that she should be excited about new clothes. At least curious about what a man would pick. But Kathleen was not. She would have preferred to do her own choosing.

So Kathleen deliberately stalled, slowly scooping oats from the sack nearby and dumping them in the manger bin. The horses snorted and plunged in their noses. Kathleen smiled to herself. She added scoop after scoop until the bins were full. When she could fit no more to the generous helping, she idly tossed the scoop back toward the sack and took her time leaving the barn.

Donnigan was just coming toward her with the team.

"Howdy," he called in good nature, then frowned slightly. "You better get in," he added. "You'll be catching your death of cold."

Kathleen wrinkled her nose but headed for the house.

Donnigan did not join her for some time. Kathleen put the coffeepot on. He would be chilled and would appreciate a cup.

She stoked the fire again so that the pot would boil quickly.

When Donnigan pushed his way through the door, his arms were filled with packages.

Looks like he bought out the store, Kathleen thought to herself, and in spite of her resolve she felt a stirring of interest.

But Donnigan looked bothered by something. Never had she seen such darkness in his eyes.

She wished to ask what was wrong, but she bit back the question. It was none of her business, was it?

Donnigan deposited all the parcels on the table. They filled the whole area. Kathleen wondered where he expected her to serve the coffee.

"Should I take—these—to the bedroom?" she asked when he turned to remove his heavy jacket and hang it on the peg by the door.

"Do whatever you want with them," Donnigan replied in a tone she had not heard him use before. "They're yours."

Kathleen's eyes widened. Something was wrong and that was for sure.

He washed his hands at the basin. She waited for the explosion she was sure would occur. She had remembered hearing that tone in her father's voice, and it had always been followed by a display of his Irish temper.

"Kathleen," Donnigan said as he reached for the towel. His voice was controlled—too controlled, as though fighting for patience with an erring child. "Don't ever feed the horses."

Kathleen stared at him in surprise. Surely—surely that wasn't a sin. Was he so possessive—?

"It could have killed them." His words were almost sharp. Blunt and stabbing.

Kathleen gasped and groped for some response. "I—I only gave them oats," she managed to say.

He just nodded.

"I've seen you give them oats." Kathleen was surprised at her own boldness. She who had determined not to cause any friction in this marriage was actually answering back to her husband. Madam would have been shocked.

"Yes," he said and returned the towel to the peg with one quick jerk. She felt that he was losing a bit of his control as well. "Very carefully measured oats," he said, his face taut with emotion. "If I hadn't happened home when I did—if those two horses had eaten what they had been given—" He stopped, seemingly unable to even think of the consequences.

He ran a trembling hand through his hair. She waited— her own hand fumbling with the parcel nearest her.

He took a deep breath, fighting hard to get himself in control again. When he spoke, his voice was low and almost pleading. As if he were talking to a child, Kathleen thought, and anger filled her whole being.

"Kathleen." He crossed the kitchen and stood close to her. "I know the farm is new to you. I know that you have never learned to—to care for stock and—and such. But please— don't—don't do things without checking with me. Oats—too many oats—can founder horses. Can kill them at times. We could have lost both horses. The mare and—and Black." He was almost white with the enormity of her misdeed.

Kathleen's own face went pale. She had not known. How could she have known?

"Sure then, and why didn't you tell me?" she demanded. "Why don't you teach me? You won't even talk to me other than telling me what I should or should not do." Her voice rose as she spoke until she found herself shouting. "You just—just keep treating me like—like I am a child. I'm not! I'm almost eighteen. And I'm not stupid either. I can learn. I'm an adult. Not a child who needs your coddling. Treat me like an adult. Give me some respect." And with the last words Kathleen's hand sought the nearest parcel of yardgoods and hurled it at Donnigan. She did not wait for his response. With sobs of anguish she ran to the little bedroom and slammed the door with such force the whole cabin trembled.

She flung herself on the bed and cried. Cried for home and Bridget. Cried for her missing father. Cried because of the empty, lonely place in her heart that would not go away. And cried for her marriage—the one she had just managed to destroy with her outburst. Surely Donnigan would never be able to forgive her for the way she had acted and the angry words she had hurled at him along with the wrapped material. She had just proved that she was indeed the child he thought her to be.

———

Donnigan lowered himself slowly to a kitchen chair and put his head in his hand. He had really done it. He had told himself all the way from the barn to the house that he must keep his control. That Kathleen did not know better. That he must not let his fright show as he spoke to her. But he had messed up the whole thing. Had really messed up. He wondered if he could ever make things right.

No, no, he guessed he couldn't. Things had never been right, not from the very beginning. This whole thing—this whole arranged marriage was a sham and a shame right from the start. He had been a fool. A blind fool to let Wallis and Lucas talk him into such a scheme.

But hadn't he become involved of his own free will? Wasn't it his decision? No one had twisted his arm that he had remembered. He couldn't go laying the blame at his neighbors' doors.

Donnigan lifted his head and ran his hand nervously through his hair. No. It was his fault. He had to take the full blame. He just hadn't been ready for marriage. Oh, he thought he was. Longed for a wife and even children. But Kathleen was so—so young and so—so— That was the trouble. He had ordered a wife and they had sent him a child.

Though he never would have dared to share his feelings with Kathleen, daily he worried that she might announce she was expecting a child herself. His child. She was too young, too frail to bear his baby. It was a fear that haunted him—that sometimes kept him awake in the darkness as he felt the strands of her dark hair touch his shoulder and listened to her even breathing as she slept.

And now—now he had hurt her deeply. So deeply that he had no idea of how to go about repairing the damage. Were they to go on and on in this marriage, shut away from each other? He didn't know if he could stand it.

He shook himself free from his dark thoughts and rose to get a cup of the boiling coffee.

He had no choice. He was in the marriage now. Whether it was a good one—or a poor one—had little bearing. Kathleen was his responsibility. He would care for her in the best way he knew how.

———

Kathleen cried until she was exhausted. At last she fell into a troubled sleep. When she at last awoke, the bedroom window told her that darkness had fallen. Unconsciously she shifted on the bed, trying to sense if Donnigan slept beside her.

She felt a pang of concern when she discovered his absence, and then another pang when she remembered what had brought her to the room in the first place.

"He will be so angry with me," she mourned and rolled back over to bury her head in the pillow for a fresh burst of tears.

"What do I do now? Oh, what do I do?"

In spite of her desire to stay right where she was with her sorrow, she forced herself to stir.

"It's past supper," she scolded herself, not one to avoid responsibility. "He'll be hungry."

Kathleen reached up to calm her tumbling hair. The pins had come loose as she had tossed in her sleep. She didn't wish to take the time to repin it, so she lifted the comb and ran it quickly through the dark, tangled curls, letting them tumble about her shoulders in girlish fashion.

"Now he will really think me a child," she said to herself, and anger burned her cheeks again.

He was sitting silently in his big chair when she quietly

slipped out to the kitchen. A newspaper was spread across his knees, but she noticed that his eyes were not upon it. At the sound of her entrance he roused and looked at her.

"Did you sleep well?" The words sounded choked. Forced. She heard him swallow.

"Well enough," she managed to respond and moved to the stove. She noticed that the parcels had all been removed from the table and were carefully stacked in a corner.

"I've eaten," he said woodenly. "There's enough in the pot for your supper."

Kathleen didn't feel like eating. She moved the pot from the back of the stove where it had been keeping warm and turned to the small cupboard. She would just do the cleaning up and then go back to bed.

But the cleaning up had also been done. The dishes were all neatly stacked back on the shelves.

The wind howled outside again, rattling the branch that always scratched against the house. Kathleen shuddered.

"Another storm moving in," observed Donnigan. "Good thing I managed to get to town for—" Then he stopped short.

He changed the topic quickly, rising from his chair and heading for his heavy coat. "Erma sent you a note," he said. "I had her help me with the—the choosing."

Kathleen's full attention was immediate. She accepted the note and pulled a chair up close to the table and the lamp and began to read the short letter.

Dear Kathleen,

I have just been dying to see you. I do hope that the weather will soon improve so you can come to town. I have so much to talk to you about.

We are going to have a baby! Lucas is so excited. He has already picked the name for his son. I can hardly wait. I've started my sewing. Lucas says at the rate that I am going, it will have to be triplets to make use of all the things.

Come and see me as soon as you can.

With warmest regards,

Erma

Kathleen carefully folded the letter and placed it in her apron pocket. How she envied Erma. Erma who was expecting a child. Erma who Lucas allowed to be a woman. Erma who now shared with a man the most intimate experience a woman could ever share—the plans and dreams and preparations of the coming of a child to their home. Kathleen felt like crying again. She dared not look toward Donnigan.

She rose from her chair and retreated to the bedroom. She was still awake when, much later, Donnigan joined her. She turned her back and feigned sleep. She wasn't sure she liked the man. She might even hate him.

Chapter Fourteen

A Long Talk

Nothing further was said about the incident. They seemed to declare an unspoken truce. Kathleen was not sure if she was sorry or relieved. After a few days of strained silence, life went on much as it had before.

Kathleen did not go near the barn again, though she longed to pay a visit to Shee. Instead, she spent her time with needle in hand, sewing up garments from the material Donnigan had purchased. She would not have let herself express her joy at having new clothes of her very own, clothes that would actually fit properly, but she felt thankfulness nonetheless. She was quite willing, in her thinking, to lay all the credit at Erma's door.

Donnigan was glad for winter chores. As every winter, the horses and cattle had been moved to the pasture adjoining the corrals so that they could be more easily cared for. The saddle horses and team were kept in the barn except on the warmer days. That meant barn cleaning, a job that Donnigan had once deplored. Now he welcomed even that, for it took him from the close confines of the kitchen. He took to talking to the black again. At first he felt awkward and embarrassed, but when the black rubbed his nose on the man's sleeve as though he had been missing the conversations,

Donnigan waved aside his feelings and enjoyed his little one-sided chats.

He did not discuss Kathleen—or his empty marriage. That was far too personal even to share with a horse. Instead, he talked about the weather, the other farm animals, or his plans for spring.

At times Donnigan found himself envying Lucas. The man seemed totally pleased with his marriage. He always spoke about how he was teaching Erma this or telling her about that. It seemed to Donnigan that the two really talked.

Donnigan missed Wallis. He would have loved to slip over to the neighbor's farm for a manly chat and a cup of the bitter coffee. But Wallis gave all indications of being more than wrapped up in his new wife. Folks joked in town about Wallis becoming henpecked. She whistled—he ran. But if Wallis didn't mind the arrangement, why should anyone else fuss, Donnigan reasoned.

No, it seemed that he was really the only one of the three who had struck out. And he couldn't blame it on the young Kathleen. He had been surprised to hear her declare that she was seventeen. Though still young, she was older than he had thought. He had feared that she might be closer to fifteen. Almost eighteen, she had said. Donnigan had known many girls who were married by eighteen. It was Kathleen's size that had fooled him. She was so tiny. So frail.

No, actually she wasn't that frail anymore. Oh, she was still a small, dainty woman, but she wasn't frail. She looked much better than when she had first arrived. And she was much stronger than she looked, he granted her that.

She had said that he treated her like a child, and with a flush to his cheeks, he admitted that he had. He had such a time thinking of her as anything else. But he was working on it. He really was.

———

They were invited to share Christmas with Lucas and Erma. Kathleen was sure that Lucas's invitation had come in response to Erma's pleading. But she was just thankful for the opportunity to get out of the house for a day.

The weather cooperated. It was still cold, but the wind was not blowing, and the sun was weakly sharing its rays with the world. Kathleen wore her favorite of the new garments and wrapped her warmest shawl closely about her shoulders. She saw Donnigan toss a couple of warm blankets in the sled, but he refrained from telling her that she should wrap up in them.

Erma was still not "showing"—except in her face that seemed to glow. Again Kathleen felt envy wash over her. Erma had so much.

Lucas, always the good host, had arranged a complete turkey dinner for them to eat in the hotel dining room rather than up in the suite. "Food odors sometimes bother Erma," Lucas explained.

But Kathleen cared not where she was served. It was so good to get out. So nice to be with other people.

After the dinner, Lucas needed his cigar, so he and Donnigan stayed to chat in the dining room while Erma and Kathleen went to the rooms above.

"I can hardly wait to show you all the baby things," Erma enthused as they climbed the stairs.

Lucas had been right. Erma had already filled a chest with carefully stitched little garments. Kathleen wondered how she would fill her next six months.

"You are really happy, aren't you, Erma?" Kathleen could not help but say.

"Oh yes!" exclaimed the young woman. "It has made so much difference to be—to be waiting for a child. My hours have meaning now. The days aren't nearly so lonely. And Lucas—Lucas comes home every morning, promptly at ten, so that I can get some fresh air and some exercise."

At Kathleen's puzzled look, Erma hurried to explain.

"It isn't proper for a woman to be out on the streets alone," she said, "so Lucas comes home and takes me for a walk."

Kathleen could only stare. Poor Erma had been virtually a prisoner in her own suite of rooms.

"When I get too—too—obvious to be on the streets of town, Lucas says that we will drive to the country, tie the carriage, and go for a little walk down some private trail."

Kathleen's mouth fell open. She quickly put aside her envy. At least Donnigan allowed her *some* freedom.

"Oh, Lucas has been reading up on it," Erma hurried on, not understanding Kathleen's expression. "One must have fresh air and exercise—for the sake of the mother and the baby."

For all Donnigan's fretting about her coming down with a cold, it was he himself who came in from chores with a flushed face and a sore throat.

Kathleen racked her brain for a home remedy that would keep the man on his feet, but came up empty.

The next morning he was dreadfully fevered. When he forced himself from the bed and tried to pull on his flannel shirt, Kathleen saw him shaking.

"What's wrong?" she asked, fear in her voice.

"I'm all right," he insisted.

"You're not all right," Kathleen flung back at him. "You're shaking all over."

"Just the chills," he responded. "I'll be fine."

Kathleen threw back the warm blankets and bounded to her feet.

"You won't be fine. Look at you."

She crossed to him and reached her hand up to his forehead. "Sure, and you're burning with fever!" she exclaimed, fear gripping her.

She pushed her feet into knitted house slippers to ward off the chill of the wooden floor.

"You'd best get back to bed," she instructed. "I'll see to the fire."

"I can't," argued Donnigan. "I've got to care for the stock."

"I'll care for the stock," responded Kathleen, already reaching for her warmest skirt.

"But you can't—" began Donnigan.

"I can—and I will," said Kathleen with boldness, the determination in her voice unmistakable. "That is—if you'll be good enough to tell me what to do."

Donnigan did not miss the challenge. He stared at Kathleen for a moment, seeing the dark flashing of her eyes.

He removed the shirt from his shoulders and tossed it on the floor by the bed.

"I'll tell you," he said meekly and climbed back under the covers.

Carefully and fully Donnigan explained the chore procedures to Kathleen. From time to time she nodded her head as an indication that she had understood. By the time he had finished his explanation, he was drenched in a cold sweat. Even he had to admit that he would not have been able to get up.

"If you need help, go for Wallis," he managed before lapsing into a fit of coughing.

"I won't need help," said Kathleen firmly. "I'll bring you something for your throat—then you stay put."

———

Donnigan was dreadfully ill, and Kathleen was dreadfully worried. She had none of the things that had been used in her London home to fight colds and influenza. She really didn't know what to do for Donnigan except to try to relieve his mind concerning the stock and to sponge bathe him to bring down his fever. She offered him soup and tea as often as she could coax him into taking a few swallows, but found it difficult to get him to try food.

It was almost two weeks before Donnigan felt strong enough to stir around the kitchen. Kathleen had put in many, many long hard days. The weather had not been kind. She had needed to fight the elements as well as his illness. And the chores had taken much of her strength and time. There had even been a cow who had calved out of season. Kathleen had put her in the barn, managed to quiet her, and promptly informed her that she would from henceforth be responsible to provide them with milk.

"She's never been milked," argued Donnigan when Kathleen told him that she had herself a milk cow.

"She has now," announced Kathleen and thrust a custard pudding in his hand.

"But how did you—?" began Donnigan.

"I bribed her with chop—and tied her legs," replied Kathleen simply.

"What about the calf?" asked Donnigan.

"The calf is drinking fine from a pail. There's plenty for all of us."

Donnigan could only shake his head and smile.

———

At last Donnigan was strong enough to return to the chores. Kathleen did not argue but inwardly she knew that she would miss the choring. She wouldn't deny that it had been difficult work. But it was a nice change to get out of the house. And she enjoyed working with the animals. She even chatted as she curried the horses or milked the now-cooperative cow. She did not look forward to being shut up in the kitchen again. In spite of the additional work, Kathleen concluded that she had never in her life really felt so good.

Much of it was due, she was sure, to the lift on the shoe. It did help her whole body to have her spine kept straight as she moved about. And when each of those long hard days came to an end, she slept as never before.

———

"We need to talk," said Donnigan, pushing back his empty supper plate.

Kathleen's head came up. Donnigan had now returned to his chores. Had he discovered something she had left undone? Or not done right? She found her mind scrambling to try to sort out where she might have failed.

"I did a lot of thinking while I lay there in bed," said Donnigan.

Kathleen still stared, not sure where he was headed.

"You said I think of you as a child," said Donnigan, and Kathleen drew in her breath. So, after all the weeks that had passed, they were finally going to go back to their quarrel. It appeared that Donnigan had a long memory. Kathleen had hoped that they could forget what had been said that evening. Now it seemed that Donnigan was going to open old wounds. Kathleen turned to face him, her chin lifting.

"I think of you as a child," he repeated. "How?"

It was the wrong question. Kathleen felt the color rush to her cheeks. She lifted eyes filled with hurt and defiance. She was right back to where she was when she had flung the parcel at him and headed for the bedroom.

"How?" she spat at him. "How? In every way, that's how."

Donnigan cursed under his breath. He was going at all this the wrong way again.

"You—you—" Kathleen was suddenly so angry again that she could not find the words to accuse him.

Donnigan reached out to touch her arm, and she flung his hand off as she faced him.

"I'm only asking so I can find out what I need to correct," he said quickly, but there was a bit of bite to his words as well.

Kathleen just stared.

Donnigan rose to his feet and began to pace the room. He rubbed his hands together in front of him as though deeply seeking answers—direction.

"I don't know about you," he said at last, still pacing, "but I'm not exactly happy with this marriage, and I might as well say it."

Kathleen sucked in her breath again. She felt that she had been slapped. She had tried so hard not to make fusses. Not to demand and now—

"And I'm not putting the blame on you," Donnigan hurried to explain. "Truth is"—he stopped pacing and faced her—"I haven't known how to be a husband."

His honest and frank confession caught her totally off guard. She had expected him to point the finger at her. Instead, he stood before her with a look of shame and embarrassment.

"I need your help, Kathleen." There was pleading in his voice.

She lowered her head so she wouldn't have to see the pain in his eyes.

"You were right," he confessed further, resuming his pacing again. "I—did think of you as a child. I still—still fight it. But I know—I've seen—that you are a woman. A woman that I would like to share my life with—but I need help."

All of the anger drained from Kathleen. She sat motionless except for the trembling of her shoulders.

"What's wrong with us, Kathleen?" he begged. "What are we doing wrong? Why aren't we happy—instead of—of just living together?"

Kathleen sat for one moment, observing the bent shoulders of the strong young man before her. She had been braced for a fight. She could not fight this.

"I don't know," she whispered, her defenses crumbling. All her loneliness and longing tumbled in upon her. Her hands came up to cover her face, and the tears dripped between her fingers.

In two quick strides he was there, gathering her into his arms, holding her close against his chest, pressing kisses against her hair.

"Oh, Kathleen," she heard him murmur over and over. "Kathleen, I do love you. I really do. Help me to show you. Please, Kathleen."

She cried against him until she had no more tears. He brushed them away with his fingers and wiped them on his shirt sleeve. When she was finally able to look up at him, she noticed tearstains on his cheeks as well.

"We'll make it," he whispered. "We'll make it—but I want us to be happy. Both of us."

He pulled her even closer and kissed her again.

"So what do we do?" asked Kathleen with a trembling

voice as soon as she was able to speak.

He shook his head. "I don't know," he answered truthfully. "I don't have the answers—but I think we need to talk."

Talk. Oh, how Kathleen longed to talk. To really talk. Not just to say, "Good morning. Did you sleep well? Please pass the biscuits." No, really talk.

She nodded and wiped her nose on a handkerchief from her apron pocket.

"Where do we start?" she managed.

"I don't know." Slowly he released her. "There is so much that we still haven't said. So much we haven't shared." Then he dared to go on. "I have longed to talk, but I thought you— you weren't ready to share your past—your heart. I was waiting—"

"And I wanted to talk," Kathleen laughed shakily, "but Madam always said a man didn't want a—a chatterer."

"Chatterer? That was one reason I sent for a wife—so I wouldn't have to talk to Black."

Kathleen laughed again. So he talked to the animals, too. It seemed funny. Ironical.

He sat down on a kitchen chair and pulled her onto his knees. "Let's talk," he said with a grin. "Let's talk all night if we want to. Let the dishes wait. I want to know all about you. I want you to know all about me."

Kathleen put her arms around his neck and drew his head against her. It was almost surprising for her to discover that she didn't hate him after all. She had never felt such deep, fervent love.

Chapter Fifteen

Erma

Once the door had been opened to real communication, Kathleen felt that she could not get enough. At times she wondered if she really was becoming a chattering woman, but Donnigan seemed to enjoy it. He nodded and smiled and made comments of his own, and night after night, before they knew it, the evening was gone and it was time to retire again.

"How much more quickly time goes when you have someone to talk to," Kathleen mused.

"Is Black missing your conversations?" she teased Donnigan one evening as they sat by the fire, she with a sock to darn and he with one of his old newspapers.

He grinned. "I talk to him now and then just so he won't feel left out," he teased back.

Kathleen chuckled. "And I still talk to Polly when I milk her," she admitted.

Kathleen had insisted that she be the one to milk the cow morning and night. It was good to get out of the kitchen and breathe a breath of fresh air. And Polly was milked in the barn, so it was never too cold.

They were silent while Kathleen threaded her needle. But the silence was no longer cold and threatening. They both knew they could break it if they had an idea they wished to discuss, a thought to share, or just an event of the day to tell about.

Donnigan's eyes went back to his paper.

"What are you?" Kathleen asked suddenly, causing Donnigan's head to lift.

"What am I?" He hesitated. "A man—I hope."

Kathleen chuckled. "I mean—what nationality? What were your kin?"

Donnigan shrugged carelessly. "I dunno."

"Donnigan *sounds* Irish," Kathleen commented.

"You know an Irishman named Donnigan?"

Kathleen made another stitch. "No," she admitted. "But when I first saw your name on that piece of paper, I thought maybe it was Irish."

"Well, I've never met another man—or boy—in my whole life who answered to the name," said Donnigan, his tone ironic.

"I wonder what nationality it is. Where it came from," Kathleen said as she placed another stitch.

Donnigan shrugged again.

"Don't you care?" asked Kathleen. "I mean, I'm an O'Malley. I've been told that all my life. My father made me feel proud to be Irish. And you don't even know what you are. Doesn't it matter at all to you?"

"Guess not. I've never given it much thought. What difference does it make? Men are—men. People are people. No difference."

Kathleen glanced up at him, surprised by his attitude.

"But wouldn't you like to know if you are French or German or British—or Irish?" she asked in mock exasperation.

"Don't think I'm Irish," Donnigan returned.

"Sure now, and you definitely are not," said Kathleen pertly, her accent strengthening for the first time in a long while. "An Irishman knows what he is, and that's the pure truth of it."

Donnigan smiled.

"Sure now," he tried to mimic her.

Kathleen threw the newly darned sock at him and he rose quickly from his chair, chasing her around the kitchen and stuffing the mended sock down the front of her gown.

"You can never be serious," she accused him, though she knew it wasn't true.

"I'm serious," he answered, but his voice still held teasing.

"Then tell me where you ever got a name like Donnigan."

He still held her around the waist. "I don't know," he replied. "My mother named me, I was told. Where she got it—or why she liked it—I'll never know."

"Don't you like it?"

He released her then. "If you had any idea how many fights I had as a youngster over this name of mine—"

"But why?"

"I've no idea. It's just—just different."

"Then why haven't you changed it? You could go by Don or—or—"

"Guess that's the reason I fought. Fellas were always trying to call me something else. Pin a nickname on me. And I kept insisting that my name was Donnigan—and that they call me that."

In their short time together Kathleen had heard Donnigan correct a storekeeper who didn't call him by his full name. He had not been rude. Just simply stated, "The name is Donnigan." At the time she had been surprised that he would make an issue of it. She was especially surprised now when he confessed he didn't even like the name.

But Donnigan had become serious. "I lost my mother when I was very young," he said with deep feeling. "My name is the one thing I have from her. Guess that seemed reason enough to fight for it."

Seeing the pain in his eyes, Kathleen wished she hadn't asked.

———

A rider pounded into the farmyard, a young boy from town. Kathleen and Donnigan were both surprised. Rarely did they have company and never anyone who came so obviously on a mission. Donnigan met him at the door.

"Is Mrs. Harrison in?" he asked, sounding out of breath.

Kathleen moved to the door, her eyes wide with concern. The young lad reached up to remove his cap.

"I've a note for you, ma'am—from Mr. Stein," the boy said, and handed Kathleen an envelope.

Kathleen's hand began to tremble. *Whatever would Lucas have to say to her that would require courier service—and at such speed,* she wondered.

By the time she had crossed to a kitchen chair and torn open the envelope, Donnigan was shutting the door. The boy was gone.

Donnigan came to stand beside her and she held the note so he could read over her shoulder.

"Dear Mrs. Harrison," the note began.

"Please excuse my liberty in calling on you, but Erma is asking for you to come. She fears she is losing the baby.

"Lucas Stein."

"Oh no," sobbed Kathleen, her eyes wide with the tragedy of it.

"I'll get the team."

"Wouldn't it be faster to ride?" asked Kathleen, already going toward the bedroom to change into warmer clothing.

He hesitated for only a moment, then nodded. "I'll get the horses," he said and reached for his Stetson.

Kathleen quickly changed her dress for one more appropriate for riding. She pinned her hair tightly and secured her bonnet. Then she reached for a warm sweater. A shawl simply would not do for riding Shee at a gallop.

Even as she hurried, her mind was in a spin. Erma might lose her baby. She would be crushed. But what could she, Kathleen, do about it? She was not a doctor. Kathleen inwardly pleaded with a God she hoped might listen that the baby and Erma would be okay.

By the time Kathleen closed the door behind her, Donnigan was bringing the horses toward the house. He helped Kathleen up into her saddle and then mounted Black. Both horses had been lacking in exercise and wanted to run.

"Hold her in check," Donnigan couldn't help but caution.

"She hasn't been ridden for a while."

Kathleen nodded. But it was hard. Not only did the mare wish to run, but Kathleen wished that she could let her. It was Donnigan who kept them under control.

By the time they reached the hotel it was all over. Erma had lost the baby. Kathleen found her sobbing uncontrollably. Lucas paced the floor beside the bed. Truly this was one event totally out of his control.

A doctor had been called from Raeford, but he had not arrived until it was too late. He did give Erma something to make her sleep and gently eased Kathleen from the room as soon as Erma's eyes became heavy.

"She needs her rest," he whispered. "That is all that we can do for her now."

Kathleen felt sick inside. It was so hard for Erma to lose the child—to pack away all her hopes and dreams along with the little garments in the chest at the end of the bed.

Kathleen longed to reach out with help for her friend. What could she say? What could she do? The ride back home was a silent one.

———

Kathleen went to see Erma often over the next weeks. Donnigan felt more and more confident with her handling of the mare and even got so he let her go alone. He may not have been quite so at ease had he known that once out of sight of the house, Kathleen often gave the mare her head. She loved the feel of the wind as it tugged at her bonnet and whipped her skirts.

Nor would he have felt at ease had Kathleen confessed that she thought—she just thought there might be a chance that she too was expecting a child.

But Donnigan knew nothing about either, and so Kathleen rode to town alone and rode at her own pace.

Each time she entered the suite of hotel rooms, she hoped with all her heart that she would find some improvement in Erma's state of mind. But always she was disappointed.

"I don't know what I did wrong. I don't know," Erma wailed again and again.

"Sure now, and you didn't do anything wrong," Kathleen tried to comfort her. "Sometimes those things just happen."

"But Lucas read all the books. We did all the things they said."

Kathleen felt impatient with Lucas and his books. It was all she could do to keep from telling Erma so.

"Lucas is so upset with me," went on Erma. "He thinks I must have done something—something to hurt the baby."

"Such nonsense!" Kathleen fairly exploded.

"Oh—I wanted that baby so much," moaned Erma. "So much."

Kathleen longed to tell her, "There will be other babies," but she didn't dare speak the words.

———

"How is she?" Donnigan asked, meeting Kathleen in the farmyard after a visit to Erma.

"Not good," she replied, frustration in her voice. "She just continues to grieve and grieve."

"I guess that's understandable," said Donnigan, taking the mare's rein and helping Kathleen dismount. "She was so looking forward to having the child."

"But she must stop her moaning," said Kathleen. "After all, she can have another child. There is nothing physically wrong with her, Dr. Heggith says. She just has to get ahold of herself."

Donnigan looked a bit surprised at Kathleen's outburst. He turned the mare toward the barn. "Maybe she will—soon," he said.

They walked a few paces before Donnigan broke the silence.

"Do you think it's that easy?" he asked.

"Of course I don't think it's easy," responded Kathleen in a quieter tone. "Of course not—easy—but necessary. One has to go on with life no matter how one feels. I know how she must be feeling. If I lost my baby—"

Donnigan stopped short.

"If you what?" he asked abruptly.

Kathleen flushed. She still hadn't told him, but she was quite sure now. She had been waiting for just the right time. She took a deep breath, then another step toward the barn.

But Donnigan's hand on her shoulder stopped her.

"What are you saying?" he asked her bluntly.

Kathleen stopped, looked at him with a flushed face, and lowered her head.

"I thought we made a promise—that we would talk to each other—tell each other everything," Donnigan said, hurt and distance in his voice.

"I was going to tell you," defended Kathleen.

"Then it's true?"

Kathleen nodded her head.

She hated the pained look in Donnigan's eyes. He looked directly at her for what seemed a terrible length of time; then he moved away to lead the mare into the barn.

Kathleen watched him go, shifting uncomfortably from one foot to the other, then turned and went to the house.

———

"Donnigan—I'm sorry," Kathleen whispered into the darkness after they had retired.

He had brushed a kiss against her cheek, said good-night in a strained manner, then turned on his side, his back to her.

Kathleen feared he might be angry that they were going to have a child. If that was so—she would also be angry right back at him. Didn't children go with marriage?

She gathered her courage and decided to try again. As Donnigan had reminded her, they had promised to talk things out.

"Don't you want to be a father?" she asked his back.

"Of course I do," he responded immediately.

"Then why—"

"I think I had a right to know—without it being a—a blunder," he said.

She knew then that she had hurt him deeply.

"I was going to tell you—soon," she defended. "It's just—just I've been so worried about Erma."

"What about my worry?" asked Donnigan, still not turning to her.

"Your worry?" she said, puzzled.

He half-turned. "About you—about our baby," he answered with a trembling voice.

"What do you mean? I'm fine. The baby is—is just beginning."

"I'm worried about you, Kathleen. You said I saw you as a child. Well, I've changed that. I'm—I'm trying hard to change that. But even if you are a—a woman, you are still—still small. Maybe too small to—to have a child."

Kathleen lay beside him, listening to his words. She began to understand his fears.

"I'm the same size as my mother was—and she had me," she informed him gently. "And her mother was even smaller, so she told me, and she had seven babies, and that's the pure truth of it."

"Oh, Kathleen," moaned Donnigan, and he turned over to gather her close. "If anything should happen—"

"It won't," she tried to assure him. "It won't."

Kathleen still went to see Erma as often as she could, but Donnigan now insisted upon driving her to town—slowly. The trips wasted a whole day and Kathleen chaffed with each step that the plodding team made. But she dared not argue. She could still read concern in Donnigan's eyes each time they talked of the baby. She wanted to give him all the reason for assurance that she could.

Erma did not show any sign of improving. She was out of bed now, but she still spent her days grieving and sorrowing over what should have been the happiest summer of her life. Kathleen sensed that the loss of the baby was putting a terrible strain on Erma's marriage. She fervently wished she could do *something* for her friend.

Chapter Sixteen

Sean

When spring finally came, Donnigan was so busy in the fields that Kathleen felt she hardly saw him. She missed him around the kitchen. But she understood about the planting of the crops.

Often on warm days she packed a lunch, filled a pail with cool well water, and walked to the fields to picnic with him while the horses munched on nearby grasses. Those were good times for Kathleen and she felt that Donnigan looked forward to her noon visits.

He had built the chicken pen as promised, and it was now filled with half a dozen hens and a cocky rooster. Kathleen hoped to increase the flock, so she set aside eggs while she waited for some of the hens to decide to brood.

She had also coaxed Donnigan for a garden and he had humored her. But he made her promise that she would allow him to do the hoeing. He was still worried about her and the baby.

———

Kathleen did not tell Erma about the coming child until midsummer when it was no longer possible to hide her secret. Erma was still grieving over the loss of her own baby. Kathleen believed that her friend should have put aside her grief and her chest of tiny garments before now, but Erma clung to both.

When the truth was finally out, Kathleen saw the hurt look in Erma's eyes. She had so longed to share her joy with her friend but realized that the joy was hers alone. The baby was only a sharp and painful reminder to Erma.

"It seems that I've truly messed up this one," Kathleen scolded herself. "I didn't really get to tell anyone. First I missed sharing it with Donnigan—and that didn't turn out well. Then I couldn't tell Erma until she guessed it herself. I sure do wish there was someone I could tell."

Kathleen thought of Risa, but she had never seemed to be able to form a friendship with the new Mrs. Tremont. Donnigan had even lost touch with Wallis, and Kathleen knew that troubled him. The crusty old bachelor had been good company at one time.

Kathleen longed to be able to share her good news with her own kin. She had tried three times to send a letter to Bridget, but each time it came back to her unopened. It seemed that the country address Kathleen had been given and the school where Bridget was to have attended had never heard of the girl. It worried Kathleen more than she wanted to let show.

The late summer, a warm one, had Donnigan often scolding Kathleen about getting too much sun. She no longer minded his fussing. She realized that it was not because he was viewing her as a child but that he was filled with concern for her and for their coming baby.

So she accepted the good-humored "chastisement" and tried her best to fulfill his wishes.

Harvest time meant that again Donnigan was busy in the fields. But he would no longer allow her the trips with the picnic lunches and water pails. He took his lunch with him, and whenever he was thirsty he stopped at the small creek that ran through the property.

"It's too long a walk. And what if you twisted an ankle on the uneven ground and went down," he worried.

Kathleen only smiled, but she did feel he was unreasonable. Surely she wasn't that clumsy.

He did let her harvest her garden, along with cautions about "overdoing it." Kathleen glowed with pleasure as she took in the vegetables, thinking how much they would improve their diet in the winter months. Some of the produce she canned. Kathleen was sure Donnigan didn't realize what a demanding job it was to spend hours cleaning and preparing the vegetables and then standing over the hot stove processing the canned goods. If he had, he never would have allowed it.

Donnigan had also prepared a root cellar in between his haying and harvesting time. Kathleen was glad to have it ready to accept her garden store.

Eventually the garden and the crops were all properly harvested and stored. Donnigan shared with neighbors in the butchering of hogs and the curing of hams. They were all ready for another winter.

Kathleen had been spending her evenings sewing her own tiny baby garments. Never had she enjoyed an activity so much. With each stitch she made she had to push away thoughts of Erma. She was coming to a new understanding of the woman's devastation over her loss. Kathleen found herself counting the days until her own special event.

Even Donnigan seemed to put his fears and concerns a little further from him with each passing month. He dared to hope that things would be fine. While Kathleen sewed, he whittled rungs for a cradle.

"When it is time, I think we should take the stage to Raeford and stay there until the baby comes," Donnigan had informed Kathleen. "That way we will be sure to have a doctor on hand."

Kathleen had not argued. A little trip to the city might

be a nice diversion for both of them.

"What about the farm chores?" she asked instead.

"I'm sure Wallis will watch things for me for a few days," Donnigan responded and it seemed to be settled. Both of the occupants of the household looked forward to what November would bring.

———

"What do you wish to name the baby if it's a girl?" Kathleen asked Donnigan as they breakfasted together one morning.

He hesitated for a moment, then responded with, "What would you suggest?"

"I rather like Meara," said Kathleen.

"Sounds just fine," agreed Donnigan with a nod.

Again silence closed in around them.

" 'Course if it's a boy he'll be named for his father," Kathleen remarked.

His head came up quickly. "You mean Donnigan?"

Kathleen began to chuckle softly. "Of course Donnigan," she said, laying a hand on his arm. "You *are* his father."

He shook his head as he lifted his coffee cup. "No siree," he said emphatically. "No son of mine is gonna carry that handle around for the rest of his life."

Kathleen looked surprised.

"I told you I had to fight my way all through my school days," went on Donnigan. "My boy might have him a fight or two—but it won't be over his name if I can help it."

"What then?" asked Kathleen.

"Something plain and sensible—like Frank or George," he answered.

"I don't like either of those," said Kathleen with a lift of her chin. She decided that she would give the matter of a boy's name some careful thought.

———

Donnigan went alone to town for supplies. The wind was chilly and the sky threatening. Kathleen looked at the gray sky and agreed with her husband that she should stay home. It made her shiver just to look outside.

"When it storms this time of year it could last awhile," Donnigan said with another glance at the sky. "I'd best go on in while I have the chance."

Kathleen nodded and made out her list while Donnigan went for the team.

It was early in the afternoon when Kathleen felt the first uncomfortable twinge. It only lasted for a few minutes and then it was gone. She dismissed it as some strange muscle spasm and went on with her baking.

When it was repeated a few minutes later, she felt some alarm.

"It can't be the baby," she told herself. "He isn't due for three weeks yet."

But in another fifteen minutes, Kathleen had another sharp pain. She looked at the clock, willing Donnigan home.

By the time he did arrive, Kathleen had been forced to take to her bed. Donnigan panicked.

"But you said it wasn't to be until the end of November," he reminded Kathleen.

Kathleen nodded mutely.

"It's only the first part of November," Donnigan said, staring at the calendar on the wall to confirm the fact.

Kathleen nodded again.

"Well—it can't be time—now," Donnigan concluded unreasonably.

"Babies sometimes do things their own way," replied Kathleen, tears in her eyes. She had not planned to be on her own for this delivery, and the very thought of it was frightening.

"What can we do?" he asked her. "The storm has moved in and the doctor is miles away."

"It's too early," moaned Kathleen again. She did wish that her baby would decide to wait until the proper time.

"I'll go for help."

"Go where?" cried Kathleen as another contraction seized her.

"I don't know—but we need *someone*."

Kathleen clung to his arm until the pain subsided.

"Don't go," she pleaded. "I don't want to be alone."

"But we need—" he began.

"Donnigan," she said as calmly as she could manage. "You have helped the stock—many times."

He looked shocked. "You are not stock," he informed her.

"But babies are born the same way," she argued. "Just—just use common sense. We can manage."

In the end it was Donnigan who delivered his son, washed him, and placed him in his mother's arms.

"Now I'm going for the doctor," he informed his pale but happy wife.

"Whatever for?" asked Kathleen, puzzled.

"To make sure everything is all right," he answered her.

"We're fine. Look at him. He's just perfect."

Donnigan looked down at his newborn son. He did look fine. Just wonderful. He was tiny—being early—but he looked wiry and strong.

The fear gradually left Donnigan's eyes—to be replaced with a look of thankfulness and pride. The baby and Kathleen seemed to have made it through the delivery in great form. He lifted a hand to brush his hair back off his glistening brow and took a deep breath.

"So what are you calling him?" he asked as he reached down and gently touched the tiny fingers with his large one.

"Sean," beamed Kathleen. "This is Sean. It is just right for him, don't you think?"

Donnigan nodded. The name sure wasn't Frank or George. Donnigan hoped his son wouldn't have to do too much fighting over it.

Kathleen's days were now more than full. Sean was a contented baby, but there were the extra chores that a baby always brings. The laundry was the biggest job. Kathleen found it hard to get things dry in the winter. She would be glad when spring would begin to make its way over the surrounding hillsides and when she would hear the song of the first robin.

––––––––

"Look at him! He'll soon be off on his own," boasted Donnigan as he walked his small son around the kitchen holding only to his fingers.

Kathleen smiled. "He will, and that's the truth of it," she agreed, her voice filled with love and her eyes sparkling with honest pride.

"He's growing so fast," said Donnigan.

Kathleen was silent for a minute. Then her head came up and she spoke with a twinkle in her voice. It was the first Donnigan had heard her thick brogue for many months. "Sure now, and he'd better, I'm thinking. He's going to be a big brother to someone before he knows it."

Donnigan stopped still.

"You're serious?" he asked, watching her face closely.

"I'm serious," she replied, her cheeks warm with the excitement of her news.

Donnigan swung his small son in the air and cheered. "You hear that, my boy?" he asked the baby as he held him above his head. "You are about to be a big brother."

"Hold on," Kathleen laughed. "It won't be for months yet. As I have it figured, Sean will be fifteen months old."

They knew the baby had no idea what the celebration was all about, but they danced around the kitchen with him anyway. Sean laughed at all the merrymaking.

––––––––

Good news came from Erma. Kathleen cried when she read her little note.

"Oh, I do hope it all works out fine for her this time," she said to Donnigan as she blew her nose. "It would be terrible if she lost another."

Kathleen cast a glance at Sean who slept peacefully in the cradle in the corner. He had almost outgrown the bed already—but then it wouldn't be too many months until he would need to pass the cradle on to another. Kathleen smiled to herself. She and Erma were due about the same time.

―――――

"How will you manage with two babies?" Donnigan asked one morning as Kathleen tried to prepare the porridge while Sean thumped his spoon nosily, calling for his breakfast.

Kathleen attempted a smile. "If they are all as good as that one, I'll have no trouble," she answered.

It was true. Sean had been a model baby. His temperament was such that he was almost always happy. Rarely was he impatient as he seemed to be at the moment.

"I'm late this morning, that's all," Kathleen went on to explain away her son's behavior.

"Aren't you feeling well?" asked Donnigan with concern.

Kathleen shook her head. "Just a little queasiness. It'll pass."

"But you weren't that way at all with Sean," reminded Donnigan. He had been expecting morning sickness, thinking that it went naturally with pregnancy and was surprised when Kathleen had shown no signs.

"It's different—with different babies," said Kathleen lightly. "I remember Madam. She was so sick with Bridget and not a bit with Charles, and then she was sick again with Edmund."

Donnigan nodded, but he still felt nervous about this second baby coming so close to the first one.

―――――

Without a conscious decision on her part, Kathleen was indeed changing the little cabin, making it into a home.

Perhaps small Sean had a part in the shaping. Baby things now appeared. A small blanket here, a pile of soft garments there, a warm wrap on the rocking chair in the corner to bundle him in while he nursed.

But other things had slowly happened as well. Soft curtains covered the windows. A geranium bloomed in a pot on the kitchen table. Warm rugs were scattered upon the floor. Pictures now broke the bleakness of bare wood walls. And always there was the warm, inviting smell of something cooking or baking or brewing. Donnigan loved to open the door and be welcomed in.

———

"I'll meet you back at the hotel," Donnigan said as he passed young Sean to Kathleen and moved to tie the team.

Kathleen nodded and they went their separate ways— she to do her shopping and then take tea with Erma, and he to make some necessary purchases at the blacksmith shop.

Kathleen hurried through her errands. She was anxious to spend as much time with Erma as she could. Now that Erma was expecting another baby, Kathleen was not so reluctant to visit her with Sean.

Not that she boasted of her small son—but then, Kathleen did not need to boast. Erma—or anyone—could see for herself what a bright and pleasant baby he was.

Erma was making progress. Oh, she still grieved of the past. She still trembled when speaking of Lucas's dark mood at the loss of their child—as though it had been her fault. She still wept on occasion over the little chest at the foot of her bed—but she also had her cheerier times. She had even smiled slightly on one or two occasions. Kathleen felt encouraged.

"Have you heard from your sis yet?" Erma asked as they sat sipping tea and watching Sean devour a tea biscuit.

"No. I've tried twice more to get a letter off to her—and they both came back again," Kathleen said, her voice filled with despair.

"It's a strange thing, it is," observed Erma, her eyes shadowed.

"I can't understand it at all. I can get my letters to the school headmistress, so the address I was given is correct. But they insist they have never heard of her."

"Oh look!" squealed Erma. "He shoved the whole thing in," and Erma began to chuckle merrily over the small Sean who had pushed such a large bite of biscuit into his mouth that he couldn't even chew.

It was so good to hear Erma laugh again—Kathleen felt like weeping. Instead she went to rescue her small son.

"You little piggy," she scolded gently. "You'll be choking yourself, and that's the truth."

But the laugh had been good for them both.

————

Donnigan's eyes were dark with concern when he met her later on, and Kathleen braced herself to hear whatever bad news he carried.

"Risa is gone," he said.

"Gone? What do you mean, gone?"

"She left. Left on the stage."

Kathleen could only stare. She knew by Donnigan's face that he wasn't teasing.

"Did Wallis go?" she asked in a half whisper.

"Wallis? No. Not Wallis," replied Donnigan.

"How—? What happened?"

"I don't know. Sam only knows that she left—and that Wallis is nearly beside himself."

Kathleen shifted the small Sean to her other arm. "That's terrible," she responded. "What can we do?"

"I've no idea—but I'd like to get home as quick as we can. I'll have to go over and see Wallis."

Chapter Seventeen

Understanding

It was true. Risa had left Wallis. She had gone to town to shop—she said—and not returned. Wallis went to look for her and was told that she had caught the two-o'clock stage heading east. Risa had talked to no one but the ticket agent. "She said she was going to Raeford to catch the train," said the man. "Thet's all I know."

"But why?" wailed Wallis. "Why?"

Donnigan spent some time with his old friend, letting him talk, hearing him out, offering his help.

"Shore, we had our times," admitted Wallis, wiping at unashamed tears. "All couples do I guess. But they weren't of much importance—an' they didn't last fer long."

Donnigan nodded. He and Kathleen had experienced their "times" as well. It took a good deal of adjusting to get things worked out in a marriage. There were still occasions when they seemed to look at the same situation with two different sets of eyes.

"She came from a big city. Didn't care much fer the farm. She called it dirty an' a weed patch," went on Wallis. He sniffed forlornly. "I thought we was gettin' things whipped into pretty good shape."

Wallis stopped to look around his little cabin and Donnigan's eyes followed his. The room bore the marks of a woman's hands. An edge of lace curtain hung at the sparkling window. The cupboard shelves were covered with a ruffle of

157

blue gingham. Woven rugs were scattered across the floor,
and the crude table's cracks were hidden by an oil cloth with
sprays of bright yellow flowers. It certainly didn't look like
the cabin Donnigan remembered. With a wry grin he noticed
that there were no bridles or pieces of harness anywhere.
Not on the pegs by the door—not on the chairs. Not even on
the floor in the corner.

It was Donnigan who put on the coffeepot. Wallis didn't
seem to be thinking too well. He hadn't eaten since he'd had
the news.

Donnigan wished he could say, "She'll be back," but he
wasn't sure if it was true.

Instead he said, "We'll see what we can find out. Surely
there is some way to trace her. Find out just why—what it
was that—" He didn't know how to say it. Didn't know how
to go on with his thoughts. Wallis didn't seem to even notice.

Wallis looked up at the smell of the boiling coffee. Donnigan went to the cupboard and found some bread and jam.
It wasn't much but it might get the man through the day.

But Wallis just looked at the bread and his face crumpled
again. "She sure could bake good bread," he said to Donnigan
and the tears were running down his cheeks again.

Donnigan supposed that the next days would hold many
memories for Wallis. It seemed that everywhere he looked
there were reminders of Risa's presence in the home.

At length Donnigan faced the fact that there was really
nothing more he could do for the grieving man, and he had
a pack of chores waiting for him at home. He bid Wallis good-
night with the promise that he'd be back the next day.

———

"How is he?" asked Kathleen.

Donnigan's shoulders slumped in discouragement. He
took off his broad hat and ran a hand through his hair. "He's
pretty badly shaken up," he said wearily.

"I know—I know it must have been hard for her. But how

could she do that to him?" said Kathleen, anger edging her voice.

"I don't think Risa was ever happy there—and you must admit that Wallis wouldn't be an easy man to live with."

"No man is easy to live with," said Kathleen.

"Even me?" he quipped.

But she was in no mood for teasing. He knew that her anger had to have vent. He only smiled to himself. Kathleen still had trouble with her temper.

"That doesn't give one call to—to just pack up and leave," Kathleen went on.

"No. No," agreed Donnigan, "it wasn't fair for her to just leave—without—without giving the man a chance—without saying her piece—or even saying goodbye. It wasn't a good way to be doing it."

He pushed his fingers through his hair again. "I need to get to the chores," he said, weariness tinging his voice again.

"I slopped the pigs and fed the hens," said Kathleen.

His eyes dropped to her waistline and Kathleen could read his thinking. "Kathleen—I wish you wouldn't—" He was trying to shelter her again.

"I didn't fill the pails to the top," she argued. "And the pigs were squealing for their supper. And I had to go to the chicken pen to gather the eggs anyway."

Donnigan nodded, but his thoughts were still heavy as he left the house. He ached for Wallis. The poor man was grieving as if he had faced a death. And maybe he had. How could a man lose what was a part of him and not feel that something—something real and important had died? And what on earth would he ever do if something happened to his Kathleen?

———

"Sure now, and that boy's not an Irishman," Kathleen commented as she and Donnigan watched their small son playing on the floor. "He's even fairer than his father."

Sean squealed as he batted at the new red ball that Donnigan had brought home from town.

"Well, he doesn't have an Irish temper—and that's the pure truth," teased Donnigan and got the response that he had expected as a towel Kathleen was folding came flying through the air.

He caught it and tossed it back, grinning in playfulness.

Kathleen sobered. "You're right," she admitted. "He's never had a temper fit."

"Well, he is all of nine months old," Donnigan reminded her.

"Sure—and a good Irish baby can be mighty good at screaming by nine months," responded Kathleen, and they both laughed.

"I wonder what this new one will be like?" Kathleen wondered softly.

"You expect it to be different?"

The ball rolled away and Sean chased it across the floor and caught up to it under a kitchen chair. Donnigan watched as the small boy maneuvered his way between the legs and rungs to retrieve what he was after.

"He's smart," he boasted to the child's mother.

"Sure now—and that's Irish," laughed Kathleen.

Donnigan turned back to his wife. "You really expect the next one to be different?"

"Well . . ." said Kathleen slowly as she lifted the laundry basket. "I've never met two people exactly alike yet. And from what I'm knowing—they mostly start out like they are going to be from the very beginning."

Donnigan nodded.

Kathleen let her eyes return to her infant son, love and pride glowing in them. "If the good Lord sent another one just like him—I wouldn't be complaining," she said and she started toward the bedroom with her clean laundry.

————

There were clouds in the afternoon sky. Kathleen wondered if Donnigan might get rained on. He was working the far field and was a long ways from the shelter of the house.

"I think it's going to rain," she said to the small boy who had pulled himself up to a kitchen chair and was playing with a ball of Kathleen's mending yarn. "Your father might get wet."

Sean gurgled and grinned.

"You're not worried?" Kathleen gently scolded. "Well, I guess I shouldn't worry either. He is a big man—he can take care of himself."

But in spite of her words, Kathleen found her eyes kept going back to the window and the approaching storm.

Then the thunder began to roll in the distance and sheets of lightning danced across the darkened sky.

"It's going to rain for sure," said Kathleen to her son. "I wish he would come in."

But Kathleen knew that Donnigan would likely stay in the field for as long as he could—fighting to beat the rain.

The storm moved in rapidly. The thunder now cracked and crackled overhead. The lightning zigzagged across the sky, ripping open the dark, tumbling clouds. Kathleen waited for the sound of rain, but there was only the angry thunder and the slashing, rending light.

An unusually loud crash of thunder shook the little cabin and Sean looked bewildered, then frightened, and his lip curled and he began to cry. Kathleen crossed quickly to him and scooped him into her arms.

"That was a close one and that's for sure," she said as she rocked the wee babe in her arms and tried to soothe him. Inside, her own stomach was churning with fright. She had never been in a storm that had struck so close. She did wish that Donnigan would hurry.

She crossed back to the window to peer out and see if he might be coming, but a frightening sight met her eyes. The nearby haystack was in flames.

"Oh, merciful God!" cried Kathleen, "we've been hit."

She wasn't sure what to do. She was thankful that the stack was far enough away from the barn and corrals that it shouldn't be a concern.

"Oh, Donnigan," she cried as she clutched Sean. "Hurry!"

And then, to Kathleen's horror she saw the little fingers of hungry flames that were reaching out from the stack and igniting grass as it moved from the stack to the ground around. The rivulets of flame were moving directly toward the house. Kathleen clutched Sean closer. What should she do? Flee—or fight?

Without time for more thought, Kathleen hurriedly placed her son on the floor and ran from the cabin. She stopped only long enough to grab a gunny sack from the nearby root cellar and dip it in the trough, then hurried toward the flames. Each time that she beat one back, another seemed to stream toward her. The heat from the burning stack was almost more than she could bear. But she had to save her home. She had to save her son.

Tears streamed down her face as she fought on. They were the only moisture with which she fought—for the rains had still not come.

"Oh, God!" cried Kathleen. "God help me. Help me."

But even as she cried she feared that it was a losing battle. The flames that reached toward the cabin seemed to be stronger than the frail woman who fought against them.

Just as she was about to faint from her exertion, the heavens opened and the rain came pouring down. Kathleen lifted her eyes to the darkened skies and cried a thank you, then returned to her fight with renewed determination. With the help of the rain, she should be able to win her war.

"Kathleen. Kathleen!"

Kathleen heard his call but she didn't answer. She didn't stop beating at the flames that were now slowly retreating.

"Kathleen," he said and he grabbed her shoulders and pulled her toward him.

Kathleen's face was white except for the streaks of dirty gray from the soot that floated around her. Her hair was dishevelled, her dress torn at the hem. She was drenched from head to toe with the rain she had prayed for, and her eyes were so filled with terror that she looked like a wounded thing—caught in a trap from which she could not flee.

Donnigan pulled her close for one brief minute and held her. "It's all right," he tried to comfort her but his own body was shaking. "The rain will stop it. It's all right."

He smoothed her hair back from her face and then moved his hands to hold her head, touching the dirty cheeks with his thumbs.

"It's all right now," he comforted again.

Kathleen nodded dumbly, the tears mixing freely with the rain on her face.

"You go in," he said. "See to Sean. I'll watch this."

Kathleen noticed that he was soaked through. Near the barn the team stood—in harness and untethered. Donnigan never left the horses like that.

Then Kathleen thought of her young son. He had been terrified by the storm. What would he be feeling now, being dumped quickly on the floor while his mother fled the house? He must be frightened half to death being left alone in the cabin.

Kathleen took one more look at Donnigan then moved from his arms.

She found her son halfway between the house and the burning stack. He had been crying. His eyes were still red and puffy, but now he sat, playing quite happily in a puddle of muddy water. The rain still washed over him, soaking his clothing, running over his blond hair, and dripping from his chin. From time to time he stuck out his tongue to try to catch the drops; then he returned to splashing the dirty water from the puddle up and over his clothes—over his face.

He squealed when he saw Kathleen coming and his hand slapped more excitedly in the puddle, making the muddied water fly even faster.

Kathleen began to cry. Then to laugh. "Look at you!" she exclaimed. "How did you get here?"

She picked up her rain-drenched son and looked toward the house. The door was wide open. Sean could not open doors. Donnigan had not been to the house. That meant only one thing. In her hurry, she had left the door open.

Kathleen hugged Sean close. "You could have been hurt,"

she murmured. "You could have been burned. I wouldn't even have seen you in my concern for the fire."

Again Kathleen lifted her head heavenward. She had something more for which to be thankful.

————

The next day she lost the baby she was carrying. The pains had started during the night. There was really nothing they could do to stop it from happening. When it was all over, Kathleen turned her face to the wall and cried uncontrollable tears. She had wanted the baby. Another little Sean. She had already learned to love him. Had been counting the months.

"We have Sean," Donnigan whispered, wiping away her tears.

But suddenly that didn't seem to be enough. She had wanted them both. Had wanted both of her babies to love and care for. One couldn't make up for the loss of the other. It wasn't that simple.

For the first time, Kathleen felt she truly understood Erma's pain. No wonder the woman had grieved. It wasn't just "hope" that she had lost. It was a child. A child she had carried, had loved. Kathleen sobbed for the baby she would never know.

It was a long time until she could fall asleep.

————

"Kathleen?" The voice was low and gentle. It was Donnigan. Kathleen waited until the voice came again. "Kathleen?"

She stirred to let him know she had heard him.

"How are you?" he asked and dropped beside her on the bed, smoothing back her hair, letting his fingers trace her cheek.

"Where's Sean?" she asked, rather than answering his question.

"Sleeping. He's fine."

He continued to brush back her long dark hair.

"Would you like some supper?"

Kathleen shook her head. She had no desire for something to eat.

"Tea? You should take something."

"Not tonight," said Kathleen, and Donnigan did not push further.

There was heavy silence in the room. Donnigan seemed to be battling with his thoughts—or how to say his words.

"Would—would you like to see—see your daughter?" he finally managed, his voice choked.

Kathleen's eyes widened. She hadn't thought about the baby's gender—nor the possibility of seeing her miscarried child.

She tried to swallow—but her throat didn't work well. She felt the tears sting her eyes. She wanted to answer Donnigan but the words would not come. So she just nodded her head, mutely.

Donnigan brushed at one of the tears on her cheek. "You—you must remember that it—it won't be like seeing Sean—for the first time," Donnigan said softly and Kathleen knew he was trying to prepare her. Shelter her again. Love swelled her heart. She felt that Donnigan would go through life trying to shelter her. She was glad.

"She's very small," continued Donnigan. "And she isn't— isn't like a newborn—exactly. But she's all there. Even her little fingers. Her toes."

Kathleen knew now without a doubt that she wanted to see her baby. Had to see her baby. "Bring her to me," she whispered.

Donnigan let his fingers trail across her cheek, rub her hair, and then he rose from the bed and left the room.

He carried the little bundle to its mother in the palm of one of his big hands. He had bathed the tiny body and wrapped her in a soft face cloth. She was far too tiny to dress in any of the small baby garments.

He did not lay her in Kathleen's arms as he had done

with Sean, but lowered his hand so that Kathleen could look at her child. And yes, she was all there. Even those tiny little fingers that Donnigan had spoken of.

"There *must* be a God in heaven," Kathleen breathed as she reached a finger out to gently touch the tiny hand, and the tears began to flow again, unchecked.

"Put her in my hands," said Kathleen when she could speak, and Donnigan gently eased the little body into the hands of the sobbing mother. "I—I would have called her Taryn," said Kathleen through her tears.

"Taryn," repeated Donnigan. "I like it. Taryn."

And both of them knew that Taryn she would always be.

"I've made a little—little casket," said Donnigan, his voice deep with emotion. "I used that cedar handkerchief box from the dresser. I lined it with some of the flannel from your sewing basket."

"Oh, Donnigan," wailed Kathleen as she suddenly leaned against him. "I wanted her so much. So much."

Donnigan held her and they wept together. Then Donnigan gently retrieved the small burden from Kathleen's hands.

"I thought—under the tree at the end of the garden," he said softly. "She'll always be with us then."

Kathleen was weeping into her pillow.

"I'll bring her in before I go."

As promised, Donnigan brought the baby in for her mother to see one last time. She looked like a tiny sleeping doll arranged on the white flannel, the folds gently tucked about her elfin face. The cedar hankie box was plenty big enough. Kathleen was glad that Donnigan had thought of it.

In the morning, the tree at the end of the garden sheltered a small mound of freshly dug earth. Later Donnigan made a small wooden cross, and on it, with his whittling knife, he carved a tiny rosebud. "For our little bud that never became a flower," he told Kathleen, and brought the tears to her eyes again.

Chapter Eighteen

Fiona

Wallis continued to grieve over Risa. In spite of Donnigan's effort, there was really no way to track the woman. The man who had driven the stage said he had let her off at the Raeford station and that was the last he had seen of her—and yes, she had been carrying a fair amount of luggage.

From sorrow, Wallis eventually turned to anger. He said some nasty things to Donnigan that were not even repeated to Kathleen.

Kathleen had her own grief. Donnigan was reminded of it over and over as he saw the sadness in her eyes when she looked toward the wooden cradle in the corner or smoothed out a tiny baby garment. He noticed the clusters of fresh flowers that were placed almost daily on the little mound at the back of the yard. The little mound that was quickly sinking to take its place with the ground around it.

"We should build a little fence," Kathleen said, and Donnigan put aside his harvest work for a day to fulfill her request.

But Kathleen's grief was no longer voiced. Donnigan felt that it would have been better for her—for both of them—if it was. She wiped away her tears—straightened her back and lifted a stubborn chin.

But part of her seemed withdrawn—shut away—angry. Only with Sean did her old tenderness really return.

"She and Wallis seem to be dealing with the same emo-

168

tions," Donnigan told Black one day. "And I don't know how
to help either one of them."

It was a heavy burden for Donnigan to carry.

For Sean's first birthday, Kathleen made a cake and they
invited Wallis to join them for the party. At first he declined
but then changed his mind. He had shared a number of supper hours with them since Risa had left him. Kathleen did
not mind the crusty old bachelor, though he was slipping
back into his former way of living. Kathleen wondered if he
had bathed or changed his shirt since Risa had left.

In spite of the heaviness of the hearts around the table,
Sean's birthday celebration was a joyous occasion and a success. The boy ate too much cake, stuffing it into his mouth
with his fingers while his spoon was held idly in his other
hand. The grown-ups laughed at his messy face and Sean
responded by beaming back at them.

"He sure is one fine boy," observed Wallis. And then his
eyes filled with tears and Kathleen knew he was thinking of
Risa again and of the son that he'd never have. Kathleen left
the table in pretense of getting more coffee.

"It wasn't fair of Risa," Kathleen fumed to herself. She
had made her promise before the God in heaven. She'd really
had no right to break it.

"Do you believe in God?"

Donnigan's question caught Kathleen totally off guard.
Where had his thoughts been wandering to produce such a
query?

"Of course," she replied without hesitation. She didn't see
how anyone could *not* believe in a God.

Donnigan remained silent.

"Don't you?" asked Kathleen, having sudden, frightening
doubts about her husband.

Donnigan thought before answering. When he did speak it was with honesty. "I've never really given it much thought," he said truthfully. "Not until Taryn died. Then—then I—I really wanted to believe."

Kathleen nodded. Vivid in her own mind was her response to the sight of her small daughter. Her statement that there had to be a God in heaven. Such a tiny little miracle could not just have happened on its own.

Kathleen was still willing to concede the fact. Of course there was a God—somewhere.

But that very admission did not bring her comfort. In fact, it filled her with anger. He was there—somewhere—and if there—then powerful. A God wouldn't be a God unless He had some power. Some authority. So why hadn't He done something? Why had He let the lightning strike the haystack. Why hadn't He brought the rain sooner so that she would not have had to fight so long—and so hard? No. Kathleen was annoyed with God. She wouldn't have dared to admit it—not even to Donnigan—lest she be smitten down and made to pay for her sin. But she felt the anger, regardless.

"I've been thinking a lot lately," Donnigan went on.

Kathleen waited, but when he didn't say anything further she prompted, "About?"

"About Sean—mostly."

Again, silence. Kathleen felt fear tugging at her. What was wrong with Sean?

"It seems—well, it seems if there really is a God—then we ought to be learning about Him—so we can teach Sean," said Donnigan.

Kathleen let out the breath she had been holding.

"What do you think?" asked Donnigan.

It was a direct question that Kathleen could not avoid.

"I—I suppose," she said without really wishing to commit herself.

She knit a few more stitches. She heard the rattle of the newspaper as Donnigan laid it aside.

"I think—the next time I'm in town I'll just check out that little church where we were married," said Donnigan, causing Kathleen's brows to lift in surprise. "Maybe we should start taking in some of the meetings."

Kathleen only nodded. She would not argue—but she really didn't feel ready to go to church, and besides, she saw no advantages in the idea.

Then she looked at her young son.

"Yes—yes," she admitted to herself. "If there really is a God—and there must be—there must be—then I want Sean to know all about Him."

————

But the next time Donnigan came home from town he looked disappointed.

"They closed the church," he told her.

"What?"

"They closed it. Weren't enough people interested."

"What's the preacher doing now?" asked Kathleen. "Would he open it again?"

"He left. Went off to some other town. No one seems to really know much about it. Weren't that many people attending."

Kathleen felt two emotions at the same time. Disappointment for Donnigan's sake and unexplained fear for the small Sean. She didn't know which feeling was the most intense.

"So what do we do now?" she asked simply.

"Not much we *can* do, I guess," said Donnigan. He hung his stained Stetson on the peg by the door and reached to lift his young son from the floor.

————

The arrival of Erma's baby was a grim reminder to Kathleen of the baby she had lost. Little Taryn should have been joining the family about the same time—not four and a half months earlier. Kathleen had a hard time fighting renewed sorrow. But she was happy for Erma.

Lucas was having a bit of a struggle. He had definitely

ordered a son. Erma had presented him with a daughter. Blond and dimpled and looking just like her mother. Erma was thrilled, but Lucas seemed confused. For the first time in his life he was dealing with something totally out of his control. First he had lost the child he wanted—then someone had mixed up his order. Poor Lucas. His grip on his world seemed to be slipping from his fingers.

Kathleen was expecting another baby. Sean, now two, was quickly becoming more and more like his father. Kathleen smiled as she watched the child follow his father around the farm, trying hard to copy everything he saw Donnigan do.

He enjoyed the farm animals, and Kathleen often took him for rides on Shee. He loved the horse and grinned his delight as soon as Kathleen placed him in the saddle.

"That boy needs a pony of his own," observed Donnigan and promptly set about seeing to it.

"Don't hurry him too fast," cautioned Kathleen. She wasn't yet ready to give up her baby.

But with each passing month, and the new baby on the way, Kathleen was more and more glad for the time that Sean spent with Donnigan. She didn't tell Donnigan about it, for fear she would trouble him unduly, but she did not feel at all well with this pregnancy. She wondered if it was just concern after having lost Taryn.

Slowly the months ticked by and Kathleen began to feel a bit better and breathe a little easier.

"I hope we can have a doctor on hand this time," observed Donnigan as he unlaced his heavy work boots one night.

"Why," teased Kathleen gently. "You did just fine."

"I was scared to death," said Donnigan firmly. "I never want to go through that again."

But he did. Just a few weeks later. There hadn't been time to send for a doctor. Kathleen was early again.

A baby girl was placed in Kathleen's arms. Her first

thought had been, *This can't be mine. There must be a mix-up.* But her own good sense told her that a mix-up was not a possibility.

"She's so—so different than Sean," she said to Donnigan.

"Wasn't that what you said—what you expected?" replied Donnigan. He still looked to be a bundle of nerves, even though it was all over.

"But not *this* different," protested Kathleen. The baby she held was dark. With lots of black hair, round full cheeks, and a face that was already screwed up in protest.

They had decided—or rather Kathleen had decided—on the name Fiona if they had a girl. Now the mother smiled at her daughter. "Hello, Fiona," she said. Then to Donnigan, "Fiona suits her, don't you think?"

"It's going to be fun having a daughter," said Donnigan, and he moved closer to Kathleen and his new baby girl.

But it was not fun. Not for the first five months. It seemed to Kathleen that Fiona fussed without stopping. Their days, their evenings, their nights were all filled with a crying baby. Donnigan tried to share the duties, but even with the two of them, it was a full-time chore.

Kathleen thought that surely Sean must resent his new baby sister, but Sean seemed to accept her just as she was. "Baby cry," he would say without rancor, just as though the small boy accepted that was what babies did.

But there were days when Kathleen wondered how much more she could take.

They took the baby off breast milk and tried a bottle. Still Fiona curled into a ball and screamed her protest.

"Her little tummy must be hurting something awful," observed her patient father. There were times when Kathleen wished the infant were big enough to spank. But even at times of greatest distress and weariness, Kathleen knew that was not the solution. There was something wrong with the child and no one seemed to be able to do anything about it.

One day Donnigan surprised Kathleen with a goat.

"Whatever are we to do with that?" asked Kathleen, thinking that Donnigan had likely brought the animal as a pet for Sean. His own "wee" cow. But to the weary Kathleen, the nanny looked like just another chore.

"Milk her," said Donnigan.

"Milk her? We scarcely have time to milk the cow."

"For Fiona," went on Donnigan. "I've heard that sometimes it works."

And it did. After being switched to goat's milk, Fiona settled down and became a laughing, bubbling, good-humored baby. Kathleen even got to sleep nights. The household returned to a normal pattern.

"Bless that nanny," Kathleen said to Donnigan one night as she carefully tucked the covers up to the chin of the sleeping Fiona. Then she lifted her head and smiled at her husband. "And bless you for finding the solution."

"I had to," said Donnigan with a teasing grin. "It was either that—or move out."

———————

Fiona grew quickly. Even Sean enjoyed her sunny disposition—as long as she didn't interfere with his time with his father.

But Sean did take care of her. Bringing her things that she should not have—things like his bread crusts, Kathleen's sewing scissors, and wiggling worms from the garden. Kathleen had to ever be on guard to intercept Sean's "gifts" to his baby sister.

Kathleen was pleased with her little family. As she became rested again, she was able to really enjoy the two children in spite of the amount of work that had come with them. She almost got to the place where she could forgive God. That is, until she looked at the little grave with its white picket fence and tiny wooden cross.

If Donnigan was in the barn or working around the yard, Kathleen did not have to concern herself with her small son. He was always following close to his father. He went with Donnigan to care for the horses, slop the pigs, or milk the cow. He watched him hoe the garden, lift water from the well, and chop the wood. Then he tried with all of the strength of his small body to imitate his father's acts. Donnigan found himself taking extra precautions. He made sure the corral gate was carefully closed. He didn't want a small boy under the hooves of the horses. He latched the barn door and double checked. He didn't want Sean kicked by a nervous cow. He secured the well lid, added a second clip that he always put in place. He hung the hoe high above the small boy's head. Donnigan was very conscious of the small lad who was watching him—copying him.

But in spite of all of Donnigan's care, an accident did happen.

Wallis had borrowed one of Donnigan's axes. In coming to call one evening he had spotted a tree down on his fence wires. It was closer to go on to Donnigan's than to go back home for his own axe. Donnigan got his axe from the woodshed and Wallis took care of the matter. Donnigan thought nothing of it when Wallis came to the door later.

"I put yer axe back," the man said and Donnigan nodded and invited the man in.

It was while they were having their coffee that they heard the young boy scream. Donnigan was the first to his feet. Kathleen was just behind him.

Sean was seated on the ground, the axe still in his hand, his small foot oozing blood.

"Oh, merciful Lord," cried Kathleen.

Donnigan scooped up the crying child and headed for the house. Wringing her hands in her apron, Kathleen followed. Wallis could only stand and stare, chiding himself for leaving the axe in the chopping block.

It turned out that it was not a deep cut—but it did cause

much concern. Kathleen feared that it might develop blood poisoning, and Donnigan used some of the same strong disinfectant that he used for the stock to assure that it wouldn't happen. Even though it was diluted, it stung sharply and the small boy cried even louder. Fiona, in her cradle in the corner of the room, heard the cries and joined the bedlam.

Kathleen longed to hold and rock her son, but he clung to his father. She knew she would have to wait her turn. Instead she went to lift the small Fiona from her bed.

Chapter Nineteen

Brenna

When Fiona was a laughing, teasing two-year-old and Sean a four-and-a-half-year-old copy of his father, another baby girl joined the family, aided by the doctor who actually made it on time. Kathleen named her Brenna and Fiona managed to call her Bwee. She was another blond baby but she had more of Kathleen's features than did Sean.

"Now you're getting it right," teased Donnigan. "A little of both of us." Kathleen just smiled.

Sean and Fiona fell in love with their baby sister at once, but it was generally left to Fiona to do the mothering as Sean was much too busy being a "farm man."

A few months later, Erma also had another baby and this one too was a girl, much to Lucas's further consternation. But his oldest girl was busy working on her daddy's heart, and though Lucas might not have admitted it, she had won him over totally. Erma shared the little tales of the doting papa with Kathleen and they both chuckled over them. Lucas tried so hard to convince everyone that he was totally and completely "all business."

Brenna was a contented baby, for which Kathleen was thankful. With two other small children to care for, her days were more than full. Sean took over the task of gathering the eggs and feeding the chickens. It was his first step toward becoming a farmer.

But the garden always needed attention, and the pile of

soiled baby laundry always loomed larger than the clean stock in the chest of drawers. It seemed to Kathleen that there was never time for rest. She was glad that her little brood was healthy and happy.

———

Brenna was now seven months old, sitting by herself and crawling all over the house. Donnigan was pleased with her progress, as he had been with each of his children. But Kathleen carried a nagging, frightening concern. The baby's eyes were often crossed as she tried to focus on what she held in her hands.

Kathleen, herself raised with a handicap that had not been properly cared for, knew how devastating it could be. Why, if Donnigan had not accepted her "sight unseen," she still didn't know if any man would have ever married her. Her stepmum had thoroughly convinced her that she had an abnormality that no man would be able to overlook. Kathleen did not want any such handicap for one of her children.

Donnigan had helped her limp by making a lift for her boot. In fact, Kathleen hardly thought of her lameness anymore, and certainly Donnigan never made mention of it. But crossed eyes could hardly be hidden under swishing skirts. Brenna's disability would be plain for all to see. So Kathleen fretted and worried and tried to make peace with the God she had been angry with so that she might evoke His intervention. Each day she watched the little eyes as they concentrated on what was held in the small hands, and still they crossed on occasion.

Kathleen kept waiting for Donnigan to speak of it, but Donnigan either did not notice or refused to admit what he saw. It annoyed Kathleen. Wasn't he concerned about his baby?

At last she had to bring it up. "What can we do about Brenna?" was the way she approached him.

"What about Brenna?" he asked innocently, and Kathleen stirred restlessly, her temper immediately roused.

"Her eyes?" she said with a bit too much emphasis.

"What's wrong with her eyes?"

Now Kathleen was really upset. "Don't tell me," she began, "that you haven't even noticed that your daughter has crossed eyes?"

"What?" he answered, his tone even and controlled in spite of her sharpness. "You mean when she holds something?"

When Kathleen did not answer, Donnigan went on. "All babies do that. They outgrow it as soon as the muscles strengthen."

Kathleen snorted. "And now you are an authority on all babies. Sean didn't do that. Fiona didn't do that."

"Sure they did," argued Donnigan.

"Not when they were as old as Brenna," debated Kathleen.

"So she's a bit slower in that area," said Donnigan, refusing to get concerned.

Kathleen said nothing more. She was still worried about her baby, but it seemed Donnigan did not share her fear.

"We'll keep an eye on her," said Donnigan. "If she doesn't quickly outgrow it, we'll take her to a doctor in Raeford."

"Outgrow it by *when*?" asked Kathleen, wishing for something definite.

"By a year," said Donnigan.

It seemed much too long to wait to Kathleen, but it had to do. She would watch Brenna carefully and then make Donnigan keep his promise when she was a year old.

But Brenna outgrew her difficulty in focusing long before she reached her first birthday. Kathleen breathed a sigh of relief—but was just a bit annoyed that Donnigan had been right—again.

———

"There's a letter for you," Donnigan said as he entered the house, a box of groceries in his arms. Sean tagged along behind him, carrying a small box just like his father.

"Can'ny?" called Fiona, running to meet them. "Can'ny?"
Donnigan laughed and hoisted her up in his arms. "I
think your mama might find a bit of candy in there some
place—you little sweet tooth, you. Maybe your mama will
let you have *one* now—and put the rest up to share later."

He pinched her chubby cheek and returned her to the
floor.

"A letter?" said Kathleen, moving forward. She never got
letters. Oh, she did hope that it was from Bridget.

The letter bore a strange address but it was from London.
Kathleen tore it open with trembling fingers, then quickly
let her eyes run down the page until they fell on the signa-
ture.

"Why, it's from Edmund," she said, and immediately felt
concern. Why would Edmund be the family member to finally get in touch?

"I'll catch it later—I have to care for the team," said Donnigan, to which Sean parroted, "I hafta care for the team,"
and the two left the house together.

Kathleen wondered if Donnigan instinctively knew that
she needed to be alone to read whatever the letter contained
of news from home. She sat down on the nearby kitchen chair
and opened the letter, totally forgetting about Fiona, who
had climbed on another chair and was busily going through
the grocery box in search of the promised candy.

My dearest sister Kathleen:

Kathleen smiled to herself. It seemed strange for the
spoiled Edmund to be addressing her in such a fashion. Then
she read on.

It has been some time since you left London to make
your new home in America. Bridget tried for some time
to get in touch but was unable to secure your address.

"Oh, Bridget," sobbed Kathleen, "I tried so hard to contact you."

She has since married and is living quite happily in

180

Belfast. The man she married is an Irishman with much concern for his homeland.

The word "his" had been crossed out and Edmund had inserted instead the word "our." Again Kathleen smiled. Edmund had never evidenced much love for Ireland. Indeed, Madam had seen that his loyalties were more toward France.

Charles left two years ago to join up with a cargo ship. It nearly broke Mere's heart. I would have thought that he could find himself a trade nearby. We have heard from him a few times since, but mostly his days are spent at sea.

So there is now just Mere and me, and our situation is rather distressful. You may wonder why we are in London. The marriage that was planned didn't take place. He proved to be a scoundrel. We shall never forgive him. At any rate, we have continued on in the city but were forced to leave the house on Carrington when we couldn't manage the rent.

Mere is pleased that she sent you to America where you were able to better your situation by marrying a man of means.

"Sent me?" sniffed Kathleen in disbelief.

Even though your going put great stress on the family here, we gladly sacrificed for your betterment. Now we are hoping that our charity will be returned. Whatever you might spare would be most appreciated.

Affectionately, your brother Edmund.

Kathleen sat staring at the page, unable to believe what she had just read. Tears formed in her eyes. It was good to hear from them—to learn that they were well. She thought of her young sister, now a married woman and back home again in beloved Ireland. And she thought of Charles at sea. Imagine that! Charles, a sailor. Perhaps on his way to becoming a captain. Kathleen smiled and wiped at her cheeks.

Fiona had found the bag of licorice and climbed down from her chair. She sat on the floor, out of view of her mother, and began to enjoy her treat. She had eaten three of the pieces before she thought of Brenna. Brenna was sitting on the floor happily playing with two of her mama's pots. Fiona picked a candy from her sack and stuffed it in the baby's mouth. It was not easy for the baby to chew, and the whole dribbling, sloppy mess soon tumbled out of her mouth again and trickled down the front of her gown. The licorice lodged in a fold in her lap. Brenna smacked her lips a few times and returned to her pots. Fiona, feeling she had shared adequately, went back to enjoying her treat. Kathleen still sat at the table, wiping her eyes and blowing her nose.

In spite of her joy in receiving news from home, she felt annoyance. "My, what a fine kettle of fish that must have been, and that's the truth," she muttered to herself as she scanned the page again. "No marriage. A scoundrel was he? And why not, I'm thinking. It takes one to draw one."

Kathleen had never dared to dwell on her feelings for her stepmother before. Now they rose up within her, surprising even her with their intensity. So the marriage for wealth had not worked. My, couldn't she just picture the anger of Madam.

Then a new thought occurred to Kathleen. "Why, if I hadn't left *how* I did, *when* I did, I'd still be there making pennies hawking buns and pastries in the dirty London streets," she murmured to herself.

A wave of thankfulness flooded through her. What she had left was so inferior to what she had gained. She closed her eyes tightly and let the emotion sweep over her whole body. What if—? What if she had never signed on to come to America? What if she had never married Donnigan?

She would still be poor and destitute and slaving for a family who did not even think to appreciate her services. She would still be limping around on a lame leg, her back aching at the end of the day, her mind convinced that she was a cripple that no one would want.

She wouldn't have a husband. She wouldn't have a family. She would know nothing about love. She— Kathleen stopped and opened her eyes to survey the family that had blessed her life. Fiona stood before her.

"A' done," she said with great satisfaction, passing Kathleen an empty sack. Licorice stains colored her chin and browned the front of her dress with ugly streaks. Kathleen gasped. "A' done," the girl repeated, dropping the bag in Kathleen's lap.

"You ate them all?" gasped Kathleen.

"No," said Fiona, shaking her head emphatically. "I give Bwee."

Kathleen gasped and jumped to her feet, fearful that she would find the baby passed out on the floor, choked by licorice candy. But Brenna was cooing to herself and fumbling with the pots. All around her mouth and dripping down her front was the evidence of the licorice she never got to fully enjoy. Kathleen breathed a sigh of relief that she was all right and hurried to clean up the pair of them before their father returned from the barn.

"You are welcome to read it for yourself," Kathleen told Donnigan as she nodded toward the letter on the small table.

Donnigan shifted the two children on his knees and picked up the letter. He read it all the way through, then read it again. Kathleen waited for his response as she moved about the kitchen getting the supper on the table.

"Sounds like they have fallen into hard times," said Donnigan at last.

Kathleen didn't dare make a response.

"How much do you think we can spare?" was Donnigan's next comment.

Kathleen looked up. Was he serious? Was he actually thinking that Kathleen owed something to Madam?

"Donnigan. Madam has always been in 'hard times'— only before she had Father—or me—to pay her way. I owe her nothing more. Nothing. Why, if she'd had her way I would still be there, walking those London streets, selling wares for that crotchety old baker."

Donnigan had never heard such bitterness in Kathleen's voice before.

He said nothing more—for the moment—but switched his attention to giving his two small daughters horsey rides on his foot.

———

When Donnigan felt that Kathleen had enough time to cool down, he brought up the matter of the letter again.

"I was thinking that we might spare a bit," he said. "We've got that extra pig money in the bank."

"If you start sending money to Madam, she'll expect it as her due," warned Kathleen.

"She *is* kin," replied Donnigan evenly.

"No kin of mine—she simply married my father—and sent my grandmother to an early grave," said Kathleen hotly.

"Your grandmother?" Donnigan had never heard that story.

"Sure now—and Grandmother O'Malley left Ireland when we did and settled with us in London. She cared for me after my mother died. Called me her little colleen. We would have been just fine too had not Madam taken a shine to my father. She worked in the local pub and he used to stop by for a pint after his day's work.

"Before long she had convinced him they should marry— and I guess he was lonely without Mother. But she couldn't leave Grandmother be. She taunted and tormented and picked on her all the time that Father was at work. Then at end of day when Father came home, she was nice as cream pudding to the old lady. I saw it all myself. Of course, Grandmother never said a thing. She didn't want to come between a man and his wife. But it broke her heart, and that's the truth of it. She just gave up and died—pining for my mother—pining for Ireland. I saw it myself."

Kathleen stopped for a breath. Donnigan reached out an arm and drew her close.

"It was hard for you, wasn't it?" he said, but it was more a statement than a question.

Kathleen found that she was crying. She had never talked to anyone about her grandmother before.

Donnigan let her cry against him. When she finally moved to dry her eyes and blow her nose, he spoke again.

"Is it too hard to forgive?" he asked her.

Kathleen sniffed and thought a moment.

"You think she deserves my forgiveness?" she asked stiffly.

"I was thinking of you—not her," said Donnigan. "Unforgiveness is a heavy load to carry."

Kathleen looked up in surprise.

"You had no choice—in what she did to you," went on Donnigan slowly, "but you do have a choice in forgiving."

"One doesn't just decide to forgive—and make it happen," said Kathleen with feeling. "You can't just—will pain away. It goes far deeper than that."

Donnigan nodded. "But somehow I think that you can choose to hang on to pain—to bitterness—sorta cling to it and coddle it and pamper it a bit so that it grows and grows."

Kathleen had never thought of that.

"Would you like to talk about it later?" asked Donnigan, and Kathleen nodded her head.

Donnigan saw it as the first positive step.

Chapter Twenty

The Continued Search

Kathleen was not looking forward to the time when Donnigan might again approach her about sending help home to Madam. She had not realized how deep her bitterness ran until she had looked at her life with the London family in light of her life with Donnigan.

"I guess I just took it all for granted when I was there," she told herself. "When you're used to a situation, you don't realize that things should be different. You just—just accept them."

But now that Kathleen had enjoyed a taste of a real home, of real love, she realized just how much she had been taken advantage of as a child and how Madam had used her for her own purposes.

Kathleen had been unaware of the bitterness she had buried concerning the grandmother she had lost when she was seven years old. It had been bad enough to lose her mother, but she'd still had her Granny to cling to. But when she lost her grandmother as well, she lost her anchor in a hostile world.

Her father had been quite unaware of what went on in the little house in his absence. Yet he should have been able to see that something was dreadfully wrong.

To Kathleen's surprise, she found that buried very deeply within herself was a resentment toward her father. The father she had loved so much. That was perhaps what pained her most of all. And it all was due to Madam. She had forced Kathleen's father into the position where he was not free to properly care for his eldest daughter. Still he should have seen. He should have sensed that things were all wrong. Kathleen felt that she could have forgiven the woman of all the sins that she had committed against her—except that one. The one of making her see her beloved father as a less than perfect man.

Kathleen struggled with her pain and bitterness, and Donnigan wisely didn't press. He knew she wasn't ready.

———

They needed more room to house their growing family. Donnigan decided he could put it off no longer. He began to order and stockpile the materials so that he could begin at the first opportunity.

"What you plannin'?" asked Wallis when he popped by one evening just as they were about to sit down for their supper.

Kathleen moved to the cupboard to get another plate. It seemed to her that Wallis ate more often at her table than he did at his own. But she would not have expressed her feeling to Donnigan.

"Time to add on to this cabin," said Donnigan as he mashed potatoes for Brenna and covered them with gravy. "We're about to burst at the seams."

Wallis nodded, looking around the circle.

"We're going to build a room for me," piped up Sean, grinning as he shared the good news.

Wallis accepted his place at the table.

I may as well set for him every night, thought Kathleen. *Seems he always ends up being here.*

"When you startin'?" asked Wallis as he stabbed a spud with his fork.

"First thing in the morning—I hope," replied Donnigan.

"I got some spare time right now," said Wallis around a bit of liver and onions. "I'll give you a hand."

That's just fine! thought Kathleen sourly. *Now he'll think he is entitled to eat here* three *times a day!*

Then Kathleen caught herself. She was getting awfully testy lately. She wondered that Donnigan could stand living with her. Maybe it was just that another baby was on the way. She hoped she would soon get her emotions back under control.

Kathleen decided not to wait for Donnigan to speak with her. She brought up the matter herself. She hoped that she would be able to keep her composure as she talked.

"About the money," she began, knowing that Donnigan would know what money she was referring to. "I know we don't have much to spare with building on to the house and all, but perhaps we could send a little bit."

"I'll see to it right away," said Donnigan, and she thought she read relief in his eyes.

"But that doesn't mean I've forgiven her," Kathleen could have said. "I've tried, but I can't. But send the money if you like—it'll make you feel better—and I guess I can grant her that much."

But Kathleen did not say the words, so Donnigan did not know what was going on in her heart. Instead she said, "And, Donnigan—when you send the money, would you please ask Edmund to send me Bridget's address?"

"Do you think there's a God?" Donnigan asked Wallis at the dinner table.

I thought he had forgotten about that, thought Kathleen, lifting her head in surprise.

Wallis, too, looked startled. He chewed on his bite of bread and butter, his eyes going darker by the minute. At last he swallowed and said in a mumbled fashion, "Used to. Kinda."

"You mean, you don't anymore?"

"Nope!" said Wallis, and he took another large bite of the slice he held in his hand.

"But if there is a God—and I've got a strong feeling that there must be—then He doesn't just come and go according to how we feel about Him," Donnigan said rather boldly.

Wallis seemed to be thinking.

"All I know is—if He's there—He sure don't run things very well," said Wallis.

Donnigan nodded. He knew Wallis was thinking about Risa.

"Do you really think *He* had a say in the matter?" he asked softly.

"Well—a God is supposed to be a God, isn't He?" declared Wallis, and there was pain and bitterness in his voice. "What good is He iffen He can't look after things?"

"Maybe it's not His business to look after *those* kinds of things," said Donnigan.

Kathleen was uncomfortable with the conversation. She rose from the table and sliced more bread.

"Then what is He supposed to look after?" asked Wallis, sounding angry and exasperated.

"Our souls," said Donnigan.

Wallis met that comment with a sneer.

"If there's a God—then there is a heaven and hell—somewhere," said Donnigan. "And I think that His business is getting us to the one and keeping us out of the other."

"So how's He do thet?" snorted Wallis.

"I don't know," said Donnigan slowly. "I don't know—but I sure would like to find out."

Kathleen cast a glance Donnigan's way and saw the shadow in his eyes. She knew then that he had not forgotten his search. That he was greatly troubled—somewhere deep inside.

———

The house was finished before the new baby made his

appearance. This boy looked much like his older brother—
except that he was dark instead of fair. But from the very
first time she heard him cry, Kathleen knew she had a child
with a totally different disposition from his brother Sean.

"My, he sounds cross," she said to Donnigan. "Do you
think he'll ever forgive the doctor for that pat on his little
behind?"

Donnigan had insisted on a doctor again for the birth and
Kathleen had not argued. There had been time for the doctor
to arrive—although certainly no time to spare.

"He's likely just hungry," replied Donnigan, handing the
baby to his mother. "He'll settle down as soon as he's fed."

Kathleen named the baby Eamon, and Donnigan accepted the name without comment.

———

Wallis was back far more often than Kathleen would have
liked, but she bit her tongue and served him his suppers
whenever he made his sudden appearance at her door.

"He needs us," said Donnigan with real feeling for the
neighbor man, and Kathleen did not try to argue.

———

"The more I see of youngsters the less confident I feel as
a parent," Donnigan observed one day just after Eamon had
thrown a real temper fit.

Kathleen nodded. She was so weary of fighting the two-
year-old. It seemed that Eamon was always upset about
something.

"He sure isn't like the others," she commented in return,
brushing back the hair from her flushed face.

"I think we're going to have our hands full with that one,"
went on Donnigan, "and I'm not sure just how to handle him.
Now, if he was a colt and acted like that I'd try gentling, and
if that didn't work I'd lay my whip on him."

Kathleen winced. It seemed to her that Eamon had already been spanked more than his fair share.

"They are all so different," said Kathleen, and reviewed in her mind her four youngsters. Sean was the easiest one. Never had he fussed and fought against their authority. He had immediately fallen in love with his father and sought to do everything just as Donnigan did.

Fiona was the spirited one. Bubbly and chattering and always on the go. She mothered and fussed over each family member and giggled and romped her way through each day.

Brenna was a loner. From the time she was little she could entertain herself for hours, sitting off in a corner or under the table, playing with whatever simple thing Kathleen gave her. She hummed little songs to herself and smiled her pleasure at family members. But then she promptly returned to her play without even asking to be picked up.

But Eamon. Eamon was out to conquer the world on his own terms even before he took his first step. Kathleen shared Donnigan's concern for their youngest son. She had no idea how to handle him.

"We need help, Kathleen," said Donnigan, and he looked weary, concerned. "I'm not smart enough to know how to raise my little ones fit for heaven, and I admit it."

There it was again. Donnigan's concern for the soul.

"I wish there was a church—"

Donnigan ran his fingers through his heavy head of blond hair.

"I don't think they're *that* bad," said Kathleen, defending her young.

"It's not a case of how good or how bad, Kathleen. I don't know what God wants. I don't know how to prepare my children for—for the world to come. There's no use bringing them into *this* world, Kathleen, and not preparing them for the *next* one. Can't you see? That's the most important thing we have to do in life. Get those little ones ready for whatever lies beyond. If I don't do that—I've failed as a father. I've failed as a man. Failed miserably."

Kathleen hadn't realized that he felt so strongly about it.

"Don't you know anything about what one is to do?" he

asked her, and there was pleading in his voice. Donnigan needed some answers.

"No. No," said Kathleen shaking her head. "I don't know anything."

Donnigan stood and moved to where his hat hung on the peg.

"Where are you going?" asked Kathleen quickly. She did hope he wasn't going to do something foolish. She was worried about Donnigan.

"To town—for some answers," he said to her. "I'm going to check out that church."

"But the parson's gone. The church is closed."

"I know. But there has to be someone left in town who went to that church before it closed. Maybe he—or she—can help us."

Kathleen wished to say, "I don't need help. I'm fine," but down deep inside, she knew that it wasn't the truth.

———

It seemed a long time to Kathleen before she heard Black coming. The young pup that Donnigan had gotten for the children made a fuss. He didn't get to bark at visitors to the Harrison farm often, so he made the most of it when he could.

Sean finally managed to quiet him. "That's Pa. He lives here, silly," Kathleen heard the boy say to the small dog.

Kathleen had to wait for more long minutes while Donnigan put the horse away and stopped to chat with the children who were playing in the yard.

Kathleen hoped that Donnigan's search had been fruitful. She was tired of seeing him with the deep concern in his eyes.

But when he entered the kitchen, she saw that his shoulders still drooped.

"No luck?" she asked, and he shook his head slowly.

"You didn't find anyone?"

"Oh, yeah. I found an old couple that used to go there."

"But they didn't have any answers?"

"Well," said Donnigan taking a chair at the table. "They did—and they didn't."

Kathleen puzzled over his answer.

"They told me what went on at the church," he began.

Kathleen waited.

"They sang songs—hymns they called them—songs about God—from a special book. They prayed. At least the parson prayed for them. And then he read from the Bible. That's the real key to it all, the old folks said. Then they listened to the parson talk a sermon."

"A sermon?"

"About how to live and what to do and all that," explained Donnigan.

"But he's not there anymore. The church still isn't planning to bring him back?" asked Kathleen.

"Nope. Not much chance of that."

Donnigan stretched out his long legs as though to work the kinks from his body and from his soul.

"Guess there's not much we can do then," said Kathleen.

"If I only had some way to get us a Bible," declared Donnigan. "I asked around town and nobody knows where to get one."

"You mean—we'd just read it on our own?" asked Kathleen. It seemed a bit presumptuous to her way of thinking.

"That's what the old folks said we could do."

Kathleen thought about it for a few minutes. There didn't seem to be any answer to their problem. She was about to leave her chair and go back to peeling potatoes for supper when she had a sudden thought.

"Wait a minute," she said, reaching out and grabbing Donnigan's arm with both hands. "I think I have a Bible."

Donnigan jerked his head up.

"In my trunk," went on Kathleen. "It was my grandmother's, and she gave it to me before she died."

Then she finished rather lamely, "I didn't know it was something you could read. I thought it was just for writing things in. Like births and deaths. That's the only time I saw Grandmother use it. When she wrote things in it."

Then Kathleen's eyes lit up with sudden understanding. "She *couldn't* have read it," she said. "Some English clergyman gave it to her, and Grandmother couldn't read English. I remember looking at the words she wrote. They looked strange, so I asked my father. He said they were Irish words."

Already they were moving toward the bedroom and the old steamer trunk.

Kathleen rummaged around, digging through discarded garments and worn bedding, and finally she came up with a faded black book.

"It *is* a Bible," said Kathleen joyfully. "It says so right here on the cover. See!"

Donnigan reached for the book. He held it lovingly, worshipfully. "Kathleen. I think we have our answer." His voice was husky with emotion.

From then on the reading of the Bible was a part of every day. Donnigan always gathered all of the family around right after breakfast and opened up the book. They began with Genesis. It was a thrill for Donnigan to discover how God had created the earth and all it contained. They discussed it with their little family.

"Did He make everything?" asked the chattery Fiona.

"Yes, He did," said Donnigan. "It says so right here."

"The birds?"

"The sky?"

"Worms?"

"Mama?"

"Washtubs?"

"Whiskers?"

"Snipper?" Snipper was their new dog.

To each of the childish questions, Donnigan offered a firm "Yes."

"Really, Donnigan. I don't think He made washtubs," Kathleen gently rebuked him later.

"Well, He made what washtubs are made of—doesn't that count?" replied Donnigan, unabashed.

Kathleen nodded. "Perhaps," she agreed.

————

The older children enjoyed most of the Genesis stories, though they did not understand them all. But when Donnigan got on into Leviticus and Deuteronomy, he had a hard time holding even Sean's attention. And the young Eamon was next to impossible.

"Are you sure we should be reading that to the children?" Kathleen dared to ask. "Maybe it is meant just for grown-ups."

Donnigan wondered the same thing. He decided to do the reading on his own and then share the easier stories with his family in his own words. It seemed to work much better.

————

"We're supposed to be praying, too," Donnigan said to Kathleen one day as he laid the Bible aside.

Kathleen just nodded.

"Do you know any prayers?" was his next question.

"No," she replied.

"I wonder where we can get some," said Donnigan.

"Maybe the old folks in town would know."

"I already asked them. They said the parson did the prayers—and he took the books with him."

"Then I guess we'll just have to do without prayers," said Kathleen.

Donnigan rubbed his hand over the cover of the Bible, saying only, "I really don't think we've got this all figured out."

Chapter Twenty-one

Family

"I was thinking—if this one is a boy—you might like to name him."

They were sitting by the table at the end of a long, exhausting day having a cup of buttermilk together.

"You run out of names?" asked Donnigan lightly.

"Oh no. We could call him Aiden or Keenan or Devlin or—"

Donnigan held up his hand.

Kathleen smiled and took another sip of the cold buttermilk.

"And if it's a girl," prompted Donnigan.

Kathleen tilted her head to one side teasingly. Her dark eyes were shining, her hair, from which she had loosened the pins, tumbling about her shoulders.

She still looks like a child, thought Donnigan to himself and felt a renewed urge to protect her.

"I might even let you name a girl," responded Kathleen after having given the matter pretended serious consideration.

Donnigan nodded. "I accept that challenge."

The baby was another son. Donnigan named him Timothy.

Eighteen months later a baby girl was added to the family.

"Well—who is she?" asked Kathleen as she pulled the wee one close and kissed her soft cheek.

"I would like to say Kathleen after her mama," responded Donnigan, "but since that might get confusing—she's Rachel Kathleen."

Kathleen smiled. Little Rachel. She pulled the baby close and gave her another kiss.

———

The years had been kind to the family. Never had they faced serious illness or mishap. Except for the loss of baby Taryn, Kathleen had brought all of her babies safely into the world with no problems. They were healthy and ruggedly hardy from farm life.

Donnigan kept their bodies toughened yet agile with a balance of work and play, and Kathleen kept their minds active and alert as they pored over lesson books.

Each morning Donnigan read from the Bible. The children had learned most of the Bible stories over the years, and Kathleen was often amused to hear their childish discussion about God.

"They talk about Him like He was—was a part of their world," said Kathleen to Donnigan.

"I hope He is," responded Donnigan—but his voice was still filled with doubts.

"I mean—like He is—is as real to them as—as I am."

Donnigan nodded. That was how he wanted it to be—but was he doing it right? Was he giving them what they needed? "Oh, God," he often groaned in times of quiet reflection, "give me wisdom. Show me what to do. It would be a terrible thing to prepare them for only this life."

———

"Why do we always read the Bible?" It was Eamon, their

difficult one, who posed the question.

Donnigan laid the book carefully back on the table.

"Because," he said with great feeling, "that is the only way that we can get to know God—who He is—and who He wishes us to be—how He wants us to live."

Eamon shrugged, seemingly unconvinced—or else just unconcerned.

"We already know about Him," said the five-year-old boy. He had been told the same stories often enough that he should know them by heart by now.

"Do we?" said his father. "Maybe we do. Let's see. Tell me what you know about God—all of you."

Eamon looked surprised.

It was the outgoing Fiona who responded first. "He made—everything." She swung her hand in a big arc to include as much as she could.

"He made the waters come down," said Brenna softly, "an' all the animals went in the boat."

"He's sorta—magic," said Sean.

"Magic? How?" prompted Donnigan.

"He can do things that no one else can do."

Donnigan nodded.

"He deads people when they're bad," said Eamon.

"Kills people," corrected Kathleen, and then felt shock at her own statement.

"He doesn't kill people," argued Fiona, casting a disgusted look Eamon's way.

"He does too," insisted Eamon. "What about the men the earth ate up? And what about when the flood came?"

"The people were already in the big boat," cut in Fiona quickly.

"Uh-uh. Nope," said Eamon, shaking his head emphatically. "Only Noah and his wife and them others were in the boat."

"There were eight," cut in Sean who always listened well to the Bible stories. "Noah and his wife and three sons and their wives."

But Eamon didn't seem to care much about the particulars.

"Well—all the other people got dead," insisted Eamon.

"That's 'cause God was mad," interposed Brenna softly. The fact didn't seem to trouble her in the least.

"I don't dead people just 'cause I'm mad," said Eamon.

"You're not God," Fiona quickly flung back at him. Her voice was shrill and angry.

"Just a minute," said Donnigan. The little conversation was getting totally out of hand and not at all what he had intended.

"Sit down—all of you. I think we need to discuss this."

The children all sat down, as told, though Eamon looked reluctant to do so and was the last child to finally take his place on the kitchen floor.

Oh, God, Donnigan found his very soul crying out, *help me with this. Please help me.*

He turned back to the ring of children—the wonderful yet frightening responsibility that God had given to him. What were the right words? Did he have the truth to share with them? Or was he still dreadfully lacking?

"God made us," he began. "And He wants us good—like Fiona said. But people didn't stay good. Remember the story about Adam. He did bad. And after that it was very easy for all men—and women—to do bad, too."

Donnigan stopped, took a deep breath and licked his lips.

"Now God didn't stop with just making this world," he went on, hoping that he had his thoughts right. "He also made a beautiful heaven. It has everything in it to make us happy—and nothing in it to make us sad. God made heaven for people. But He also made a hell. He made it bad. In fact, He made it just as bad as it could possibly be so that no one would want to go there. So that people would try *very hard* not to go there."

Donnigan stopped again and looked at the little faces around him.

"I don't want to go there," put in Fiona, shaking her head emphatically.

"But people were still bad," went on Donnigan. "God told them and told them to be good—but they liked being bad, better.

"From time to time, there was a man who wanted to be good. To do what God told him. So when God would find a man like that, He would talk with him, help him, and sometimes God even felt that it was important to get the good man away from the bad people."

Donnigan stopped and looked straight at the squirming young Eamon.

"It is very easy for even good people to be—be followers of bad people. God knew that. So sometimes He took the good people away from the bad place where they lived. Like He did with Abraham when He called him away from Ur. Like He did with Noah and his family when He had them build the boat. He sent the flood of water to save Noah and his family from the evil around them. If Noah had stayed with the bad people, his family might have soon become bad, too.

"But sometimes, God used other ways. There were many good people—and bad people mixed in with them. Well, God knew that if the bad people were allowed to stay there and do the wrong things—then it wouldn't be long until other people would be doing wrong things too.

"So God took the bad people away. Like the big earthquake that swallowed them up. Yes—they were killed. That was the way God could be sure that they wouldn't—wouldn't spread their evil—their bad to others.

"You see—God didn't really kill the bad people because He hated them and was in a temper. Oh, He hated the sinful things they did—the way they lived. But God destroyed them so that they wouldn't destroy others—so that others wouldn't learn to be bad, too."

He looked at the little faces before him. Sean sat listening carefully, seeming to take in every word. Fiona listened with her head tipped to one side, her fingers twisting in the folds of her dress, her toes wiggling impatiently in the worn boots. Brenna sat quietly, one arm cradling her doll. She appeared to be listening, but Donnigan wondered if Brenna, the little dreamer, might silently be humming a little tune to her baby.

Eamon stirred restlessly. His eyes were not on his father's face. He was watching a spider that crawled up the outside of the window. Donnigan prayed inwardly that Eamon might have heard more of his words than he had let on.

Timothy, at three, wiggled and listened by turn, seemingly catching a word here and there that interested him, then turning his attention back to the small hole in the knee of his pants.

Their baby Rachel, sitting on her mother's lap, paid little attention to her father's words, though she was intent on studying his face.

Six children—all different—all in need of heaven, thought Donnigan. *God, help me to get them there.*

———

Eamon continued to be their "tester." Often they heard the same defense: "You didn't tell me not to."

When he cut all the tops off the early spring carrots to feed the bush rabbits in the woods along the creek, when he cropped baby Rachel's silky curls with Kathleen's sewing scissors, when he threw a hen off the barn roof to see if she could fly, when he left the poor pony out in the pasture blindfolded to test if she could see in the dark. At all of these times, and many more, Eamon would shrug his shoulders with the same answer: "You never told me not to."

How could their minds possibly keep ahead of the young boy's?

Timothy, on the other hand, was cheery and cooperative. He followed along after his older siblings, grinning at their accomplishments, clapping at their exploits, seemingly thinking that everything they did was terribly right and brilliant.

Kathleen rejoiced in the small boy. He was such a delightful change from the rambunctious, ever-pressing Eamon. No challenging, no arguments, no talking back.

But Donnigan watched his small son and felt concern.

Kathleen could not understand his worry. "He's so easygoing and pleasant. All the others dote on him."

"That's just the point," replied Donnigan. "He might get the idea that's what life's about. Pleasing others. Being fussed over. You can't always please others, you know. Sometimes you have to take a stand for what is right. You have to be one person against the crowd. Timothy is too quick to try to please. Too quick to do whatever he is urged to do. No. I'm thinking that boy might take more wisdom to raise than we think."

———

Rachel, dear little dark-curled Rachel, began by being a happy, docile baby, seemingly content to watch the actions of the older children. Kathleen was quite surprised to discover when Rachel reached about eighteen months that her independence took a nasty turn.

"I do it!" she would scream and insist on doing her own thing—her own way. Though usually happy if left on her own, she was stubborn and difficult to discipline.

"Why didn't I stop at five?" Kathleen asked herself more than once. But inwardly she knew that she loved the baby dearly and couldn't imagine life without her.

———

"We really should pray, too," Donnigan told his little family as he closed the Bible one morning.

"What's pray?" asked Fiona.

"Well, it's—it's—" began Donnigan.

"Talking to God," said Kathleen to help him out.

"Then let's," said Brenna simply.

Donnigan felt ashamed. How could he tell his children that he didn't know how to pray? Didn't know the words— the procedure? Didn't have any of the prayer books or hadn't learned any of the prayers? Little did Donnigan realize that what he cried from the deepest recesses of his heart—many times every day—was prayer.

He was about to try to explain when Brenna spoke again. "I'll talk to God," she said simply.

"She does it all the time," explained Fiona to her parents.

"But—" began Donnigan. He did not want his child to do anything sacrilegious.

"God," said Brenna, folding her hands in her lap and looking heavenward, "we read all about you in the Book. Sometimes we understand—and sometimes we don't." She gave her shoulders a slight shrug. "I liked the story about Jesus making the bread grow. And Fiona liked the story about the lions with their mouths tied shut. And Sean—" She stopped and looked at her oldest brother. "What did you like, Sean?" she asked him.

"Making things," Sean said, his voice almost a whisper.

"And Sean likes how you made everything—like the animals. He likes the horses best. And—" Brenna stopped and looked around the circle. "Eamon likes the—the way you dead people." Eamon wiggled, then grinned. It made him feel important to be talked about to God.

"And—Timothy likes—"

"The Three Bears," called Timothy excitedly.

"That's not the Bible," said Fiona with chagrin. Timothy looked surprised at the put-down and lowered his face, his lip coming out.

"Timothy likes the bears you made," Brenna changed it and Timothy lifted his face again, a grin replacing the pout.

Brenna cast one last glance around the room.

"And—Rachel likes— She's still too little," she explained to God, shaking her head.

Then she lifted her hands in front of her, looked around the room once more, shrugged her little shoulders and announced, "And that's all."

The prayer was over.

From then on, Donnigan encouraged his children to pray their own simple and original prayers.

Chapter Twenty-two

Eamon

Donnigan eventually knew the Bible well enough to know where to turn for the stories the children would understand—the stories that he thought they needed to know.

They had covered both the Old and the New Testaments a number of times. But Donnigan found himself flipping back to the New more and more often. The stories about the Son God sent to earth held fascination for him—and interested the children.

Kathleen hardly realized how much she had changed over the years she had spent with her family in studying the Bible. She no longer felt the same bitterness, the same resentment toward God, that she had when she had lost baby Taryn.

But when the letters came from Edmund wondering if "they would be kind enough to share the wealth that America had afforded," Kathleen would rage inwardly, looking at the six children round her table that had to be fed and clothed. But she said nothing, and knew without asking that Donnigan always managed to find some way to send a bit of money from their meager savings.

Deep inside there was still an uneasiness in Kathleen. Why did she have to struggle so? Why did her temper still flare when things irked her? Why wasn't she able to put the past behind her and forgive Madam? She believed the Book that Donnigan read each day. She even tried to live by it. So why didn't God help her with her struggles?

Donnigan, too, had inner battles. He had never been troubled by deep anger. It simply was not his temperament. But there were other things that bothered him. He wondered if his offspring didn't get some of their independence from their father. Donnigan always liked to be in charge—make the decisions for those in his care. Hadn't he nearly smothered Kathleen in the first year of their marriage? Was he doing the same now with his children? No, surely not. It was important for them to have the right training. Donnigan felt strongly about it. It was the most important thing in the world to him. But was he doing it right? Doing all he could? He was sure in his heart that God really existed. Sure that the Bible held the truth. Why then didn't he find peace for his own soul?

———

"I don't understand it," said Sean thoughtfully.

He and his father were excitedly surveying the new colt that had just made his appearance in the far pasture.

"Don't understand what?" asked Donnigan, turning to the boy.

"If—God—creates everything—then why—why—how come animals keep making them? Who really makes them— the mothers or God?"

Donnigan smiled.

"God created all things—in the beginning," Donnigan explained. "But when He did—He designed them special so that each thing—in all His creation—could reproduce itself. That is, could make a baby—of whatever it is. The pigs have pigs—the horses have horses." He didn't need to go on. Sean was a farm boy, he knew about reproduction.

"God still has a very real part in everything that is born. He is the 'giver of life' just like the Bible says, but He allows the parents to bring forth young. That's how He made them. Remember those words God spoke in Genesis, 'Be fruitful and multiply'? That's what they mean."

Sean nodded.

"That's how life continues on," Donnigan went on. "Animals, birds, fish, even plants, are still obeying God's command. Are still reproducing. Why, I'm told that the drive to reproduce is even stronger than the drive to eat," he went on frankly. "But without it—life would cease. The old would die off and there wouldn't be any young—any new life—to take their place."

Sean nodded again, willing to accept whatever his father told him. His eyes had not left the new foal.

"He looks like Black," he said, turning Donnigan's attention back to the new colt.

"Young often look like their fathers. Or mothers," said Donnigan, nodding his head in agreement. "But sometimes they don't. Guess the important thing—and sometimes the scary thing—is that they often act like their father—think like their father."

Again Donnigan felt keenly his responsibility to his children.

A young gelding approached the new colt in curiosity and the mare tossed her head, bared her teeth, and flew at him, turning him aside and driving him away with nipping teeth and flashing hooves.

"Why did she do that?" asked Sean. "She knows him. He's just another horse. He wouldn't hurt the foal."

"Parents can be very protective," said Donnigan. "A new mother will often give her life to save her young."

Sean nodded his agreement. He had seen new mothers protect their babies before.

"Guess she'll take good care of him, huh?" he commented as they prepared to leave.

But Donnigan continued to ponder their conversation even after they had turned their mounts and were on the ride home.

Reproduction? It was a strong drive. Animals risked their lives to fulfill the inborn command of God. And that was just to bring an offspring into the temporary world. How much more important that one reproduce spiritual children—children who could be taken to heaven for that eternal life that the Bible spoke of.

That was *his* job—as a parent—and yes, he would be willing to give his life to see that it was accomplished—that his children not be barred from the heaven God had prepared.

Yet, what he was doing—what he was struggling to accomplish—somehow seemed to be falling short. And Donnigan did not understand why.

———

Of all of the children, Eamon seemed to need the tightest rein. Donnigan often felt at a loss as to how to properly guide the young boy. To discipline after the fact seemed like shutting the barn door after the horse got out. If he could only instill in his son a *desire* to do right. But how? Eamon seemed to thrive on controversy—on bucking authority—on testing his parents. Why? Why? Donnigan asked a dozen times a day. Why so much defiance in a child who was loved?

Eamon was not all bad. In fact, he had many good qualities, and Donnigan and Kathleen continually pointed them out to each other and to the young boy, reminding themselves daily to keep those good points ever before them. But so often the rebellion seemed to struggle with the good.

Another thing that caused Donnigan concern was small Timothy. He followed Eamon everywhere he went, copying the actions of the older child, taking whatever order Eamon cared to give.

If Eamon said, "Here. Throw this rock at that old gobbler," Timothy threw the rock. If Eamon handed him a stick and said, "See if you can hit hard enough to break that window glass," Timothy broke the window glass. When Eamon was disciplined for telling Timothy to do such things, he became more clever. He began to say, "Do you think you can tie the goat up by her tail?" Or "Do you think you could make an *A* on the house with this red paint?" Of course Timothy always thought he could, and Eamon could stoutly declare, "I didn't tell him to do it."

It was a bad combination and one that worried Donnigan and Kathleen.

"Mama, come quick. Eamon is hurt!"

It was Fiona screaming as she ran into the kitchen. Kathleen dropped the bread dough she was kneading and rushed to follow the young girl, her eyes wide with terror. What had happened?

"He played in the fire," Fiona shouted over her shoulder as they ran.

The fire. Donnigan and a neighbor man were getting set to butcher one of the farm pigs. A tub of boiling water was needed for dipping the carcass so they could scrape away the tough bristles. All the children had been thoroughly warned time and time again to stay away from the fire.

Kathleen found the boy in the garden shed, curled in a ball, trying hard to keep from screaming over his damaged hands.

"Oh, dear God," she said after taking one look. Then she turned to Fiona, "Go get your father. Quick!"

She managed to get Eamon to the house. He had given up on being brave and was crying in pain by the time she laid him on the kitchen table. The palms of his hands were fiery red with smears of black soot across them. Kathleen could already see angry blisters beginning to rise.

"Oh, dear God," she cried again. "Both of them. Both of them."

Donnigan arrived and took over. Kathleen felt sick to her stomach. She moved along the table and tried to calm the boy by speaking to him, pushing back his unruly hair, and running her hand over his flushed, tearstained cheeks.

The other children began to gather, eyes wide, voices one minute filled with excitement, then silenced by the enormity of the injury.

"He's hurt bad," Kathleen heard Brenna whisper.

"He shouldn't have played in the fire," responded the

motherly Fiona as she wiped away her own tears.

Timothy just stared—wide-eyed. Then he started to cry. He backed away from the cluster and ran sobbing to the boys' shared bedroom. Kathleen wanted to go to him, but she felt that she was needed where she was.

They cleaned up the damaged hands as best they could, applied some healing salve generously, and bound them with white strips of a sacrificed pillow case.

"I wish he could see a doctor," said Donnigan.

"But that would take hours," responded Kathleen.

"Let's just do the best we can," said Donnigan, shaking his head. "I hope we can keep the infection out of them. If we see even a hint of it—we'll have to take him to Raeford by stage."

Kathleen nodded. They would need to be most vigilant in watching the boy.

———

The story came out later. Eamon had said to Timothy, "Do you think you could drop this big rock in the hot water?"

Timothy had accepted the rock and taken the dare.

But as Timothy approached the fire and its boiling tub of water, he had stubbed his toe on a piece of firewood left to stoke the flames.

Eamon, who was near his side to watch what the boiling water would do to a stone, saw the younger boy fall forward. He lunged to push him aside, and in so doing lost his own balance, falling with his hands right in the hot coals.

So it was Eamon who took the consequences of his own disobedience. And young Timothy saw firsthand the cost of defying orders.

———

The hands were slow to heal. Donnigan worried. First, that the hands might not heal properly at all. Then, how the disobedient, rebellious boy would accept having his natural independence totally taken from him. He had to be dressed, he had to be fed, he had to be groomed and cared for. He could not so much as take himself to the outside privy.

At first he found it very hard. Fiona hadn't buttered his bread right. Brenna hadn't cut his pancake the right size. His shoe came untied the way Sean had tied it. His bed had wrinkles. People were never there quickly enough when he needed them. He grumbled and complained about almost everything. Donnigan would just say quietly, "If you hadn't damaged your hands, you could be doing things for yourself."

Gradually the boy seemed to settle into his circumstances and accept his temporary handicap as his own responsibility.

"I'll sure be glad when I get these bandages off," he would declare, but he didn't chafe and fuss as before.

Kathleen, who daily changed the bandages and clipped away dead and damaged skin, watching closely for signs of infection, knew that she would be glad also.

———

As Eamon waited for his hands to heal, his attitude changed considerably toward the other members of the family. There seemed to be some special bonding taking place between him and each of his siblings. Sean helped him with his clothes and did his farm chores while Eamon tagged along to supervise. Donnigan always insisted that Eamon at least go through the motions of choring. He didn't want him sitting around sulking and being bored.

Fiona took her nursing duties seriously, mothering the boy and making sure that everything that he needed was done just right. Brenna made little games of what she did. "Open your mouth wide so the bumble bee can come in," or "Shut your eyes tight while I wash the freckles off your nose," she would tell him, and then giggle when he obeyed.

Timothy tried to help his older brother, but almost everything that he attempted didn't turn out quite right. Timothy likely taught Eamon more about patience than any other family member. For Eamon did adore his younger brother, in spite of the fact that he often led the smaller boy into trouble.

"When you get all better—" Timothy would often say, and then follow the words with some elaborate plan. Eamon would look at his damaged hands and his eyes would cloud. "I don't think that's a good idea," Kathleen heard him say on more than one occasion. "We might get hurt."

Kathleen figured that Eamon had experienced quite enough "hurt" for some time to come.

By the time Eamon's hands healed enough to use in some fashion, he seemed to be much quieter of spirit.

"Maybe God has used this terrible accident to bring Eamon a—a miracle," Donnigan dared to say to Kathleen as they prepared for bed one evening.

"Oh, I do hope good will come of it," breathed Kathleen as she slipped her long gown over her head. She moved toward the bed and threw back the covers.

"But it is so hard—so hard to see his hands scarred like this," she said with heaviness.

"Better his hands than his soul," replied Donnigan.

Kathleen nodded her head in agreement.

"Now," she said to her husband, "what are we gonna do with Rachel?"

Chapter Twenty-three

The Discovery

Donnigan was poring over the Scriptures again. It seemed to Kathleen that he spent most of his evenings reading portions, scribbling down notations and cross-checking verses.

"What are you looking for?" she asked him, using her teeth to bite off the thread that had just been sewn on a button.

"You shouldn't do that," Donnigan reminded her as he looked up.

She nodded. She knew she shouldn't do it, but the scissors were across the room in her sewing basket.

"We're missing something," Donnigan went on in reply to her question. "I'm sure it's here. I'm sure. If I can just get it all sorted out."

Kathleen made no reply so Donnigan went on, scanning down his notes as he spoke. "God made man—man sinned—so God brought in the Law. If man sacrificed the animals and tried to obey—God was pleased."

Kathleen nodded in agreement. Donnigan's brow was still furrowed.

"You don't think we should still be making sacrifices, do you?" asked Kathleen, a bit appalled at the thought.

"No—" replied Donnigan tapping his paper with the pencil. "Remember the verse that says, 'Obedience is better than sacrifice.' And Christ didn't ask for sacrifice in the New Testament church."

"So all we need to do is obey?" responded Kathleen, somewhat relieved.

"Yeah—but the problem is—none of us do."

Kathleen wished to argue that statement. "I do," she said quickly. "At least—I try."

"That's the point," said Donnigan. "No matter how hard we try—we still don't quite make it. Here in Romans it says, 'For all have sinned.' And again over here, 'There is none righteous, no, not one.' And the verse that really settles it is this one that says, 'All our righteousnesses are as filthy rags.' "

Donnigan laid down his pencil and looked at her. Kathleen's hands had stilled in her lap. It sounded to her as if there really wasn't much hope.

"But something changed," she reminded him. "All those verses about Jesus—why He came to earth—to die. Remember it said that He was the sacrifice—once—for all."

"That's why we no longer need the lambs and bulls," said Donnigan, nodding.

"Then what's missing?"

"I don't know," replied Donnigan slowly, leaning back in his chair and gazing at the open Book before him. "I don't know what's missing—except peace. Why don't I have peace, Kathleen? Why am I still struggling?"

Kathleen did not reply. She did not have the answer.

———

Wallis called—just at mealtime. Kathleen should have been used to it—in fact, she was—but it always managed to irk her just a bit when she had to leave the table and get another plate for the neighbor man and crowd the children even closer together.

"Wondering how yer crops are doin'," Wallis explained to Donnigan as though that were the reason for his visit.

Kathleen lowered her eyes quickly to her plate so her irritation wouldn't show.

"Fine—just fine," Donnigan replied. "And yours?"

"Fine—just fine." Wallis reached for the bowl of carrots.

Wallis had never really gotten over Risa's leaving. He didn't seem as angry anymore and he had progressed to the point of weary acceptance. He knew she would never be back, as he had hoped for so many months—so many years.

"God made the crops," piped up Rachel. Then returned to her eating.

"Ya sure got a nice-lookin' bunch of spring calves," Wallis said around a bite of warm biscuit.

Donnigan nodded. They were nice.

"God made the calves," said Rachel.

Wallis frowned and took a big bite of potatoes and gravy. After he had chewed for a few minutes, he lifted his head again.

"Did ya get much outta thet rain shower last night? I figured it sure did come at the right time."

Before Donnigan could answer, Rachel said in a sing-songy voice, "God made the rain."

Wallis, dumbfounded, looked at the child. Then he turned back to Donnigan. "What do you do, Donnigan? Spend all yer time religioning yer young?"

"Not *all* my time," replied Donnigan evenly.

The silence hung heavy in the room for several minutes. Even the children seemed to sense it and stopped their usual prattle.

Donnigan was the one to break it. "You don't seem to put much stock in religious training," he said to Wallis.

Wallis continued to chew; then he lifted his eyes and replied dourly, "It's not I'm *all* agin it. My folks were plenty religious. I had more'n my share in my growin' up—but a man can go too far with it, seems to me."

Donnigan would have liked to ask, "And how far is too far?" but his attention had been caught by Wallis's earlier statement.

"You've had your share? What? What were you taught?"

Wallis shifted uneasily. He reached up and scratched his uncombed hair with the blunt end of the fork he held in his hand.

"Well, I—I don't know as I recall all the—the— You know the usual, I guess."

"Like," prompted Donnigan, leaning forward in his eagerness.

Wallis still hesitated.

"Go on—please," said Donnigan.

"Well—you know the stuff. God made everybody and—"

"We know that story," called out Timothy. "It's in the Bible."

"Then Eve et the apple—and she gave some to Adam—and he et a bite and then God sent them from the garden and told 'em never to go back."

All Donnigan's children could have told those stories—likely better than the grizzled man.

"Then—" prompted Donnigan.

"Well, then ya got all those stories 'bout those other fellas, Noah and Joseph and Elijah and sech," went on Wallis.

With a look Donnigan silenced his children, who seemed about to explode with their own knowledge of those Bible characters. He was anxious to hear what the man had to say. Maybe he had the last piece to the puzzle.

"And then ya get to the next part," went on Wallis slowly. "Where Jesus is born."

"Go on," said Donnigan.

Kathleen had stopped eating. She leaned forward almost as eagerly as did Donnigan.

"Well, He went about healin' people and helpin' the poor and trying to teach what was the right way to live an' fergivin' their sins an'—"

"How?" broke in Donnigan. "Forgive sins—how?"

"How?" Wallis sounded caught off guard. He also sounded puzzled. "How?" he repeated. "Guess God Almighty is the only one who knows thet."

Donnigan felt acute disappointment. But he refused to give up. "Did you ever have your sins forgiven?" he pressed the older man.

Wallis blushed under his bearded cheeks.

"Me? Not me," he hastened to answer.

"Did you see anyone else?"

"Well—sure—lots of folks." Wallis sounded a bit put out. One wouldn't have attended his church, with his folks, without seeing a good number of folks praying for forgiveness.

"How?" asked Donnigan.

"Well—ya gotta go up front of the church—or wherever—sometimes it was at one of them there tent meetings, an' kneel down and cry some, at thet—they call it an altar, I remember now—ya gotta go to the altar—an' cry and ask God to fergive ya fer the bad ya done."

Donnigan eased upright in his chair. An altar. They did not have one. Kathleen met his eyes.

"I wonder if there's an altar left behind in that church," she said aloud.

"Oh, I'm sure they is," said Wallis. "Church always has an altar."

Donnigan's memory began to stir. The Bible spoke of an altar. When God gave the people the tabernacle, and later the temple, He spoke of the altar. The altar was where the sacrifices took place.

"Did they—did they make sacrifices at the altar?" he asked hesitantly.

"Sacrifices? Ya mean like slayin' things? Naw. They didn't do nothin' like thet. Preacher said we was to give ourselves—a livin' sacrifice."

"A living sacrifice? What does that mean?" asked Kathleen.

"I don't know. Preacher talk, I guess. I don't know."

"A living sacrifice," said Donnigan. "You know, there's a verse that talks about that. I saw it again just last night. In Acts. No—no. Romans, I think."

Donnigan hurried away to get the Bible. He spent a few minutes turning the pages while the rest of the people around the table sat in perfect silence.

"Here it is in Romans 12:1: 'I beseech you therefore, brethren, by the mercies of God, that ye present your bodies a living sacrifice, holy, acceptable unto God, which is your reasonable service.' "

Donnigan frowned—reread the verse, then shook his head.

"It says 'service,' " said Kathleen. "Do you think—?"

"It must mean something about living to serve God," said Donnigan, still studying the verse.

Then he lifted his eyes again to Wallis.

"Do you understand it?" he asked the man.

Wallis scratched his head again. The whole conversation was making him dreadfully uncomfortable—and it was so close and warm in the room. He reached up to loosen his shirt and run a finger around his collar.

"Well, ya can't serve Him when ya got sin—thet much I was told," went on the man. "I don't think He really wants much to do with ya when—when ya ain't yet made yer confession."

"Confession?" asked Donnigan.

"Sure, confession," said Wallis, looking a trifle upset with their lack of understanding. "Ya gotta confess yer sins— thet's what ya go to the altar fer."

Donnigan knew there were many verses that spoke of confession. He made a mental note to look them up and study them that evening.

"Then ya just—just—I think they say—accept," went on Wallis. "Thet's how ya be born agin."

Jesus had used those words with Nicodemus, Donnigan remembered. Born again. Born of the Spirit, Jesus had gone on to say. Donnigan felt excitement. The pieces were slowly falling into place.

"An' thet's all there is to it," said Wallis, wishing to get himself out of his present situation.

"You were taught that—in your church?" plied Donnigan.

"Yep. Shore was," said Wallis without hesitation.

"But you didn't confess?"

Wallis looked up slowly, then shook his head.

"But—why? I mean—if you had the teaching—if you knew it worked—why—?"

To their surprise the man began to shift nervously on his chair. He looked down at his calloused hands and rubbed them together in agitation. When he at last looked up his eyes were clouded.

"It worked—fer others. I saw thet. But—well—I was young. I wanted to—well—to do things my own way—be my own boss. I figured there was plenty of time fer religion when . . . someday," he replied simply.

He raised his arm to wipe his sweaty forehead on his shirt sleeve.

"Weren't thet it didn't work," he went on to say. "It was me. I got feelin' kinda ornery like. Wanted to sow my oats. My mama—" He stopped again. "I was about ready to think on it agin when—when—Risa—"

He stirred again.

"But it ain't been a smart thing to do," he finished lamely. "I ain't had me much peace."

"But—others? You've seen others with peace?" asked Donnigan softly. He just had to know.

"Ya mean when they went to the altar and confessed? Yeah. I did. I sure did." The old man managed a wobbly smile and brushed again at his forehead.

I've got to find us an altar, thought Donnigan. *For all of us. That's what we need—a place to confess—and accept.*

———

Donnigan made a trip to town. The church door was still bolted shut. In fact, there was a double lock on the door. Donnigan rattled the locks, but knew there was no way to open them without the proper keys.

He walked around to the window, pressed his face against the glass and peered in. He could see nothing that he understood to be an altar. There was only a small stand at the front where one could maybe lay a book, and a little railing that went around it. Donnigan was disappointed. If he knew what an altar looked like, perhaps he could build his own.

Sadly he turned away. Then he thought of the elderly

couple he had visited a number of years before. Maybe they would know about an altar. Maybe they even had the key to the door.

But when he knocked on the door, it was a new face that greeted him. "Oh, ya mean old Joseph Reed?" said the woman. "They moved off to somewhere. We been in the house for 'most a year now. No, I don't know where they went. He was rather poorly. 'Spose they went off to kin somewhere."

Again Donnigan felt disappointment. As a last resort he headed for Lucas.

After a time of small talk and inquiring of Erma and their four girls, Donnigan dived right in.

"You're a man who has lots of knowledge about lots of things. What can you tell me about an altar?"

"An altar?"

Donnigan nodded.

Lucas sat quietly thinking, seeming to be reaching for answers.

"Well, the Incas used them for their—"

"I'm not talking Incas here," said Donnigan. "I'm talking the Lord's altar, the one church folks use."

Lucas was silent for a minute; then he confessed with no seeming shame, "I've never researched religion," and Donnigan was disappointed again.

———

Donnigan went back to the Bible. He studied the altar in the Old Testament that had been built of shittim wood and overlaid with pure gold. Was that really the kind God demanded? If so, it was no wonder it hadn't been left behind in the locked-up church, and if so, there wasn't much chance of Donnigan getting one.

Donnigan shifted instead to the study of confession and acceptance.

He found a lot of verses. He began to put them together. As he studied they began to make a lot of sense. He reread many of the New Testament stories. The preaching of John, the calling of the twelve, the conversion of Paul—then the ministry of the disciples. As he read there seemed to be a new understanding coming to him.

Confession. Rebirth. That was what was really happening. Over and over—the people who were told of Christ and became His followers were being received through confession of their sin and acceptance of His forgiveness. And Donnigan didn't find one verse where it talked about needing an altar in order to be "reborn." He jotted notes quickly as he went from passage to passage. His fingers were trembling and his face pale. Was that it? Was that the answer he had searched so hard to find? The one that should have been so obvious from the beginning?

It was all there. There were no missing pieces. It all fit beautifully together. You bowed before a merciful God, confessed your sins, and begged His pardon. Then you accepted, with thanksgiving, His sacrifice on the cross on your behalf. He was the Lamb. The Lamb killed and offered up for every sinner. He washed away your sin stains with His own blood and made you clean so that you could present yourself as a living servant of God the Father. And you did not need an altar. God accepted you wherever you were. At whatever time you came with your confession.

God had accepted Saul in the middle of the dusty road to Damascus. The Philippian jailer in the dank, dark dungeon. The Ethiopian in the carriage under the hot sun of the desert.

"Kathleen. Kathleen," Donnigan said excitedly. "I've found it. I've found it. It was here all the time. Look—right here. You don't need an altar. There can be peace—real peace for all of us. All you need is here in this verse. Look! 'If we confess our sins, he is faithful and just to forgive us our sins, and to cleanse us from all unrighteousness.' "

Donnigan looked up, his face flushed with excitement. "Now all we need is to find the prayers so that we can pray them," he said.

They were getting closer.

———

Donnigan shared the verse with his family the next morning, the thrill of his new discovery edging his voice.

They looked at him, some eyes uncaring, some showing confusion, and others registering no response at all.

"What does it mean?" asked Fiona candidly. "What's confess?"

"Well, you remember that we talked about Adam sinning—and then every one of us since that time finding it very easy to sin after that?"

Fiona nodded.

"Well—confessing is admitting that you have sinned. Here—here's another verse. It talks about repenting. Repenting is feeling sorry about what you have done wrong and turning away from doing it anymore. So you admit to God that you have done wrong—and you feel sorry about doing it."

"Like Eamon and the fire," put in Timothy. "He told Mama he did it—and he was real sorry."

Donnigan could not help but wonder if young Eamon would have been sorry if he had not burned his hands in the incident.

"God hates sin," Donnigan went on to get the lesson back on track. "Sin spoils everything. He can't allow sinful people to go to His heaven. The sin would spoil heaven, too."

Donnigan intended to continue his explanation, but a quivering voice stopped him. It was the small Brenna who broke in. "Daddy."

Donnigan turned to look at his child and was surprised to see that her eyes were filled with tears and her chin was trembling.

"I want to tell God sorry," she sobbed.

For one long minute Donnigan seemed to hold his breath. He was about to say, "But we don't know the prayer—yet." Then he looked at Kathleen. He noticed that her eyes were misted, but she nodded her head. It seemed quite right to let the young Brenna tell God that she was sorry in her own childish way.

A short time later Brenna walked away with all traces of tears gone and a smile lighting her petite face.

"I told God sorry and now He's not cross at me anymore," she informed Fiona.

"But you have to be good now," warned Fiona, "or He'll get cross again."

For one brief minute Brenna frowned and then her face brightened. "Daddy said that Jesus will help me to be good—and if I really do something wrong, then I'll tell God sorry again."

"Well—you can't just *plan* on doing that, you know," said Fiona matter-of-factly. "You have to really, really, really try to be good."

Brenna shrugged her tiny shoulders. "I will," she said with a toss of her head. "I don't want to make God sad again."

That seemed to settle it.

Donnigan went to his outside work and the children all went to play or to care for chores. Kathleen was left alone in her kitchen with the events of the morning filling her mind. At the thought of young Brenna, her eyes filled with tears. The child had really seemed to understand what she was doing. She had been so filled with sorrow as she cried out her plea for forgiveness. And she had been so filled with joy when she felt her little prayer had been answered.

Kathleen kept thinking about it as she kneaded the day's batch of bread.

"That's really what I need," she told herself. "Perhaps it would take care of the heaviness of heart I've been feeling. I've been trying so hard to be good since we've been reading the Bible. I've been trying so hard to forgive—Madam—but I can't. I guess it's just like the Book says, our righteousness is as filthy rags, because we never quite are able to do what we try so hard to do."

Tears were running down Kathleen's cheeks at the troubling thoughts. At last she turned from the bread dough, wiped her hands on her apron, and made her way to the bedroom. She knelt down beside her bed and turned her face heavenward. "God," she cried, tears streaming down her cheeks, "I'm like Brenna. I want to tell you I'm sorry. For all the wrong—all the—the sin in my life. Forgive me, Lord. Please forgive me—and make my heart clean like you have promised—through—through the blood of your Son, Jesus."

There were a few moments of silence—followed by a softly whispered, "Thank you, Lord. Thank you."

Kathleen could not have explained the deep feeling of peace that was stealing over her whole being.

———

Donnigan tossed another fork of hay into the manger for the milk cow. He was still shaken by Brenna's simple prayer. Was that what Jesus had meant when He had spoken of becoming like a little child? Donnigan concluded that it well might be. Her faith had been so simple—so complete—her prayer so earnest from her childish heart—and she had walked away with a smile on her face and a lightness to her step.

"That's what I've been wanting—longing for," Donnigan told himself. "But I've been making the whole thing so difficult. Trying to sort it all out—make sure I was doing everything right. And it is as simple as that. Calling out to God—telling Him we're sorry."

Donnigan shook his head. His cheeks were wet with the wonder of the discovery.

"So what am I waiting for?" he suddenly said to Black. "Now that I know—why don't I just—?"

And Donnigan tossed his fork into the pile of hay and fell on his knees in the bedding straw.

"Oh, God," he began. "I come like Brenna. Thank you that you showed us the Way through a little child. We don't need fancy prayers. Special words. We just need to come to you with honesty—and talk to you, Lord.

"Forgive me, Lord. Forgive me and give me your peace and cleansing. Help me to be the husband—the father—that I need to be. Help me to be a living sacrifice. Acceptable to you for the sake of Jesus—your Son—our Lamb. I love you, Lord. Help me to show it—through my life—through obedience."

Donnigan waited in silence—his head bowed—his hands clasped in front of him.

A strange and gentle calm seemed to move into the crude farm structure and surround him. He couldn't have explained why, but he knew that his prayer had been answered.

———

Kathleen ran from the little house. "Donnigan. Donnigan." He would be so happy to learn that she had found the Way—the One that they had been searching for.

But before she had crossed the small yard she saw the barn door open and Donnigan was running toward her.

"I found it—I found Him!" he called across the short distance.

She could tell by his glowing face that he had something exciting to share.

"You, too?" she called back as she continued to run to meet him.

"And you?" he responded.

"Yes," she laughed, the joy bubbling up within her. "Yes!"

"Oh, Kathleen," he managed just before he reached her.

With shining eyes and overflowing hearts, they threw their arms around each other and joyfully laughed and cried together. Nearby, several small heads lifted and little eyes watched in curiosity and awe.

Then Fiona said simply, "Guess they're happy 'bout something."

"I think *I* know," replied Brenna, her eyes glowing again.

JANETTE OKE

HEART OF THE WILDERNESS

BETHANY HOUSE PUBLISHERS
MINNEAPOLIS, MINNESOTA 55438

Cover by Dan Thornberg,
Bethany House Publishers staff artist.

Published by Bethany House Publishers
A ministry of Bethany Fellowship, Inc.
11300 Hampshire Avenue South
Minneapolis, Minnesota 55438

Printed in the United States of America

Library of Congress Cataloging-in-Publication Data

Oke, Janette, 1935–
    Heart of the wilderness / Janette Oke.
        p.   cm.
        1. Orphans—Fiction. 2. Grandfathers—Fiction. I. Title.
PR9199.3.O38H4   1993
813'.54—dc20   93–5338
ISBN 1–55661–362–8   CIP
ISBN 1–55661–363–6 (Large Print)

To those I lean on
throughout the writing process—

Mrs. Katherine Hamm,
who never ceases to assure me
that she is praying for me
Bethany House Publishers' Staff,
who gently prod me
through each new endeavor
My family members,
who understand and encourage
And especially Edward,
my constant supporter,
companion and friend.

Contents

1. For Love of Family.............................. 9
2. Belonging....................................... 18
3. A Difficult Decision............................ 26
4. An Exciting Adventure......................... 34
5. Nonie.. 44
6. Wilderness Child 53
7. The Ugly Side.................................. 63
8. Acceptance..................................... 72
9. Fire 81
10. School 91
11. Pain of Separation 98
12. Adjustments 108
13. Home Again................................... 120
14. Plans... 124
15. Visitor.. 133
16. Hard Winter 142
17. More Trouble.................................. 150
18. Going Out..................................... 157
19. Stirrings...................................... 164
20. Amy.. 173
21. Encounter..................................... 182
22. A Meeting 194
23. Back to the Wilderness........................ 202
24. Change of Plans 213
25. A Heart at Rest 229

Chapter One

For Love of Family

"Where is she?" The question seemed to pull from the depths of his anguished soul.

The gray-haired woman opening her door to admit the tall, dark-bearded man standing on her step felt tears form beneath her eyelids.

"Come in, George," she said softly, waving her hand at the simple room behind her. "You look worn out."

She sensed his deep impatience and feared for a moment that he would refuse. Then with a sigh, he nodded his head and moved past her into the room.

She closed the door, stopping first to look out on the busy street already bustling with the activities of another day. The world seemed to be going on as usual—yet she knew things would never be the same again for the man who had just come.

She turned to him. She had known him for many years. Had seen him suffer before. Yet she had never seen the strong, manly face so tightly drawn, the broad shoulders so slumped, the clear, dark eyes so filled with pain. Today he who had never shown his years looked much older than the fifty she knew him to be.

He was slumped in a chair across the room from her. Head lowered, he brushed at his beard with a large calloused hand, a habit she recognized. He always brushed at his beard when he was anxious or agitated.

9

"She's fine." She answered his question as she moved toward him. "She's in that little Home on Park Street."

His head came up, his eyes darkened. Was he angry? With her?

"I tried to get them to let me keep her here, but they wouldn't allow it. Said that with things like—like they are here—and such . . ." She paused, shrugged, then hurried on when she saw his eyes burning intensely, though not with accusation. "They said they could do nothing until—until they had been in touch with kin. I—I got word to you in the quickest way I knew. Isn't a very good way of communicating—"

"How long has it been?" he cut in.

She stopped for a minute and did some mental calculation. "Almost three weeks since—"

"Three weeks? Terribly long time—for a child."

She nodded at the grief and anger and frustration in his voice, feeling his pain.

He stood suddenly, his dark eyes shadowing more deeply. "I've got to get on over there, Maggie," he said brusquely.

"You look worn out," she hastened to repeat, wanting to keep him from doing anything rash. "You'd better take the time to eat some breakfast—rest a bit. They won't open for another couple of hours anyway."

She was afraid she had lost the argument as he took a step toward the door. Then his hand came up and he began to rub his beard in agitation. At last he retreated and slumped back into the chair and nodded his head solemnly.

"I've traveled day and night since I got your message," he admitted. "I must look a sight."

"Well, I will admit if I hadn't known you, I may not have opened my door." The words were spoken lightly. He managed a bit of a smile.

"You clean up and I'll get us some breakfast," she went on. "Henry will be stirring soon and—"

He lifted his head and looked at her, apology replacing the grief and anger in his eyes. "How is Henry?" he asked simply.

The woman shrugged. There was really very little to say. Henry hadn't changed over the months. The days came and went with little difference in his condition. He seemed to get no better—perhaps a little worse, but it was hard to tell.

"About the same—I guess," she said, her shoulders sagging.

"Can I see him?" the man asked softly.

She nodded toward the small room off the sitting area. "Go ahead. He's likely still sleeping. He doesn't usually wake for another half hour or so. Sometimes he wakens earlier— or during the night. But—but if he is awake, you won't know much difference. He may not respond. He—" She stopped, knowing the man needed no explanation about Henry. He paid a visit to the sickroom whenever he was in the city.

They had been good friends for years. Both big strong men who knew what it was to put in a good day of hard, back-breaking labor. As a younger man, Henry had been George's yardstick, as he had been for most of the community where they'd been raised. Anyone who could keep up to Henry was considered to be a good worker and worthy of his hire. And now Henry lay on the same bed that had taken him to its bosom four years earlier. He could not even lift a hand to feed himself or brush the annoying tears from his eyes. Since the accident in the lumber mill, Henry had been paralyzed—totally paralyzed—and Maggie had to do for the big man all those things he had at one time done for himself.

The visitor moved toward the door, his body showing his dread at seeing again his lifelong friend in such a crippled state.

But Henry was still sleeping. George stood for some moments watching the rise and fall of his friend's shallow breathing. Henry had lost even more weight since the last visit. Gaunt and pale, he looked so wasted that George barely recognized him as the same man who had won the log-sawing contest nine years running.

George crossed to the foot of the bed and spoke softly to the unhearing man who slept restlessly. "I'm here, Henry. Been a long time. Should have come oftener—I know that.

But I've been so busy—" He stopped. Would Henry want to hear of his busyness? Henry who couldn't even move.

He shut his mouth on the whispered words and studied the thin, useless right hand that lay pale and helpless on the coverlet. The callouses were gone now. The warm, deep tan from the summer sun had long paled. George stepped forward and took the thin hand in his own. The scar was still there. More visible than ever against the tissue-like skin.

In spite of his resistance to tears, George felt them gather now. Were the tears for Henry? For himself? He didn't know. He only knew that suddenly his world seemed filled with so much pain. Pain he tried desperately to keep within himself.

He looked back again at the hand he held. That hand had been scarred on his behalf. He remembered the day well. Henry had risked his life to save him. And now Henry lay withering away on his bed, and there wasn't one thing George could do about it.

He placed the hand gently back on the patchwork coverlet and quietly left the room.

————

"What do you plan to do?" Maggie asked the question as they lingered over another cup of breakfast coffee.

The sigh seemed to begin somewhere deep inside him and gradually make its way through his whole being, ending with a little shudder.

What did he plan to do? The words echoed in the air between them.

"I must see her—as quickly as possible," he answered Maggie, but both of them knew that his words did not really address the question.

Maggie nodded and waited for him to go on.

He shook his head, his eyes looking deep and troubled. His left hand stole to his beard again.

"It's so—so—so unfair," he almost spit out. "For a child's father and mother to be taken and—and leave her—alone."

Maggie nodded again.

His head jerked up and his eyes filled with anger as he turned to her. "What were they thinking of, Maggie," he demanded, "to leave a child and go off on some—some helter-skelter expedition into the wilds? Had they no—no thought of—?"

Maggie reached out and placed her hand gently on his trembling one. "Now," she said softly, "you know better than to think like that. After all, you're the one who taught Mary to love those wilds. They'd made trips like that over and over in the past and nothing had happened. It was an unexpected accident, George. An unexpected and unexplained accident. Nothing more. It—it does happen. It doesn't mean that they were uncaring or—or irresponsible parents. They loved her. Did everything for her."

"But—but—*both* of them. Why both of them? The two of them could swim. Why both of them? And why—why take on rapids that they couldn't handle? Mary knew—they both knew the danger of—"

He had to vent his feelings. He had been burying them deep inside ever since he had gotten Maggie's message. He had to let those feelings out. And who better than Maggie to share his pain—his confusion.

"The Mountie said there was a snag under the water," Maggie explained softly. "A broken tree—with a jagged break. The canoe caught it and spun out of control. When they went in—well—they figure he swam to shore. He made it. His heavy boots were found there—on the bank—together. He must have placed them there. But—Mary. I know she was a good swimmer. But for some reason—she got into trouble. Maybe got a bump as they were thrown out. Guess we'll never know.

"But he went back for her." She stopped and sighed. "We'll never know," she said again. "They went down together. Found their bodies downstream from the rapids. He was still holding her. Still had shreds of her clothing clutched in his fingers."

Hearing the story of the death of his daughter—his only daughter—and his son-in-law filled him with such pain and sorrow that some of the anger was pushed from his heart. There was simply no room for him to hold all the feelings. No room. He felt as if his heart would burst with pain. He wanted to bury his head on his arms and sob until the hurt went away, but he knew it was not that easy. It would be a long, long time until his heart began to mend and memories of his precious Mary would bring pleasure—not sorrow.

Maggie wiped at the tears that ran down her cheeks. George wished he were free to express his grief as easily. He swallowed, hiding his eyes, brushing with an angry hand at the beard that shadowed his face.

"Where are they buried?" he managed to ask, his voice shaky with emotion.

"Beside their cabin—just at the base of the stand of spruce to the west."

He nodded. It was the place he felt Mary would have chosen.

He stood up quickly, two conflicting desires drawing him. He longed to visit the grave of his daughter. The grave of the young man she had learned to love. The man who had given his own life in his unsuccessful effort to save her. Stu Marty. The man George felt he had hardly known—and now would never really know, though he had longed to claim the young man for the son he'd never had. But the miles—the miles had kept them apart. He could not leave his own wilderness—nor could he ask them to share it with him.

And he also wanted to rush to his little grandchild. Little Kendra—now an orphan. His daughter Mary's only child. The child he had not seen since she was little more than a baby. How he chided himself for his error. How he wished that he had taken the long journey, visited his daughter, her husband, her baby girl, more frequently. But there was no going back. No reclaiming of the years that had slipped by so quickly.

"I need to go," he said to Maggie. "I need to—" He stopped and licked his lips. He still had not answered her deeper question.

"Sit," she said, nodding her head toward his vacated

chair. Only Maggie would have dared to address the big man in that fashion.

He sat down. Silently. Dutifully.

Maggie waited until she sensed he was ready for her to speak.

"Have you made any plans?" she asked again, softly.

He shook his head, his left hand working vigorously on his beard.

"Shouldn't you?" she persisted after a pause.

"I—I don't know. I—I don't know what to do—how to plan. I'll need to work it through. Figure it out."

Maggie nodded, her expression telling him she knew it was hard to make plans. Hard for a man to be able to think when he had traveled so many miles in such a short time. To know how to properly respond to the present situation.

"Where was she when—?" he began, and Maggie guessed his question.

"They had left her with one of Mary's friends. A neighbor. I—I think she might have wanted to keep her, but she is expecting her first baby. Had to come to the city for delivery."

He nodded.

"She may be willing to take her . . . after," Maggie went on.

He brooded over her words. It seemed so—so difficult to think of trying to arrange for his grandchild. To "place" her. To farm her out. Just as though—as though she were some—some animal that needed care. He shook his head.

"You know I would have taken her—would still take her," went on Maggie softly. "But—but Henry—he needs so much care." She hesitated, studying her thin hands as she rubbed them together in helpless agitation. "I—I really don't think that—that this house is—is the right place for a child to grow up," she finished lamely. "You understand?"

She sounded so remorseful. So filled with shame that she couldn't reach out to her friend in time of need. Her words wounded him. It was his turn to reach for her. He took her two hands in one of his own and gently squeezed in understanding. His tears did fall then. Full and unrestrained tears that made soft damp trails down the weathered cheeks and hid quickly in the heavy, dark beard.

"My dear Maggie," he said huskily. "I know that you'd help me if you could. I know that you loved Mary almost as much as I did. As Polly did. You couldn't take the child in—with Henry needing you like he does. I don't know—I'll never know—how you manage to keep going day after day with all the care he needs. I—I—should have been here to help you. To—"

"Nonsense," said Maggie stirring restlessly in her chair. "I haven't minded the caring for Henry."

She withdrew her hands and blew her nose noisily on a sturdy cotton hankie.

He wiped away his own tears and fought to get himself under control again.

"You still haven't—" began Maggie.

"I'll just have to find a good home—I don't know how—or where. I won't leave her where she is, I know that. I couldn't. Not in a Home."

"They do give them good care," put in Maggie softly. "Mrs. Weatherall is a good woman."

He nodded, glad to hear the words and at the same time rejecting what they implied.

"I can't leave her in a Home. She needs family. A sense of belonging to—someone. It's important to a child."

She nodded her understanding.

"She won't know me," he went on almost absently. "It's been almost two years since I've seen her. She was just a toddler. She won't even know me—her own grandfather."

Maggie said nothing.

"Do you think the beard will frighten her?" he asked, sudden alarm in his voice. Before Maggie could answer, he spoke again. "Perhaps I should shave it off."

"She wouldn't be frightened of a beard," put in Maggie. "There are bearded men all around. Her own papa had one. Not dark and bushy like yours—but a beard nonetheless."

He looked relieved. Then he stirred restlessly, dreading what lay ahead. Seeing little Kendra in the charge of the matron at the Home would be such a final recognition that his Mary was really gone.

Maggie placed a hand on his sleeve, willing him some of her strength for the ordeal. "Come back," she said, compassion coloring her words. "Come back—whenever— Stay with us for a few days. As many days as you like."

He nodded his head and reached for his coat and hat. The mornings were still chilly in spite of the fact that they were moving into spring.

"I'll be back," he said. "Tell Henry. I'll be back."

He moved through the door and closed it softly behind him. Then he lifted his shoulders and braced himself for what lay before him. He was facing one of the most difficult days he had experienced in all his life.

Chapter Two

Belonging

"I understand you have my granddaughter," he said to the prim young lady who sat behind the wooden desk in the little room that served as reception area and business office.

Her expression did not change. She still wore the smile with which she had greeted him.

"You will want to speak to Matron," she said, the smile tilting her full lips. He did wish she would wipe the silly look from her face. This was not a lighthearted matter.

"Matron?" he repeated.

"Mrs. Weatherall."

"Mrs. Weatherall?"

"Yes. You will need to speak with her. She answers all inquiries concerning our wards."

He nodded and waited, expecting her to summon the Mrs. Weatherall referred to. She sat where she was, still smiling.

He shifted his weight to his other foot, twisted his hat in his big hands, then lifted the left hand to rub at his beard.

"Mrs. Weatherall?" he repeated.

"Yes," said the smiling young lady.

"Does she come to me—or do I go find her?" he asked impatiently.

"Oh—she'll come. When summoned."

"Then summon her," he ordered, a bit too gruffly. Too impatiently.

"Yes, sir," she responded, and for the first time he saw

18

the smile slip. She quickly regained her composure and returned the smile to its rightful place, rose from her desk,
gave him a brief nod and an even bigger smile, and left the
room.

He paced the small space. Two steps to the window, three
back to the door, three to the window, and back again to the
door.

A tall, full-figured woman with a kind face entered the
room followed by the still-smiling younger woman. *The Matron,* he thought, and felt that she indeed looked the part.
She moved directly to him and reached out a hand. For such
a small one, he was surprised at the strength in the clasp.

"Won't you come into my office," the woman invited, and
nodded her head toward the door that she had just entered.
Without a word he followed her.

She indicated a chair and he took it while she proceeded
around her desk and sat down facing him. There was no smile
pasted on her lips. He thought he read compassion in her
eyes.

"Miss Wilson says that you have a grandchild with us."
Her voice was full, yet soft with feeling.

He nodded his head, finding it hard to come up with
words. She waited, seeming to know that he was fighting
hard for control.

"A—a granddaughter," he managed at last. "A little
girl."

He didn't stop to think that his few words were redun-
dant.

She nodded patiently, waiting for him to go on.

"They called her—" For one moment he choked, thoughts
of his Mary flooding over him. Mary with her head bent over
a new baby girl. Mary with laughter in her voice and love in
her eyes. Mary, his little girl, as a mother. He pushed away
the thoughts and tried to speak again. "Kendra," he managed. "Mary named her Kendra."

"Kendra Marty?" asked the woman softly.

He could only nod.

"You must be George McMannus," she went on easily.

"Mrs. Miller told us that we could expect you—once you got the word."

He nodded again and swallowed hard. So Maggie had already prepared the way.

"Let me offer my condolences. I am so sorry about your daughter and her husband," the woman said, and he could sense the deep and honest sympathy in her voice. He wondered if she had lost someone to be able to feel his pain in such a fashion.

He couldn't answer. He toyed with his hat with the fingers of his right hand and reached his left to his beard. He could not look up. He could not face even understanding eyes.

"I will have one of the attendants get little Kendra," she went on as she rose from her chair. "We have a comfortable little room just for such meetings. Or would you rather meet in the garden?"

"The garden," he said quickly. He was pleased he could escape the closeness of the stuffy rooms. He needed air. He needed space.

"You go ahead. Right through the door at the end of the hall. I'll bring Kendra out to you."

She turned to go but he stopped her quickly. "She won't remember me," he blurted. "She—I haven't seen her for almost two years. She'll have forgotten—by now."

The woman nodded. "Perhaps I will stay nearby for your first meeting," she answered, and he knew she was thinking of the little girl and her many exposures to pain and strangeness in such a short time.

"That would be good," he said simply and left the room for the garden.

He paced about, trying to quiet his troubled thoughts and get control of his mixed feelings when the same gentle voice spoke behind him.

"Grandfather McMannus. Kendra is here to see you."

He stiffened. He wished to wheel around and embrace the child now within his reach. At the same time, he longed to flee. It would be so hard to see Mary's baby—alone.

Reason told him that he had to be careful. Cautious. Slow

and deliberate and gentle or he would frighten the little one half to death. She had already been through so much. So much, for such a little tyke.

He knew that the title "grandfather" had been for the sake of the child. To perhaps stir some memory. Make her realize that the stranger before her was somehow connected to her. That they belonged together, the big man and the little girl. Inwardly he was grateful to the woman who seemed to understand so much. If only—if only he knew how to approach the small child. How to let her know he loved her. If he could only reach across the span of time—and miles—and be a—a real grandfather. Could let her know what he felt in his heart.

He turned slowly, took a deep breath and looked first at the woman. She stood silently, seeming to will him her strength. He knew that tears were in his eyes, threatening to spill down his cheeks. Would they alarm the little girl? He mustn't cry. He mustn't. He almost choked on the intensity of his feelings, then let his eyes drop to the little person who clung to the matron's hand.

She was such a tiny thing. So small. So—so vulnerable. One small child, clutching firmly to a worn rag doll. He remembered the doll. Mary had made it. Kendra had toddled about the cabin, dragging the doll behind her when he had visited them the last time. Mary's baby—smiling and gurgling over her own baby. Dollie.

She had grown so much since he had seen her and held her in his arms. Yet she was still so—so small to have lost so much. He shuddered, fearing that he would not be able to move—to speak. And then she lifted large green eyes to his face. Mary's eyes. His Mary in miniature. He felt the pain rend his heart. He wanted to sweep this child into his arms. To hold her and weep and weep for what he had lost. For what they both had lost. But he could not move. He could not speak.

Kendra broke the silence. But she did not speak to him. She spoke to the matron. Her words were clear, but confusion made the little voice tremble. "Is this my grandfather?" she asked simply.

"Yes," the woman replied in a firm, soft voice. "You have not seen him for some time, so you might not remember him well. But he is your grandfather. Your mama's father. He remembers you when you were a baby—and as you grew a little bit bigger."

Her eyes turned back to him again. He still had not moved.

"Hello, Grandfather," she said, and again her voice trembled.

"Hello, Kendra," he managed. He didn't think he ever remembered speaking such difficult words.

They looked silently at each other.

"I've asked Miss Jane to bring milk and cookies to the garden," the woman said. "We can have them together."

For the first time the large green eyes took on a sparkle. It was clear to him she thought milk and cookies a wonderful treat.

"Shall we sit down?" offered the matron, moving toward a small bench. Kendra did not release her hold on the hand she clutched tightly.

Kendra did not sit. She stood, holding Dollie under one arm, leaning up against the knee of the woman. George McMannus could not take his eyes from her little face. She looked so much like his small Mary. Only the shape of her mouth and the color of her hair were like her father's.

He longed to talk to her, but what could he say? *How are you, Kendra?* He knew how she was. At least he felt he knew. *How do you like living here?* That didn't seem like a proper question for a little girl who had been taken from a loving home and thrust in with a group of strangers. *What arrangements would you like to make for your future?* No. The child knew nothing about the difficult decisions that were ahead. The decisions that he, as her grandfather, must make on her behalf.

He raised his eyes to the face of the woman who sat on the small bench. Her hand rested lightly on Kendra's back, pressing the child up against her knee. There was caring in the touch. Caring in the eyes. If Kendra could not be in her own home—then perhaps—perhaps the best place for her was here.

He stirred restlessly, brushing away the thoughts. He couldn't leave her here. He knew he couldn't.

A young woman in a stiff, clean uniform arrived with a tray. There was tea for the man and the woman, milk for Kendra, and cookies for all to share. He was glad for the distraction. Though he had never cared for tea, he was willing to accept the cup offered to him. At least it would busy his hands.

Kendra seemed to relax as well. She settled on the bench with her milk and cookies, her too-short little legs swinging back and forth as she prepared herself to enjoy the refreshment.

George saw her tilt her head and look up into the branches when the song of a bird lifted against the late morning sky.

Just like Mary, he thought, and the pain stabbed him again.

"Is that a robin?" she asked the matron, interest in her voice.

"That was a chickadee," responded the woman. "I have not seen or heard a robin yet this spring. But they should be coming back soon."

Kendra looked pleased at the fact. Then she said merrily, "Mama and I like the chickadees best anyway. Papa likes the crows, he says. But he's just teasing. He doesn't like the crows. They make an awful squawk." She giggled at her own little joke.

Her words surprised her grandfather. *Didn't she know?* Had no one told her? She was speaking of her parents in the present tense. Surely—surely he wasn't expected to be the one to tell this little child that her parents were both gone and that she was alone in the world. That she really had no one—except for one errant, distant trapper grandfather who came to call so seldom that she didn't even know him.

He lifted his eyes to the woman, accusations deepening his gaze.

But the woman looked unperturbed. She was stroking back Kendra's soft curls and repeating the child's words, but in her way. "So your mama used to like the chickadees and your papa used to tease about liking crows," she said, her smile warm and friendly.

Kendra nodded but her eyes became serious. "They used to," she agreed with a solemn nod, her eyes becoming clouded.

"Your mama and papa liked the birds," the woman went on. "They loved everything about the outdoors."

George McMannus looked again to the woman. He wondered how she knew so much about his Mary.

"It's nice to be in God's outdoors," went on the woman. "It's nice to enjoy His creation. Perhaps when you are older, you'll love it and know about it like your mama and papa did."

Kendra nodded. She was quiet again.

The woman stirred and lifted her eyes to the man who sat silently staring at his delicate teacup. He looked up.

"Did you tell your grandfather that you will soon be four?" the matron prompted Kendra.

The little face took on a sparkle again. She carefully raised a little hand and tucked her thumb against the palm. "I will be four—this summer—in August," she informed him.

Yes—it had been August. He remembered it well. Mary had hoped that Kendra would be born on his birthday, but the infant had arrived eight days later. "Your 'almost' birthday present," Mary had teased as she handed the small Kendra to him on his first visit to see them after the baby had been born. Even at that time he had thought she looked like Mary. He remembered that now.

He nodded to the small child. "August seventeenth," he said, keeping his voice as even as he could.

"How did you know?" she asked, both curiosity and excitement edging her voice.

"I'm—I'm your grandfather," he reminded her. "I—I remember when you were born."

"Were you there?" she asked quickly.

"No. But I came as soon as I could."

"Came from where?"

He hesitated. How could he explain the "where" to the child. There wasn't even a known name for the wilderness he called home, though the locals referred to the small post and settlement as Bent River Crossing.

"From where I live. From the—the mountains and the woods and the—the rivers—where I live."

To his surprise her eyes widened. Something was going on in the small head.

"Are you *that* grandfather?" she asked him, the green eyes widening with puzzlement, then with understanding.

He hardly knew how to answer her question. What grandfather? He knew that she only had one in Canada. Her papa's folks were in England.

Before he could answer she spoke again. "My trapper grandfather?"

His heart leaped. They had some connection. Bless Mary! She had linked them in the short time she'd had with her daughter. With his granddaughter.

"Yes. Yes," he answered quickly before the moment was lost. "I'm that grandfather."

She smiled at him. The first tentative little smile she had given to him. It stirred his very soul.

Chapter Three

A Difficult Decision

"I'll need some time," he told the matron after Kendra had been taken back inside by one of the uniformed attendants. "I haven't had a chance to make any arrangements. I just got into town."

He did hope she wouldn't push for him to take the child before he had a chance to carefully select a place for her. He couldn't place her just anywhere. She needed love. She needed family. She needed more than just care.

"I understand," said Mrs. Weatherall. "You need time— and Kendra needs time."

His surprise must have shown on his face.

"Kendra has been through a very emotionally devastating time for a child," went on the woman evenly. "She has faced pain and confusion to the fullest measure. She has been brought to a house filled with strangers. Caring strangers— but strangers nonetheless. She has just begun to adjust to this new life here—and we are going to ask her to make another big change. It will not be easy for her—and should be done as slowly and carefully as we can manage."

He nodded, swallowing the lump in his throat.

"You are very important to Kendra," she continued. "You are a link with her past. Even though she does not know you well, she does remember her mother speaking of you. That is important. It not only gives her family—it gives her a living memory of her mother. Something to tie to—to anchor

26

her. She is not totally alone now. Do you understand?"

He nodded again. It was all so hard for him. To see the child—to remember Mary. He was still wishing for a quiet place where he could let the tears flow. Ease some of the pain.

"We all need some time," said Mrs. Weatherall. "I know you are a busy man, but I do hope you can give us some time. Time for you to just spend with Kendra—while she is still here. Then when she is ready—and moved—time to let her become adjusted in her new home—before you leave her. That will make such a difference for her—to have that transition spanned with love."

He silently agreed with the wisdom of the words. He determined in his heart that he would be there—for Kendra. He would make it as easy for her as possible. Already he felt such love for the brave little waif.

"I'll be here—for as long as she needs me," he managed to say.

"Good," said the woman and she seemed relieved. "Take as long as you need to find the right home. In the meantime you can visit Kendra as often as you like. It will be good for her to have her grandfather. I'll tell her that you'll be calling. Tomorrow?"

He was about to agree when he thought of Mary. He had to go to her. He just had to. His heart would find no rest until he had made that final call.

"Not—not tomorrow," he mumbled through stiff lips and saw the disappointment in the eyes of the woman.

"I have to—have to go see my daughter," he tried to explain. "It's a full day's trip—each way. I—I have to see—I have to," he finished lamely.

"I understand," she replied, her voice low and echoing his pain.

"You can tell Kendra that I'll be here first thing Friday morning," he went on.

"I'll tell her," agreed the woman. "And with your permission I'll also tell her where you have gone."

"Do you think—?" he began to question.

"I think it is important for Kendra to know that you loved

her mother and father. That you are sharing in the pain of their death."

"Do you think—?" he began again, then quickly checked himself. "No, I guess not," he answered his own question.

"Think what?" the woman pushed him.

He shuffled uneasily. "Well, I was just wondering—just thinking—but it wouldn't be wise."

"Yes?" she prompted.

"Well, I was wondering if the child—Kendra—if she'd like to—to go with me, but I don't suppose—"

"Could you wait?" asked Mrs. Weatherall frankly.

"Wait?"

"Could you put off your trip for a few days—until you and Kendra have a chance to know each other a bit better—and then decide if it would be wise to take her or not?"

He thought about his answer before he voiced it. It would be hard to wait. He had longed to go to Mary ever since he had heard of the accident. Then he pictured Kendra. Would the trip be right for her? She was only a child. Would it be right to take her to the grave of her mother and father? To her former home? He didn't know.

He lifted his eyes to the woman. "What do you think?" he asked frankly. "I'm willing to wait—if it would be the right thing."

"Kendra has not been back to the cabin since the accident. Perhaps it would be healing for her to see where her parents have been laid to rest. I don't know. We can only judge that when we—when we see how she learns to feel about you. I think—I think that Kendra herself will be able to tell us. We'll have to let her take the lead."

He nodded, his heart still heavy.

"Then I'll be here tomorrow," he said simply and rose to go.

"I'll tell her," said the woman.

With a nod he left the small office and moved out into the sunshine of the spring day, glad to fill his lungs with clear, fresh air.

———

"I don't seem to be getting anywhere," George McMannus said to Maggie across her kitchen table. George had just fed Henry his supper of broth and custard. Now they sat down together to partake of the meal Maggie had prepared.

"It might take time," Maggie responded. "You'll have to be patient. She has been through so much for such a little tyke. It might take a while until she is ready to warm up to anyone."

"Oh, it's not that. Not Kendra."

Maggie looked at him with puzzlement.

"I mean—she's chatty and friendly. Seems glad to see me whenever I arrive. It's this—home situation. I've followed every lead I've been given, and I still haven't found a place I would feel right about leaving her."

Maggie stirred the soup before spooning some into their bowls. She knew George had spent most of his days making calls throughout the city trying to find a suitable place for the young child.

Maggie nodded. It was hard to see her old friend carry such a heavy burden.

"Did you check with that pastor Mrs. Leed told me of?"

He nodded.

"He gave me two names," he answered. His hand stole up to his beard, and Maggie's expression mirrored his deeply troubled one.

"Both fine enough folks, I guess," he went on. "One man has no work right now. Finding it hard to feed his own family. 'Course I could pay him for Kendra's keep—but would the money meant for her be used to feed the others? Could hardly ask a man to feed an outsider better than his own offspring. And the other—I think they mean well enough—but, well— she's rather a sour person. Mary was always so—so bright and cheerful that I don't know if Kendra could—could live comfortably with dour sternness."

"Something will work out," Maggie said, trying to console him. "These things take time."

He nodded. But he was impatient. The days were slipping by so quickly. Days spent hunting for the right place for the child. Days spent with the little girl who was so quickly claiming his heart. He felt as if he were being torn asunder.

"Do you know what that is, Grandfather?" she quizzed as they took a walk along the riverbank hand in hand, Kendra holding tightly to her rag doll. "That is a boon."

"A boom," he corrected. "A log boom."

"Yes, a boom," she repeated. "Papa told me. A boom."

It was one of the many things her papa had told her and she had repeated in their few days spent together. George McMannus was getting the feeling that the son-in-law he had hardly known had made a good father for Kendra. She spoke of him constantly. Just as she chatted about her mother.

Her grandfather noticed that she still interchanged past tense and present tense as she discussed them. At times she even spoke of the future. It worried him. Did Kendra really know that her folks were gone? That they wouldn't be coming back to pick her up? He hardly knew how to deal with the child. Should he remind her each time that she would not see her parents again? Was that too harsh for a child to bear? He did not have the answer, but the small child's desire to live in the past tore at his already wounded heart.

He turned his attention to her now as she pointed at the log boom that moved slowly down the river.

"Do you know what that man does?" she asked him. "He makes sure they don't jamp."

Jam, he was going to correct her, but he let it go.

"And sometimes he runs all across the logs—jumpin' and jumpin'," she went on. "Papa showed me a jumpin' man once."

"When did you see the jumping man?" he asked her softly.

"Once—when Mama was home with a tummy ache from the fu and Papa took me with him for a walk by the river."

He didn't correct her word for flu either.

"Mama was real sick that day," went on Kendra. Then brightened. "But she got better. She doesn't got any fu now at all."

He winced. Would she never remember? he wondered.

"Kendra," he began slowly, not knowing what to say, not knowing how to say it, but sensing that this might be a good time to feel his way, "I'm goin' to make a little trip—"

He saw the questions darken the large green eyes. Had she heard those words before? Had he chosen his words poorly?

"Where?" she asked quickly.

"Well, just—just—up to where you used to live—with your mama and papa."

The eyes changed dramatically. He saw the light in them.

"Can I go?" she asked before he could even continue.

He stopped walking. He felt his hand tightening its grip on the small one that was slipped in his. She stopped him and looked up into his face, her eyes pleading. He reached down and lifted her and sat her up on one of the posts that lined the river dock.

"Kendra—" He struggled for the right words. "It—it won't be like it was—you know that. Your—your mama and papa are no longer—they no longer live at your old home."

She looked at him solemnly, then nodded her head in understanding, tears forming in her green eyes.

"They're dead," she said with candid frankness.

It was his turn to blink away tears.

"Yes," he agreed when he could trust his voice to speak. "Yes, they are dead. Do you—do you know about—about what it is like to be dead?"

She nodded slowly.

"Have you seen anything that was—dead?" he pressed further.

She nodded again.

"What?" he asked her.

"When—when Papa shoot things—they be dead," she answered him.

So her father had been a hunter. At least the child had an idea of what death was.

"But nobody shoot my mama and papa," went on Kendra, shaking her head vigorously. "They got dead in the river rapids."

He nodded in agreement.

When he found his voice, he went on. "Do you know what—what happens to people who—who die?" he asked with difficulty.

"They get buried—in the ground. They make a grave and they—they bury them in a special place so that we always know where they are."

He bit his lip to keep it from trembling. He knew that someone had been trying to explain to her what had happened. He was thankful for that "someone."

"I'm going to your old home to see—to see the graves of your mama and papa," he told her. "So that—so that I'll always be able to remember—where they are."

"Can I come?" she asked again without hesitation.

"Do you—do you really think you'd like to do that?" He still wasn't sure if it was the right thing to do.

"I want to," she said simply. "I want to see where they really are, too."

He nodded. "I'll talk to Mrs. Weatherall about it," he promised her. "We'll see what she thinks."

He lifted her back down from the post and they turned their steps toward the Home.

————

He told Mrs. Weatherall about the conversation he'd had with Kendra that afternoon. The woman said very little as she listened. Just nodded her head occasionally.

When he finished his little account he was stroking his dark beard vigorously. "What do you think we should do?" he asked.

She turned the question back to him. "What do *you* think?"

"I don't know. Honestly, I don't know. She—she seems to understand. But I don't know."

"How do *you* feel—about visiting your Mary's grave?" asked the woman.

His head came up quickly. "I have to go. You know that," he responded.

"Why?" she asked softly.

"Well—because—" He stopped, impatience edging his voice. He had felt that she understood him, and now she was asking this—this question to which the answer should have been so obvious.

"I need to see her one last time." He hesitated. "Oh, not her—I know I won't see *her*. But I mean I have to—to sort of make that last contact. I have to—to know where she is—to say that final goodbye before—before I can have any rest—get on with life."

She did not speak. She just sat silently, letting his words hang in the air between them. Letting them echo back in the big empty space that had been Mary in his own heart and mind.

"And Kendra?" she asked softly. "Do you think she might need that too?"

"She's a child," he argued, but his tone was thoughtful. "She's so young."

"But she's also a person," spoke Mrs. Weatherall. "A person—a very small person—with a great big loss."

"I don't know," he said after the silence between them had lingered long enough.

"I don't know either," said Mrs. Weatherall. "Perhaps we'll have to let Kendra guide us."

He nodded and rose to his feet. Already he knew in his heart that when he visited Mary's grave, Kendra would be at his side.

Chapter Four

An Exciting Adventure

"I 'member that house."

There was excitement in the small girl's voice. The building she pointed out was nothing more than a log shack along the riverbank, but the sight of something familiar seemed to please her.

She released one hand from holding her doll and swatted at the mosquitoes that buzzed about her face, then turned her little face behind her. "Grandfather. Do you 'member it?"

"Can't say that I do," he answered as he took a long stroke on the canoe paddle. "But then I haven't been up this way in a long time."

"I 'member it," she said again. "When we went by it before, there was a red shirt on that line."

He marveled at her memory.

"Grandfather," she said again, "do you 'member the red shirt?"

He smiled and shook his head. "No," he responded, "I don't remember the shirt either."

She swatted another mosquito. "These 'skitoes are a pesky nuisance, aren't they, Grandfather?"

Surprised, he couldn't hide the smile that played about his lips.

"That's what Mama says," she added.

Yes—Mary had said that. And his Mary had borrowed the words from *her* father. His words were now coming back

34

to him through the grandchild who shared his canoe.

"Grandfather—do you know what I think?"

"Well," he said, resting his paddle against the side of the small craft. "I know what I think. I think that grandfather is an awfully big name. Do you think there might be something else you would like to call me?"

She puckered her brow, deep in thought. He studied the seriousness of the green eyes, thinking back to another little girl who had shared his canoe such a long, long time ago— but that only seemed like yesterday.

"I know," she said, her face brightening. "I could call you Papa Mac."

The words caught him so totally off guard that he heard his own soft gasp. "Where'd you—?" he began, but she was bubbling on.

"Mama used to call you Papa Mac—so I will call you Papa Mac. Okay?"

Another link. Another pull at his heart. He couldn't answer her because he was so choked up, so he just nodded his head.

"How much longer?" she asked, seeming totally oblivious to the sweet pain she had just caused him.

"A long way yet," he managed to answer, clearing his throat. "But I think that it's about time to take a break and eat the lunch Mrs. Miller sent, don't you?"

She agreed wholeheartedly. He eased the canoe up against the bank of the river and helped her from the craft. He was surprised at how easily she seemed to adjust to the sway of the small boat. He wondered where she had learned the rhythm of a canoe. Never once on their trip upriver had he needed to caution her to sit still or not to lean over the edge or never to move quickly. Worried about it, he had been prepared to rescue her from the water should they have a spill. But she seemed to know instinctively how to move.

"Have you been in a canoe before?" he asked her as she stood beside him on the riverbank.

"Oh yes," she enthused. "Mama used to take me. And

sometimes Papa used to take me. And sometimes we all went together."

So that was the secret. Already Mary and Stu had been raising a little girl who would love the wilderness just as they did.

They ate their simple lunch in silence. It was the first she had stopped chatting since they had left the city behind. He watched her as she tilted her head and listened to the song of a bird.

"What was that, Papa Mac?" she whispered. He couldn't believe how easily she had adapted to the name.

"That was a wild canary," he replied.

"Mama was teaching me the birds," she said sadly.

The bird called again, and Kendra tipped her head to listen. "A wild canary," she said to herself as though to implant the words firmly in her mind. Then she shrugged her shoulders. "Guess I'll never know the birds now." She spoke quietly, but her voice broke with the words, and he saw her chin quiver.

When she lifted her head again there was strength and determination in the little face. "They don't have many birds in the city anyway," she informed her grandfather. "I don't think the birds like all those houses and all that noise and stuff."

He wondered how *she* felt about all the houses and all the noise—and stuff. He felt his own chin tremble.

"I guess we should be going," he said to her to break free from the pain he saw in her face. The pain that spilled over into his own heart.

She nodded and climbed to her feet, but much of the excitement of the morning seemed to have left her.

———

In the afternoon, she slept, her rag doll, Dollie, held closely to her chest. He worried about the sun shining down upon her and managed to make a shelter of sorts to shade her face. He also worried about the mosquitoes that buzzed endlessly about her, but there was very little he could do about them.

He still wondered if he had done the right thing. Should he be bringing her on this journey of sorrow? Could he hide his own pain enough to be a source of comfort for one lost, bewildered, heartbroken little girl?

Many times during the day of paddling, he felt a strong urge to turn the canoe around and beat a hasty retreat back to the city. He wondered if he could face the pain that lay ahead in seeing Mary's grave. It was too much. Too much to add to the pain of the past. The pain of losing Mary's mother. He had to get away. He had to brace himself against all the anguish he was feeling. He had to get back to the mountainous wilderness where he was sure he could find some measure of calm and serenity and begin to heal again.

But what of Kendra? He looked at the slight body, the pixie face, as she slept. She still clutched her worn rag doll that Mary had made for her. She had called him her trapper grandfather. She had also dubbed him with Mary's pet name. They were linked together as surely as they would be if actual chains bound them. It brought him joy—and deep sorrow. What would he ever do about Kendra?

———

The two stood, heads bowed, hands clasped tightly. Before them were two mounds of scarred earth. At the head of each a small cross stood, carved from the nakedness of a forest tree. No words were on the crosses, just simple initials. On one was carved M.M., on the other, S.M.

The lump in his throat was so intense that he feared he would choke. He did not even dare let his gaze rest on the silent little figure beside him. She was so still—so quiet. Even in his own grief he was thankful that the child did not understand—could not possibly grasp the meaning of the two mounds.

"Which one is Mama, Papa Mac?" a small, trembling voice whispered.

His body gave a start. Perhaps she did understand. He swallowed, trying to gain control of his voice that he was sure wouldn't work properly. "That one," he managed to answer, fighting to keep his voice even.

"Can I hug her?"

"Hug her?" He did not understand.

She pulled her small hand free, moved from him, and with one quick motion fell beside the mound, reaching out with little arms to embrace the dark, bare earth. Tears came then. Not just the tears of the little girl, but the tears of her grandfather as he dropped down beside her and gathered her close. They cried together for the mother, the daughter, they had lost. They cried until they were finally able to whisper a goodbye and move on to the next silent grave to cry and whisper again.

When their tears were spent, he picked her up in his arms and cradled her close. She put her arms around his neck and held him tightly. At last he turned from the two graves and carried her down the hill the short distance to the small cabin that had been her home. They did not speak. He longed to say words of comfort. To ease her pain. But what could he say?

He did not know what the little girl might be thinking. She could not share her thoughts of loneliness and sorrow with him. But he knew what he was thinking. *They belonged together*—the two of them. There was nothing that could change that. He should have known it from the first time he looked into her large green eyes. She was his. He was hers. There was no way he could ever turn his back and walk away from her. Not if he found the best home in the city. No, she would never be alone again if he could help it. She was going with him—back to the wilderness. Back where she could hear the song of the birds. Away from the "many houses and noise—and stuff." He would teach her to identify the bird songs. He had taught her mother Mary.

He held her tightly and wiped the final trace of tears from her cheeks.

"We need to have our supper and get a good sleep," he

said softly to her. "We have a big trip to make tomorrow. And then—after that, we have to get ready for an even bigger trip."

Her eyes widened. "Where?" she asked him.

"Home," he said simply. "Home."

She looked at the little cabin they were about to enter.

"A new home," he hurried to tell her. "A new home—with me."

For one moment she looked at him and then her arms tightened about his neck. He couldn't see her face, but he had the feeling that some of the pain had left the large green eyes.

———

"Are you sure you are doing the right thing?" Maggie asked in a hushed tone. Kendra lay sleeping on a makeshift bed nearby. The days since their return from the trip upriver had been busy. There were always supplies that were needed when he visited the city, but now that Kendra was going home with him, there were so many more things he would need.

They had gathered up her few possessions that had been left behind at the small cabin. The remainder of her clothing, her toys, and a few reminders of her mother and her father. It had made a cumbersome load for the little canoe on its return trip, but he would not have denied her anything that she had wished to take. She needed all that was available to keep her parents' memories alive in her mind.

As the mound of articles from his daily shopping trips grew and grew, he knew his trip back home was going to be slow and costly. He would need to hire another boat or two. There was no way the supplies could be contained in his own small craft when he reached the end of the freight line.

But he did not worry about it. There were always trappers or Indians willing to make a little extra money by paddling freight upstream. He'd have no problem finding someone to share the load.

So he continued to pile up supplies, and Kendra continued to chat excitedly about the long trip she would soon be making with her grandfather and the fact that she would be living with him in his wilderness home.

He had feared that he might have to fight it out with Mrs. Weatherall. She did question him.

"Do you think that is a good place to raise a child?" she had asked soberly.

"No. No, likely not," he answered honestly. "But her own folks gave her a good start in the wilderness. And I can't abide the city—besides, my livelihood is out there."

"And Kendra—?"

"I won't leave her behind," he said firmly. "She needs me."

He didn't say what he could have said quite honestly. That he also felt a need for the little girl. He knew he would never be able to stand being separated from her now.

"And her schooling?" asked the woman.

"I bought books," he replied. "I can teach her for the first years—and then—then she can come out to one of them girls' schools."

The woman had not argued further. He was surprised at how easily he had won. "I'll have her ready," was all the matron had said.

And she had kept her word. When the last of the purchases had been added to the collection and arrangements made for them to board the big paddle boat, George McMannus went for his small granddaughter and found her bag packed, ready for the trip ahead.

"Goodbye, Kendra," said Mrs. Weatherall, and she put her arms around the small girl and held her close. She did not say, "I will miss you." She had far too many other small children who needed her love and attention. She did not say, "I hope you will be happy." She seemed to know as she looked at the two of them together that the best way for Kendra to put her past behind and find a measure of security and happiness was with her grandfather. So she just said again, "Goodbye, Kendra. Whenever you return to the city, I would love to have you visit me."

"I will," promised the little girl, then solemnly added, "but we might not come for a long, long time. Papa Mac doesn't come very often to the city."

The good woman smiled. George McMannus held out his hand. He knew that his eyes were about to betray him again.

"Words can't say what I'm feeling," he said. "But I do thank you for taking her in. Easing her pain. Hugging away some of the hurt."

The woman blinked hurriedly, not wishing to show the depth of her feelings.

"That's why we are here," she said, her voice steady and her eyes direct. "I wish—I wish that all of our children had such a—such a happy ending to their days with us."

He gave her hand a slight squeeze and turned to pick up Kendra's little suitcase.

The long, long journey began with the paddle-boat trip up the broad river. Kendra's excitement ran high. Her grandfather, more accustomed to the quiet of his wilderness, was chatted at and led about until he felt exhausted. Relieved when it was time for her to be bedded for the night, he tucked the blankets around her and the rag doll she clutched to herself.

After three days of river travel, they docked and hired a wagon to haul their belongings overland. This meant a four-day journey with frequent stops to rest the team, but the pauses only served to agitate the man. He was anxious to get back home. He had been away far too long.

At last they reached their own river and the group of small shelters that had been built close to the stream.

"Is this our city, Papa Mac?" Kendra asked him.

"We don't have a city," he answered. "This is an Indian settlement."

She looked about with candid curiosity. Children ran back and forth on the riverbank, yelling at one another with strange-sounding words. Dogs barked and women peered shyly from behind draped doorways. In the shade a few men lolled and whittled, looking up now and then to study the wagons that had pulled up in front of the small outpost store.

George McMannus reclaimed the canoe he had left behind with the man who ran the post and managed to find two fellows with sturdy canoes who were willing to move his freight upriver to his cabin home.

"You go on ahead," the big man called to the men in the other two loaded canoes. "I'll only be a short while—then we'll catch up."

"Why are we stopping here, Papa Mac?" Kendra asked, but there was no alarm in her voice, only interest.

"We are going to see Nonie," he answered, reaching for her hand.

As they passed the village inhabitants, he called out greetings. Kendra had never heard the words before and did not understand them. Some of the men rose to their feet and answered him with strange words of their own. They often chatted for a few minutes before the pair moved on, Kendra's hand held firmly in her grandfather's.

They came to a small, ramshackle home at the edge of the little settlement, and George McMannus called loudly, then stepped up to the door. Without a knock he bent his head and ducked under the tanned moose hide that had been pulled back to let the sun shine in.

A voice from inside answered him softly and Kendra ducked her head just like her grandfather had done, though she was much too short to have necessitated such a move, and followed him into the dark, smoke-smelling room.

A woman sat on the floor. She worked over a large bowl she held within her bent legs. She did not even lift her head but spoke rapidly in her own tongue.

"Speak English, please," George McMannus answered her. "So my granddaughter will understand."

The woman lifted her head slightly and took one brief peek at the small girl before her.

"This is Kendra," George said to the woman.

"Kendra," she repeated, her native tongue making the

name sound strange yet appealing.

"Kendra, this is Nonie," the man went on.

Kendra held back shyly. She wished to duck behind her grandfather's long legs, but she wasn't sure if that would be acceptable. Instead, she turned her face against him.

"Say hello," her grandfather bid her.

"Hello," she said shyly, still feeling uncomfortable in the unfamiliar house and in the presence of this person who was a stranger—and strange—to her.

The woman on the floor chuckled softly, lifting her hand to hide the sound. She was no longer young, but her wrinkled face held serenity, her deep eyes soft merriment. Graying hair hung down over her shoulders in two neat braids.

"Nonie, I need help," the man went on without any preamble. "I need to pick up my dogs as quickly as possible, and I can't leave Kendra alone. Can you stay with her?"

Nonie lifted her head fully and looked from the man to the small girl. She shrugged her shoulders and nodded.

"Good," said the man. "I will look for you tomorrow—at first sun."

Nonie nodded again, then turned her eyes back to her bowl.

Kendra felt a tug on her hand and realized that her grandfather was now leaving the cabin again. He said one last word in the strange language and the two made their way back to the canoe that bobbed up and down with each movement of the river.

Though Kendra had not fully comprehended the exchange, the arrangements had been made. Nonie would be the one who would care for the child while her grandfather tended to some other duties.

Chapter Five

Nonie

"Where's Papa Mac?" A sleepy Kendra peeped out from a tangle of blond curls at the woman in deerskins who worked near the cabin fireplace. The woman did not lift her head at Kendra's question.

"Gone," she said.

Gone. The single word brought terror to the child's heart. First her parents—now Papa Mac. *Gone!*

For one moment she stood frozen—then with a cry she leaped forward and ran to the door of the cabin. Tearing at the door, cries lifting to the rafters of the small cabin, Kendra fought to get out. Fought to escape. Fought to run after Papa Mac.

The woman watched her, silently, motionlessly, and then she slowly stood and brushed off the bits of swamp reed she had been weaving. She crossed to the child in silent steps and gently laid her hands on the small shoulders.

"Tush," she said gently. "Tush."

But Kendra paid no heed.

"Tush," the woman said again and gently but forcefully turned the little girl around to look into her face.

"Tush," she said again. "He come back. Tush."

When Kendra still wailed wildly and tried to turn back to the door, the woman firmly drew the child into her arms and held her tightly. Kendra had no choice but to weep against the smoky-smelling shoulder of deerskin.

The woman's hands gently soothed as they brushed at the head of tangled hair and patted the thin, shaking shoulders, then stroked the arms, now still.

"Tush. Tush," she said over and over, the word calm and soothing. "He come back. Soon. He come back."

When the words finally got through to the little girl, her struggling ceased, her tears lessened. At last she pushed back, brushed her hair away from her face, and took another look at the woman who held her. She remembered her from the day before. Papa Mac had said that she would be cared for by this woman. She remembered now. He had said he was going to get his dogs.

With the memory of Papa Mac's words, Kendra's fears began to be alleviated, though her little body still trembled and her heart pounded within her. She had not really understood Papa Mac's words. She had not expected to wake up to a stranger in the small cabin.

"Hungry?" the woman asked her now.

Kendra nodded her head.

"First—" The woman pointed to the bunk where Kendra had slept. At the bottom of the bunk some of her garments had been laid out carefully. Kendra didn't know if the woman had chosen them or if her grandfather had put them there before he left the cabin, but obediently she followed the pointing finger and slipped out of her flannel nightgown and into her simple garments.

As soon as Kendra had finished, the woman beckoned her over so she could work on the tangled hair. As she combed and plaited, she clicked her tongue in strange sounds and chuckled. Soft, silvery laughter that almost made Kendra wish to join her.

When the woman was finished and had laid the comb aside, she turned the small girl back to face her and looked deeply into her eyes. "Amo-chika," she said softly. "Amo-chika." She drew Kendra close against her and held her for a long time. For a reason that Kendra could not explain, she felt comforted. The strong, dark arms that held her promised such love. Such security. Kendra buried her face against the rough, skin garments and breathed deeply of the strange smell of woodsmoke.

The woman held her back at arms' length again and spoke softly, pointing at herself, "Nonie."

Kendra nodded. She remembered the name now. "Nonie," she repeated, trying hard to give the name the same soft lilt that the woman had.

The woman smiled.

Then she pointed at the wee girl. "Kendra," she said. "Amo-chika."

The name—her own name—sounded strange to the young girl. And the new Indian name sounded even stranger. But she liked the sound of it. She repeated it, trying to make it sound just like Nonie had said it. It was different to be practicing one's own name. But she tried it again and again as Nonie led her to the small table by the room's one window and sat her down, soon bringing her a dish of breakfast porridge.

Kendra did not like the taste of the simple meal and would have refused it, but she was hungry and Nonie said "Eat," so Kendra ate.

After she was finished, they gathered up the few dishes from the morning's meal and went to the small creek that ran close by. Nonie hiked her skirts, tucked them in, and bent over the fast-flowing water, washing the dishes in the cold stream. Then she set them in the warm morning sun. Kendra ran about on the shoreline, discovering pretty wild flowers hidden among the grasses.

When the dishes were warm and dry, Nonie gathered them together and they returned to the cabin.

"Now—we go," said Nonie and she picked up a basket that was beside the door and reached for Kendra's hand.

They spent the entire morning out of doors. For Kendra it was a delightful day of exploration. For Nonie it was serious gathering. As they walked, her eyes were ever alert to plants that grew about their feet. Often she would stoop and search out hidden leaves with her fingers. She seemed to sense just where to look for them. Sometimes she took the leaves. At other times she cast the leaves aside and dug the roots for her basket.

"Why do you do that? What do you want that for?" Kendra asked on more than one occasion, and she was always given an answer.

"Good medicine," Nonie would say, or "Makes good to eat."

"Can I pick some?" asked the child.

"Yes. I show," said Nonie.

And Kendra began her own search for special plants and wild herbs.

"This one?" she would ask, holding out a plant to Nonie. More often than not Nonie would laugh merrily and shake her head. "No, no," she would say, "not that one. That one p-f-f-t."

It was a strange sound. Almost a cross between a spit and a hiss, but Kendra quickly got the message that those leaves were throw-aways.

It did not discourage her, for Nonie would show her again just what they were looking for. When Kendra did happen to return to the woman with a few of the right leaves, Nonie clapped her hands gleefully and rewarded the girl with clicks of her tongue and a huge smile. Kendra fairly burst with her success.

The sun had climbed high into the sky when Nonie said, "We go home now." Kendra's short legs were weary with all the walking, the scampering here and there in her search for special plants, but she was reluctant to return to the darkness of the cabin. She wished with all her heart that she could protest, but even at her young age, Kendra had been taught to obey orders without argument. She turned slowly to follow the woman back through the woods.

They had not gone as far from the cabin as Kendra might have guessed. Their search had been leisurely paced, with frequent stops. Now on their way home, though unhurried, they walked steadily and soon the cabin came into view. Kendra was almost glad to see it, for she suddenly felt tired. Yet she could not hide the sigh that escaped her lips as they neared the door.

"You like sit?" asked Nonie, pointing to a grassy place in the shade of a tall spruce tree. Kendra nodded.

"You stay," said Nonie softly.

Kendra nodded again and dropped down on the grass. It was so nice and cool. So soft beneath her. Above her head, clouds floated across the sky and birds darted here and there among the branches. She heard one call across the small clearing and another answered from the other side. But Kendra did not know what bird was calling. She clamored quickly to her feet. She would run and ask her mama. And then Kendra remembered. Mama was gone.

Her face puckered and she threw herself back down to the ground and buried her face in her arms. Nonie found her crying when she returned with their simple meal.

"Tush," she said, laying aside the plates. "Tush."

"I don't know the bird," wept Kendra, not able to explain to Nonie the full meaning of her tears.

"Bird?" replied Nonie.

"I don't know which bird—that sang," she sobbed.

"One does not cry—over birds that sing," said Nonie, still sounding bewildered.

"Mama would tell me."

For a long moment Nonie puzzled over it, her brow knit in a frown, her eyes intent upon the small girl's face. Then a sudden light seemed to brighten her eyes. She nodded and reached to draw the little girl into her arms.

"Nonie tell," she said, her hands gentling and soothing. "Nonie tell—everything. Nonie be here. Always. You see."

Gradually the tears stopped and when Kendra had ceased crying and had wiped her eyes on the hem of her skirt, Nonie offered the plate.

The bird called again and Kendra lifted her head, tilting it to one side as she listened.

"That mountain bluebird," said Nonie without being asked. "Someday I show you. Maybe we find his nest."

Kendra smiled.

It wasn't the name of the bird that brought the smile. Though Kendra already had a deep love for all things of nature—it was the fact of being comforted after the death of her parents. It was the renewed feeling of security after the terrible shattering of the world she knew. And it was especially the sense of being cared for after having lost the people she loved the most.

————

It was almost sunset when Kendra heard dogs barking and ran to the cabin window.

A team of dogs was coming quickly down the trail that led up the creek. They pulled a strange sleigh that ran on small wheels instead of runners. A man ran behind them calling out orders. Kendra wondered if they could even hear above their yapping. But they stopped suddenly and lay down in the harnesses, tongues dripping and sides heaving.

It wasn't until then that Kendra noticed who was driving the team.

"It's Papa Mac," she squealed. Already she had forgotten that he was coming home, back to them. In her little heart she had expected him to be gone just as her parents were gone. Without realizing it, she had accepted the fact that now it was to be she and Nonie in partnership.

For one moment she stood—torn. She loved her Papa Mac. But already she felt drawn to the kind woman who had held her close and comforted her with such understanding. She looked over her shoulder at Nonie. Which one would she choose? Which one could she choose? Confusion filled her heart and showed in her eyes.

She turned again to the window. Papa Mac was unharnessing the dogs and tethering them about the clearing. The wagon-sleigh stood deserted—empty.

Kendra swung back to Nonie, her green eyes wide with fright. Was her world to be one of constant change?

"Are you—you goin' to go?" she asked the Indian woman, fear making her voice tremble.

Nonie, not understanding the full import of the question, nodded her head matter-of-factly and answered, "I go now."

The terror deepened in Kendra's eyes and with a loud wail she threw herself at the woman and wrapped her small arms around the pungent-smelling skirts. "No," she wailed. "I don't want you to go."

Gently Nonie unwound the arms and lifted the child up against her shoulder. Understanding filled her dark eyes as she stroked the soft blond head and crooned her soft "tush" in the child's ear.

"I go tonight. I come in morning. You see. You see. I come in morning. Didn't Nonie say, 'I here always'? You see. You see. Tush. Tush."

What was Nonie saying? Kendra hushed her crying so she could listen more closely.

"Papa Mac here. Nonie go. Papa Mac go. Nonie here. You see. You see," promised Nonie over and over. "Tush. Tush."

Kendra's tears stopped. Was this really a promise? Would she be able to keep both Papa Mac and Nonie? Dare she hope that Nonie could keep her word?

Kendra pressed more closely against the woman and wrapped her arms tightly around her neck.

The door behind them opened and Kendra knew that Papa Mac had entered the cabin. She felt more than saw the exchange of glances between the trapper and the Indian woman. A message seemed to pass between them without a word. Then Papa Mac spoke, his words sounding loud after the soft voice of the woman.

"Kendra—I've missed you. How about a big hug?"

Kendra eased back slowly, studying the face of the woman before she was lowered to the cabin floor. With one last glance at the dark face she had already claimed for her own, she turned and looked at Papa Mac. He offered outstretched arms and Kendra smiled and ran to them.

"So, did you and Nonie have a good day?" he asked as he settled her on his knee.

Kendra nodded. Then she turned to her grandfather.

"I don't want Nonie to go," she stated simply.

"Nonie has to go," he said, and Kendra saw a look pass between the two again.

"Look," said her grandfather, sweeping the entire cabin with a wave of one long arm. "Where would Nonie fit? There isn't room for three people here. It was all I could do to squeeze in your little bed in the corner. There isn't room for another person."

Kendra frowned. "Nonie can have my bed," she offered generously.

Her grandfather laughed and gave her a hug.

"Nonie has to go home. Back to her own cabin," he explained further. "Nonie likes her home. She wouldn't want to leave it to live with us."

Kendra looked at Nonie, her big eyes questioning the woman, challenging her.

Nonie dropped her eyes to the cabin boards. She moved silently toward the potbellied stove that stood in the corner of the cabin and pushed more sticks of wood into the firebox.

"Nonie will come again tomorrow," promised the grandfather. "Whenever I am not here—Nonie will be here."

That was what Nonie had said. Nonie had promised. One or the other of the new people in her world would always be with her. Dared she believe them?

The strong arms of her grandfather tightened about her. Kendra snuggled down against his chest and studied Nonie who moved a stew pot back over the hidden flames.

This arrangement wasn't what Kendra would have preferred. She would have liked it much better if both her grandfather and Nonie could be with her constantly. But perhaps she could accept them—one at a time. She laid her head against her grandfather's chest. She could hear the gentle rhythmic beating of his heart. It was a comforting sound. Slowly her head began to nod in assent. If that's the way it had to be, then she would accept it. Just as long as they kept their promise. Just as long as she had one or the other. Kendra felt secure.

"I brought the dogs back home," her grandfather was saying. "Would you like to see them?"

Kendra's attention was quickly diverted. She loved dogs.

"Are they yours?" she asked her grandfather.

"Ours," he answered. "Ours."

Kendra grinned as she took his hand and led him from the cabin.

————

Almost daily, Nonie and Kendra took treks through the woods. Patiently Nonie taught the young child to recognize the plants that were useful and would be placed in the gathering basket. Over and over the lessons were repeated until Kendra began to understand just what it was she was looking for. Always she was rewarded by an enthusiastic Nonie. Kendra tried hard to mimic the soft clicks of the tongue that expressed approval and soon had the little sounds added to her own vocabulary.

"She's a bright little thing," her Papa Mac informed Nonie, and Nonie nodded her agreement, her eyes, though turned to the floor, sparkling with the thoughts of Kendra's quick achievements.

There were many days over the summer when Papa Mac did not go away and Nonie did not come. Kendra never knew when those days were to be. She sometimes wondered how the two people in her life knew. How did they get their message from the one to the other? Would the day ever come when there would be confusion and they would both be there at once? The thought made her little heart skip with anticipation. And then a chill passed through her. What if, in confusion, they both would be gone at the same time and she would be entirely on her own? It was a frightening thought and it made her heart pound within her.

But as the days passed and those fears were never realized, Kendra forgot them. Perhaps—perhaps her world was not about to turn upside down again, after all.

Chapter Six

Wilderness Child

Kendra's fourth birthday was not spent as a child would normally spend a birthday—but it was not forgotten. Papa Mac even made her a cake. A rather lopsided, strange cake with no icing and no candles, but a cake. No four-year-old could ever have been more excited than Kendra as she looked at the simple creation.

Then Kendra was given a birthday gift. Papa Mac told her to close her eyes and not open them until he told her. She felt something soft and furry in her arms. A puppy! Her very own dog. It was from the litter of one of the dogs in the Indian village. Her grandfather had paid the man dearly for the choice of the pups.

Now as Kendra held the squirming puppy in her arms and squealed over the fact that he was really hers, Papa Mac felt the price he had paid was a fair one after all.

Kendra called the small pup Oscar. A strange name for a sled dog. But Papa Mac did not argue with her choice. He named his dogs as he desired. He saw no reason to deny Kendra the same privilege.

"That not good," said Nonie, pointing to one of the berries in Kendra's basket. "Make sick."

"It was right there with the other berries," she argued.

"Not good. Make sick," Nonie insisted. Then spit out her word, "P-f-f-t."

Kendra picked up the berry, studied it for a moment, then let it fall from her fingers into the grasses at her feet.

"Guess a bird can have it," she said, hating to give up the red plumpness.

"Bird know better. Make sick," Nonie said and turned her attention back to her picking.

They had spent many of their days together picking berries. Kendra had already learned to recognize most of the berries that were "good." She had also been taught to recognize many of the berries that were "bad." Now she had added another one to the list. She did not want a berry in her basket that "made sick."

A bird called.

"That's a loon," spoke Kendra without lifting her head.

"Brother loon," said Nonie.

Kendra was becoming used to Nonie's family references to the woodland creatures, but when she told her grandfather he just chuckled.

"Nonie trying to put silly notions in your head? Trying to make a Cree out of you?" he had asked the young girl.

"Uh—uh. Nonie's not Cree," Kendra had said.

"I really have no idea. I wonder if Nonie knows. She was born mixed blood. Mother was Peigan. I don't know what tribe her father was. She was raised by the Blackfoot and then married into the Stoney tribe. Now she lives with the Cree. She speaks several languages. I'm not sure if Nonie has figured out just what she is."

Kendra was far too young to understand all that her grandfather's words implied. She shrugged her shoulders and said simply, "She's Daughter of the Earth. She told me."

Papa Mac had laughed good-naturedly. Kendra had said the words the same as if she were announcing her own name as Kendra Marty.

Now as the young girl and the Indian woman picked berries together and listened to the mournful cry of the loon from the nearby lake, Kendra was quite willing to accept the bird as Nonie's brother loon. Just as the sleek mountain lion was her brother lion and the marauding grizzly was her brother bear.

But Nonie interrupted Kendra's picking and her listening for another cry from the lake.

"We go," said Nonie. "Storm come."

Kendra lifted her head to the sky. The sun still shone down upon them. Fluffy clouds skittered across the expanse of blue, seeming a bit more in a hurry than normal, but Kendra could see no threatening rain clouds.

"The sun is shining," said Kendra.

"Storm come," said Nonie again. "We go."

Kendra did not argue further. Although she loved to be outside, she was weary of picking berries. She nodded in agreement and stood to her feet. Nonie led the way back through the forest. There was no trail to follow. Kendra followed closely behind her. The growth was heavy, and Kendra did not wish to be left behind.

They were just nearing the cabin when a loud clap of thunder seemed to rock the very ground they sped over. Kendra lifted startled eyes to the heavens and was surprised to see that dark, menacing clouds had gathered over them. The child felt a moment of fear and hastened her step to catch up to the scurrying woman. She grabbed a handful of buckskin skirt, her eyes turning again to the sky.

They rushed into the cabin just as the first large drops of rain began to fall. Kendra whirled at the entrance and pushed the heavy door soundly shut behind them, glad to be in where they were safe.

Never had she heard it thunder as it did in that storm. Her wide green eyes grew large and intense in the small face. Kendra trembled, her whole being filled with fright.

Nonie had been busy clucking over her berries and had paid little attention to the young girl, but when a small hand again clutched at her skirt, Nonie turned. For one moment quiet dark eyes met troubled green ones and then Nonie began her little comforting noises. "Tush. Tush," she soothed, gathering the small child into her arms. She held her close for a long time while the thunder crashed and rumbled overhead and the lightning ripped through the sky above them, piercing their small clearing with jagged flashes of light.

"Tush. Tush," said Nonie. She carried Kendra to the rocker in the corner of the room and held her close against the cured buckskin with its strange and comforting smell.

"Father Thunder," she said. "Father Thunder."

Kendra's trembling lessened. The storm moved slowly on until the thunder seemed to echo off the mountain ridge across the valley and no longer shook the small cabin with each clap.

"I tell of Father Thunder," said Nonie, and still holding the little girl close, she began her story.

"Once, before there were people, all animals and trees lived and talked with one another.

"Bear think he was biggest and strongest of all animals, but Fox think he was smartest. He keep telling Bear it was better to be smart than to be strong and that make Bear angry.

" 'We'll see,' said Bear. 'We'll have contest.'

" 'What contest?' asked Fox.

" 'There is not Fire on Earth,' said Bear. 'We need Fire to keep us warm, but there is only Fire in Heaven. We must steal Fire from Sun. But first we must go to Sky and find Fire. Sun keep it hidden in wooden box with three leather thongs around it.'

" 'How will we get to Sky?' asked Fox.

" 'That is part of contest. We must find a way,' said Bear.

"So they both sat down to think and think. They think all day and they think all night. They think all next day.

" 'I'm strong,' said Bear. 'I will build myself a road to Sky.'

"So Bear went to Cedar. 'Will you give me your long trunk for poles for building a road to Sky?' he asked.

" 'If I do, I will die,' said Cedar.

" 'What does it matter?' said Bear. 'You are not strong like me.'

"So Bear took Cedar to build road. And all other forest cedars cried.

" 'I need thongs to tie my poles together,' said Bear, so he went to Deer. 'Will you give me your skin to make thongs to tie my poles together?' he asked.

" 'If I do, I will die,' said Deer.

" 'What does it matter?' said Bear. 'You are not strong like me.'

"And Bear took Deer to make thongs to tie poles, and all other deer cried.

"Fox watched Bear build a long road to Sky with strong poles from Cedar and tie them together with thongs of Deer.

" 'This is not right,' thought Fox. 'Bear will destroy our forests and our friends to win his contest.'

"Sun saw what Bear was doing. It made Sun angry. 'What are you doing?' he said to Bear.

" 'I must get to Sky,' replied Bear. 'I am building a long trail.'

" 'Why do you climb to Sky?'

"But Bear would not tell Sun.

"That night when Sun was sleeping, Bear climbed the long, long cedar trail. He climbed all night. Next morning, just as Sun awoke, Bear made a hole in Sky with one long claw. Bear did not know, but Fox was close on his heels ready to sneak past him and into Sky to steal the firebox before Bear could find it.

"But Sun was angry when he saw Bear. He stopped him.

" 'Why do you come here?' asked Sun, but Bear would say nothing.

"Sun did not see Fox, who hid behind Bear in his shadow.

"Bear went along Sky in search of the firebox. But Fox ran ahead and found the box first. He was ready to climb back through hole and run back down the long, long trail made by Cedar when Sun saw him.

" 'Where are you going with my firebox?' asked Sun.

" 'Bear is trying to steal it,' said Fox. 'I am bringing it to you so Bear cannot find it.'

" 'Thank you, small brother,' said Sun.

"Then he turned to Bear who was close behind Fox. Sun was very angry.

" 'You try to steal my firebox? I will give you Fire,' he said and turned his strong medicine on Bear and sent out great fingers of fire that chased Bear back and forth across the heavens."

Kendra's eyes were wide as she listened and imagined all that was happening in the story.

"Bear began to roar in anger and pain," Nonie continued. "And Fox quietly slipped down the long, long trail of poles from Cedar with the firebox under his arm.

"Sun is still searching for his firebox. Now and then he becomes so angry he chases Bear across Sky. Bear roars as the fingers of fire burn his tail and ears. We call it thunder when Bear roars and we see lightning flash as Sun throws his fire at Bear.

"Fox gave Fire from firebox to all animals. The animals shared Fire with man and that is how we keep warm when the nights are cold.

"So it is better to be smart than strong. And it is better not to treat one's brothers in evil ways."

Kendra decided that the thunder seemed so much less frightening with Nonie's soft voice finishing the story.

"So," said Nonie simply. "Father Thunder is only angry with Bear."

Now the thunder was a distant rumble. Kendra could almost enjoy the sound. She no longer felt fear.

Nonie lowered her to the floor and stood to return to her berries. They needed to be picked over and put to dry as soon as the sun would shine on them again. Nonie would have them ready.

As they moved into the winter months, Kendra's grandfather was never there when she awoke in the morning. He left on the trapline long before the sun had touched the horizon. Nonie was always there, sitting before the fire, her braiding or weaving or buckskin work in her gnarled fingers. Occasionally Kendra was already in bed and sound asleep before her grandfather returned in the evening, but always he came to her bed, roused her gently and kissed her on the cheek, then stroked her hair until she had fallen to sleep again.

Oscar, playful and teasing, was a constant companion. Kendra spent hours playing with him, and Papa Mac, when he was home, showed the little child how to teach the growing dog to obey simple commands.

Nonie paid little attention to the animal. She seemed to feel that dogs were not her brothers. She treated the puppy with tolerance, not affection, and he accepted her in the same way.

Kendra coaxed to allow the puppy to sleep in a corner of the cabin, though Papa Mac made it clear that it was totally against his principle to pamper an animal in such a fashion. But, he never did open the door and thrust the animal out into the night, even after Kendra had fallen asleep.

She still slept with Dollie tucked tightly against her, but now she often left it behind when on an outing with Nonie.

So the first winter came and went. Papa Mac came and went. Nonie came and went. But Kendra no longer feared that she would be left on her own again, deserted and frightened and without someone to care for her.

Not swiftly, but slowly and silently spring's sound gradually swelled to spill over in the rush of the stream that passed by their cabin door, the song of the birds that filled the forest stillness, the rustle of molding leaves as small animals scurried to retrieve berries missed in their fall gathering, and soft breezes that waved the swelling tender buds on the arms of forest trees.

"Mother Earth stirring," said Nonie, pleasure in her voice.

"Who is Mother Earth?" asked Kendra innocently.

"Long ago, before stars, even before Sun and Moon, Old One made Mother Earth. All was dark and no birds sang. No stream ran through the forest. No animal brothers walked in the shadows. There was nothing.

"Old One did not like nothing. He woke Mother Earth. 'Be mother of all people,' he said.

"Mother Earth took some of her flesh and made creatures. Some were like us. Some walked on four feet and were creatures of the forests. Some had wings and flew about the heavens and others swam in the rivers and great waters. All living things come from Mother Earth. When we look around we see part of Mother Earth everywhere. Like us, the animals, birds and fish are made of Mother Earth. So we are all earth brothers. That is why we care for one another.

"Mother Earth is old, old woman who has seen many moons," Nonie went on with her teaching. "She was before Moon. She lives still, but she has changed much since Old One first made her to be his friend. The soil is her flesh. The rocks are her bones. The wind is her breath. The trees and grasses are her hair.

"Many people do not care for Mother Earth. They tear at her flesh and bones and pull her hair up by roots. But we must love Mother Earth. We must treat her kindly if we do not wish her to be angry. If we love and respect her, she will thank us by giving us food and shelter. She will always be there to care for her children."

Kendra's eyes were wide, her heart full. She loved Nonie's stories. She resolved that she would always be kind to Mother Earth so she might be accepted as a worthy child.

When summer came again, Kendra saw much more of Papa Mac. He even took her with him to the outpost store where he sold his stock of winter furs and purchased the supplies they needed for the months ahead.

He informed Kendra that she could choose a new pair of shoes, but after studying them carefully she shook her head slowly. She wanted shoes like Nonie wore. Soft, supple moccasins. Papa Mac laughed and then nodded his head. He promised he would speak to Nonie about the new "shoes."

Kendra did pick out some yard goods for a new skirt. And some soft flannel for a new nightgown. Papa Mac was sure Nonie would agree to do the sewing.

Kendra enjoyed the excitement of the trip, but she was glad when they climbed from the canoe and she could stretch her cramped legs and take Oscar for a romp along the bank of the stream. And she could hardly wait to show Nonie the new material.

————

George was home a good deal over the summer months, not a time for trapping. All the traps were brought home on the wagon-sleigh and carefully checked and oiled to make sure that they were ready for the next winter's catch. The summer was also spent in other activities. A garden was planted and cultivated. Wood piles were refurnished. Knives were sharpened. Meat and fish were stripped and dried in the sun. Dog harness was repaired with newly tanned moose hides. Never did there seem to be a day when George did not have something with which to busy his hands.

If his work took him away from the cabin, Nonie came. Kendra and Nonie spent many days back in the berry patch or looking for "good" plants to gather in their baskets. Kendra carried her own basket now. Nonie had fashioned it for her from marsh reeds and stained it with a pattern of red, yellow, and brown. Kendra felt proud as she filled her basket with roots and leaves that would be useful.

Whenever she was in error, Nonie showed her the plant and uttered her little sound "p-f-f-t." The next time out, Kendra watched carefully as she gathered. She did not want to pick the offensive plant again.

But when her grandfather's work kept him around the cabin, Kendra was close beside him. He taught her the bird songs, along with many facts about their habits. Often they searched for nests together, though they never disturbed the tiny warm eggs. If the nestlings had hatched, they sat silently together and watched the parents feed the nosily demanding babies whose beaks never seemed to be silent or their tummies filled.

Another birthday came and went for Kendra. This time her grandfather had made her a harness for the now-grown Oscar. In the days that followed, they spent time teaching the young dog to pull a small training cart. Kendra giggled with delight as Dollie went for her first ride in the small wagon behind Oscar.

As the first snow of another winter whipped around the corners of the snug cabin, Kendra felt her heart stir restlessly. The cold meant that her grandfather would return again to his traps. She hated to see him go. At the same time, it would mean more time with Nonie. Kendra had been missing those long, quiet winter days filled with stories about the Old One and Mother Earth. Kendra was not quite sure whether to be happy or sad to see the snow shut the door on the outside world.

Chapter Seven

The Ugly Side

Another spring was sneaking slowly through the mountain passes, filling the streams and washing away the drifts of snow that had covered the trails and nearly buried the small cabin.

Nonie was anxious to get out to the meadows to catch the early growth of new plants, tender and potent and good medicine for her herbal cures. Kendra was just as anxious to escape the cabin site as well. It had seemed like a long winter of confinement to the five-year-old. She was glad the days were lengthening, the sun stronger in the sky.

"Mother Earth is coming awake," she said to Nonie one morning as they stood in the cabin door drinking in the freshness of the spring air.

Nonie nodded, making no return comment to the child.

"We go," said Nonie after sniffing at the air and studying the sky.

They wrapped themselves in their deerskin jackets. Nonie had made Kendra a long-fringed buckskin of her very own. Then Nonie wrapped their moccasins with strips of leather thongs and rubbed them generously with bear fat to keep the dampness of the trail from penetrating. They collected their baskets, ready to go.

Nonie chose the trail along the banks of the stream. Kendra was fascinated with the tumbling, frothy water that bubbled and splashed its way over the rocks she knew lined the

63

bottom, though they could not be seen now through the foam.

"Sister River is in a hurry," she said to Nonie.

Nonie nodded silently. She never had called the stream "Sister River," but the child seemed to have taken all of nature into her family.

They were nearing the point where the stream made its sharp turn and headed almost back in the direction from which it had come, giving the Indian people the name of Bent River, when a strange moving in the water caught Kendra's eye.

She stopped short, knowing that the movement was unusual but not able to figure out what was different about it.

She turned to Nonie and saw that the woman had also stopped, her dark eyes clouding as she looked toward the same spot. Strange words escaped the woman's lips. Words Kendra had never heard before. Nonie seemed upset.

Then Nonie's chilling cry filled the air and she raised her arms over her head and began to call to the heavens. "Aiyee—aiyee," she wailed, making Kendra's eyes fill with fright, her spine tingle.

She didn't know whether to cling to the woman's skirts or turn and flee toward the cabin.

"Aiyee," called the woman again, entreating the sky in a nameless petition.

Kendra began to cry. In the water the strange thrashing continued, and Nonie kept up the pitiful cries to the skies.

Soon Kendra was frightened into action. She darted to Nonie, yanking on the woman's skirts, her own wails filling the air around them.

Nonie stopped her strange chants and reached her hands down to the child. She still moaned from somewhere deep inside her.

"What is it? What is it?" Kendra cried, shouting her words above the cries of Nonie and the noisy gurgling of the stream.

"Brother Beaver," moaned Nonie. "Brother Beaver."

Kendra's eyes widened. She had seen many beavers. Many times. That had never caused concern before. She liked to watch them. Nonie liked to watch them. They had spent many hours on the banks of the stream watching the beavers fell their trees and build their dams. Nonie had never wailed before.

"Trap," said Nonie. "Trap."

Kendra knew of traps. Her grandfather had traps lining one entire side of the cabin. Traps had never been cause for lamenting either. She was puzzled by Nonie's strange behavior.

Her eyes dropped to Nonie's moccasined feet. Her grandfather had warned her to watch the trails for hidden traps, though he had assured her that no trapper would set a trap on the foot paths used by the people of the area. Still, he had told her of the dangers of traps and had set and sprung some in her presence to show her their strength. They had snapped small sticks as if they had been kindling wood. Kendra had vowed to watch carefully for traps.

But there were no traps attaching themselves to Nonie's feet. Kendra lifted her eyes again.

Nonie was still moaning and swaying, rocking the body of the small girl along with her.

Kendra looked back at the stream.

And then she saw it. A large beaver had managed to pull itself to the bank of the stream. On one front leg dangled a piece of red-wet ugly metal. The beaver thrashed and pulled, its tail whipping the water, its large eyes wide with terror. A strange agonizing sound escaped its throat. Kendra had never seen anything so awful. Never heard anything so pain-filled.

"What happened? What happened, Nonie?" she cried. "How did it get in the trap?"

"Aiyee," wailed Nonie, letting go of the child and lifting her hands again.

"We've got to help it, Nonie," said Kendra, her eyes filling with tears. "We've got to get it out."

But Nonie had turned them both around and was moving down the trail away from the beaver—away from the stream—away from the ugly sight.

"We've got to help it, Nonie," Kendra said again, trying to pull back from the hand that pulled her along.

They had gone some distance before Nonie stopped her wailing and lifting her hands to the sky. The dark eyes were still shadowed, but the woman now hurried Kendra along the trail, and nothing more was said about the trap.

But the fearful event did not leave Kendra's thinking. All day as she played with Oscar or watched Nonie move about the cabin, she kept reflecting on the scene and wondering why Nonie had done nothing to help the entrapped beaver.

When Papa Mac came home, Kendra would be waiting on the doorstep. Nonie talked when Nonie chose to talk. Kendra had the feeling that Nonie would not be discussing with her the incident that had spoiled their day.

But Papa Mac talked. Kendra felt that she could ask him anything. Tell him anything—anything, that is, except the stories that Nonie shared with her about Mother Earth and the Brothers of the forest. Already Kendra had caught the displeasure of her grandfather regarding Nonie's strange tales.

So Kendra waited patiently for her grandfather while Nonie stirred about the cabin behind her. Oscar lay at her feet, chewing on a piece of well-worn bone. Kendra wondered absently why he continued to chew. All the meat had been removed long ago.

As attentive as Kendra was, it was Oscar who alerted her to the coming of the team. He lifted his head and sniffed at the air, a whine starting somewhere deep inside him and escaping his dark, curled lips.

"They're coming," said Kendra to the dog as though she had been the first to know.

She reached her hand out to Oscar to hold him to his spot. She didn't want the dog to be the first one to greet her grandfather and the approaching team.

In spite of her hand, Oscar rose to his feet, his whine deepening, his ears perked forward.

Soon Kendra could hear the soft yapping of the dogs, the rumbling of the wheels as they stumbled over the rocks of the trail.

She waited. She knew that it wouldn't be long until the team would come into view at the far end of the clearing.

Just as she had expected, the dogs entered the clearing first, her grandfather close at the rear of the sleigh-wagon. She could see the pile of darkness that meant her grandfather had had another good day at the traplines. She was pleased because she knew he would be pleased. He had told her that the final catches of the spring were important. That soon the trapping season would be over for another year.

Normally Kendra ran to greet him, her voice calling out words of excited welcome, her moccasined feet beating a rhythm on the soft ground as she hurried to him to be scooped up into his arms and carried back to the cabin on broad shoulders.

But tonight she sat where she was, her fingers tangled in Oscar's heavy coat, willing him to wait with her.

The sled dogs raced directly to where her grandfather always parked the sleigh.

"Well," he called across to her, "are you too weary to meet me tonight? Has Nonie been dragging you through the woods all day?"

Kendra shook her head quietly. She did not stir from her seat on the step.

With an order to his dog team to lie down on the spot, he moved toward her, sensing that something was wrong.

He lowered his big frame down on the step beside her, pushing back Oscar who wished to get a share of the attention. His arm slipped around the slight body and drew her close.

"You look sad," he said after holding her for a moment. "Did something happen today?"

Kendra nodded her head, her eyes filled with tears.

"Did you and Nonie have a spat?" he continued.

Kendra did not know what a spat was. She had no one to spat with. She looked up at him, her eyes questioning his words.

"Did you and Nonie have a fight?" he asked her again.

Kendra knew what a fight was. She had seen her grandfather separate sled dogs on more than one occasion. But she couldn't imagine getting into such a fuss with Nonie.

She shook her head slowly, the tears spilling over as the picture of the trapped beaver filled her mind again.

"A beaver," she managed, "a beaver got caught in a trap."

There was total silence. The arm about her tightened.

"He got caught," explained Kendra, her eyes large, her lip trembling. "Nonie wouldn't help him."

Her tone was accusing. Kendra had not been able to understand why Nonie hadn't rescued the animal.

Again silence. The arm around her was joined by her grandfather's other arm until Kendra was encircled. She heard him take a deep breath and then he spoke softly, slowly. "Nonie couldn't rescue it," he said, and there was pain in his words. "She would have been in big trouble if she had."

"But why?" sobbed Kendra. "He was caught and he was bleeding and—"

The arms lifted her up onto his lap, where he cradled her against his chest.

"No one can ever interfere with someone else's trap," he explained.

"But the beaver was caught—by its foot. It was crying and—" The small girl was sobbing too much to go on.

"I know. I know," her grandfather tried to soothe her. "But Nonie couldn't let him out. He was already hurt too bad to be—to be set free anyway, and when whoever owned the trap came to get his animal, he would have been very angry with Nonie. He—he needs the money from the pelt. He—"

But Kendra sat bolt upright and pushed away from him. The word pelt had caught her attention. She had watched her grandfather many times as he had worked with pelts, cleaning them, stretching them, sorting them according to worth. Never once had Kendra thought of the piles of warm, thick furs as animals. Never once had she seen the traps on the walls of the cabin as instruments of horror. Never once had she dreamed that her loving grandfather was capable of causing suffering—to anything.

Now her eyes opened wide as she began to put the words,

the images together. Her green eyes grew larger, her sobbing stopped. She stared at him as the truth began to sink in to her childish mind, and then she pushed back from him, her eyes wide with terror and anger, her voice choked with the intensity of discovery.

"I hate you!" she cried, springing from him. She stood in front of him, her green eyes flashing, her small body trembling. "I hate you!" she screamed at him again. "You hurt our brother animals. I hate you."

With a look of pain, anger, and defiance, Kendra lifted her arms heavenward and screamed out the strange and eerie cry, "Aiyee! Aiyee!"

It came from the depths of her troubled spirit—just as it had from Nonie's.

"Aiyee," she wailed again and ran from her grandfather, across the wooden porch, through the door to the cabin, past a startled Nonie, and threw herself upon her moss and pine-bough bunk bed in the corner of the room.

———

"I think we need to talk."

They had finished the supper that Nonie had left for them before she returned to the village. It had been a silent meal. He had tried to coax conversation from her a time or two, but she had been unresponsive. Now she sat sullenly before him, picking at her food with her fork.

She raised her eyes and nodded. Already she knew that the pain deep within her needed attention. She didn't want to be angry with Papa Mac. It made her hurt all over.

He pushed back his chair from the table and held out his arms. "Come here," he invited.

She went to him, prepared for another good cry in his arms.

When he had soothed her and the sobs had stopped, the tears had been wiped away, he began to talk.

"Trapping is not—not nice for the animals. I know that. But—but people need the furs—the pelts—to make things.

Like coats and moccasins. Oh yes, the moccasins that you like to wear, they came from animals, too.

"Animals get killed. We don't like that. But they do get killed. Some of them by man, some of them by other animals. Some of them get old and hungry and can't hunt anymore—and they die. It's not nice—but it's the way it is.

"Traps can be—can be terribly mean things. Like the trap that caught the beaver. Good trappers know how to set the traps so that the animal doesn't suffer as much. But they always suffer some. I admit that. And I don't like it either. But I need the money from the pelts. That is how I live."

Kendra did not stir. He wondered if she was listening. He wondered if she was still hurt. Still angry with him.

"I am always sorry about the animal. About the fact that I take their life in order to make a living—to have pelts to sell so that people can have warm clothes for our harsh winters. But I try—I try hard not to make the animals suffer very much."

Kendra sat in silence, thinking seriously about what he had said.

"I wish—I wish that I could tell you I won't trap anymore. But I can't. And I don't want to lie to you. So I won't tell you that it doesn't hurt the animals. I know it does. But trapping—trapping is a way of life. If we raised animals—cows or sheep or even chickens—for our use—our food and our clothing, they would have to die too. Traps are perhaps a more cruel way to die, but if one is a good trapper the animals can be spared suffering. I'm sorry, Kendra, but that's the way it is."

Kendra sat quietly in his arms, pondering what he had said. The beaver with its dangling paw and plaintive cries still disturbed her. She shut her eyes tightly, trying to block out the sight—the memory. Then she stirred and turned to face her grandfather, her arms stealing about his neck.

"I don't hate you, Papa Mac," she said, her words trailing off in sobs.

He rocked her back and forth, holding her close, wishing

that he could shield her from the ugliness of the trapline. Wanting to shield her from the ugliness of life. But he could only hold her and weep, his tears mingling with the blond hair that rested against his cheek.

Chapter Eight

Acceptance

Kendra's sixth and seventh summers varied little from the previous ones. She and Nonie worked together as a team gathering leaves and tender shoots, roots and berries in their baskets. Kendra's sharp eyes were often the first to spot the wild produce, and her keen nose the first to smell the pungent odors that led them in the right direction.

Oscar, big for his breed, had grown to full size and with Kendra's patient training had become a dog that quickly obeyed her commands. Kendra's grandfather, Papa Mac, teased that Oscar ate better than anyone else in the cabin. It was true that Kendra fussed over him and fed him accordingly. The dog was also strong and sturdy, his chest broad, his legs sinewy. Papa Mac, voicing pride in the dog, declared that he would make an outstanding lead dog for a sled team.

The words were not lost on Kendra. In her mind was the picture of the team she hoped to one day have as her own.

She managed to find it in her heart to hope for a good winter's catch on her Papa Mac's traplines, though she still inwardly cringed at the thought of the instruments of death. But she never could run her hands over the softness of the pelts with pleasure as she had done as a small child. She could not see them now without thinking of the animals that they had once been, roaming free and wild in the mountainous forests.

But more and more Kendra was understanding the words

72

her grandfather had spoken—the truth of the laws of nature. Life was hard. Life was violent. The strong took from the weak. Indeed, took of the weak. Kendra had witnessed a wolf pack bringing down a moose. She had seen a lioness dragging a new kill back to her den of cubs. She had watched the bears sweeping salmon from the stream. "The weak will feed the strong," her Papa Mac had explained simply, and though Kendra had at first hated it, had fought against it, she gradually learned to accept it.

Nonie did not lift her arms and cry her chilling lament of "Aiyee" over the kills of nature. She reserved her plaintive cry for the acts of men. Kendra wondered about it and wished to ask the elderly Indian woman, but something held her back. Kendra did not feel free to question Nonie. She did feel she could ask her grandfather.

"Papa Mac," she said one night as they sat on their porch watching the sun dip behind the outline of distant mountains, "why does Nonie say 'Aiyee' like she does?"

"That is her people's way of expressing grief," he answered her. Even then his memory went back to the younger Kendra who had troubled him deeply by echoing Nonie's cry.

"She did it for the beaver—but she didn't do it for the moose," puzzled Kendra.

He sat for a moment in silence, not that he didn't know the answer, but because he wasn't sure how to explain it to the young girl.

"Nonie—and her people—accept the ways of nature. That is normal . . . and right." He hesitated. "But Nonie—and her people—fear that—that their gods—nature—might be angry with man for taking for himself. Oh, they know that animals are here for man to use. They hunt. They fish. They must or they would never survive. But when an animal dies—on behalf of man—then Nonie—and many others—feel that they must mourn that animal so that the spirits—whatever they are and wherever they are—realize that they did not take pleasure in the death of their animal brother. If they don't mourn sufficiently, they are afraid that the spirits might decide to take their lives."

"Is that right?" asked Kendra, her eyes large in her childish face.

"That's the story I was told," said Papa Mac.

"But it is right? Do the spirits really do that?"

"What spirits?" Papa Mac's words were abrupt. Then his tone softened. "Look, Kendra. I don't mind Nonie telling you her little tales about the loon or the mountain lion—but I don't like her filling your mind with all that stuff about spirits and taboos and evil omens. That's all nonsense, Kendra. Indian myth. The earth is not our mother. The beaver is not our brother. Animals don't have spirits that prowl about at night looking for revenge. These are all just—stories—like the ones I read to you at bedtime. Just stories. I don't want you to think of Nonie's tales as anything but—tales. That's her way of life—and at times I think she really believes all that nonsense—but we don't, Kendra. We know better."

Kendra felt a strange stirring somewhere deep inside. She had believed Nonie's stories. She had let them become a part of her. Now Papa Mac was saying that there was no truth in them. But she wanted them to be true. She wanted to feel akin to nature. To have that sense of being a part of something so much bigger than herself.

She wished with all her heart that she could turn to her grandfather and say stoutly, "You are wrong. They are not just stories. There *are* spirits. Good spirits and bad spirits—just like Nonie says. I know. I can—can feel—something."

But Kendra did not say the words. Looking into the intense, dark eyes of her grandfather, she did not dare to say the words. Papa Mac knew about such things. Papa Mac did not believe. Papa Mac might be angry with her if she believed.

She swallowed away the lump in her throat, but deep within herself she felt a sudden pain—an empty spot where something had lived before. What had it been? Belief? Hope? Kendra did not know. She just knew that now it was gone—slain by the words of the grandfather she loved. But what would she ever find to fill its place?

———

The long summer evenings were a joy to Kendra, for it was then that her grandfather told her to get out the books and they would read and study together.

Kendra loved the books. She loved the words on the pages. It was a marvel to her when she first learned to read and discovered for herself that she now had the key to unlock the mysteries of those pages.

The lessons in sums were not as popular with Kendra. All of the numbers made little sense to her. Then her grandfather began to use more realistic equations. "If you had three weasel pelts, four lynx, two wolves, and three beavers, how much flour, salt, and coffee could you purchase?"

On the wall in her grandfather's cabin was an updated list of the worth of a pelt. He changed and posted it as frequently as the prices fluctuated. Kendra always ran to the list and figured out the worth of the furs, then scrambled back to the table to his last journal entry on the prices of the kitchen supplies at the local store. It made the problems fun to solve, and Kendra always felt proud when her grandfather praised her work.

But the simple problems in arithmetic also did something else for Kendra, though neither her grandfather nor she were aware at the time what was happening. But something was being born within her—the desire to have her own trapline. To add up those pennies and dollars from the furs to her own account. It seemed to the young girl that with all the furs she watched her grandfather pile carefully in the sturdy shed behind the cabin, her grandfather must be getting terribly wealthy in his trade. Someday, she decided silently as she worked the sums, someday she would be counting out pelts of her own.

———

"Mother Earth mourns," said Nonie, and Kendra lifted her head and looked about. What did Nonie mean? But Kendra did not ask. Over the years they had spent together, Kendra had learned from Nonie many of the ways of the

Indians—and one of those ways was to wait in silence for an elder to speak further.

"I saw black crow—blackest crow ever. But sad. His eyes were dark. His feathers no longer glistened in sun."

The words that at one time would have filled Kendra with a delicious chill failed to stir her. Papa Mac had said that Nonie's tales were untrue. Just Indian myth. They no longer had the power to move her.

"He speaks," went on Nonie. "He speaks of Mother Earth. She mourns in sorrow. Soon we too will mourn. All will mourn."

Kendra turned her back and lifted her chin. Nonie's story was a bit silly. Just as Papa Mac had said, it was just a foolish omen. Something that the elderly lady was making up to try to frighten her.

"We pick—for Mother Earth," went on Nonie. "Berries of all kind. We scatter them by the first moon in the moon ripples of the lake water. Maybe Mother Earth will forgive."

Kendra wanted to argue. They needed the berries for themselves. They needed to clean and dry them in the warm summer sun so they would have them to sweeten their porridge on the long, cold winter mornings. The berry bushes had not yielded as well as in other years. They had to fight with the birds and the animals for their possession. To pick them and scatter them on the moon ripples of the lake was ridiculous.

But Kendra did not argue. Nonie spoke with such confidence. What would happen if they did not appease Mother Earth? Would she turn on them with thunder and lightning? Would the skies pour down balls of icy hail that would destroy their already shriveling garden plants? Kendra wished to deny the words that Nonie was speaking, but in her heart she felt a tingling of fear. What if? What if Nonie was right and her grandfather was wrong? What then? Could they really afford to challenge Nonie's strange gods?

When Kendra had filled her basket with the luscious wild fruit, she silently passed it to Nonie. She wouldn't take part in the little ritual herself, but if Nonie had the power to protect them from the anger of the gods, then Kendra would not interfere.

————

"Would you like to go with me?"

George turned to his young granddaughter, who was watching him load the canoe in preparation for a trip to the post. It had been some time since Kendra had made the trip. She seemed to prefer to stay at home with Nonie, roaming the nearby woods and meadows, gathering her berries and herbs, studying the wildlife that teemed around them.

But today her eyes held wistfulness. Was she getting bored with her life in the woods? Was she longing for a bit of excitement? Civilization?

At his question, Kendra's eyes seemed to deepen in their green intensity, but no other change took place in her countenance.

"Choosh," said George under his breath, "she's been isolated in the wild too long. Now she doesn't even let her feelings show."

He lifted his head to study his granddaughter and asked again, "Would you like to?"

She nodded mutely. She longed to go. Something within her was stirring. She knew not what. Maybe it was just a silent longing to spend extra time with her grandfather.

"Go tell Nonie. She won't need to stay. Get your things. We may get caught in the rain, so you'd better take an extra coat."

Kendra ran to do his bidding, and in spite of herself a smile played about her lips.

"You'd better tether Oscar," her grandfather said when she returned, breathless and carrying a small bundle under her arm.

Kendra hated to tie her dog. All the sled dogs were tied about the clearing, but Oscar did not like to be tethered. Kendra lifted her eyes to her grandfather and pleaded silently.

"What if he runs off?" he asked in answer to her unasked petition.

"He won't," she dared to promise.

She turned to Oscar and pointed to the porch where he often lay in the sun. "Stay," she said firmly.

Oscar crossed to the porch and lay down, but a whine of protest lifted his sides and seemed to be reflected in the shadowing of his eyes.

"Stay," Kendra said again as she stepped from the bank into the loaded canoe.

It was wonderful to feel the gentle rock and sway of the canoe as they glided over the swift flowing water. Up and around the sharp bend they went, and Kendra could picture again the sight of the beaver fighting for its life against the trap that held it. Though the picture still made her feel sick inside, she pushed it firmly from her. It was a way of life. Acceptable. Ugly—and painful—but acceptable.

She let her glance fall to the pile of carefully wrapped pelts. The returning canoe would bear flour and salt and coffee and yard goods and all the other supplies they so desperately needed for survival. Kendra sighed deeply and reached out a hand to let it trail in the cool stream.

They passed by the Indian village, and Kendra nodded greetings to the children who played about the bank. She recognized a few of them by name. Nonie had provided the information on the few trips they had made together to the little settlement. But George did not like Kendra to spend much of her time with the other children. He feared that if she learned more of their ways, she would have even greater difficulty when she had to go back to the city for her education.

George had been putting off sending Kendra out. He knew that it had to be done. He knew that he had waited longer than he should have. But she was doing well. She could read almost anything he handed her—with understanding. And she was quicker at working out sums than many of the adults he knew. Still, she did need to go out. Back to the city. She needed to learn about her own culture.

Her own people. She needed to learn the social graces that would identify her as civilized. He knew that. But it was so hard to let her go. To think of the long days without her about the cabin.

George rested the paddle for a moment and let the small craft drift as he studied the face of his grandchild. She was doing fine—wasn't she? She was happy. Content. Nonie was caring for her. Nonie with all of her ridiculous scare stories. He did hope that she had stopped feeding the child all the nonsense about ghosts and wandering spirits. He had talked to her about it on more than one occasion. Kendra hadn't brought the tales to him of late. Did that mean they had stopped—or had Kendra chosen not to discuss them with him anymore?

Kendra felt his eyes upon her and lifted her head to look at him. The green eyes were so large and intense. The small oval face so much like his Mary's. He could not hide the love—the pain—that he was feeling inside. He forced a smile to crinkle the corners of his eyes, make his mustache twitch at the sides of his mouth. "Happy?" he asked simply.

Kendra nodded. She was happy. Totally at peace with herself and her world. She tilted her head and listened for the return call of the whiskey jack, then nodded again.

"Except for poor Oscar," she said to her grandfather. "I wish he could have come. He hates to stay alone."

"He has all the other dogs for company," her grandfather answered.

"But he doesn't want the dogs for company," argued Kendra. "He wants us. He thinks he's people."

George threw back his head and laughed good-naturedly. It was the first time Kendra had heard him laugh so generously for a long time. A smile played about her lips, and before long she felt a little giggle rising in her own throat.

From then on the trip became a shared delight. They chatted and laughed and teased each other as they had not done for a long time. Both of them enjoyed it. It was a breaking of silence. A bonding together. A release from a thought prison that had held back full communication.

We need to do this more often, thought George. *She needs to be able to talk and laugh. She is not silent by nature. She should not be forced into that mold. She needs to talk and to be free to share her feelings. She needs to be with me more. Be less with Nonie.*

And George decided that he would find ways to integrate the child more into his style of living.

Chapter Nine

Fire

There were visitors at the fort. The trader's brother and sister-in-law had come from a city somewhere to visit him in his "wilderness."

Kendra tried not to stare at them, but she could not help feeling interested. As her grandfather accepted a cup of hospitality, the trader's thick bitter coffee, Kendra sat on a pile of furs and listened to the conversation and studied the faces before her.

"Your granddaughter?" Kendra heard the visiting woman ask. "How nice." Then she turned to Kendra and gave her a big smile.

"How long has she been with you?" the woman asked.

George had to stop and do some calculating. "Past four years now. Almost five," he answered, surprising even himself at the time that had quickly passed.

The woman cast another glance at the slight young girl in her simple shirt and buckskins. Her blond braids were in sharp contrast to her tanned cheeks.

"'Course she goes out every winter," speculated the woman.

"Oh no," George said quickly. "She has been with me the whole time."

The woman's eyes showed her surprise. She did not hold back but spoke her mind quickly. "Where does she get her schooling?"

It was more than a question. It was an accusation.

"I teach her," George answered, his voice getting deeper with his need to defend the circumstance.

"But—" began the woman.

"And I dare say she can read better for her age than any of those city kids," he went on, tempted to call Kendra to him to show off her ability. He did not do so. He felt it would be unfair to the child to drag her into their little dispute.

The lady cast another glance at Kendra and seemed to concede the point. Then she licked her lips, doubt still showing in her eyes. "What about her religious training?" she challenged further.

George stirred uncomfortably. He put no stock in religious training, whether one was raised in the wilderness or the middle of the city. Did he dare to speak his feelings to the woman before him? Would he take the stand of an infidel in front of the whole trading post? If he did, how might it affect the future of Kendra?

He swallowed the words he wished to say and replied simply, "You think the wilderness has no God?"

The woman nodded in silent agreement. She could not argue that point. She saw the work of God everywhere she looked in this wide, open, beautiful country.

The subject was dropped, the coffee finished, and the bartering begun.

————

"I have something I would like to give you," the woman said, approaching Kendra as her grandfather was loading the canoe for their return trip.

In her outstretched hand she held a silver chain, and on the chain was a strange, delicate figure.

"What is it?" asked Kendra.

"The cross," said the woman. "You wear it about your neck—like this."

She placed the necklace around Kendra's neck and fastened it securely.

"Is it an amulet?" asked Kendra.

"A—a what? No—no nothing like that. We don't wear it like a—like a charm. We wear it simply as a—a remembrance."

"Oh-h," said Kendra. But she had no idea what the woman was talking about.

"You are a very pretty girl," went on the woman, reaching out to stroke the blond head of hair. She smiled. "And rather intriguing too. A young Scot in Indian dress. You make quite a picture."

Kendra did not fully understand the words. She had no idea what the woman was carrying on about.

"Are you a Scot?" Kendra asked. She knew the woman was not Indian.

"Oh no." The woman chuckled merrily. "I'm German," she said.

Kendra supposed that the words should mean something to her—but they did not. She had nothing with which to identify them. So she tucked the word away for future reference and studied the woman carefully.

She looked kind. Her eyes were clear and direct. Her mouth curled easily into a smile. She was neat and pleasing. Her body looked strong and sturdy. Kendra concluded that it must be fine to be German.

George McMannus was approaching. The woman stepped back and smiled at Kendra again.

"Perhaps we will see you again sometime," she said pleasantly.

Kendra nodded, then turned to follow her grandfather to the canoe. Her fingers reached up to feel the cross that dangled from the chain around her neck. It was a pretty thing. Shiny and simple. Kendra had never had anything like it before. She was anxious to show it to her grandfather.

The two pushed off in the canoe for their return up the river. Papa Mac was much too busy easing the canoe out into the stream and around all the other canoes that bobbed up and down on their moorings to be distracted by Kendra's new possession.

Kendra watched, noticing how skillful he was with the paddle and subconsciously noting how to handle the oar with the most efficiency.

When they had waved for the last time to the group clustered at the water's edge and the canoe dipped behind the first bend in the river, Kendra sat back and relaxed. It was all paddling upstream now, but her grandfather had made the trip many times and seemed not to tire as the paddle dipped rhythmically into the cool, clear stream, thrusting them ever forward against the pull of the current.

"Look what the lady gave me," Kendra finally said, her fingers still on the silver cross.

"What lady?" he asked absently, not even glancing up at her. He was intent on easing their way around an outcropping of rock in the stream bed.

"The German lady," said Kendra. "The one visiting the post."

But before her grandfather could even respond, Kendra changed the topic with, "What's a German?"

His eyes still on the rocks as he steered the canoe carefully through the maze, he replied, "A race of people. They come from Germany."

"Where's Germany?" asked Kendra.

A frown furrowed his brow. He had been priding himself on Kendra's advanced education. But the truth of the matter was there was so much that he wasn't teaching her. So much that he couldn't teach her. She needed lessons in geography. In history. In social studies. He didn't have the time or the ability to teach her what she needed to know. No—he would have to send her out. It wasn't fair to the child to keep her from school.

Deeply troubled, he sighed. He did not wish to spoil their time together by bringing up the subject. When they had spoken of it before, Kendra had always begged for a bit more time. But now—? The woman had been quite right, though it galled him that she had dared to question him on the raising of his granddaughter. But she was right. Kendra needed to go to school.

He would keep her with him throughout the summer, but he would write a few letters and when the fall arrived again, he would take her to the city.

———

"Where'd you get that?"

For a moment Kendra was puzzled by her grandfather's question. They sat at their evening meal together, Oscar stretched out on the floor beside Kendra's chair. Then Kendra noticed that his eyes were studying the chain with the lovely silver cross attached hanging around her neck.

"The woman gave it to me," Kendra explained, eyes shining.

"What woman?"

"The German woman—at the post." Kendra fingered the cross and lifted it so that she and her grandfather could get a better look. "She brought it to me when I was waiting for you to put everything in the canoe. She said it's a cross."

"I am well aware of what it is," he responded, but he didn't sound pleased or excited about Kendra's gift.

She looked at him, not understanding the gruffness in his voice.

"Don't you like it?" she dared to ask, disappointed.

"I guess it's harmless enough," he replied carelessly. But Kendra could sense that he was not pleased with the gift.

Still, he had not said that she couldn't keep it.

Perhaps he just didn't think it was pretty. Already Kendra had noticed that her grandfather was drawn to things she and Nonie were not; the reverse was also true. She would show the cross to Nonie. She felt quite sure that her response would be quite different.

———

"Look what I've got."

Kendra had run down the path to meet Nonie. Grandfather was still at the house preparing the dogs for a trip to the bush to haul firewood. Nonie approached the cabin slowly, her ever-present herb basket on her arm.

"Look!" said Kendra again and lifted the silver cross for the woman to see.

Nonie's eyes brightened. She may not have understood the cross, but she did understand silver jewelry. "Good!" she said to Kendra.

Kendra was quite pleased with herself. Nonie had pronounced the gift as something worthwhile.

"A lady gave it to me," she explained as she skipped along beside Nonie toward the cabin. "A German lady."

The old woman stopped short, stared at Kendra with dark, brooding eyes, then said, "German. P-f-f-t." She spat in the dust of the trail.

Kendra's eyes shadowed. She did not understand the response. Nonie had liked the gift. Now she looked at it with contempt, spitting out her word with the one angry exclamation.

"P-f-f-t," said Nonie, and she spit again.

Then without another word to the girl, she resumed her silent steps toward the cabin.

Kendra turned to follow, her eyes troubled with questions, her mind filled with deep confusion and sorrow.

There was something bad about Germans. Maybe she shouldn't have accepted the gift. Maybe she should take it off now and throw it into the lake as an appeasement to the moon ripples. Would Mother Earth—or some other unseen being—be angry with her? What might be the consequences? Kendra shivered at the thought.

Wordlessly she followed Nonie. When she reached the cabin, she cast a glance at the woman. Noticing that her back was turned, Kendra reached up and slipped the silver chain over her head. She would take no chances.

For a long moment she stood and looked longingly at the pretty cross. She hated to give it up, but she really had no choice. Tonight she would steal down to the edge of the waters, and when the first moon cast its gold over the ripples of the lake, she would cast her gift into the deep. She hoped

there would be a loon. If a loon cried at just the right time—
the time that the moon first turned the ripples gold—it would
be a good omen. Any spell that might have been cast over
her would surely be broken.

Kendra hoped that she would never again have to face
the curse of a German.

————

There was a strange crackling sound up on the roof. Kendra wondered if a bird or squirrel was doing something quite
out of the ordinary. She listened for the sound to come again.

Nonie had stopped what she was doing and tilted her
head to listen too.

The sound came again. This time Nonie's head jerked up
quickly. "Come!" she said to Kendra and reached out to
nudge her toward the door.

Kendra frowned in puzzlement—not because of the command but because of the urgency with which it was spoken.

"Come," said Nonie again, and the two of them pushed
through the cabin door at the same time.

It was then that Kendra noticed a different smell. In the
air about the cabin a new color of smoke drifted leisurely.

"What is it?" Kendra asked, fright making her voice
tremble.

"Fire," said Nonie. "Fire on roof."

Kendra lifted her eyes to the sloping roof of the cabin.
Sure enough. The smoke was curling upward, caught by the
gentle breeze and spiraling around the chimney.

"Get pail!" shouted Nonie, and after one wild glance at
the woman, Kendra ran for the pail that stood on the bench
by the door.

"Water," barked Nonie.

With terror making her heart constrict, Kendra dashed
for the stream and scooped up a pail of water.

Nonie had already placed the ladder against the side of
the house. Now she took the pail from Kendra's numb fingers
and turned to mount the ladder. Her knees were stiff, her

shoulders bent. Kendra feared that the woman would fall in her attempt.

"Let me," she said, taking the pail back. "I will do it."

When Kendra looked over the side of the roof line, she could see that the fire had started in the chimney. The flames were now extending beyond the stonework and reaching angrily toward the sky. Kendra pulled herself up onto the roof and struggled with the heavy pail of water.

She crept as close to the flames as she dared and flung the water with all of her might. She heard the sizzle and sputter as the water collided with the fire, but even as she watched, the hungry flames flared up again. The water had little effect.

By the time Kendra scrambled back down the ladder, Nonie was there with another pail of water. They exchanged pails and Kendra remounted the ladder.

Again and again she climbed the ladder—up and down. The flames had escaped the chimney now and were licking at the dry shingles of the roof.

But each time Kendra threw another pail of water on the flames, she seemed to make a small bit of headway. Not much. But as the dry shingles soaked up more and more of the cold river water, the fire seemed to lose a bit of power in the struggle.

Kendra's face burned. Her arms ached. Her back felt as if it were broken, and with all the trips up and down the ladder, her legs seemed like jelly. She wondered if she would be able to fight on.

But she did. She climbed and dumped every pail that Nonie dragged up to her. And finally the flames flickered, struggled, then ceased.

Kendra was ready to collapse. What if they had lost their cabin? What if they had lost their home? The traps? Her books? Their supplies? Everything they owned was in that cabin. What if they had lost it all?

She climbed stiffly down the ladder for one last time and collapsed on the cool ground beside Nonie. Both were exhausted, soot-covered, both flushed from the heat of the fight.

"Mother Earth angry," said Nonie between gasps for breath.

Kendra immediately thought of the silver cross given to her by the German. Her grandfather had said that it was harmless. But Papa Mac had not understood about Nonie's gods. Had not realized how angry they could be.

She had thrown it away. Given it to the gods of the lake. She had been careful that the first light of the moon was tinting the ripples of the water. But no loon had called. There had been two loons on the lake. Kendra had pleaded in her heart for one of them to call to the other, but they had stubbornly refused. Was that the problem? Were the loon brothers also angry?

Kendra buried her head in her arms and began to weep. It was so hard. So hard. So hard to keep all the spirits happy. She hadn't meant to make them angry. Had tried so hard to undo the damage. It seemed there was just no way to live at peace with the spirit world.

———

George McMannus spent the next two days patching the roof of the cabin, and as he worked he often shook his head in wonder. How had the elderly Indian woman and his young granddaughter managed to save the structure? He couldn't imagine the number of trips she must have made up and down the ladder. Again he was thankful that he kept the tall pines and spruce from encroaching too closely on the space around the cabin. If the fire had spread to tree branches, they would never have saved the cabin. There would have been a forest fire that might have taken a large sweep of the area. He might even have lost his little girl to the flames.

He should not have been so careless. He knew well that chimneys need frequent cleaning. He knew that a buildup of soot and wood tars could be disastrous. Why hadn't he paid closer attention? Why hadn't he checked it sooner?

It was another reminder to George that his cabin, miles from civilization, was really not a proper place for a young girl. He pulled out the letter he had penned a few weeks earlier and went to the post to send it off to the head mistress of the girls' school. He had to make proper arrangement for Kendra. He could put it off no longer.

Chapter Ten

School

"Why do we need to go to the city?"

He was sure Kendra already knew the answer to her question. He had explained it carefully to her before they left the cabin. But he answered her again, "So that you may go to school."

"But why do I have to go to school?" she argued. "You teach me."

"Yes—I have taught you—some. But there is so much more to learn than I've been able to teach you. You need to learn about lands and peoples and discoveries and inventions. I can't teach you all of those things. I don't know about them—and I haven't got the maps or charts or books that tell about them."

Kendra was silent. To his relief she had not resisted the trip when he had first told her about it. But he did wonder if she was feeling the change more deeply than she dared to let on.

"You will like it at school. There will be other girls of your own age. You will make many friends."

"I already have friends," said Kendra stubbornly.

"What friends?" He wondered if Nonie had been sneaking her off to the village when he wasn't around.

"Nonie," said Kendra. "Nonie and Oscar."

George McMannus smiled, but he also felt sadness. He should have brought the young girl out earlier and let her have a chance at being a part of the real world.

"When do I go to school?" she asked him. "How many more days?"

"We'll have a whole week before school starts," he answered, trying to put some enthusiasm into his voice. "Mrs. Miller is going to help us get you ready for school. She knows how to shop for young girls. We might even pay a visit to Mrs. Weatherall—if you'd like. Remember her?"

Kendra did remember. Slightly. She had liked the woman well enough. But she wasn't sure she wanted to pay a visit.

"Would you like that?" her grandfather pressed.

"I don't think so," Kendra replied simply, her head turning from him. He did not push the subject further.

"We will do your shopping then," said her grandfather. "That should be fun."

Kendra looked down at her soft buckskin garments. Her feet were still comfortably shod in her moccasins. She wasn't sure if she wanted to shop or not. Oh, she supposed it would be nice to have new things instead of the clothing that Nonie had sewn for her. But she just wasn't sure she wanted to give up the things with which she was familiar.

"Who is Mrs. Miller?" she asked instead.

"She is a friend of mine from many years back."

Kendra knew that. What she really wished to know was what kind of a person the woman was. Was she old? Young? Kind? Difficult? Talkative or silent? Who was Mrs. Miller?

"You will like Mrs. Miller," her grandfather continued. "She never had a family of her own but she . . ." He hesitated. They had not talked of Mary for many months. At last he willed himself to continue. "She loved your mother very much," he said softly. "Almost like she was—was her own daughter. After your—your grandmother died, Mrs. Miller helped your mother with her clothes and—and even her wedding."

Kendra stirred. It was the first in a long time that she had been reminded of the mother she could barely remember.

"Is she Scotch too?" she asked, wishing to have some point of contact.

"No. No, she is German."

Kendra's head came up, her eyes reflecting her deep shock.

The man had no idea what the one simple word meant to Kendra. Again she saw the flashing dark eyes of Nonie as she spat in the dust of the path and hissed out the words, "German. P-f-f-t." And spit again.

"What's wrong?" asked her grandfather, sensing her discomfiture.

"Germans are bad," she said in a whisper.

"What do you mean?"

"They're bad."

"Who told you that?" he asked her. "Where did you get that idea?"

"Nonie. Nonie spit. She—"

"Nonie?" His mind scrambled to try to figure out the meaning of her words. Then a light dawned.

"Oh, that. Nonie shouldn't say such things. Should know better."

"But—"

"There was a trapper in the area once," he went on to explain. "He was a bad trapper. He stole from other traps and made a great deal of trouble for everyone. Including Nonie's husband, who was still alive at the time and trapping south of the settlement. Eventually the Mounties came and got the man. They put him in jail somewhere, I guess. We've never heard of him again. He was German. It's true. But, Kendra—you never should judge a whole race of people because one of them is bad. It doesn't work that way."

Kendra still looked doubtful.

"I knew a bad Scotsman once," her grandfather went on. "He drank whiskey—all the time. Then picked fights with anyone who came along. He was a Scot. I am Scot. Does that make me bad?"

Kendra knew that it didn't. Still she could not voice a reply.

"And I knew a bad Indian once," her grandfather went on. "He never wanted to work a trapline. Never hunted for food. Never wanted to do anything except steal from his neighbors. He watched the other cabins, and whenever the people were not at home, he slipped in and stole from their traps and belongings, their food supplies and leggings. He was Indian. Nonie is an Indian. Does that make her a bad Indian?"

Kendra shook her head slowly. She knew that it didn't. She loved Nonie.

"We must never—*never* judge a race by one person—or a person by a race. Each individual must be allowed to be good—or judged bad—on their own merit, their own behavior. Do you understand, Kendra?"

The words were spoken softly but firmly. Kendra sensed that her grandfather felt very strongly on the matter.

She nodded her head again.

"Maggie Miller is about the finest woman you will ever meet," her grandfather went on. "She nursed your grandmother for months before—" He couldn't finish the thought. "And Henry, her husband, another German—he risked his life to save mine. He still bears the scars on his hands. No, Kendra. One bad German does not make a race of bad Germans any more than one bad Scot makes a race of bad Scotsmen."

Kendra looked at him solemnly. When it came to taking sides with the one or the other, Kendra was willing to accept the word of her grandfather over Nonie's.

———

"George. Come in! It's been a long time."

Kendra judged the woman at the door to be Maggie Miller. The long journey had finally ended, and she and her grandfather stood on the stoop with small cases in hand.

"Come in. Come in," the welcoming voice continued. "I'm so glad to see you. It's been such a long time."

She drew them in. There was a strange and delicious aroma in the room. It smelled spicy and warm—reminding Kendra of a warm summer day in the berry patch.

"And this is Kendra?" The woman's arm reached out to draw Kendra close. "My, how you've grown! And such a pretty girl, too. Your mama would be so proud of you."

Kendra felt herself pulled close. She could smell the scent of the woman. So different from the way Nonie smelled. There was no hint of cured leather. No odor from open fires. No lingering smells of the cooking pots. Kendra did not recognize any of the strange aromas, so she felt neither welcomed nor repelled by them. They were simply new. Different. Like the house that enclosed her. It was strange. With furnishings and "things" all around her. Pictures on walls, more chairs than there were people. Books. Lamps. Baskets cradling various objects. Coats on hooks. Blankets draped here and there. It looked cluttered and busy to Kendra, who was used to stark simplicity.

She kept her eyes to the floor in the manner she had learned from the Indian women, but she was so tempted to peek around her, taking in all of the strange sights and feelings.

Mrs. Miller released her, and Kendra stepped back, not really feeling comfortable in the arms of the woman.

"Sit down," Mrs. Miller said to them both, and George moved to an overstuffed chair with a multi-colored blanket draped over it and lowered himself with a sigh of contentment.

"How's Henry?" he asked before his body had even settled in.

"Not good, I'm afraid." The woman's eyes shadowed. "He gets a bit weaker every day."

George did not allow himself the comfort of the chair. He rose quickly and crossed to the bedroom where he knew the man to be. Mrs. Miller nodded and moved toward the kitchen. Kendra did not know what to do, so she followed her grandfather.

"Hello, Henry," he said to the man who lay prostrate on the bed. "It's George. I should have come sooner . . ." The words trailed off.

Kendra saw her grandfather reach down and take the

limp, wasted hand in one of his strong, sun-browned ones. He turned the hand over and stared for a long moment at the scar on the back of the hand. Kendra too saw the scar. The scar that her grandfather had told her about. She saw her grandfather's jaw working with emotion as he held the motionless hand. Then he laid it gently down on the covers and reached to brush the scanty gray hair back from the man's face.

He turned then, surprised to see Kendra standing so near to the bed of the invalid.

"This is Henry," he said quickly, as though he felt an explanation was in order. She nodded. She knew. She also saw in her grandfather's eyes the terrible pain he felt in seeing his friend so helpless.

———

George stayed with Henry while Mrs. Miller took Kendra shopping for the new clothes she would need for her school year.

In a way, it *was* exciting. Kendra saw things she had never dreamed existed. Pretty things. Delicate things. Colorful things. Over and over she wished she could share her experience with Nonie. She wondered if Nonie's eyes would light up and pronounce them good, or if she would stop and spit in the dust.

Kendra wasn't quite sure what she thought about the new world. The world that she had quite forgotten. It fascinated her and seemed to draw her, yet she felt strange and uneasy with all the strangeness.

When the week was up and time to enter the new school approached, Kendra's wardrobe was ready. Mrs. Miller herself had done much of the sewing. The new nightgowns and undergarments were ready. The stockings, shoes, and school uniforms were already carefully packed in the new case.

But as Monday drew closer, Kendra was more and more sure that Martha Adams' School for Girls was not where she wanted to be. She wanted to climb aboard the boat with her grandfather and return to the place that was familiar. She wanted to go home to Nonie. To bury her face against the warm, soft side of Oscar. But Kendra did not even try to tell her grandfather how she felt. She did not speak with the German woman who fussed about her, hemming skirts and fitting bodices. Kendra buried the feelings deep inside, but at night when she went to bed, she pulled Dollie from her worn suitcase and later cried into the plump, soft body of the old rag doll.

Chapter Eleven

Pain of Separation

It was terribly hard to say goodbye. George consoled himself with the fact that he was doing what was right for the child. Kendra had no such consolation. She saw the separation as a painful situation totally beyond her control. Nor could she see that there was anything to be gained by the whole endeavor.

She did not weep. Not as she was held in the arms of her grandfather and commended for being such a brave young lady. She did not even weep as she watched his tall back disappear beyond the strong wooden door of the girls' school.

The tall, stern-looking young woman whom she was to call Miss Bruce said a crisp, "Come," and Kendra turned to follow, much as Oscar followed her commands.

"This will be your room," the young woman said. "You will share it with three girls. Stella Lange, Ruth Winters, and Rebecca Joyce. That bed will be yours. You may use the two bottom drawers in the chest by the window. Unpack your things and place them neatly in the drawers. Your case will be picked up for storage.

"Mind you hurry now. It will soon be time for the lunch bell."

She turned on her heel and was gone.

Kendra stood, her whole body trembling. But she did not cry. The words of the woman had come so fast, so brisk, that Kendra wondered if she had understood them. She couldn't think. Couldn't remember. What had she said? Kendra looked at the bed. Had she said something about the bed? Oh yes. This was her bed. The three other beds in the room belonged to—to somebody else.

Kendra let her eyes wander over the room. They lighted on the case that held all her new things. The woman had said she was to unpack her new things. Where was she to put them? She couldn't remember. Couldn't unscramble all the words that had poured out in such quick and utter confusion. In storage? But storage where?

Kendra knew about storage. Her grandfather had a loft in the cabin for storage of supplies. He had a shed out back for storage of pelts. He had another little shed for storage of materials for mending sleighs and harness and all sorts of other things. It held some tools too. Simple tools.

But where were the storage sheds for the girls' school?

Kendra opened her suitcase and carefully took out all the new items. She piled them on the bed that she was told would be hers. The little piles kept toppling over, and she knew she would never be able to keep them together to carry to the storage shed.

There was a nice white sack over the pillow at the head of her bed. Kendra decided to borrow it. Item by item she began to load all her belongings into the case. All except Dollie. Kendra looked about the room to make sure she wasn't being watched and stuffed the rag doll under her pillow. She had the feeling she was going to need her precious companion over the coming days.

The pillowcase was getting full by the time Kendra finished, but she managed to stuff the last pair of long stockings into the sack.

"I do wish I didn't have to store them," she whispered to herself. "I think Papa Mac was expecting me to wear them." She looked down at the dress she was wearing. She guessed that it would have to do—maybe for a long time. She wished she had brought her buckskins.

"Now, where is the storage shed?" she asked herself, and lifting her bundle she traveled the long hall and pushed her way out the door that led to the rear of the property.

She managed to find a shed, but the door was locked. Kendra did not know what to do, and then she spotted a window above her that was slightly open.

"If I could find a ladder," she murmured. She laid down her sack with all of her belongings and looked about. There on the side of the shed was a ladder. Kendra felt relieved to find that her problem would be solved so quickly and easily. She placed the ladder against the side of the building, hoisted her bundle and started up. Difficult climbing with her arms so full, she nearly lost her balance and fell.

She managed to push her bulky load through the open window. She heard the funny sound as it landed on the floor in the shed. Then there was a tinkling sound as though something else had landed on the floor as well. Kendra held her breath—but nothing more happened.

By the time she climbed back down the ladder and placed it back where she had found it, she was panting from her excursion. Somewhere a bell was ringing. Kendra puzzled over it. She was not used to hearing bells.

Then she remembered the words of the woman. There was to be a lunch bell. What did that mean?

As Kendra entered the building through the door from which she had left, she could hear scurrying feet off in the distance. Someone else was in the building. They were on their way—somewhere.

Kendra studied the puzzle of doors. She couldn't remember which one had been hers. She made her way down the hall, peeking in room after room. She was totally confused. The young girl who could have found her way through the forest trails without benefit of compass was thoroughly mixed-up by all the doors that looked alike yet led to different places.

At last she noticed a bed with a different pillow. It looked lumpy and bare and out of line. "That's mine," she said with some satisfaction. All the other pillows still had their cases. All the other pillows were placed evenly and neatly at the head of each bed.

Yes, it was hers. Dollie was still hidden under it. Her open valise was still sprawled across the floor. She closed the case and fastened the clasp.

What was she to do now?

She decided that the only thing she could do was to wait. She pulled Dollie out and tried to straighten the pillow to match the other ones on the beds in the room. Perhaps she should have dumped her things through the storage window and brought back the case so that her pillow wouldn't look different from the others.

It was too late now. There was no way she could retrieve what she had deposited in the shed.

With a deep sigh she looked for a place to sit. There was only one chair in the room and it was across the floor from her. What if it belonged to someone else? Perhaps it would be safer if she sat on the bed. But the bed was so white and smooth that she didn't dare sit on it.

At last she sank down to the floor, Dollie clutched tightly in her arms.

But Kendra had no idea what she was waiting for nor how long she might have to sit there. She didn't think much of this girls' school. She had been told that she was sent here to learn. She had expected to be able to use all the new clothes Papa Mac and Mrs. Miller had provided. She had been told about books and maps and all manner of interesting things that would help her to learn about the world.

But there was nothing. Nothing but a room with stark white beds. Papa Mac was gone and she was all alone. She didn't know where she was or how to ever get back to Bent River Crossing again. She didn't know how to find Nonie. Or Oscar. She was alone. Alone. And so frightened and lonely. Besides all that—her feet hurt in the tight, stiff new shoes. Kendra reached down and slipped them off. She hated them. She wanted her comfortable moccasins back. She wanted to go home. She just wanted to go home.

Kendra curled up on the hard board floor with Dollie held tightly in her arms. She longed to cry, but she refused to allow herself even that small comfort.

———

George McMannus walked slowly. He had delivered Kendra as he had known he must do. Martha Adams' School for Girls was known to be a good one. It would be good for Kendra. The first few days might be hard, but she would quickly adjust. She was a bright little thing. She would soon have everything in the place all figured out. She would soon make friends with the other little girls.

He had done the right thing. He knew that. But he had not done the easy thing.

No. He was miserable. He knew that he would likely be miserable for months to come. How long? How long was the school term before Kendra could come home again? Not until spring. Not until almost summer. He didn't know if he'd ever be able to stand it.

He knew that the winter ahead would be the loneliest winter of his life. He hoped that he would be able to endure it. That he could make it through. He wouldn't even have Nonie moving silently about the cabin. There would be no need for Nonie to come now. There would be just him and Oscar. He thought of the sled dog. He was really too big to be taking up room in the cabin. It was totally unnecessary. He had a warm, thick coat. He would be as comfortable out of doors as any of the other team members. But for the first time, George felt thankful that Oscar was a cabin dog. It wouldn't be quite as lonely. At least he would have the pampered dog to talk to.

It was going to be a long winter. An awfully long and lonely one.

———

"Kendra! What are you doing?"

It was the stern-looking young woman who stood over Kendra, her brow furrowed, her eyes flashing frustration. "You missed your lunch."

Kendra struggled to her feet, Dollie hanging limply from

her hand. She had no words to answer. She wasn't quite sure of the question.

But it came again. "What are you doing? You were told to put away your things and come for the lunch bell. We have strict rules. If you miss the lunch bell, there will be nothing to eat until the supper hour. And if you miss that—nothing until breakfast. Do you understand?"

Kendra nodded. There was so much she did not understand, but she felt she had understood those few severe words.

"Come now," said the woman. "It is time for your first class."

She wheeled on her heel and Kendra obediently stepped forward to follow.

"And leave that—that worn-out—rag—behind," hissed the woman, motioning toward Dollie.

Kendra looked down at the doll that still dangled from her hand. Then she looked about the spotless, bare room. Dollie would look so out of place.

"Put her in the drawer where you put your clothes."

Kendra stood stark-still. She remembered then. She was to have put her clothing in the chest. In the chest with the drawers. She was to have the two at the bottom. But she had put her clothes in the storage shed. She had made a dreadful mistake.

"And where is your pillowcase?" a disturbed and angry voice demanded.

"I—I needed it," Kendra stammered. She still stood holding Dollie. Slowly the doll was lifted until Kendra was clutching her tightly against her chest. Her large green eyes were dark. There were no tears. Kendra was beyond that.

"And get your shoes back on," ordered the woman, totally beside herself.

Kendra didn't know what order to try to fill first. She lowered Dollie to the wooden boards of the floor and sank down beside her, reaching for a shoe as she did so. She hated to put the miserable things back on her aching feet. They hurt. And they made noise when one walked.

"Now—about that pillowcase—where—?"

Just then another woman entered the room. She was shorter than the blustering woman who stood before Kendra. And she was not as thin, nor as straight. Nor did she look quite as sour.

"You have found her," the woman said, and there was both concern and relief in her voice.

"She was right here in the room—the whole time," answered the younger one, annoyance still evident in her voice.

Kendra was sitting on the floor struggling with her shoe. She said not a word, though her thoughts reminded her that she had not been in the room "the whole time." She had gone to the shed.

"I told her plainly to come at the lunch bell, Miss Jennings." The woman went on to explain to her elder that she had done her job properly but had not been obeyed.

"Perhaps she didn't know where the dining room is. Did you tell her that?" the older woman inquired softly.

The younger one seemed flustered. "Well, we must get her to her class. We don't want her late so she disturbs the others," Miss Jennings said. The one called Miss Bruce bent and snatched Dollie off the floor from Kendra's side and moved quickly to the chest of drawers.

"She has done something with the pillowcase." The thin one fairly spat out the words. "I was trying to get to the bottom of it."

She leaned and jerked open the drawer, then straightened with a horrified look on her face.

"She hasn't even unpacked her clothes!" she exclaimed, then wheeled back to Kendra.

"Why didn't you unpack as you were told."

"I—I did," floundered Kendra.

The woman turned back to the empty drawer before her. "No, you didn't," she denied hotly. "There's not a thing in here."

Miss Bruce spun around and lifted Kendra's case from the floor, opening the latch with hands that trembled with anger.

"There's nothing here either," she said, her face filled with unbelief. "What did you do with them, child?"

"Perhaps she put them in the wrong drawers," suggested the other woman.

"They wouldn't fit." But even as the younger woman said the words, she crossed to the chest and pulled out one drawer after another. Kendra's things were not there. "What did you do with them?"

"I—I—" Kendra could not meet the angry eyes. She lowered her head, her eyes on the floor.

The older woman, Miss Jennings, had not left the room. She seemed to sense Kendra's deep discomfiture. Kendra heard the swishing of skirts and felt a hand placed on her head.

"What is it, child?"

Kendra longed to weep but she stood silent. As tall as she could. Completely still.

"Did you unpack?" asked the woman. Her voice did not sound harsh and angry, just concerned.

Kendra nodded her head.

"Where did you put them?"

"In the storage shed," answered Kendra.

"What storage shed?"

"The one at the back—down the hall."

"But the shed is always to be locked."

Kendra nodded again. It was locked.

"How did you get in," the voice above her went on.

"I put them through the window," said Kendra in a small, trembling voice.

Kendra heard a sharp intake of breath. It came from the tall, brisk, angry woman.

"Miss Bruce—find the gardener and check the storage shed," ordered the older woman, her voice even and controlled. "Kendra—come with me. We'll have a little talk."

Kendra was led from the room with its four beds, through the hall, down some steps, and to a small office.

"Sometimes first days can be confusing," Miss Jennings commented as they walked.

Kendra sat down on the big chair indicated to her and nodded her head silently.

"Miss Bruce asked you to unpack your things and put them in the drawers?" It was more a question than a statement. Kendra nodded again.

"So why didn't you?" The question was direct and firm but without accusation.

"I got mixed up. I thought she said to put them in the storage shed."

"In the storage shed? Why did you think that?"

"I forgot. She—she—I think she said the case was for the storage shed."

"The pillowcase?" The woman sounded confused.

"No. The clothes case. When it was empty," explained Kendra without looking up.

"The suitcase?"

"I don't have suits," replied Kendra, and for the first time she lifted her eyes.

A small smile played about Miss Jennings' lips. She lowered her own eyes to the hands that were clasped together on the desk in front of her. "And the pillowcase?" she asked Kendra.

"I couldn't carry the clothes. They kept unpiling," said Kendra. "I borrowed it."

The woman nodded.

"Did you hear the lunch bell?" she went on, changing the direction of their conversation.

"I heard—something," admitted Kendra.

"But you didn't to lunch. We have rules that one must be at lunch."

Kendra nodded. She had heard about the rule. Even talking about lunch made her stomach growl. She'd had nothing to eat since early morning.

"Were you shown the dining room?" asked Miss Jennings.

Kendra nodded her head. She and her grandfather had been given a tour of the school. But it was so big and had so many halls and doors and steps up and down. It wasn't like her familiar home area where one could travel by landmarks.

"Would you take me to the dining room?" Miss Jennings stood as she asked the question and motioned for Kendra to lead the way. Kendra knew she must obey, so she nodded again and stepped from the door.

But she couldn't remember. She had no idea which way to turn. She went to her left and started down the long hall. They came to steps and Kendra didn't know whether to take the ones that went up or the ones that went down. She decided to go down.

Another long hall. Should she go left—or right. She took a deep breath and turned left.

"Kendra—" The voice stopped her. "Kendra, you will never get to the dining room this way. It's on the bottom floor at the end of the hall."

Kendra wasn't sure what to do. What would the woman do with her now? She didn't know. Along with her confusion and loneliness a new emotion filled her. Fear. Kendra was quite unaccustomed to fear, but it shook her young body now.

"Come," said the woman, and she extended her hand. "It's already too late for you to join your first class. We will get you some soup and bread. But this must not happen again—understand. I am waiving the rule this one time because you did not know where to find the dining room, but in the future we will expect you to be at meals on time. There will be no bowl of soup should this happen again."

Kendra trembled. She had no intention of missing a meal in the future.

"We will henceforth appoint a classmate, a big sister, to help you get acquainted with the layout of the building."

There were a few words that Kendra had not understood, but she felt that she knew the woman's meaning.

She was glad to accept the offered hand and be led to the dining room.

Chapter Twelve

Adjustments

It was not a good start for Kendra. The feelings of being left on her own in an alien environment lingered with her even after she had eaten her bowl of reheated split pea soup and a slice of dark bread. The bread tasted fine, but Kendra didn't like the soup and wished she could refuse it. But she was hungry, and the lady who sat down opposite her told her that she was to eat. Kendra ate obediently, but she did not enjoy the strange soup and felt her stomach threaten to refuse it on a couple of occasions.

When the bowl was finally empty, Kendra pushed it back with no intention of asking for more.

"Now—we must show you the classroom. We won't go in. The rule is that one must be on time for class. If students don't get there before the door closes, they do not get in."

It seemed to Kendra that there were rather a lot of rules.

Miss Jennings stood up and Kendra stood with her. As soon as the woman took a step, Kendra was at her heels. She was reminded of Oscar, and with the thought came another wave of loneliness. How was Oscar doing without her? Was the dog as lonesome as she?

They walked together down the hall. Kendra heard her unfamiliar shoes clicking against the hard board floors, a strange sensation to be hearing each step. She was used to walking silently except for the possible rustling of dried leaves that had tumbled to the trail.

She missed the sound of the leaves. They whispered to her as she walked through them—not the loud clunk, clunk as did the solid boards.

They came to some steps. These, too, were wooden, and Kendra noted the hollow sound as they thumped their way up the stairs.

Then they traveled down another hall, and Miss Jennings stopped and pointed at the door with one hand and raised the other to put a finger before her lips. Kendra had no plans to utter a sound. She wouldn't have needed the warning. But with the pointed finger and the quiet "sh-h-," Kendra did not even dare to breathe.

"This is the classroom you will be attending," the woman whispered.

Kendra's eyes grew larger. If there was one redeeming factor about going to school, she felt she would discover it behind this closed door. Her grandfather, Papa Mac, had spoken excitedly about all the things she would get to learn and be able to share with him when she returned to their home at Bent River Crossing. Kendra could hardly wait.

"Since class has already started, you may go to the library," Miss Jennings went on. "We mustn't waste precious time. I will give you a reading assignment and expect a report at the end of the normal class time. When rules are disobeyed we give library assignments. This is your first day and there seems to be some excuse for your failure to follow orders—but we cannot set new precedents. The other girls will expect to see you studying—not loafing."

Kendra had no idea what the library was. She did understand that she was going there as a result of her failure to obey instructions, so the library must be a place of punishment.

Dejectedly she followed the woman. They traveled the hall and Miss Jennings pushed open a large wooden door with a word on it that said "Library."

"Remember the rule," spoke the woman before they entered. "There is to be no talking in the library. Any communication with the librarian must be written clearly on a slip of paper and handed to her in silence."

More rules. Kendra began to wonder if there was ever an end to them.

Miss Jennings stepped in and Kendra followed. She had expected a horrid place—one of some kind of wicked torture, but instead what she saw was a room with shelves and shelves of books. To the side were two long tables with straight-backed wooden benches tucked along them. At one end was a desk where a woman sat with her head bent over a book. Kendra could see nothing but a pile of red-gold hair and the tip of an oval-shaped chin. In front of the woman was a lettered sign that read "Miss Dorcas. Librarian."

Miss Jennings motioned Kendra to one of the benches. Kendra went obediently and sat down quietly while the woman moved on. She searched along a shelf while Kendra's eyes traveled over the room. Never had she seen anything so breathtaking. Papa Mac had been right. She would be able to learn all sorts of things.

Before Kendra was able to take in all that was around her, Miss Jennings was back. In one hand she held a book and in the other a sheet of paper and a pencil. The paper said "Report," and then some instructions. "Complete your report on your assigned reading, sign your name, and hand it to the librarian before leaving the library." The rest of the sheet was blank except for faint lines across the paper.

Kendra stared at the sheet. She wished she could ask what a report was, but she had already been told sternly that one was never to speak in the library. She looked up at the silent woman before her and said nothing.

Then the woman leaned over, and with the pencil still held in her hands she wrote on Kendra's sheet of paper: "Assigned reading—pages 1–20," and handed the sheet and the pencil to Kendra.

Kendra was still puzzling when Miss Jennings left the room. But she turned her attention back to the book that had been laid on the table before her.

She had never seen the story before. It was called *The Mystery of the Yellow Crow.* Kendra had never seen a yellow crow. She couldn't even imagine one. She began the book with some reservation.

By the time she reached page twenty, the story had barely begun. Hardly noticing that she had completed the assigned pages, Kendra kept reading. The purpose of reading a book was to discover what happened.

Somewhere a bell rang. Kendra scarcely heard it. The farmer and his wife had just decided to paint their house a nice bright yellow.

Kendra kept reading, turning pages quickly in her growing enthusiasm over the story. The blank paper still lay on the desk before her. From somewhere in the distance Kendra could hear the voices of children playing as they took their playground break from classes, but the sound did not even register. The story now had her totally enthralled.

She was almost to the end when she felt a presence near her. The librarian was standing close to her table, looking down with a frown at the blank sheet of paper. She pulled a pad and pencil from her skirt pocket and wrote in big letters: "Where is your report?"

Kendra held her breath. She took the offered pencil and put in small letters on the bottom of the pad: "I don't know."

The woman frowned even more deeply. Then she pointed to the sheet that had been left on the table beside Kendra's book. She wrote again. "You have not written your report. The library is closing for the supper hour. You should have finished the twenty pages easily."

Kendra looked back at her book. It had one hundred and six pages. She had two more to go.

"That will be two demerits," Miss Dorcas's long white slim fingers wrote on a fresh sheet of the little pad.

Kendra had no more idea about demerits than she did about reports. She shrugged her slim shoulders, anxious to return to her book.

The librarian was nodding toward the door and reaching for the book that Kendra held. Kendra realized that the librarian wanted the book. Reluctantly she handed it over. The last two pages would unlock the mystery, but the book was being taken from her. Mutely, Kendra watched as it was returned to a shelf.

Miss Dorcas turned and came back to the table. She pointed to a line that said, "Place your name here," and Kendra picked up the pencil and wrote in neat script, Kendra Marty. The woman took back the pencil and wrote in big letters all across the page: REPORT NOT COMPLETED. TWO DEMERITS. Then she took the paper with her and returned to her desk. With one more nod of her head she indicated that Kendra was to leave the room. The girl got up and moved toward the heavy wooden door. She didn't know where she was or where she was to go next. She had no idea what the rule was about leaving the library. She only knew that she was confused and alone and that she had not been able to finish the story. She would never be able to tell her Papa Mac what had happened.

"Are you Kendra?"

A girl stood beside the big library door seeming to be waiting for her to exit. Kendra was surprised to see her and even more surprised to hear her question.

She nodded silently, wondering what was going to happen now.

"I'm to be your big sister," the girl went on, but she didn't sound one bit happy about her assignment.

Kendra just nodded again.

The girl was older than she was. Perhaps eleven or twelve, Kendra decided.

"It's almost supper," the girl went on. "Have you washed?"

Kendra had washed that morning before she had left Mrs. Miller's house. She was about to say that she had when the girl spoke again.

"It's the rule that we all have to wash our hands. We get a demerit if we don't."

Kendra still wondered what a demerit was.

"Have you washed your hands?" asked the girl again.

"I washed this morning at Mrs. Miller's," Kendra managed to say.

"Not this morning," said the girl in exasperation. "We have to wash before every meal."

Kendra hung her head. She had not washed.

The girl led her to a large room with many basins and a long row of towels hanging on pegs on the wall.

"That's your towel," said the girl, pointing to a peg. "Hurry or we'll both be late and we'll both get demerits."

Kendra washed quickly and was soon hurrying along behind the briskly walking figure in front of her.

"We can't run or we'll get a demerit," the older girl informed Kendra over her shoulder.

They were breathless by the time they reached the dining room, but they did manage to duck in just before the big door closed.

"That was close," said the older girl under her breath. "We were almost late—and I'm starving. I never would've lasted 'til breakfast. Next time don't be so slow."

Kendra nodded.

"That's your place," said the girl and motioned to the empty chair beside the one she moved toward at the table. Kendra was about to take her seat, but the girl hissed crossly, "Don't sit down. We haven't said grace."

Kendra looked around the room. All the other girls were standing silently behind their chairs, their hands placed on the chair back.

Kendra imitated what she saw.

"Bow your head," whispered the girl beside her sharply, and Kendra bowed her head.

Soon someone began to speak. "For all we are about to receive, may we truly be thankful. May we honor thee in our walk, our talk, and our thought. Amen."

As soon as the last word was spoken there was a scraping of chairs, and the girls all around her took their seats. After a moment of confused hesitation, Kendra followed.

The food was served by two older girls who walked up

and down the tables and spooned a portion onto each plate. As soon as Kendra had received her scoop, she picked up her spoon and took a bite.

"Don't eat yet," the girl beside her ordered in a harsh whisper. "We have to wait until everyone is served."

Kendra cast a nervous glance about the room and dropped her spoon beside her plate. She didn't know if she should spit out the food or swallow it quickly. Which action would reap the least demerits? She dared not chew. Some pair of stern eyes would surely see her.

"And don't use your spoon," the voice beside her continued. "Use your fork."

From then on Kendra watched the older girl carefully. She did not make one move until her leader had made it.

The supper was green beans—fixed in a very strange way that made them taste funny—mashed turnips and a small slice of roast meat. The meat was bland and tough to chew. Kendra did not like that either.

Silently she ate her supper. She longed for some of Nonie's good stew. It had so much more flavor with its garden vegetables and its herbs from the forests. Kendra was sure she would not be able to swallow the stuff that had been set before her. She did enjoy the half slice of bread.

Gradually Kendra began to understand about the life at the girls' school. When in doubt, she watched the other girls. Her sharp eyes and quick wit kept her from more demerits. As it was, Kendra had amassed far too many demerits before she had learned the system. And she had discovered, much to her dismay, that a total of six demerits could earn one cleaning duties, and eight demerits sent one to the office of Mrs. Adams herself. Ten demerits meant a strap, and with a dozen demerits the doors of the esteemed school closed on you forever, sending you home totally disgraced.

As much as Kendra longed to return home, she did not wish to disgrace her grandfather, so daily she tried her hardest to evade the dreaded demerits.

She enjoyed the classes, even though they were a puzzlement to her in the beginning. She wished she could just read and do sums, but the teachers seemed to expect all manner of strange procedures. Kendra did discover what a report was and once she knew, she did the assignment well and on time.

Her favorite place was the library, and while other girls often seemed to think of the room as some specialized form of school torture, Kendra could not get enough of the books on the shelves and would gladly have spent her recess times buried in a book rather than shyly standing back from the games on the playground.

But rules were rules. Each girl had to have daily exercise, so Kendra reluctantly made her way to the backyard as well.

Kendra did not feel at home with her new roommates. She was not used to having the company of other girls. And the girls from the school already had their special friends. Nor were they inclined to befriend someone new. Instead, they teased and giggled and picked on Kendra when no one else was around to admonish them.

Kendra never fought back. Never told her superiors. Instead she withdrew, becoming more and more the butt of cruel jokes and girlish pranks.

In spite of her determination to comply with the wishes of Papa Mac, Kendra was unable to shake her deep loneliness. Day after day she yearned for home. At first it was just a hollow, empty longing somewhere deep inside her. A feeling of not belonging with all the busy, noisy girls who already had their friends and did not really need or welcome a young stranger. The shared bedroom seemed crowded and stuffy at night. The clothes she wore were uncomfortable and stiff. Her shoes hurt her feet constantly. She could not remember all the rules. People frowned at her and prompted her and gave her orders that she could not understand. She just didn't like it. She didn't like it at all, and she longed with all her heart to go home to Papa Mac and Nonie and Oscar.

Day by day her longing increased until it was so painful she couldn't sleep at night or swallow her food at mealtime.

She became pale and listless—even her schoolwork suffered for lack of concentration. Miss Bruce always seemed to be fussing at her for one reason or another, and her teacher, Miss Spooner, fretted and stewed and sent repeated reports to the office of Mrs. Adams. At length Mrs. Adams herself called the girl in.

"Are you not feeling well, Kendra?" she asked.

Kendra shook her head. Her eyes looked dull, her face, tanned and healthy at her arrival, now looked wan and pale.

"Where are you sick?" asked the woman.

Kendra could not answer the question. She felt sick all over. Right from the very depth of her soul—the very pit of her stomach—the very core of her being.

At last Mrs. Adams, as the head of the institution, felt it her duty to notify George McMannus. In her letter she tried to assure him that she was sure the illness was nothing serious. That the girl would soon perk up again. They now had her on tonic morning and night.

But Kendra did not improve. Most of her food was still left on her plate, and when a staff member insisted that she clean up the plate, she promptly brought it all back up again. She was not forced to eat again.

Mrs. Adams was about to send off another letter when there was a knock on her door.

George McMannus stood there. It was already the trapping season. He could ill afford the time to make a long trip to the city. But he had to check on Kendra. He had to know what was ailing his little girl.

———

"I'm taking her home, Maggie."

George had just tucked his granddaughter into the bed made for her on Maggie's cot and sat beside her until she dropped off to sleep. She had lost weight and looked so pale that he feared there must be something terribly wrong with her.

"Shouldn't she see a doctor first?" asked Maggie, who

agreed that the child was not well.

"Mrs. Adams said that she had her thoroughly checked by the school physician—twice. He could find nothing wrong with her."

Maggie sighed and poured buttermilk into two tall glasses.

"I should have kept a closer eye on her," she berated herself.

"You couldn't. Not with Henry needing you full time here," George quickly responded. He sat in reflective thought for a few minutes and then went on. "I'm not sure that it would have helped anyway. I have a feeling she is just pining for home."

"So what will you do?" asked Maggie. "She does need schooling."

George sat stroking his beard. Maggie noticed that it showed faint streaks of gray. They were all getting older.

"Mrs. Adams said that Kendra is a smart little thing. She already has the basics. With extra books to study, she feels that Kendra will be able to get most of what she needs. At least she won't be illiterate."

"She reads everything," chuckled Maggie. "I heard her reading that *Almanac* while I was getting supper on and you were feeding Henry."

There was silence for many minutes. With a sigh, George broke it with, "Henry's getting weaker, isn't he? I could scarcely get him to swallow a little soup."

Maggie nodded her head. Every day it seemed that Henry lost a little more of his strength. Tears moistened her eyes.

"It's hard," she said. "Hard to just watch him waste away day by day."

George nodded. He didn't know how Maggie kept on going. She must be worn to exhaustion.

"Can I ask for further hospitality?" he asked her, sorry that he could be a burden but hoping he might be able to give her a hand with Henry's care for a few days and let her get some much-needed rest.

"Of course," replied Maggie. "You know you can."

"I need to do some shopping for books for Kendra. And a globe. Mrs. Adams said that it is important for her to have a globe. Get the feel of the world around her. Especially since she is so isolated. And history books and . . . There is so much she needs that I can't get for her out there. Mrs. Adams said she should have a weekly newspaper. Wouldn't do much good. The mail only comes in about once a month. Sometimes less if it should storm or the rivers flood."

He sighed deeply and rubbed at his beard again.

"I've not done right by her, Maggie," he said with remorse.

"You've tried," responded his friend. "You've done your best. No one can do better than that."

"But she looks so frail. So pale. They said she hasn't been eating—or sleeping. That she just sat around looking forlorn and forsaken."

"That'll all change quickly," Maggie dared to promise.

"You should have seen her when they brought her to the office. I'll never forget her eyes. They—they looked like she couldn't believe I was really there. Like I was a ghost or something. And then she just threw herself into my arms and hung on. Like she was afraid to let go. She didn't even cry—just clung to me. I—I—it was almost more than I could take."

He brushed the back of his hand against his cheek. "If I had only known—how bad it really was—I would have come for her sooner," he finished.

"But you didn't know."

Silence again. He stirred restlessly in his chair. "No," he said at last. "I didn't know. I figured that she would adjust and be happy. I thought that I was the only one—suffering."

"You missed her, didn't you?" said Maggie softly. It was not really a question but an observation.

"Terribly. I—for the first while I thought that I was going to—to go stir crazy. And that dog of hers sure didn't help. He kept pacing the cabin, whining and moaning, and then he would go to her bed and cry like she was dead or something. I couldn't stand it. I spent as much of my time away from the cabin as I could find excuses to leave."

"You'll both be much happier with her home again," Maggie assured him.

She looked toward the door that led to the bedroom. Henry had not really been able to offer companionship for many months. Years. And yet he was still with her. She knew he would not be with her for much longer. He was so weak. She knew it would be better for him. But my! How she would miss him. Just to know that he was there brought her a measure of comfort. Just to be able to talk with him. Tell him about her day. Even if he couldn't understand or respond. She did not look forward to being alone.

"We weren't made to be alone," said Maggie softly and reached into her apron pocket for a hankie.

Chapter Thirteen

Home Again

They left for home as soon as George was able to find the needed books and school supplies for Kendra. George remembered their first trip and the excited, chattering young girl. Now she was quiet, studying everything about them with wide, haunted eyes. He tried to draw her out, tried to coax back some of her former merriment, but she did not respond. George hoped that once they got back to Bent River Crossing and Nonie and Oscar, she would return to being his beloved Kendra again.

———

"Look," said Kendra, and for the first time on the entire trip George heard excitement in her voice. "There's Nonie!"

"Where?"

They were still some distance from the Crossing, but they could see a number of figures moving about the shore. George found it hard to believe that Kendra could actually pick out Nonie.

"Right there," insisted Kendra, "by that clump of willows."

And she was right. When the wagon neared the small post, a lone figure moved silently from among the willows across the river and waded right into the water toward them. Kendra didn't wait for Nonie to come to her. She jumped from the wagon before George could even summon her to be careful and plunged into the stream to wade toward Nonie.

They embraced each other, the elderly lady in her deerskin garments and the young girl, whose thin face made her large green eyes look even bigger and greener. The shallow, cold waters of the Bent River swirled and eddied about their skirts. The tears that had not been free to fall when Kendra had welcomed her grandfather were now released. Nonie just held her, one hand on the blond head, the other pressing Kendra to her as she rocked back and forth. "Nayeea, nayeea," she cried over and over. George recognized it as Nonie's prayer of thanks to the spirits for bringing back the child.

"I suppose we'll have to go through that all over again," he muttered to himself. "If the old woman has her way, she'll make a pagan of the child."

George promised himself that he would watch more closely and try to keep Nonie from putting foolish notions in the young girl's head.

Kendra was anxious to get back home to the cabin. George knew that the main reason was to see Oscar. The girl could hardly wait to hug her dog again.

"Do you think he will remember me?" she asked her grandfather, apprehension edging her voice.

"Oscar?"

She nodded.

"Do you remember him?" asked George, teasing her a bit to try to get her to talk more.

Kendra nodded her head. "Of course," she said. Her voice was little more than a whisper.

"Well, dogs have even better memories than humans do," said her grandfather. "Guess there's not much chance that he will have forgotten you."

Still Kendra's face did not relax or her eyes lose their look of fear.

"He won't be at the cabin when we get there, you know,"

her grandfather reminded her. "I left all the dogs with old Two Tooth."

Kendra remembered. She was sorry she'd have to wait, but she knew that her grandfather could not have left the dogs at home with no one to care for them.

"When will we get them?" she asked softly.

"I'll go for them first thing in the morning," he promised.

She sighed. It would have to do. Then she turned and let one hand trail in the cold river water. She was very tired. It had been a long, long trip—but she would be so glad—so glad to be home.

———

True to his promise, George left early the next morning to go for the dogs. He was gone long before the sun had stirred itself from the night's repose. Nonie silently entered the cabin and crossed to the bed. She stood and watched the child as she slept. She was so pale and thin. Nonie's thoughts went to her medicine baskets. She knew the very thing to get Kendra well and strong again. She would make up the herbal tonics that night and bring them with her in the morning. She would be sure to put some in the stew and porridge each time she cooked. Soon Kendra would be running and smiling again.

Nonie let the two big tears that rolled down her withered cheeks go unheeded. To interfere with one's tears might make the rain gods feel they had been slighted. Next spring they might hold back the rain. Nonie did not wish to risk their wrath.

Nonie crossed to the rocking chair near the fire and eased her body into its wooden embrace. The warmth from the open fire felt good on her chilled bones. It would not do to stir about. She would sit quietly while Kendra slept. The girl needed her rest.

———

Oscar bounded into the cabin, seeming to be well aware that Kendra had returned even before he reached her little corner bed with its mattress of fresh moss and spruce boughs. With an excited yip he pushed his nose against her and rooted at the covers that partially hid her face.

Before her eyes were even open, Kendra's hand came up to clasp a handful of the long, silvery coat. Oscar licked at her cheek and her eyes opened wide.

"Oscar," she squealed and bounded up to hug him and bury her face in his long hair.

Nonie rose from her chair. It was time to stir now. Time to put on the breakfast porridge. Time to carry on with life. Things were back to what they should be.

It took several days for the old way of life to be reestablished. George had to return to his traplines, and Nonie came to stay with Kendra. She was always there when Kendra awoke in the mornings and they spent their days together, sometimes chatting, sometimes silent, often taking their baskets and heading for the woods. Gradually a feeling of security and peace began to steal over the young girl. She began to eat again and put on the weight she had lost. She romped in the out-of-doors with Oscar or helped Nonie with the chores. The late autumn sun and cold fresh air flushed her cheeks and added vitality to her body. Kendra was at home again.

Chapter Fourteen

Plans

"I'm going to build onto the cabin," George announced one morning while they shared their breakfast porridge.

Kendra lifted her head.

"You need your own room," he went on. "On which side of the cabin would you like us to build?"

Kendra couldn't keep the shine from her eyes.

"My very own room?" she asked him.

They were crowded in the small cabin. Especially since Kendra had so many books and school supplies to spread about.

"Your very own. This makeshift curtain stuff doesn't work too well."

It sounded too good to be true. Kendra took her time thinking about it. She wasn't sure where the best place would be. If her room was to the east of the cabin, she could watch the morning sun, while on the west of the cabin, she could watch the sun set beyond the mountain range. The east was closer to the stream. On warm summer nights she would be able to open her window and listen to its laughter. Yet the west was closer to the groves of forest trees. The birds would be so close it would seem that their singing was with her in her room.

"I'll—I'll check," said Kendra, going outside to walk slowly around the cabin.

At length she made up her mind. Her room would be built

on the east. It was not a large room, but it was plenty big enough, with its own fireplace and two windows. Two windows, Kendra exulted. One that looked to the east and another that looked to the south. She could hardly believe her good fortune.

George made a built-in bunk, and Nonie and Kendra gathered the spruce boughs and soft moss for the mattress. George also built a simple table-desk close to the fireplace and put a number of shelves along one wall.

Kendra moved in all her books and lined them up so she could read the titles. It was so much nicer than having them in stacks on the floor.

Nonie gave her a large bearskin rug that she placed in front of the fireplace. She could picture herself curled up there on long winter evenings, her head bent over the pages of one of her books. It made a nice picture. Kendra felt contentment wash over her.

When Kendra was totally moved in and settled, she heaved a deep sigh, then turned to her grandfather, who stood studying the work of their hands. "You can visit me sometimes, Papa Mac," she informed him generously.

He laughed heartily. "I'll just be beyond the door," he informed her.

Secure and happy, Kendra felt a world apart in her own place.

———

The year that Kendra turned eleven included a cold, damp summer. The garden did not produce as it should have. Even the berry trees in the nearby woods had been caught by a late frost so were producing little fruit. Nonie and Kendra tramped the trails gathering herbs and roots, but Kendra often saw Nonie lift her face toward the sky, fear filling her voice as she uttered words of pleading.

Nonie had ceased telling Kendra Indian tales. In a way she missed them. At times it had been frightening, knowing that one's life was in the hands of the unseen spirits. Spirits that seemed so difficult to please. But Kendra knew her grandfather did not approve of the stories. He dismissed them as fairy tales and informed Kendra that they had no foundation of truth.

There were so many mysteries. So many unanswered questions. Something deep within Kendra longed for answers.

"If the Old One didn't make the world, how did it all get here?" Kendra dared to ask her grandfather.

"There are theories," he answered vaguely. Personally, George McMannus didn't put much more stock in some of the usual theories than he did in the Indian tales. They didn't quite add up to logical conclusions.

"What theories?" asked Kendra.

"I'll get you a book on it the next time I am in the city," the man replied. Kendra was impatient to study about the theories. Would they answer her burning questions? It was hard for her to wait. She knew that grandfather might not go to the city again for many months—or even years.

She nodded. She would have to accept her grandfather's answer.

"What would you like for your birthday?" Her grandfather surprised her with his sudden change.

Kendra did not hesitate. She had been thinking of what she wanted. "I want to go with you on the trapline," she said quickly.

"You want to—? Why?"

Kendra did not back down. "So I can learn to help you—with the traps and the skinning and the caring for the pelts."

He looked thoughtful. He shook his head slowly. "The trapline is no place for a child," he said, his voice soft.

"But I'm getting big now," protested Kendra.

He smiled. She was getting tall for her age. But she was still a child.

"It gets pretty cold and stormy sometimes," he went on.

"I won't go on those days. Just the nice ones," put in Kendra.

He thought for a moment longer. "We'll see," he said slowly.

"That isn't a birthday gift," protested Kendra. " 'We'll see' means maybe. A birthday gift has to be real."

George chuckled softly. "Okay," he said. "I'll take you— at least—at least three times. How's that?"

It wasn't all that Kendra had hoped for, but it had to be enough for now.

Word came from Maggie that Henry had passed away. George mourned his friend, but he was not able to make the long trip out for the funeral. He knew that the news should bring relief. Henry would not be suffering any longer. Maggie would not be driven to exhaustion caring for an invalid. But even so, even with his reason telling him that things were better now, he could not help but grieve. Maggie was going to be so lonely in the days ahead. He sat down and wrote her a long, long letter.

George chose the first of Kendra's trips on the trapline carefully. The sky was clear, the day bright, and the temperature moderate for a winter's day in the area. Even so, he had misgivings. He had not forgotten the words of a very young Kendra when she had turned from him, pain in her eyes and screamed, "I hate you. I hate you."

How would Kendra respond to seeing animals caught in the traps? It was not a pretty sight.

But Kendra surprised him. She turned her eyes from the first animal, an otter, curled and frozen, his head resting on the very trap that held him prisoner on the red-stained snow.

From then on, Kendra spoke of the animals in terms of the price of the pelt. Her knowledge surprised George. He had not realized just how much she had learned about the worth of furs and how to tell a fair skin from a superior one.

He took her again the next day. It was fun to have her company on the trail. George lost count of their trips after their third time out together. From then on, she went often. Kendra was soon more than company. She was actually a great help.

————

A storm moved in, dropping the temperature and swirling snow about the cabin.

"I don't think you'd better come with me today," George announced firmly. Kendra looked out on the storm. It was one of the worst she had seen in her few winters.

"I don't think *you* should go either," she told him.

"I have to," he answered without even giving it thought. "The traps need to be checked every day."

Kendra knew that George always traveled the line each day when he had the traps out.

"Why?" she asked now, surprising her grandfather. "The animals won't stir about in this weather anyway."

"But there may be something in a trap already."

"You can get them when the storm is over," said Kendra.

"I don't want them to suffer needlessly," put in her grandfather.

Kendra looked up, her eyes big. "They're dead," she reminded him frankly.

Her words caught George totally by surprise. Yes. They were dead. Any trapped animal would be dead in a very short time in the frigid temperatures. But what if—what if—? No, he wouldn't take that chance. He would not have an animal suffering through a storm.

————

Nonie no longer made her trips to the cabin when George was away from home. Kendra did not need child care. But the girl missed Nonie. Often on the days that she didn't go with George to check the traps, she paid a call on Nonie in the settlement. The elderly woman always welcomed her with smiles and soft words. Kendra knew she was loved.

The years were telling on Nonie. She seemed to much prefer the fireside to stirring about outside in the cold.

George made sure the elderly woman had a constant supply of wood. He often wished he could stack the fireplace logs up beside her door and then be done with it. But he knew that wouldn't work. Any of the other residents would feel quite free to use from the pile as well, and Nonie would soon be out of fuel for her fire.

So every other day George had to take Nonie another load, which he placed in her cabin. The time cut dreadfully into his workday, but he feared that Nonie would go cold if he didn't care for her.

Kendra also helped, gathering wood from the nearby forests and carrying it in her arms to the old woman's cabin. It was a chore that kept both George and Kendra busy over the winter months.

———

When Kendra was thirteen, one of George's team members produced a summer litter. Kendra spent much of her time playing with the puppies. By the time they had been weaned, she had made her picks. "I want this one and this one and this one . . ." she told her grandfather. She didn't stop until she had pointed out five of the eight puppies.

"What are you planning to do with all those dogs? They do need to be fed, you know."

"I'll make them work for their keep," Kendra said confidently.

"Work. How?"

"I'll use the old sled," said Kendra. "I can haul the firewood to Nonie and get supplies from the trading post and— and—"

"Whoa," laughed her grandfather. "I get the picture. But are you sure? A dog team is a lot of work."

"I know," replied Kendra. "But they are a lot of help too."

Kendra got her pups and could hardly wait until they were big enough to start training for the sled.

————

Kendra sat at the table close to the crackling fire. The night was cold again. She could hear the wind moaning outside the log frame, but she paid little attention to its mournful song. Her nose was buried in a book. George had sent for a new supply by mail. Kendra drank in the information, but it never seemed to be quite enough. She had so many unanswered questions. If Nonie's stories were just myth, then how did things really come to be? Kendra had studied nature enough to be dissatisfied with trite answers. There had to be a logical reason for the universe with all of its complexity and intrigue. There just had to.

She lifted her head suddenly. Her eyes looked off into the distance, past the shadows of the flickering lamplight, her thoughts far away.

"I want a trapline of my own," she said suddenly, turning to her grandfather.

The wish was out. She had dared to voice it.

George looked up from the trap he was cleaning, surprised by her words. She had been working with him on the traplines now for three winters. She handled the snowshoes as if she had been born with them as an extension to her feet. She could mush the dogs and handle the sled. George had spent time with her in rifle practice until he had total confidence in her ability to wisely and accurately use the gun. She knew the rules of the trail, could read the signs, and knew the laws of survival. She had become skilled at skinning without damaging the pelts. She could work the skins carefully over the stretchers, putting on just the right pressure without causing rips or weak spots. Kendra was a real product of her wilderness setting and quite at home in her surroundings.

Still George hesitated. Was he ready to let her have her own trapline? It didn't seem the right place for a young girl.

He knew the dangers. Many an experienced man had lost his life to the trapline.

"Do you really think—?" he began, but Kendra stopped him.

"You've been my teacher," she said frankly. "And I think you've done it well. Nonie says I know as much as some of the village men."

George could not hide his smile. In his thinking, Kendra knew a good deal more than most of them.

"I don't know," he said again. "Some of those traps—"

"I won't use the biggest ones. I'll just go for the smaller game," offered Kendra.

"But the—the weather? The cold?" George thought of the bitter winds and the times when he had feared that he himself might perish in a storm.

"I'll be careful," put in Kendra. "I'll keep my line closer to the cabin."

"Of course—if it was really cold you could leave things go for a day or two," her grandfather thought out loud. "Lots of trappers do."

"I—I wouldn't want the animals to suffer," Kendra echoed her grandfather's own words. "I'll be careful."

George nodded, still reluctant to let the young girl have her own traps. But he was the one who had raised her in the wilderness—taught her the only way of life she knew. Was it fair of him to deny that she use what she had learned?

"I'm going to save my money," went on Kendra. "I'm going to go out to school."

George was caught off guard by her statement.

"But you—you didn't like school."

Kendra had said nothing about wanting more schooling. Had she been thinking about it? Longing for it? Why hadn't she spoken? He would have sent her.

But even as the thoughts raced through his mind, he felt a stab of fear follow them. If Kendra left, his own life would be so empty. So void of any meaning. He quickly chided himself. He had to think of the child—not his own selfish desires.

Kendra looked at her grandfather, her eyes clear, her

gaze steady. "I think I am ready now," she said frankly.

"But—but you will be—be older than all the other girls. They—" George was stroking his beard, his eyes intent on the face of his granddaughter.

"Oh—I don't plan to go to *school* school. I want to go to university. There is one in Edmonton—and they let girls attend. I read about the graduation exercises in that paper that came midsummer," said Kendra. "If I study real hard, and read all the books I can find—then I think I can be ready for it. Maybe by the time I am seventeen—or eighteen."

George let out the breath he had been holding. Seventeen—or eighteen. That still gave them a little time. He wouldn't have to face the thought of losing her for some time yet. He relaxed.

Then his mind switched back to the traps. He supposed it would not be fair to refuse her request. After all, because of him she was who she was.

"We'll see," he answered with a nod of his head.

Kendra smiled to herself. When her grandfather responded in that fashion, she most always got what she wanted.

Chapter Fifteen

Visitor

Kendra stamped her feet on the wooden step and pushed the door open with a mittened hand. It was cold. Even colder than she had expected it to be. She was glad to be home. Glad to be back to the comfort of the cabin, though it too would be cold until she got a fire going.

She closed the door behind herself and pulled off her heavy fur-lined mittens. Even with the protection of the fur, her fingers felt numb. She blew on them as she crossed to the fireplace and knelt to arrange kindling wood in a little pile for lighting. She was glad that there was never a shortage of fuel. Her grandfather saw to that.

With thoughts of her grandfather Kendra frowned. She wished he were home. She hoped he was okay. He had so many more miles to travel than she did. His trapline took him the entire day. It was now shortly past noon—and bitterly cold. He would be kept busy coaxing the dogs along. They would wish to bury themselves in the snow and curl up to keep warm.

"I wish he'd just forget the rest of the line and head for home," she spoke aloud, her words sounding strange in the stillness of the cabin.

She reached for the can that held the matches and removed one. Never did she need more than one match to start a fire. Now as she held the match to the tinder-dry kindling, she noticed that her fingers still felt numb. Her fears con-

133

cerning her grandfather deepened.

"He likely won't even get anything in the traps. It's too cold for the animals to be moving about."

She had checked her own traps and found nothing.

A dog barked, followed by a chorus of yelping. Kendra lifted her head. For a moment her heart quickened. Perhaps her grandfather was returning early. But she quickly changed her mind. Her dogs were not welcoming her grandfather's team. The barking indicated that a stranger was approaching.

Kendra looked up at the frosted window. She knew that she would see nothing through the iced-over pane of glass, so she rose and crossed to the door. They never had visitors unless another trapper dropped by for a cup of coffee and a bit of a chat, and that happened so rarely that Kendra couldn't remember the last time.

A team of only four dogs pulled up before the cabin. Kendra was not used to seeing a sled pulled by a team of four. All the trappers around their area used at least six dogs on their sleighs. She did not recognize anything about the fur-bundled figure who moved around the sled, then spoke sharply to the dogs who dropped down quickly to the snow. His head bent into the wind, he moved forward toward the cabin.

Kendra stepped back, holding the door open for the stranger. He didn't see her until he was about to step up onto the small porch. Then his head came up and he paused.

"Thank the good Lord!" he uttered with a strange accent. "I feared I would never reach a cabin alive."

Kendra said nothing, just nodded the man inside and closed the door quickly behind him. He pushed back his fur parka. His beard was covered with ice.

"I thought I would die on the trail," he added. "I prayed for a cabin. Someplace to take shelter."

"I'm sorry," said Kendra indicating the fireplace. Her little flame had burned up the kindling and gone out while she was at the door. "I just got in. I haven't even got the fire going."

"Well, at least I am out of the frigid wind," the man went on, drawing off his heavy mittens. "Here—let me start the fire for you," he said.

He bent before the fireplace and reached for kindling. Kendra bit her tongue. He was using far more of the precious fuel than was needed to get a fire started.

"Where are your matches?" he asked.

Kendra handed him the coffee can. He struggled with the lid. Kendra noticed that his fingers were clumsy. Likely he was even colder than she had been. With the fourth match he finally got a flame. Kendra wished she could ask him to move aside so she could carefully add larger pieces of wood to the fire. She was afraid to speak so watched as he bumbled the job and had to start all over with fresh kindling, depleting their precious supply still further.

"Why don't you thaw your hands in water," said Kendra, indicating the basin in the corner. "Your fingers must be half frozen." The man nodded and got up from his knees, and Kendra seized the opportunity to take over the fire lighting.

"The water's frozen," the man said as he turned from the basin.

Kendra had thought that it might be. "I'll get some snow," she said. "It works just as well."

But she didn't go for the snow until she was sure the fire had taken hold and would be ready to receive larger chunks of wood.

"It will soon be warm," she told the man. "I'll build a fire in the stove too."

She hastened to start the second fire and then took the basin from the shelf to scoop up some snow.

"Just use a little at a time," she said. "Frozen fingers need to be thawed slowly."

"I don't think they are frozen—yet," said the man. "But they sure are cold. It wouldn't have been much longer until more than my fingers would have been frozen."

Kendra nodded. Again she thought of her grandfather.

"Are you here alone?" the man asked her.

"No. My grandfather is out checking the traps," replied

Kendra and reached for her heavy mittens. "I've put some water on for tea," she said. "You take off your wraps and sit by the fire as soon as it starts giving off some warmth. I need to care for the dogs. I'll tether yours at the north side of the house."

The man nodded. "You are an angel of God," he told her.

Kendra puzzled over his strange words as she stepped out into the cold air and began to unharness and tether the sled dogs. As soon as her own team was unharnessed, she moved to care for the four dogs of the stranger. When she had them all securely tied, she went to the shed for frozen meat for the dogs.

A loud clamor greeted her as she returned with their daily portions of meat, but soon all the dogs were much too busy eating to be making further noise. Kendra cast one last glance around the circles to be sure she hadn't missed any animal and returned to the cabin.

She could feel the heat as soon as she opened the door. It was a pleasant welcome on such a cold day. She shrugged from her furs and hung them on the peg on the cabin wall.

The man was standing in front of the fireplace, his furs tossed on the floor behind him, his hands spread to the blaze.

"Don't warm up too quickly," Kendra cautioned him.

"I couldn't warm up too quickly," he replied with a laugh.

Kendra did not wish to argue. She crossed to the stove and added a bit more wood under the kettle. It would soon be singing and she would be able to make them tea.

"My name is John Blackman," he told her.

Kendra responded with her name and then said, "I'm going to start a fire in my room. Why don't you pull the rocker up to the side of the fire?" *At least then he won't get faint and collapse,* thought Kendra as she went to build the fire in her bedroom fireplace.

When she came back to the room, the man was sitting in the rocker. His face was flushed, his eyes glazed. Kendra hastened to make the tea. She wished to coax him away from the direct heat.

"This will help warm us," said Kendra. She placed the

tea on the table and drew two cups from the shelf. Then she sliced some bread and spread it with blueberry jam.

Mr. Blackman left the rocker and joined her at the table. Kendra breathed a sigh of relief.

For several minutes they sipped their tea in silence. The warmth of the liquid seemed to loosen his tongue.

"I just came from Bent River Crossing," he told her. "I'm on my way to Kenakee Falls."

Kendra looked up. Kenakee Falls was a long way from their area.

"Fellow at the trading post tried to talk me into staying on there until there was a break in the weather. I should have listened to him. Didn't realize how cold it was."

Kendra nodded.

Kenakee Falls was another Indian settlement. There was not even a post there as far as Kendra knew. Why would this white man be heading there?

It was not polite to ask another's business, so Kendra waited for Mr. Blackman to go on.

"We are going to start a church there," he said. "Take religion to the Indian people."

Kendra felt her eyes widen. The Indians had religion. Her grandfather maintained that they had far too much religion for their own good. Why would this outsider want to take them more?

Kendra poured more tea.

"We hope to start churches all through the area," the man went on.

Kendra remembered pictures of churches from one of her books about Europe. They were huge buildings with spires and turrets and beautiful windows. But Kendra wondered how, and why, this man and others would build such a building for the Indians.

"We have asked God to bless us so that by 1930 there will be no more pagans in northwest Canada."

Pagans. Kendra did not know the word. But the man was speaking with such intensity that she knew his cause touched him deeply. Kendra made a mental note to look up the word in her dictionary later that evening.

"Have you always lived here?" Mr. Blackman asked, changing the conversation.

"No," replied Kendra. "I came from north of Edmonton when I was almost four."

"Have you been back?" asked the man.

"To Edmonton. Once," said Kendra. "To school."

"Of course," said the man with a nod of understanding. Kendra did not bother explaining further.

"And you live with your grandfather?"

Kendra nodded.

"No grandmother?"

"My grandmother died before I was born," replied Kendra.

"And your folks?"

"I lost them the spring before I came with Grandfather."

Mr. Blackman shook his head sympathetically. "You poor thing," he said solemnly.

"I've liked living with Grandfather," replied Kendra simply. "He's been good to me."

The man seemed about to get up, and Kendra was afraid he would cross to the fire again. He'd had a chance to warm up a bit and the tea would have helped considerably. Still, she worried that it might be too much heat too soon.

"Would you like to lie down on Grandfather's bed for a while?" she asked him. "There's a heavy blanket there that you can just pull over you."

To her relief he nodded his head. "I am a bit done in after the trip," he said. "That wind was almost more than I could fight against. Might not hurt to just rest for a few minutes."

Kendra watched with relief as he settled himself and pulled the blanket up to his chin. Soon soft snoring filled the room. Kendra was relieved to hear the sound. She turned her thoughts back to her grandfather. She did hope he would soon be home.

———

The man slept the entire afternoon. Kendra moved about

quietly as she prepared the evening meal. She wondered if the aroma might waken him, but still he slept.

Kendra kept an eye on the faint sun that hung listlessly on the western rim of the sky. She longed to hear the sound of her grandfather's team. It would soon be dark. Was he okay?

Kendra was placing another log on the fire when she heard Oscar cry out. Oscar was always the first of her team to be alerted to something. His yip was quickly followed by welcoming staccato yaps. Kendra knew that her grandfather would soon be home. She reached for her fur jacket and heavy mittens. She would take care of the team and let him enjoy the warmth of the cabin.

After the supper hour the two men had a long visit in front of the fireplace. George had many questions to ask Mr. Blackman about the world outside.

"Edmonton is growing quickly," the man informed him.

George nodded. He had not been out to Edmonton for some time. He had been getting all of the supplies he needed at the local post or else ordering them in. He had not even been to see Maggie since Henry had died. He chided himself about that fact.

"And Calgary is becoming quite a city as well," the man went on.

"But you are from the East?" asked George.

"From England originally," replied the man. "But I've been in Canada for seven years now."

The visit continued. Kendra listened quietly as she washed up the supper dishes and melted the snow she would need for the next day's water supply. She found the discussion of the outside world most interesting, and it served only to intensify her longing for answers.

Why was this man coming from the cities to the far reaches of the wilderness? Why did he think that the Indian people needed more religion? Her grandfather assured her that religion was of no consequence. Why bother with it then?

Kendra finished the last of her chores and went to her room to look up the word *pagan* in the dictionary. "A heathen; idolater," the book told her. Kendra frowned and flipped back through the pages until she came to the word *heathen*. This had a bit more. "Heathen. One who does not believe in the God of the Bible; one who is neither a Christian, Jew, nor Mohammedan; an irreligious person; pagan."

Kendra read it over again. "One who does not believe in the God of the Bible," she said to herself in a whisper. "What is the Bible?" She had never heard Nonie speak of the Bible. Yet her grandfather said that Nonie could find a god under every stone and behind every bush. It was all very strange.

———

The next morning the wind had calmed and the sun was shining feebly, though it was still cold. After their visitor had been breakfasted and sent on his way back to the trading post to wait for better weather before traveling on to Kenakee Falls, Kendra dared broach what had been troubling her mind.

"Papa Mac," she said, "are we pagans?"

"Pagans?" His head came up and his eyes darkened. "That fella say something?" he asked her.

"No. Not really about—about us. But—he said they hope that by 1930 there will be no pagans left in northwest Canada," said Kendra.

Her grandfather surprised her by chuckling. "He did, did he? Seems to me he's taking on a pretty big job."

"He's going to Kenakee Falls," went on Kendra.

"I know. He told me," said George, shrugging into his heavy coat. It was time to check the trapline again.

"I looked up pagan in the dictionary," went on Kendra.

"And—?" prompted her grandfather.

"It said 'heathen.' And then it said that a heathen is a

person who doesn't believe in the God of the Bible. Which one is that?"

George couldn't help but chuckle again. Nonie had introduced Kendra to so many gods. Yet none of them came from the Bible. At least not to his knowledge—though he would have admitted that he knew very little about what the Bible contained.

Then he quickly sobered. Maybe it wasn't so amusing after all.

He answered slowly, "Really doesn't matter much as far as I can see," said George as he drew on a mitten. "It's all just a bunch of stories. Just different versions, that's all."

"So we are pagans, then?" pressed Kendra.

He reached out and pinched her cheek. "Some folks might call us that," he answered truthfully. "Isn't the way I think of it."

"But who—who is the God of the Bible?" asked Kendra.

Her grandfather turned to the door and Kendra knew that he would soon be out on the trail again. "Just the white man's version of the Indian myths," he told her, and with a nod he left the cabin, closing the door firmly against the cold.

Chapter Sixteen

Hard Winter

The cold snap continued. Kendra now dreaded the daily round of checking the traps. She feared more for her grandfather than for herself, but he insisted that they needed the money from the furs and went out each day as usual.

Kendra, too, left the cabin each morning as soon as it was light enough to see the trail. In spite of the weather, she did have fair returns from her traps. Each day she tallied the little account she was saving toward her schooling. She really had no idea how much money it would cost, but she knew she would need to work hard to save enough if she wished to go in her eighteenth year.

The cold weather was hard on their wood supply. Kendra watched as the pile that had seemed so big in the fall grew smaller and smaller every day. She still took Nonie a sleigh filled with wood every other day. The cold made it necessary for her to pile the wood a little higher on the sled. The dogs sometimes complained about the load, but Kendra preferred one hard trip to two lighter ones and helped ease the burden by throwing her weight behind the sleigh on the upgrades. Nonie needed to have wood for her fire.

It seemed that every task was just a bit harder in the inclement weather. Kendra's fingers often felt numb, her cheeks close to freezing in spite of her efforts to keep exposed skin from frostbite. The river ice had to be chopped to reach water for the pail or else she had to thaw snow to fill the water buckets. She didn't know which task was the most difficult to take and alternated the one with the other.

Kendra began to wonder if there would ever be a break in the weather. Just after the first of the new year, there was some relief when the temperature climbed and the sun actually shone on the frigid world.

"Have you had any trouble?"

The words came from the red-coated Mountie who shared their supper table. He was the second visitor they'd had in the space of a few months.

"No," said George after giving the question some thought. "I haven't noticed anything out of the ordinary."

"Well, we've had reports that someone has been tampering with traps in the area. I'm going on up to Wingate to ask a few questions and see what I can find out. I'll be back through in a week or two. I'll stop around and see if there's any reason for concern."

George nodded. Stealing from traps was a serious offense. Trappers would not tolerate it. If, in fact, someone was caught in the act, the person making the discovery might well take matters into his own hands. It was no wonder that the Mountie was concerned.

The conversation was not lost on Kendra. She said nothing, but a few discomforting thoughts began to whirl in her thinking. Her traps had not been doing as well of late. She had feared that perhaps she was trapping out the area—that the smaller animals had moved on to another range. But maybe—maybe someone else was taking advantage of her traps.

After the Mountie had thanked her for the meal, shrugged back into his heavy parka and left the cabin, Kendra still mulled over his words. Had she missed something? Were there signs that she should have caught?

"Papa Mac," she said after George had returned to the

cabin, "I wonder if I have had someone bothering my trapline."

George looked up from the moccasin he was lacing. "You've spotted something?" he asked.

"Well—no. That is—nothing in particular, but it does seem as if I've had poor catches lately. I've been very careful when setting the traps to hide them well and cover the scent and sprinkle fresh snow over my tracks. And I never take the team too close.

"There are still animal tracks through the area. It seems the game is there—I'm just not having the catch that I should have. At least I'm not *getting* the catch."

George lowered himself to the chair by the table and proceeded to put on his other moccasin.

"Well—keep a sharp lookout," he advised. "If anything looks suspicious let me know."

Kendra nodded.

They both put on their warmest outer wear. They were facing another day on the trail to check the traplines.

————

"I knew it," said Kendra, bent over her trap. "Someone *has* been stealing."

Anger filled her. It was hard work running the trapline. If someone wanted the benefit of trapping, they should be willing to do the work for themselves. It wasn't fair to reap from another's labors.

Kendra lifted the tuft of hair that clung to the sprung trap, indicating that an animal had been caught. But there was no carcass anywhere to be seen.

The next trap held an otter. Kendra noted that the fur was at its prime. It should bring a nice price on the market.

But as she left the packed trail and neared the next trap, she noticed that the snow had been rearranged as though something had scuffled around in it. There had been a new fall of snow and Kendra saw no footprints or snowshoe indentations showing through it. But perhaps the culprit had been sly enough to use a small twig to brush at the spot or else had sprinkled handfuls of powdery snow to cover any tracks that might have been left behind.

The more she studied the area around the trap, the more sure she was of her suspicions and the more incensed she became. She took off her mitten and brushed her hand through the new layer of snow. There were blood stains and scattered pieces of hair just beneath the surface. There *had* been an animal caught here, and it was now gone.

Who would do such a thing? Surely it wasn't one of the area trappers. But it had been a hard winter. Every trapper was finding it difficult to travel out in the intense cold. Perhaps someone had decided that there were easier pickings closer to the settlement. Surely, though, the people in the area knew whose trapline lay so close at hand. But maybe that was the problem. Maybe they reasoned that a young girl would not be smart enough to read the signs. Maybe she was being taken advantage of simply because she was a girl.

The thought made Kendra even angrier. She found her mind reviewing each trapper in the area, white and Indian alike, trying to sort out which one might stoop to such lowness.

It was a mental exercise that disturbed her and really profited nothing. She tried to push aside the troubling conjectures.

"Someone has been bothering my traps," Kendra said to George that evening. Her green eyes flashed anger as she spoke the words.

"You're sure?"

"I'm sure. Two of them had catches that had been taken before I got to them."

"Did you find prints?"

"No. The thief is smart. He covers his tracks well. All I found were signs of the animals."

"What animals?"

"It was hair from a lynx at the first trap. The second was a fox. It had snowed enough to hide the prints, and whoever was there had disguised things pretty well."

George sat silently. "I don't like it," he said at last. "Anyone who will rob a trap will be desperate enough to do almost anything. I'm not sure that you should go out again until after that Mountie has been through."

"But I have the traps set. I need to check them," argued Kendra.

"Maybe I should take your line tomorrow."

"You have your own line to care for. The day isn't long enough for you to cover both."

George knew that was true. He really couldn't argue further.

"Well, I don't like it," he said. "Not one bit."

Kendra did not like it either. If someone was stealing from her traps, then someone was desperate and dangerous. She would have to be doubly cautious as she made her daily run. She hoped she could depend on Oscar to alert her if danger was about.

The next day Kendra did her run with a loaded rifle near her on the sled. She hoped she would not need to use it, but she must be ready to take action if it was necessary.

"Just bring your traps on in until this is settled," her grandfather had suggested, but Kendra hated to give up the peak trapping season when she needed the money for her schooling.

"I'll be careful," she promised, and he reluctantly agreed to let her go.

Nothing unusual caught her attention. She picked up four catches and reset her traps. She was glad to hurry home. Nonie needed another load of wood.

Four days later Kendra had another trap robbed. Again there had been a snowfall, so she had little hope of picking up any signs. But it made her uneasy in spite of herself. She decided not to tell her grandfather. He would just worry. She did hope that the Mountie would be back soon. The whole thing made her feel edgy. She traveled with the loaded rifle slung over her shoulder.

———

Oscar shifted in his harness and sniffed at the air. Kendra, who traveled closely behind the team, saw the hackles rise along his neck.

"He senses something," she said to herself and reached for the gun on her shoulder.

There was a bend in the trail ahead, and just beyond, a small windfall where Kendra had carefully concealed a trap. Oscar's lifted head pointed in that direction, his sharp ears upright to catch the faintest stirring. He lifted his nose and sniffed at the air. Kendra heard a quiet growl come from his throat.

"Lay," she ordered softly and Oscar dropped immediately to the snow, and the other team members quietly followed suit.

Kendra hesitated. Should she leave the entire team where it was or might she need Oscar? She hesitated for only a moment, then fell to her knees and with a few quick movements had Oscar out of his harness.

"Heel," she commanded in a whisper, and Oscar dropped in close beside her.

The trap was out of sight beyond a stand of spruce. It had been hidden from view along an animal trail that crossed through fallen timber. Kendra knew that once she rounded the bend, she would be exposed to full view. She stopped and slipped off her snowshoes. She did not wish to be encumbered if there should be a tussle. On moccasined feet she moved slowly forward, Oscar following her like a silent shadow. The hair on his neck stood raised, his teeth were bared and ready, but no sound came from his throat or his softly padded paws.

Kendra cocked her gun. She was ready to face whoever was at her traps. She hoped with all her heart that it wouldn't be someone she knew. It would be hard enough to pull the trigger if it was a stranger in the sights.

"Go for his left shoulder—but well above the heart," she told herself as calmly as she could. "If he still threatens, take his right arm."

Then what would she do with him after she had wounded him? It would be a race with the dog team to get him to help before he bled or froze to death. Perhaps she should just turn and flee for home in the hopes that he would not spot her, for if he did he would most certainly be the one firing his gun and he wouldn't be shooting to wound.

No, it was too risky. Better to face him than to turn her back. She had to follow through now.

She took a deep breath and stepped out into the open. Her trap lay just ahead.

For a moment Kendra saw nothing. Whoever was at the trap was apparently bending over close to the ground. Kendra lifted her rifle and sighted toward the spot. Had he already been alerted? Was he hiding behind the fallen log with his sights trained on her? Kendra willed her hands to remain steady even though she was trembling inside.

A head rose above the log. Kendra squinted against the glare of the morning sun on the whiteness of the newly fallen snow. She had to see clearly—to focus on the face of the enemy.

Curious and challenging eyes stared back at Kendra and Oscar. A deep growl crossed the space between them, and Oscar echoed it with a growl of his own. The wolverine snarled more loudly, his teeth bared around their grip on the animal carcass he held in his mouth.

Kendra stood transfixed. So here was the thief. The dreaded wolverine. For one moment she held steady, and then her finger squeezed the trigger. He might charge—or he might bolt for cover. She could not wait to see. He had to be stopped. There would be no peace for any of the trappers as long as he prowled the woods stealing from them.

As the report of the rifle echoed across the still morning air, Kendra's whole body shuddered. It was hard enough to shoot a hated forest thief. She was so thankful that it hadn't been a fellow human in her sights. She lowered the gun, hands trembling. Had it not been an animal, she knew she never could have pulled the trigger.

———

The Mountie stopped by again on his way back through. Kendra gave her report. He nodded his head solemnly.

"One wolverine can cause an awful lot of havoc," he admitted, "and they can cover several miles. Stealing here—stealing there. Making trapper doubt neighboring trapper. I've seen it before. I'm glad you got him."

Kendra smiled. She was glad too. He'd had a remarkably fine fur. It would add to her funds for university.

Chapter Seventeen

More Trouble

Kendra finished her morning run and prepared the two pelts taken from her traps. She was getting ready for a trip to see Nonie when she heard Oscar setting up a howl.

From the sound of Oscar's greeting it was her grandfather's sled entering their clearing. But it was just past noon. Her grandfather should not be returning for several hours. He could not possibly have finished his run. Kendra moved to the door, a frown creasing her smooth forehead.

Her grandfather was not running behind the team as she expected him to be. Surely his team had not deserted him. That was unheard of. But where was he?

Kendra strained to see up the trail. Was he following somewhere behind the sleigh?

But as the team drew near Kendra noticed that the sled had a load. Was the morning catch that profitable to make such a pile in the sleigh?

Kendra hurried forward as the dogs pulled up to the front of the cabin and dropped to the snow. Their sides were heaving, their tongues lolling to the sides of their mouth. Kendra knew they had been pushed hard on the trip.

"Give me a hand."

Kendra's attention jerked from the team to the sled. The mass in the sleigh bottom was her grandfather.

"What happened?" she asked, panic in her voice as she reached out to him.

"A moose. A moose came at me. Got my leg."

Kendra heard the pain in his voice. Terror seized her. How badly was he hurt? How could she ever get help?

"Can you make it to the house?" she asked him.

"I think so. If you help me."

He was a big man and heavy to lift. With a bit of help from the strength still in his arms they managed to get him up and on his one good leg. Then with Kendra for support, they moved slowly to the cabin.

"Get Nonie," George said with a husky voice as Kendra lowered him to his bed.

"Let me see first," said Kendra. She had noticed that one pant leg was soaked with blood. She could not leave him bleeding while she traveled to fetch Nonie. He might bleed to death before she could return.

Kendra reached for the skinning knife she carried in the side of her moccasin and slashed away the pant leg. The wound beneath made her shut her eyes and fight against fainting. The moose had given her grandfather an awful gash.

"How is it?" George managed to ask between clenched teeth.

"It's bad. Deep, I think. But if we can keep the infection out, it should heal okay."

"Get Nonie," George said again.

"Nonie is sick in bed," replied Kendra. "I was just leaving to take her some broth and firewood."

"What will we do?" George groaned as he asked the question.

Kendra tried to quiet her racing thoughts. She had to think clearly.

"I have medicine here," she said, trying hard to keep her voice calm in spite of her trembling. "Everything that Nonie has, I have. You lie still and I'll fetch it. It's in my room."

Kendra went for her roots and herbs. She had to think carefully, to sort out which use each one had. She had to be sure that she didn't make an error and use the roots for stomach pain in place of the roots for clotting, or the herb for toothache in place of the pain-killer. She also needed the bitter herb to fight infection and the gum from the spruce for healing.

It took some time for Kendra to clean the wound, treat it, and get it bandaged. George was in a cold sweat by the time she was done. She covered him with the blanket and moved to put her supplies back where they belonged. She still had not cared for the dog team, and Nonie still needed wood for her fires and the broth for her meal.

Her grandfather's trapline had not been covered, but she could not possibly see to it before dark. For the first time, it would not have its daily checking.

Kendra pulled on her heavy coat. "Try to rest," she told her grandfather. "I will put your team down for the night and make a fast trip to Nonie's. I'll be back as soon as I can."

George opened his eyes slowly. He tried to smile but it was more of a grimace. "Pesky nuisance," he managed. One hand stole up to tug at his beard. Kendra moved forward and tucked the covers up around his chin.

"Sleep," she whispered. "I'll be right back."

When she returned from the dogs, she was thankful to find him sleeping. He needed to rest. He had lost a fair bit of blood, but Kendra was thankful that the bull's antlers had not seemed to break any bones or tear any muscles. With time he should heal. But it would be a while before he could travel the trapline again. Kendra prepared herself for some difficult days.

It was impossible to care for both traplines alone, so Kendra brought in her own traps and took the trail daily to cover the trapline of her grandfather. He fussed and fretted but there was little he could do. They needed the furs from the winter catch to make it through to another season.

Spring was making promises to return to the land.
George had not yet taken over his trapline again, but when
it came time to take the pelts to the post, he informed Kendra
that he was well enough to drive one of the teams.

"Are you sure?" cautioned Kendra.

The leg had been healing nicely, but Kendra did not wish
to take any chances.

"I'm sure," he insisted. "Stop pampering me."

They loaded the furs on the sleds and hitched the teams.
Both of them knew that the winter had not been a good one.
Usually their winter catch was twice as big as the one they
now took to the post for trade.

"Well—it's not much," said George as he lashed the pelts
on the sled, "but it might get us through until another season. Maybe our next winter won't be as bad as our last one."

Kendra nodded. She did hope things would improve. If
they didn't, she might never get out to school.

With a shout to the dogs, both the sleds moved out onto
the trail. They would follow the packed trail through the
trees until they came to the bend in the river, and then they
would travel the river ice into the settlement.

The morning held a hint of warmth. The snow had not
yet left the area, but the sun now shone with some strength
in its rays.

Kendra looked up at it and could not keep the smile from
her lips. Nonie would have told her that Father Sun was
getting over his anger with the world and was willing to give
them all another chance.

They reached the river and moved out onto the windswept
ice. It was much easier for the dogs to pull on the level. They
increased their speed, and Kendra was afraid her grandfather's injured leg would make it difficult for him to keep up.
She coaxed Oscar to set a more leisurely pace.

"We'll have to watch it around the beaver dam," George
cautioned and Kendra nodded. She knew that the beaver
dam could be dangerous. The water was deeper and the animals often made channels that would freeze over lightly.
The channel ice could not carry the weight of a loaded sleigh.

Once they neared the dam, they slowed the dogs, and George walked slowly ahead of the teams, sounding the ice with a stout stick. Kendra followed carefully, her eyes ever alert for thin ice that might lead to trouble.

They were almost beyond the spot when there was a sickening sound of cracking ice. Kendra cried out to her grandfather, but it was too late. Another crack. She watched in horror as his sleigh broke through the ice and slowly began to sink from sight in the gurgling water. The team struggled to hold it, pulling frantically against their leather harnesses. Kendra held her breath. Would the sled pull the entire team into the icy stream?

The dogs continued to scramble, their frightened yips filling the crisp morning air. Sharp toenails clawed at the slippery surface; then Shanoo went down with a cry, splashing nosily as she hit the water. She struggled against the current but it was no use. Kendra watched as the dog was dragged under, the water closing above her head with a satisfied gurgle.

Kendra's eyes jerked back to Natook who still fought for a foothold on the slippery ice that seemed to keep crumbling beneath him. He was losing ground quickly. Kendra looked on in horror, frozen to the spot, her thoughts whirling too quickly to make much sense. How much, and how many, were they to lose?

It was her grandfather who brought her back to her senses.

"Cut the harnesses," he called. "Cut the harnesses."

Kendra looked up to find George at the head of his team, clutching the harness of the lead dog and trying hard to keep the team from slipping farther into the gaping hole.

Kendra dropped to her stomach and inched her way across the ice. As she moved she reached down for the knife in her moccasin. Natook was still clawing and scratching at the edge of the breaking ice, about to slip into the river. Kendra was sure she would not make it in time.

She reached for the frightened dog and gave him a boost with all the strength she could muster. At the same moment her knife sliced through the strap that held him prisoner to the sleigh. She heaved again and the dog increased his scrambling, his claws digging at the icy surface. Kendra heard the ice groan beneath her. For one awful moment she was sure it would break again and she and the dogs would slip into the chilly water. She held her breath as she hoisted at the sled dog again.

Natook managed to get his feet back under himself as Kendra slashed at the harness that tied the other dogs to the weight of the sled.

At last the final strap was severed. Kendra lay panting. She heard the sound of the dogs as they scraped and scurried their way to the shore, fright still echoing in their whines.

"Get out of there," George called sharply and Kendra opened her eyes and forced herself to move, inching backward slowly in her prostrate position. She did not dare to try to stand. She did not even dare to draw herself up on her knees.

Where was her team? Had they gone down?

When Kendra thought she had slid far enough away from the danger zone, she rolled over slowly and looked around her. Oscar had the team in check. He stood before them, his eyes alert, ears back. The rest of the team lay silently where she had left them. The ice around them was still intact, but Kendra did not trust it for a minute longer.

She continued to slide her way back from the widening hole until she could safely rise to her feet. Then she called to Oscar and ordered him to bring the team off the ice to the safety of the riverbank.

Once they were all ashore, Kendra sank to the snow-packed ground. She was breathing hard and trembling from head to foot.

"We could have lost them all," said George, his voice edged with strain.

Kendra thought of Shanoo. The dog had no chance against the strong current. She had been swept under the river ice and carried downstream. Kendra closed her eyes tightly. It was too awful to even think about. But, like her grandfather had said, they could have lost them all.

Then Kendra thought of the load of winter furs.

"Is there any chance at all—?" she began, but George was already shaking his head.

"We'd never get it out," he answered her.

Kendra buried her head against her raised knees. It was so unfair. So unfair. They had needed every pelt. They'd already had a bad winter. What would they ever do now?

She felt a hand on her head. "We'll make it," her grandfather soothed. But his voice was tight with worry. She wondered if he really believed his own words.

"We'll make it," he said again. His words held more confidence now, as though speaking them gave him some assurance. Kendra lifted her head and looked at the teams lying about them on the snow. At least they still had their dogs. All but poor Shanoo. And she still had Oscar. The ice had not broken under her weight while she fought at the edge of the hole to rescue the team. And, most important, her grandfather had not gone down. For that she was thankful. Perhaps they had a good deal to be thankful for after all.

Chapter Eighteen

Going Out

The summer was much kinder to them than the winter had been. Kendra planted a garden and tended it carefully. The vegetables kept their table supplied and produced additional food for canning and for their root cellar. Kendra spent day after day in the woods finding edible roots and berries. That, with the meat brought in from the hunt, kept them going over the summer and far into the fall. They got to the place where the flour and coffee ran out, but they managed to have food for their table.

Kendra did not even suggest that they pick up some supplies on credit as many of the other families in the area commonly did. She already knew her grandfather's feeling concerning spending money that one did not have. George believed in paying at the time of purchase and preferred to make do with less rather than run up a bill at the post.

It was almost Christmas when they took their first pelts of the season to the trading center and bought supplies they needed to get them through the rest of the winter. They both breathed a bit easier with the cabin's shelves stocked once again. It had been tough—but they had made it.

Kendra made a batch of fresh biscuits to go with their usual meat and vegetable supper, and they ate them all at one sitting. It had been so long since they had enjoyed the taste of any kind of bread.

———

The catch that year was a good one. Kendra began to hope she would be able to go out for school, after all. George brought the matter up every now and then to let the girl know he had not forgotten her plans.

"When do you want to go?" he asked one day as they worked together on next winter's supply of wood.

"I've been told classes start mid-September," replied Kendra. She did not have to ask her grandfather to what he was referring.

"And how much time will you need to be ready for classes?" he pressed further.

Kendra placed the wood length on the pile and straightened. She reached her hand up to brush wisps of blond hair back from her moist brow. "I don't know," she responded. "It's rather scary. I haven't been out for years."

George leaned his saw against a young sapling and dropped to the grass. It was hard work felling trees and sawing them into stove lengths. They could both use a rest. He patted the grassy ground beside him and Kendra took the few short steps to lower herself at his side.

"I've written to Maggie. She says you can stay with her for as long as you like," George said.

Kendra nodded. She was glad that Maggie Miller was in the city. She let her eyes drop to her worn and simple clothing. She certainly wouldn't be wearing these to the classroom. What would she wear? None of her clothes were suitable. Her wardrobe consisted of a strange combination of deerskin and simple cloth garments. Most of the materials for her skirts and blouses had been woven by the local Indians or purchased as yard goods at the trading post. In fact, she dressed just as the Indians in the settlement did. Practical clothing, made to endure and keep one warm.

Her eyes traveled farther—to the tips of her moccasined feet. Another change and one that she did not look forward to. She remembered when she had gone out for school before and how uncomfortable the stiff, awkward shoes felt. She would have to adjust to the shoes this time.

"I don't know," she said again as she stretched the ache from between her shoulders. She had some nagging doubts. Perhaps she shouldn't go out, after all. Her grandfather did need her to help with the work. It took both of them working hard just to survive.

"Would you rather I stayed here?" she asked him, her eyes still on her feet.

"Oh no," he assured her quickly. "I think you should go to school."

She didn't know if his words were encouraging or disappointing. Did she really want to go? Could she make it?

He seemed to sense her mood. "Of course, there will be some adjustments—at first," he commented. "But you're bright and quick—remember, I was your first teacher." They smiled at each other at those memories. "You'll adjust quickly," he went on. "And once you do—I think you'll really like it."

"You think so?"

"I'm sure you will. Just think of all of the new stuff you can learn."

Kendra longed to learn, but she still felt agitated.

"And you'll be all right?"

"Truth is," he said slowly, "I don't know how in the world I'm ever going to get along without you. Don't know how I ever got along without you before you came. I'm going to miss you—so much." He turned again to her. "But I want you to go—honest. I want you to learn about that big world out there. You won't want to live back here forever. It isn't fair. You need to know people. Other people. People your own age. You've never even had a playmate. Never even had a chance to play. I feel bad about it, Kendra. I—"

But she interrupted him. "There's no reason to feel bad. I couldn't have chosen a better way to live. Honest. I can't imagine living a life where you just—just sit around all day—being bored—and useless. I love it here. And I'll be back. I promise you that. I'll be back."

She leaned over and kissed his whiskered cheek.

———

They left in the middle of August. Kendra fretted and stewed as she checked the woodpile, the storage shed, the supply shelves. Would her grandfather really be able to handle things all alone? She would be gone for the whole winter. Maybe two or three winters before she returned to the cabin. Would he really be able to manage?

The trip out meant days of weary travel while Kendra silently wondered over and over if she was doing the right thing. George, silent as well, was sure his granddaughter was doing the right thing—the only thing—but he also knew that it was going to be awfully quiet and lonely when he returned home to the empty cabin.

When they finally reached the city, Maggie greeted them warmly. She had aged since Kendra had seen her last. George noticed it as well and knew that losing Henry had been terribly hard for Maggie.

Still, she was able to smile and chatter and inform them of all the new happenings in the city.

"We've got some lovely shops, dear," she told Kendra. "Whenever you wish to go shopping, I will be most happy to go with you."

Kendra was glad to hear that. She wasn't even sure what she should be shopping for. How did the young women who attended university dress? Did Maggie know? Would the sales ladies help her or were they just out to sell as many dollars of merchandise as they could? Kendra trembled every time she thought of her upcoming shopping trip.

George busied himself about Maggie's small home, fixing this and repairing that while Maggie and Kendra went out on shopping excursions. It wasn't quite as bad as Kendra had feared. The sales clerks were most helpful, though Kendra did feel that they would gladly have helped her spend every cent she had. She would not let them pressure her, and when she decided that the purchases for her wardrobe were sufficient, she gently but firmly said no to further suggestions.

The sewing of garments was the next step. Maggie was

a good seamstress, but because she was afraid she was not up on the latest styles, she took advantage of the help of a neighbor. Between the two of them, they presented Kendra with an adequate and attractive wardrobe.

Kendra spent days trying to adjust to the shoes. There were many times she wished to lean down, slip them from her aching feet, and retrieve her worn moccasins, but she did not allow herself the pleasure. She had to learn to wear them or be the laughingstock of the classroom.

Another adjustment came in changing her hairstyle. Kendra was used to wearing it in two long braids that hung down over her shoulders. If her task was such that she didn't want the braids dangling in her way, she simply wound them around her head and pinned them securely.

But braids would not do on the university campus, however. Kendra knew that. But she wasn't quite sure how her hair should be worn. Again the young neighbor came to her rescue. She set about trimming Kendra's long blond locks.

"You have lovely hair," she said over and over. "Such a beautiful color—and so shiny."

Kendra had never given it much thought. It was just—hair. Different from the Indian neighbors, but hair nonetheless. Now she looked at it a bit more closely. It was a nice color. She was pleased about that.

"Now," the neighbor woman went on to explain, "the younger women are wearing it a bit looser at the front—with soft waves. You have a real advantage there because yours is naturally wavy. You bring it back like this. Give it a twist, then wrap it like so. Then you bring this section over here, fold this back this way, bring this around, tuck this in, and put pins in like this."

It looked so complicated. Kendra was sure she would never be able to do it. She regretted that she wouldn't be able to just braid her hair the way she was used to.

————

George accompanied Kendra when she went to the school to enroll. She did not tell him, but it was the most frightening experience of her life. She wanted to cling to his hand, to plead with him to take her home again, but she did neither.

It was not a large school, but to Kendra the halls felt strange, the many unknown faces slightly threatening.

"There's nothing to be afraid of. Stop your trembling," she chided herself over and over. But her heart pounded, her stomach hurt, and her hands shook anyway.

She was quizzed about her knowledge. That made her tremble even more, but the results seemed to satisfy the officials, for soon she found herself being handed the papers that told her when and where she would be expected to show up for her classes. She was in.

———

She decided to accept the gracious invitation and stay with Maggie. At least she could save herself one additional adjustment—and perhaps a few dollars as well. Besides, Maggie expressed a genuine desire to have her company, and George seemed most anxious that she agree to the arrangement.

George stayed on until she was settled into her new surroundings and schedule. Kendra knew he would need to leave soon to prepare for the winter trapping season. He knew it as well, but he seemed to hate the thought of leaving.

Along with Kendra, Maggie hated to see him go. "I didn't realize how many little things needed fixing," she told him. "Henry—Henry wasn't able to care for such things his last years, and I didn't know how to go about them. Seems one broken or worn-out thing just leads to another. It is so nice to have everything in good order again."

"I was happy to do it," replied George. "Gave me something to do while you ladies were shoppin' and snippin'."

Kendra laughed. She knew he would have been terribly bored if Maggie hadn't found little chores for him around the house.

A full week of Kendra's classes had passed before George announced that he would be returning to Bent River Crossing. Kendra was adjusting well, though she occasionally had moments of intense nervousness. She still often trembled as she thought of how much "catching up" she had to do in some of the subjects. But she was willing to work hard.

She hadn't as yet made any new friendships, but she did have a few nodding acquaintances. In one class the teacher had singled her out for introduction to the entire class and asked her to share a bit about life in the wild. Kendra, blushing with embarrassment, had managed to give a brief report. It must have created interest, for after she was done a number of students had questions. She fared far better in giving direct and informative answers to the queries, and when she finally took her seat there was appreciative applause. Kendra felt that the students were friendly and open and that, given a bit of time, she would be able to make friends. She told her grandfather so and he seemed pleased.

"The belle of the classroom," he beamed. "I knew you would be."

"Oh, Papa Mac," said Kendra, hanging her head, her cheeks flushing, "it's not like that at all."

"Well, it will be. Just you wait and see. It won't take those teachers—or the other young people—long to see that you are a very special person."

Kendra smiled in spite of herself.

And then her glance fell on her hands. She had soon realized that hers were the only rough and calloused hands among the school's young women. Embarrassed, she wriggled uncomfortably on Maggie's sofa and ended up with her hands tucked under her new gray wool skirt.

Chapter Nineteen

Stirrings

"How are your classes going?"

Kendra frowned at Maggie's question. The classes, for the most part, seemed to be going just fine. Yet for some reason Kendra couldn't explain, she felt she was not enjoying them as she had anticipated.

"Perhaps it's just that I miss home and Papa Mac and Oscar so much," she told herself night after night when she was tempted to cry silently into her pillow. "I will get used to the noise and commotion of the city. It will just take a while."

But every day added to Kendra's discontent.

Now as she hesitated, Maggie read in her eyes her secret yearnings.

"You miss home." Maggie's simple statement was filled with understanding. "Some of these adjustments are hard and they take time," Maggie went on. "But it will come. You haven't had time to make friends yet."

Kendra wondered if time was the issue. Perhaps she just didn't fit in. She had been raised so differently. She thought differently, liked different things. Even dressed differently in spite of the fact that she had tried so hard to imitate the other girls.

"I don't know, Aunt Maggie," she finally answered with a deep sigh. "I—I just feel that—that something is missing. I don't quite fit. I'm like—like a hawk trying to swim. I just

164

don't understand some of the ideas. I—"

"But you will," said Maggie with complete confidence. "It takes time."

Kendra thought for a while. Perhaps her problem was that she really didn't *want* to be like the others. They all seemed so—so patterned. So programmed. If one said something was so, all the others agreed. Did she really want to be like that? She wasn't sure. Perhaps that was her problem. Maybe she just wasn't open to change.

"I don't know," she said hesitantly. "I think it might just be me."

"Nonsense," said Maggie, rising from her chair to bring the apple cobbler. "Don't rush yourself." As though still carrying on the same subject, she added, "I had a letter from your grandfather today."

Kendra lifted her head. She'd already had three letters from her grandfather in spite of the inadequate mail service. Two of them had arrived together. Every letter made Kendra so lonesome she wondered if they brought pleasure or added to her misery.

"How is he?" she asked quickly.

"Oh, he's fine. Just fine. He's missing you awfully though. Says that Oscar still sits and whines."

It was almost more than Kendra could bear. She clenched together the hands that lay in her lap and willed tears out of her eyes.

"He says they've already had some snow," Maggie continued, unaware of Kendra's struggle as she cut the cobbler. "Not too cold yet. Just a flurry. He doesn't think it will stay."

"No," Kendra murmured. "It likely won't stay. We get those storms that move through and it always gets nice again."

"Says Nonie's doing well," Maggie added. "He was over to take her some wood the day he wrote. He knew you'd be wondering about Nonie, so he said for me to be sure to tell you."

Kendra longed to see Nonie. The Indian woman had been like a grandmother to her in many ways. Kendra did not know what she would have done without Nonie in those early years.

"Nonie had a flying squirrel drop down her chimney and scatter fireplace ashes and soot all over the place. Luckily the fire had died out and the squirrel didn't suffer none from the fracas. But Nonie sure had a mess to clean up."

Kendra couldn't help but smile. It must have been quite a shock for the squirrel. She could picture the little creature being greeted with a loud shrieking, "Aiyee! Aiyee!" It must have been frightened half to death.

"Not much other news, I guess. He was just wondering how we are getting on."

Kendra accepted the dish of apple cobbler. Maggie was a good cook. Kendra was enjoying all sorts of new and delicious food. But tonight she didn't feel much like eating.

———

"Miss Marty. May I walk with you?"

Kendra looked up to find a tall young man standing beside her, books tucked under his arm just as she did. Kendra had noticed the young man before. He sat just behind her and to her left in English Literature class. Other students shifted from one seat to another, but this young gentleman, like Kendra herself, always got to class early and always chose the same seat.

Kendra nodded and resumed her steps. They didn't have much time between classes.

"May I introduce myself," he said as they walked. "I'm Carl Mandrake."

Kendra nodded, aware of that fact.

"So how are you enjoying the class?" he continued.

Kendra dipped her head slightly. She always loved literature. Yet if she were to be honest, she was not overly impressed with the professor, so she wasn't sure how to answer the question.

"Personally," he went right on, "I find old Prof Flanders absolutely"—He stopped and glanced around to make sure there was no one else within earshot—"boring," he finished conspiratorially.

Kendra couldn't help but smile. He had echoed her own feelings. She felt it a shameful waste for a professor to take an interesting subject and treat it with such lack of enthusiasm.

"Hear he teaches philosophy as well," the young man went on. "I'm avoiding that one if I can."

"Thanks for the tip," Kendra replied with another smile. "I think I'll try to do likewise."

They had almost reached their classroom.

"I was wondering," said the young man, suddenly sounding rather out of breath and in a hurry, "if you would like to join us on Friday night. We're having a party at Nancy's house. I've been invited and she said we might bring a guest."

Kendra stopped walking. She had never been invited out before—never been to a party. What would she wear? How should she act? Did she really wish to go?

"That would be very nice," she heard a voice answering and was surprised to discover that it was her own.

"Good," he said. "Write down your address and I'll get it after class. I'll pick you up at eight."

All through class Kendra's mind kept whirling. What had she done? She hardly knew the young man. She had no idea what sort of a fellow he was. She had even less of an idea of how the young entertained themselves at a party. She should not have said yes. Perhaps she should just write him a little note and tell him she had changed her mind. Several times during the class Kendra felt his eyes upon her. She dared not turn her head even slightly for fear their eyes would meet.

At the end of the class period she slipped him a note with Maggie's address. She wanted to avoid looking at him, but it didn't seem the polite thing to do. She glanced at him briefly and was rewarded with a warm smile. Kendra flushed and hurried off to another class. She would not see him again until the next day. In the meantime she hoped she would have a chance to chat with Nancy, a girl she knew slightly. She just had to learn a bit more about the coming party.

Normally Nancy was surrounded by a noisy, fun-loving group of her five or six special friends. But this time, Kendra noticed, she was sitting alone in the small cafeteria. Kendra breathed a sigh when she spotted her and concluded that the others must not have been dismissed from their final class yet. She took a deep breath, walked forward, and put her best smile in place. "May I join you for a minute?" she asked.

Nancy looked surprised, then nodded.

Kendra took the seat opposite the girl and sipped at her cool drink. Then she swallowed quickly and decided she had better talk fast. Nancy's crowd might soon be arriving.

"Carl has asked me to accompany him to your party on Friday night," she began, noting the surprised look that crossed Nancy's face.

"Good," she smiled, and Kendra hoped she truly meant the single word.

"I was wondering," continued Kendra before she had a chance to lose her nerve, "what we plan to do—so I'll know how to dress for it."

Relaxed again, Nancy smiled a second time and leaned forward.

"Oh, we won't do much. We mostly just hang around and talk and eat and maybe dance a bit to the gramophone. I have some great records. Papa got them the last time he traveled to Chicago."

Kendra nodded, her own smile still carefully in place.

"So you aren't dressing formal?" she asked. She had heard the word used and finally figured out what it meant in terms of present-day wear.

"No. No. Just come—comfortable. Whatever—" said the young woman with a flick of her wrist.

Kendra could hear a chattering group entering the room. She looked up to see Nancy's usual bevy of cohorts. Nancy stood and waved wildly. "Over here," she called across to them.

Kendra stood and smiled. "Thanks," she said.

"Oh, you don't have to leave," put in Nancy. "There's room for you to join us."

But Kendra gathered her armful of books.

"Thanks," she said again, "but I really have to go. I have loads of homework."

"Homework?" said Nancy with a shrug of her shoulder. "I really can't be bothered." She laughed.

———————

Kendra was so nervous as she dressed for Friday evening's outing that her hands trembled. She was ready much before eight and sat on Maggie's couch watching the clock and nervously fidgeting.

"I think it's so nice that you can go out with the young people," Maggie exclaimed for what Kendra judged must have been about the tenth time. "And you look so nice," enthused Maggie. Kendra again felt doubts that she may have picked the wrong outfit.

"What did you say this boy's name is?"

Kendra licked dry lips and swallowed. "Carl," she said. "Carl Mandrake."

"Mandrake. I don't believe I've heard that name in the city."

"No. No, I believe he is from out of town. Somewhere south, I think," replied Kendra. She had a vague recollection of a comment made in class, but she couldn't remember what it was. She had paid little attention at the time.

"Well, I do think it's so nice," said Maggie again as she reached for her scissors to clip a thread on her needlework.

"Your grandfather will be pleased as well," went on Maggie. "He has worried some that he kept you in the woods too long."

Kendra smiled. But it was a halfhearted one. She was too nervous to fully appreciate Maggie's comment.

"Well, I told him that I was sure you'd do fine. It just takes time, that's all. One can't come into a new situation and feel perfectly at home immediately. It takes time."

Kendra thought she heard steps on the wooden sidewalk. She rose swiftly to her feet and crossed to the window. There was no one in sight.

She sat back down and fiddled with the buttons on her shirtwaist front. Was the shirtwaist too plain? Too tailored for such an outing? She glanced at the clock. She did wish she had decided on the other one, but she wouldn't have time to change now. It was almost eight o'clock.

Kendra, beginning to hope that she had been forgotten, didn't hear a knock till twenty past eight. But when Maggie opened the door, Carl Mandrake stood on the step. He smiled congenially and introduced himself to Maggie. Kendra grabbed a light shawl and went to meet him. If Maggie got started talking, they would never get away, she reasoned.

Carl made no reference to the fact that he was late and no apologies for keeping her waiting. Kendra tried to shrug it off. Perhaps that was how young people generally made arrangements—with a great deal of flexibility.

It was fifteen blocks to Nancy's house, but it was a nice evening and Kendra enjoyed the chance to stretch her legs and breathe in the fresh evening air. She walked farther than that each day to get to classes. Maggie had fretted about the distance to the university, but Kendra felt it was a short stroll after being used to following the dog team for miles each day.

As they walked, Carl made light conversation. He was easy to listen to. His little puns made Kendra laugh. She began to feel that the evening might not be so bad after all. Perhaps she had done the right thing in agreeing to go out.

When they reached Nancy's house, there was a noisy crowd already gathered in the backyard. Carl led Kendra directly down the sidewalk, past the flower garden, and to a back patio. Kendra could tell that he was familiar with the place.

"Hi, Carl" greeted them over and over as they neared the group of revellers. "Hey, Carl." "How you doing?" "What took you so long?"

Kendra listened to the boisterous shouts. It seemed that

Carl was popular with the crowd. It made her feel rather good to be out with such an important young man.

But the feeling didn't last very long. Though a good deal of attention was showered on Carl, Kendra was rather ignored. She managed to find a spot to sit on a low bench almost in the shadows, and from her perch watched the party going on around her.

Kendra wasn't sure what she had expected, but certainly more than the chattering, bantering, teasing, and flirting that went on. Now and then a couple drew back into the shadows, more interested in each other than in the rest of the party guests.

There was lots of food. And drink. Much of it was alcoholic. Kendra had never seen people drink before. Her grandfather abhorred the use of alcohol. But the young people at the party did not share his perspective. Even some of the young women present shared the bottles passed around.

Now and then Carl seemed to remember her. He would look around, spot her on the bench she had not left all evening, and wave his hand at her merrily. Once he brought her some of the party food. It tasted strange to Kendra, and she was glad she had taken only a small portion. At least she wouldn't have to force down a lot of something she didn't like.

The hour got later and later. The air became chillier. The party grew noisier. Kendra suppressed yawn after yawn. She began to shiver. She was afraid the neighbors would soon be complaining. She longed to go home.

"Hey, Kendra. Join the party," someone called.

"Come on, Kendra," said Nancy, finally acting the hostess. "We are going in to dance."

There didn't seem to be anything else to do. Kendra followed.

The dancing was even noisier and livelier. Kendra wished she could cover her ears. She was used to quiet, to silence—except for the sliding of the sleigh runners over the crisp winter snow or the call of a loon in the cold evening air. Even the whole dog team baying at once wasn't as loud as this group.

"Want to dance?" The young man who spoke to her was a stranger to Kendra. She did not know him even from any of her classes.

Kendra shook her head. "I'll just watch," she replied and tried to smile. She had no idea how to take part in one of their dances. All she had ever seen were the dances connected with the Indian festivities at the settlement.

He shrugged and left to find another partner.

Carl was having fun with a young woman in a full navy skirt and a puffy-sleeved blouse. When she twirled, her skirts lifted, both surprising and embarrassing Kendra. But the young woman did not seem to mind. Round and round they whirled, laughing and breathless.

The party went on and on, and Kendra's desire to go home nearly overwhelmed her. But Carl was having such a good time she feared he would never wish to leave.

"You wanna dance?' he asked her breathlessly between pieces played on the gramophone.

Kendra shook her head.

"Can I get you a drink?" he asked solicitously.

Kendra shook her head again.

He nodded. It seemed to be fine with him if she wished to just sit. He looked around for another dance partner.

Kendra waited until the music started and the couples began to swing and sway; then she gathered her shawl about her shoulders, slipped quietly from the room, and started the long walk home.

Chapter Twenty

Amy

At first Kendra was angry—angry with Carl for asking her to the party and then nearly forgetting she was even there. Angry with Nancy for not making more effort to include her in the evening's activities. Angry with the other young guests who gave her a nod and then went about having a good time. But, mostly, angry with herself for not fitting in. They had already branded her as a girl "from the sticks." She had just proved to them that she was.

Tears threatened to form, but Kendra willed them away in the manner she had learned from her childhood. She would not cry.

"I just don't fit," she scolded herself. "I just don't fit. I'm as—as awkward and—and different as a—a crow with a flock of bluebirds."

Kendra was almost halfway home when a new thought came to her.

"I don't need to fit. I really don't. If I'm not comfortable with the 'in crowd,' I don't need to fit. Why was I trying to fit with them anyway? They aren't what I want to be. What I wish to become. They don't even take life seriously. They don't study. Half of them will never make it through the year. They party. They drink too much. They—" Kendra stopped. She need not go on with her accusations. She had no more right to judge them than they'd had to judge her.

"I don't fit!" she said to finish her tirade. "And that's that!

They have a right to be who and what they want to be, but I don't have to try to mold myself into their way of living. I can still be me."

Once she had worked it through, Kendra felt much better about the evening. Perhaps good had come of it after all. She now did not feel so pressured to be part of this strange new world. She could take it one day at a time, and pick and choose what she liked from it and feel perfectly free to reject what did not suit her. She was here to learn—to become a wiser and better person because of the experience. There was no reason for her to throw that away just to be one of the crowd.

"Besides," she reminded herself honestly, "there are lots of young men and women who are here to learn. Perhaps—in time—I will get to know some of them."

———

"Did you have a nice time?"

Maggie was still up, clad in a warm fuzzy robe and pretending to be reading.

Kendra managed a smile. The night was a bit chilly and she had only had her light shawl along. She felt cold in spite of her brisk walking pace. She shivered slightly.

"It—it was different," she managed.

Maggie laid aside her book, concern filling her eyes.

"Oh, it was all right," Kendra quickly added to ease the woman's fears.

"Would you like a cup of hot cocoa," asked Maggie, "or have you been eating all evening?"

"No. No," said Kendra. Some of them had been eating for a good part of the evening, but she had not. "I haven't eaten much at all, and a cup of cocoa sounds wonderful."

They went to the kitchen and Kendra was glad for its warmth. Maggie had kept the fire going in the big cookstove. The teakettle was still humming contentedly on the back of the range.

Kendra lowered herself into one of the wooden chairs, and

Maggie went to stir up two cups of cocoa.

For a few moments silence settled over them. Maggie broke it, seeming to search carefully for words. "That—that Carl—seems like a—a nice young man."

Kendra wanted to laugh. All the anger and frustration had totally left her. She had drawn back—distanced herself from the laughing, celebrating party-goers. It seemed strange now that she had even tried, or thought of trying, to be one of them.

And then quite suddenly, catching her unaware, she felt an unusual sadness. Carl *was* a nice young man. Sort of. He had been fun to talk with. He had asked her out. He had tried to look after the young girl half-hidden in the shadows, unable to come out and join the crowd. He had brought her something to eat. Had checked now and then.

She didn't feel angry with Carl now. Nor did she feel superior to him. But she did feel sorry—in a strange way. Carl was failing. In almost every class. It was not a well-kept secret. She was sure it was not because Carl needed to fail. He had a good mind and would do well if he chose to use it instead of spending his time partying. She felt sorry about Carl and wondered what the future held for him.

Maggie placed the steaming cup on the table in front of her.

"Yes," said Kendra as she stirred the frothy brew. "He *is* nice. It was good of him to invite me tonight." She lifted her eyes. "But, Maggie—I'll not be going to one of their parties again. I don't—don't have anything in common with them. I've decided to take my time and—and pick my own friends. It might take a while—but good friends are worth it—don't you think?"

Maggie nodded, then smiled slowly. Her eyes looked off into the distance seeing another time and other faces. "George and Polly McMannus were friends like that with Henry and me—for ever so long," she said, looking at Kendra. "They stuck through thick and thin—even when we didn't see one another that often. When one has friends like that—you don't really need many." She smiled at Kendra and wished such a blessing for her.

———————

"You're still lonesome too, aren't ya?"

George ruffled the fur of the big dog beside him and then patted the large, soft head. Oscar responded with a whine and a tongue licking at the hand.

"Thought we'd have got used to it by now," the man murmured. "But we haven't—have we? Cabin still feels just as empty. Sometimes I wonder if I'll ever be content to be alone again."

George continued to stroke the head. He had never allowed a dog in to share his cabin until Kendra had coaxed to have Oscar inside. Now it didn't seem right to make the dog go back outside with the others. Besides, George rather needed his company on the long, cold winter nights cooped up inside near the fire.

"What did I use to do with my time?" he went on. "I don't remember the time dragging like it seems to do now. How did I spend those long evenings? Reading? Working on the furs? Just loafing? I don't know. It seems like I now have more hours than I have jobs to fill them. I don't like the feeling, Oscar. Not at all."

George was not conscious that his left hand reached up to stroke agitatedly at his full beard.

From somewhere out in the night a lone wolf howled and the sled dogs set up a chorus in response.

Oscar pulled away from the man's hand, a deep rumble starting down in his chest.

"What's the matter? The wilderness calling? You wish to be out? Free?"

But no. George was sure that Oscar would not welcome freedom. He was restless. Lonely. That was all. Oscar did not wish to rush out into the night in answer to what he was feeling any more than George himself did.

The big dog returned from his pacing and pressed up against George's knee, still whining.

"She'll be back," George said as he reached out to stroke the silky fur. "She'll be back. Before we know it spring will come again and she'll be back."

But even as he spoke the words, George wondered. Would Kendra really want to return to her home in the wilds? Would she ever be content again to dress in buckskins and furs and mush a team of huskies? He half hoped that she would not. She deserved more than what life here could give her. He really didn't want this hard and lonely life for his little girl. But oh, how he would miss her—did miss her. The very thought of her not coming back brought a lump to his throat that he could not swallow away. He curled his fingers deeply into the fur of the large animal. He needed something to hang on to.

———

At Monday morning's English Literature class, Carl dropped into his usual desk, breathing hard from hurrying. His eyes, a bit hesitant, lifted to Kendra's. He looked a bit apologetic.

Kendra smiled. He responded quickly, easily, seeming to be relieved that she was not angry. "Hi," he said, shifting his books around on the desk top.

"Hi," she replied, then turned her attention back to the front of the room and the professor who had just entered.

Nothing more was said between them until the class ended. The teacher had called for assignments, and Kendra noticed that Carl had nothing to turn in. Another assignment missed. Kendra could not help but wonder how much longer Carl would be allowed to stay in the class.

As she gathered her books to leave, Carl fell in step beside her.

"So what did you think of poor Walter?" he asked, referring to the story they were studying in class.

Kendra laughed lightly. "I think he made his own problems," she answered.

"You don't think he was a victim of circumstance?"

"No more than you or I—or anyone, for that matter," responded Kendra.

"But look at the poor ol' chap," went on Carl in mock sympathy. "Married to that woman. Needing all that money. Having that poor job."

Kendra smiled. "He married the woman—he spent money he didn't have. He picked the job because it was undemanding."

Carl chuckled. "So you won't give the unlucky ol' boy a break?"

Kendra shook her head. "We all make our choices," she replied. "He made bad ones."

Carl sobered suddenly. They walked in silence. At length Carl spoke again.

"Do you think that's what the author is trying to say?" he asked seriously.

"No," replied Kendra after some thought. "I think the author was trying to picture Walter just as you have described him. A victim. But I don't agree. There are victims in the world, of course. Real victims. But they are the people who've never had choices to make. Not the ones who have made bad choices."

"Youch. You're tough," said Carl with a mock grimace, and they both chuckled.

Nothing was said about the Friday night before. No reference. No apology. No accusations. Kendra was happy to forget the whole event.

"See you on Wednesday," said Carl when they reached the end of the hall where Kendra turned one way and he the other.

Kendra nodded and smiled. She was glad that things could continue just as they had been.

———

On Tuesday Kendra hurried to tuck her books together and follow the class from the room. She did wish she didn't have classes back-to-back that were located from one end of the building to the other. She always reached her late-afternoon biology class breathless and flushed. She was feeling frustrated with the class anyway. What she had hoped would provide her with many answers was instead filling her mind with troubling thoughts and even more questions.

Just ahead of her, two students nearly collided, jostling to avoid each other, smiling in embarrassment and fighting to stay in control of their armloads of books.

"I'm sorry," Kendra heard the young man apologize, but it was obvious he was in a big hurry to get to his next class.

"My fault," replied the girl. "I was too deep in thought." She managed a smile. He gave her a smile in return and they both hurried on.

Kendra was about to push the little incident from her mind. It happened frequently in the narrow halls as students rushed back and forth to classes. But just as she neared the spot where it happened she noticed some sheets of paper on the floor. They must have fallen from the books of one or the other of the students. She stopped to scoop them up. They might be important. She stood and looked down the hall in the direction both students had gone, but they were no longer in sight. She did not have time to run after them nor did she have time to check the papers at present, so she slipped them into one of her own class books. She would try to sort it out later. She did hope that if they indeed were important, there would be a name on one of the sheets.

It wasn't until Kendra was doing her homework that evening that she remembered the sheets of paper. She pulled them from her text and scanned the page to look for a name. At the bottom of the one page was one word, written in smooth, elegant script, "Amy."

Amy? Was that the name of the girl? Was this a class assignment? Would she be looking frantically for the copy? Kendra had so little to go on. She didn't remember seeing the girl in any of her classes.

"It looks like poetry," mused Kendra. She began to read the lines.

Trees
So new-born
They still look
Sticky-wet.
They
Haven't
Even gathered
Any air—dust yet.

Kendra reread the little verse. She liked it. It was strange to her, this new form. But she liked the thought. She had seen trees like that. In the spring. With the new green leaves just unfolding, looking fresh and new—and yes—just a bit sticky as they uncurled from the firm wrapping of the bud.

Kendra turned to the next sheet.

Who put the stars in the evening sky?
Who gave the waters their azure blue?
Who set the rainbow up on high?
And sprinkled the grasses with morning dew?

Who hid the fawn with its dappled sides?
Who taught the salmon to swim the brooks?
Who buried gold in the heart of the earth?
Planted wood violets in shadowed nooks?

Who told the crocus that spring had come?
Brought the butterfly from the cocoon?
Who put the song in the robin's heart?
Governed the tides by the distant moon?

Kendra felt a strange stirring of her heart in response to the poem with its reference to the nature she loved and the questions it raised. She was so moved she could scarcely continue reading. This was what she wanted to know. This was what her heart cried out for. The answers. She needed the answer.

She let her eyes fall back to the page she held in a trembling hand.

Who put the "wonder" within my breast?
Set off the "joy bells" within my soul?

Kendra turned the page, but the back of the sheet was empty. Was there another sheet? There had to be. The poem had not given her the answer. There had to be more. There just had to.

But there was nothing more. Kendra turned the page again and slowly reread the poem. Line by line she pondered the thoughts. Here was a kindred spirit. Here was someone who thought as she thought. Wondered as she wondered. Had she—this Amy—found the answer to all the unasked questions? Oh, she must have. Kendra could sense a—a contentment—a peace in the writing. It was not written as by one who was still searching in frustration to find the answers. There had to be more to the poem.

Kendra looked again at the last two lines. Yes. There was more. The meter, as well as the content, called for it. There were at least two more lines to the poem. Perhaps they held the secret. Kendra scrambled through her textbook hoping to find another page of script. But there was none.

"Oh, I do hope she hasn't lost the last part," cried Kendra inwardly. "What if she dropped another sheet and I didn't see it? What if she dropped it farther on?" The very thought made Kendra feel panicky. Maybe she would never find the answers to her questions.

She had to find Amy. She had to. She focused mentally on remembering the girl she had seen briefly in the hall. She was of medium height, with dark hair and eyes, a nice, rather shy smile, glasses—yes, glasses. Not many of the students wore glasses. Perhaps she could find her by her glasses. She had to find her. Somehow.

Chapter Twenty-one

Encounter

For the next two weeks Kendra walked the halls scanning faces. She was so intent on trying to find Amy that she could hardly concentrate on her schoolwork. She even went to the office and asked if anyone had inquired about missing assignment copies.

"No," came the answer. "I suppose we could hold the sheets here in case anyone asks concerning them," he added, but Kendra was reluctant to give up the pages.

"I'll just keep looking for her," she replied hurriedly. "I'm bound to run into her again."

But Kendra was beginning to doubt her own words. Would she ever find the girl? Had the unknown Amy needed the pages to fulfill an assignment?

By the end of the third week, Kendra wondered if she must give up. It seemed that Amy was not to be found. Dejectedly Kendra loaded her arms with her homework for the weekend and started home. She would never find her now. She wondered if she would even remember what the girl looked like.

It was a cold day. The wind blew from the north and whipped at Kendra's heavy coat as though trying to tear it from her shoulders. Kendra braced herself against it and pulled her collar snugly up to her chin. It was on days like this that she wished she still had her fur parka.

"I wonder how Nonie is doing?" she asked herself. She

missed Nonie. Missed the smile and the friendly chatter.
Even missed her silence as she moved wordlessly about the
cabin. Nonie had been like a grandmother. A replacement
for the woman Kendra had never known.

Kendra's thoughts then turned to her grandfather. She
wondered often how his winter's trapping was going. He had
helped considerably with her university costs. Had he kept
enough money back to get himself through the long, hard
winter? Did he have ample supplies? Kendra did hope so, but
she had been reluctant to ask. She worried about her grandfather, and she felt some guilt for leaving him on his own
just so she could fulfil her selfish desire to learn at the university.

"I may as well have stayed at home," she said sadly. "I
really have not found answers anyway. Not to the real questions. It—it seems that the answers are—are as lost as I am."

Kendra fought against a sudden gust of wind that
whipped sharp ice crystals against her exposed cheek, making it sting.

"I think I'll just go home." She surprised even herself.
"Back to Papa Mac and Nonie and Oscar."

But as quickly as her heart began to beat with the excitement of the thought, Kendra dismissed it. She couldn't
quit in the middle of a term. That would be a waste. That
would not please her grandfather. He had not raised a quit-
ter. Kendra amended her statement. "I'll go home just as
soon as I finish my first year," she told herself and felt sorrow
and loneliness fill her being again. It seemed such a long
time to wait.

Had Kendra been one to give way to tears, she would have
let them fall now. She felt deep, inconsolable sorrow. She was
so lonely for the life she knew. So disheartened over what
she had failed to find. All she wanted was her own familiar
room with its Hudson Bay blankets, its kerosene lamp, its
crackling fire in the hearth, and Oscar lying on the bear rug
beside her moss and fir-bough-covered bed. All she wanted
was her shelf of books and the stirring of her grandfather in
the small room beyond her door.

But Kendra knew she must finish what she had started.

She was glad for Maggie Miller. The friend of her grandfather's had been most kind. Kendra was sure that, despite her strong resolve, she would never have been able to finish the year were it not for Mrs. Miller.

Another gust of wind caught her, almost wrenching the books from her arms. She clutched them closer and turned to ward off the chilly blast.

Just as she turned back she bumped into someone. Startled, Kendra caught herself and looked to see who it was. A young woman was returning her gaze, her eyes as wide open in surprise as Kendra's.

"I'm—I'm sorry," said the young woman quickly. "I—I'm afraid I wasn't watching."

"My fault," replied Kendra, but the wind seemed to snatch her words away.

"It's the wind," began the girl and she pushed back her heavy scarf. Kendra found herself looking at the girl from the university hallway. She had found her.

"Amy?" she said in unbelief.

The girl looked even more surprised. "Do I know you?" she asked simply.

"No. No," said Kendra, shaking her head. "But I've—been looking for you. For weeks."

Amy looked confused. "Why don't you come in," she offered, turning to indicate the small house in front of them.

"You live here?" asked Kendra. It was only a few blocks to Maggie's house.

"Yes," replied the girl and took Kendra's arm.

They hurried toward the house against the push of the wind.

Once inside, the door firmly closed behind them, they turned to face each other again. Amy pulled off her scarf, revealing her face. Yes, it truly was her. Kendra saw the same dark eyes, the same soft smile. Kendra took a deep breath and grinned.

"I thought I'd never find you," she admitted.

"Come in," said Amy, pointing to the sitting room. "Take

off your coat—and tell me why you've been looking for me."

Kendra quickly shrugged out of her coat and picked up her textbook with the folded pages that bore the two poems.

"You dropped this—in the hall one day. You ran into someone and I found these on the floor."

She handed the pages to the girl.

"Oh—these. I wondered where they went." Amy looked up and smiled. "Thanks—for returning them."

"I was afraid you'd need them for an assignment, and I'd get them back to you too late," continued Kendra.

"Oh—no. Just—just some of my—musings. I'm always—scribbling down thoughts here and there. I just—"

"Do you have the rest of it?" asked Kendra before she could check herself.

Amy looked down at the sheets she held. The short poem about the trees was on the top.

"Not that one. The other one," put in Kendra. "The one with—with all the questions."

Amy turned to the second sheet and let her eyes fall to the bottom lines.

"Did you finish it?" prompted Kendra.

"Oh—yes. Yes, I finished it."

"Would you—would you mind terribly if—if I saw the—ending?" asked Kendra. She wondered if she was being terribly rude. If it was right to ask someone to share something so personal. She flushed at her own boldness.

"That is—if you wouldn't mind," she finished lamely.

Amy's chocolate brown eyes met hers evenly. "It's not really very good," she apologized. "I just—just scribble things down to—to sort things out for myself."

"It's beautiful," enthused Kendra. "I could almost see it. Hear it. Just like—" She stopped.

"Sit down," invited Amy. "I'll see if I can find the last few lines."

Amy was gone for several minutes.

When she returned she was shaking her head. "I can't find it right now," she said. "I'm sorry. It must be with some of my other books."

Kendra stood, disappointment filling her whole being. She had been so close to an answer. Now she had nothing.

"Would you like a cup of tea?" Amy asked.

"Thank you—but I must be going. Aunt Maggie will be worried if I don't show up soon."

The girl nodded.

"Well, I'll keep looking for the lost sheet," she promised Kendra. "If you live nearby, then stop again and perhaps I will have found it."

"Oh yes, could I? You wouldn't mind? I don't want to be a—a pest."

"I wouldn't mind at all," Amy began and then quickly added, "You say that you do live nearby? And you go to the university? It's strange that we haven't met before. We must walk the same sidewalk every day."

She was smiling again and Kendra smiled in return.

"It seems strange that after searching and searching for you for three weeks that I would find you living almost in my own backyard," Kendra acknowledged.

"I stay here with my aunt and uncle," Amy said. "I'm really from out of town. A farm kid, actually. I'm hoping to be a teacher."

Kendra was pulling her heavy coat on again. She did hate to go, but she didn't wish to worry Mrs. Miller.

"What are you majoring in?" the girl asked.

"I—I haven't decided on—on anything yet. Just a general course. Though I admit I picked the subjects that interest me."

"Like?"

"Literature—and the sciences."

"Ugh," said Amy. "My most *un*favorites. I like math and history."

"I guess that explains why we haven't met before," said Kendra as she leaned to pick up her books.

"Well—we must remedy that," put in Amy. "Now that we are acquainted, we must make the most of it. I could use a friend."

Kendra did not trust herself to speak. The words spoke

to her very soul, and it responded with all the longing that was within her. But she could only nod her head.

She was about to leave when Amy spoke. "Wait. I don't even have your name—or where you live."

"It's Kendra. Kendra Marty," she replied. "And I live on Ninety-Sixth Street with Mrs. Maggie Miller—a friend of my grandfather's."

"What time do you go to class on Monday?" asked Amy.

"I—I walk past here about eight o'clock," replied Kendra.

"I have to leave by seven-thirty," continued Amy. "It's a shame we couldn't walk together."

"Oh, I can be here by seven-thirty," quickly promised Kendra. "No problem at all."

"Are you sure?"

"I'm sure."

Kendra turned back to the door. She really had to go.

"I'll see you on Monday then," said Amy. "Oh, but before you go, you must meet my Aunt Sophie. Just one minute," and she dashed through the adjoining door. Kendra heard voices but she couldn't make out the words. Soon the door pushed open again and a matronly woman made her appearance as she wiped her hands on her printed apron. Amy followed closely behind her.

"Aunt Sophie, this is Kendra. She goes to the university too. We just rather—rather bumped into each other."

The last words were said with a grin. Kendra smiled and reached to shake the hand that was extended.

"We are going to walk together on Monday," went on Amy. She sounded as excited as Kendra felt.

"It's nice to meet you, Kendra," said the older woman.

Kendra thought the lady had such beautiful warm eyes. She hated to turn from them.

"I must go," she apologized. "Mrs. Miller will be waiting."

"Do stop in anytime," the woman offered, and Kendra could feel the sincerity of her words.

"Thank you," she managed to mumble, then turned to go out into the cold.

She could scarcely slow down her anxious feet. She could

hardly wait to get home to tell Mrs. Miller. She had a strange, wonderful feeling that she had found a friend.

Over the weeks that followed, the two new friends exchanged many ideas between them. The girls walked to and from university with each other almost every morning. They visited back and forth, studying together, sharing hot cups of cocoa and freshly baked ginger cookies.

The deep, dark empty feeling that had been loneliness gradually began to leave the heart of Kendra. It was so much nicer when one had a friend.

"I've finally found it," said Amy breathlessly as she waved a sheet of paper under Kendra's nose. "I had almost given up."

Kendra's brow furrowed in perplexity.

"The rest of the poem," Amy reminded her and Kendra took a deep breath. She had almost forgotten the poem. She had been so relieved to have a friend that her quest for answers had been temporarily set aside.

"Oh!" she exclaimed now, almost squealing in her eagerness. "The poem."

"I brought the first page too," put in Amy. "Just in case you have forgotten how it starts."

Kendra accepted both sheets and began to read aloud.

Who put the stars in the evening sky?
Who gave the waters their azure blue?
Who set the rainbow up on high?
And sprinkled the grasses with morning dew?

Who hid the fawn with its dappled sides?
Who taught the salmon to swim the brooks?
Who buried gold in the heart of the earth?
Planted wood violets in shadowed nooks?"

Who told the crocus that spring had come?
Brought the butterfly from the cocoon?
Who put the song in the robin's heart?
Governed the tides by the distant moon?

Who put the "wonder" within my breast?
Set off the "joy bells" within my soul?
Who gave a reason to even exist?
Made earth a "mission" and heaven a "goal"?

Mere chance occurrence? Complete mystery?
Of course there's a reason, if only we prod.
Nature demands it—and so does my heart.
There's only one Answer. Only one God!

Kendra looked up from the page. She liked the poem. Something within her responded to it. But she didn't understand it. Not really. She felt a moment of deep disappointment. She still didn't have her answer. Even Nonie had told her this much.

Her eyes returned to the last few lines. She read them over again.

Mere chance occurrence? Complete mystery?
Of course there's a reason, if only we prod.
Nature demands it—and so does my heart.
There's only one Answer. Only one God!

Only one God! Did Amy really believe that?

"I—I really don't understand . . ." began Kendra hesitantly.

"I told you I'm not a very good poet," shrugged Amy. "I—I guess the poem was—just for me. To express how I feel about—about God creating everything. About—the—the purpose of life."

"But—" began Kendra. That was exactly what she didn't understand. Who was God? Her grandfather had told her that God existed only in the myths of the white people. The Indians called Him by another name—The Great Spirit or the Old One or some other rather mysterious title of honor.

"I like the poem," Kendra was quick to assure Amy. "I really do. But I— Do you really think—? I mean, do you really believe—about—about God?"

Amy's eyes widened. "You don't?" she asked, incredulous.

Kendra opened her mouth and then closed it again. Somewhere deep within her was a little voice that wished to say that she did believe. But how could she believe in One she had never known? She shrugged her shoulders and tried to smile.

"I really don't know much about Him," she informed the other girl, trying hard to make the words sound casual and of little importance.

Amy seemed to have recovered. "How about this?" she said. "Would you like to come to church with me on Sunday?"

"Church?"

Kendra had doubts about church. She had heard some very strange rumors about what went on there.

"Yes. I go with my aunt and uncle to a church near here. It's not big—but they really are nice people. I felt at home almost at once."

Kendra hesitated. "I don't know," she stalled. "I promised Mrs. Miller that I'd give her a hand with a quilt on Sunday."

"Maybe another Sunday then," replied Amy easily, seeming quite willing to make it another time.

There was something different about Amy. The more time they spent together, the more Kendra sensed the difference. Even though Amy was buoyant and outgoing, she was just so much more settled than others her age. So at peace with herself and her world. So confident that things were under control.

But whose control? Amy admitted to not being in charge of her own life, her own fate. She made frequent references to God. She talked just as though she herself knew this mystic being. Yet there was no fear in her voice when she spoke of Him as there had been when Nonie talked of one or another of the spirits.

Kendra was puzzled.

"How did you—learn—so much about—about this white man's spirit?" Kendra dared to ask one day.

"Who?" asked Amy, puzzled.

"This—this God," replied Kendra.

"God? Oh, He's not the white man's spirit. Or the white man's God. He's everyone's God—the Creator God. He doesn't belong to the white man any more than the—sun or moon belongs to the white man."

"But—?"

"He created all men. All things."

It sounded like more myths.

"But how do you know this?" asked Kendra.

"It's all in the Bible—the whole story," replied Amy, not one bit put off by Kendra's asking.

"The Bible?"

"You don't have a Bible? I'll lend you one. You can read it for yourself."

———

Kendra did read it for herself. Over the weeks that followed she spent every minute she could spare reading the account for herself. Deep within her she felt she had finally found the answers to her questions. It was not a myth. It was *truth*. There really was a God in heaven—just as she had wondered, had suspected all along. He really *did* create the universe. All the things that Amy's poem had referred to and so much more. Kendra was glad to discover such a God—but she was just a bit afraid of Him, too.

———

"I think I'd like to go to church with you on Sunday," Kendra surprised Amy by saying. They had been doing homework together on a Saturday afternoon. Kendra thought she might as well say the words before Amy asked her again. Amy always seemed to offer another invitation each Saturday.

Amy's eyes lit up. Kendra knew that she was pleased that her standing invitation had finally been accepted.

———

As Sunday followed Sunday, Kendra began to put all the pieces together. There was a God. Not a mystic, unknown someone, out there somewhere. A real Person, a revealed and understandable God. He created people, who sinned. This caused a chasm between human beings and their Creator. They hid from God and at the same time turned their backs on Him and wished to be left on their own.

But God loved the creation of His mind, His hands. He knew that the people He had created were lost—blinded— and left to the devices of the Evil One. He had a plan whereby mankind could once again be restored to a place of fellowship. Sin had to be dealt with, had to be justified. Kendra supposed that it must have been the hardest part of the plan for a holy God to carry through. It meant sending His Son, His only Son, to take the penalty of death for people—the sinners.

No one had to tell Kendra about the reality of sin. Deep within her own heart was a feeling of guilt. She wasn't sure she could have listed the things that made her guilty—but she knew that her heart was not right in the eyes of her Creator. The knowledge troubled her, but she wasn't sure what to do about it. She knew one thing. She could not stop attending the services. She hungered for the truths that were taught. Nor could she quit reading the borrowed Bible. She was sure that it was the only place where the true answers might be found.

———

"I know you are well familiar with the text of the morning," said the pastor, "but I feel we should return to it often so that we might never lose the wonder—the marvel—of what it says to us. That an Almighty, Eternal, Holy, and Just God would love us—me—and you—so much as to send His only Son to Calvary to bear the penalty for our sins and grant to us, through the name of Jesus Christ our Savior, forgiveness of our sins and life everlasting. Turn with me to the third chapter of the gospel of John."

Kendra did not stir. She held the open Bible in her hands silently as others about her rustled with the pages of their Books. Something had clicked in her mind with the words of the speaker. That was it. That was it! God loved her. God had sent His son—for her. Kendra Marty—that she might have her sin forgiven and be granted everlasting life.

A sob arose in her throat. Her head dropped and before she hardly knew what was happening she was saying, "God, please forgive me—please help me—" The prayer quickly turned to one of thanksgiving. "Thank you—oh, thank you, Father," her heart cried. "Thank you, Lord Jesus."

A peace, a warmth began to steal over her soul, washing away doubts, confusion, and frustration. It was true. It was true. She knew it as surely as she knew anything. It was not a myth. There was a God. He loved her. He sent His Son to take her penalty of death. She was free. Free and forgiven.

The tears rolled down her cheeks as she turned the pages of her Bible to locate the morning text. The preacher was beginning his sermon. But Kendra was already marveling over the truth of the message.

Chapter Twenty-two

A Meeting

"You look all bubbly this morning," Kendra remarked to Amy as the two fell into step for their walk to morning class.

"I am. I'm going home for the Easter break. I can hardly wait. I haven't been home since Christmas and it seems an awfully long time."

Kendra's eyes shadowed. She hadn't been home for what seemed like ever so long. Now that she had answers—the real answers to life—she longed to get back to her grandfather so she might share her good news. She had written him a long, long letter, but it had been so hard to try to express all that she felt, all she was discovering, on paper.

And she wished to see Nonie again. To tell the dear Indian woman that she now knew just who the Great Spirit was that Nonie spoke of. The woman was so close—yet so far from the truth. There weren't lots and lots of gods dwelling in the hills, the trees, the sun, the moon. There was only one God—who made all things. And human beings were not fashioned by Mother Earth who took from herself to bring people forth. Humankind was designed by the Creator who breathed into the new creation the breath of life, making each one the only created being with a living soul.

Kendra could hardly wait to explain it all to the woman who had been her guardian, her mother, her grandmother— all in one.

Kendra turned her attention back to Amy, happy for her upcoming visit.

"They are picking me up tomorrow night," Amy went on excitedly. "And Mama suggested that I bring you along. Oh, can you, Kendra? I would so love to have you."

Kendra stopped walking. Was she hearing right? Was Amy really asking her to share her wonderful long Easter week at her farm home?

"Can you?" prompted Amy again.

"I don't know," replied Kendra. "I'll have to talk with Aunt Maggie."

"Oh, I hope you can. I would love to have you meet Mama and Papa and Reynard and Thomas and Carry and Nell. I would—"

But Kendra had grabbed her hand to stop her. If Mrs. Miller didn't agree, it would be difficult enough to endure without making lots of plans that would never happen.

"I'll ask," promised Kendra, her whole being filled with excitement. She had heard Amy speak of her family many times and always thought how wonderful it would be to have brothers and sisters. A real family.

All during the classes of the day, Kendra kept thinking about the possibility of going home with Amy. Would Mrs. Miller think it was okay or would she hesitate to take responsibility for the decision? Kendra prayed, as she had learned to do, many times throughout the morning and afternoon. She finally came to the place where she could honestly leave her deep desires in the hands of her newfound God.

"As you will," she whispered and felt a measure of peace. Whatever God worked for her would be for her best good.

"Do you want me to come with you to ask Mrs. Miller?" asked Amy on their return home. "I will—and explain everything—if you wish."

Kendra shook her head. It was in God's hands. "Aunt Maggie is not unreasonable," she hastened to say. "If she feels that she isn't stepping out of line by giving permission, she'll let me go. I know she will. After all, I'm not a child."

Amy nodded. "Oh, I do so hope you can come," she said.
"I do hate to leave you here all alone—and Easter week, too."

———————

Mrs. Miller did not even hesitate to grant her permission,
even though she had a few reservations about the new "faith"
that Kendra often spoke about. Mrs. Miller had never been
a religious person and she knew that George McMannus was
not in any way religious either. What would George think of
Kendra's embracing of a faith?

Mrs. Miller had written a letter to George. Hers too was
a long letter, trying her best to describe what had happened
to Kendra. But Mrs. Miller really didn't understand what it
was.

"She has not gone 'off,' " her letter stated. "She was lonely
before and seemed a bit disturbed. Now she is more settled
and seems to enjoy the little church where she goes. I think
that having Amy Preston for her friend has been good for
her. There doesn't seem to be anything to worry about. I will
keep my eyes and ears open and let you know if anything
happens that doesn't seem right."

George had written back to Maggie through the first
available post.

"When Kendra went off to university," he wrote, "I fully
expected that it would change her thinking on many things.
Though, I admit, I didn't expect this. But she is a bright girl.
She has her own life to live. She must make up her own mind
on such things. I will not try to sway her or change her
thinking. I do hope that she continues to hold steady. I
wouldn't want her becoming fanatical or mystical about this
new religion she has taken on."

Kendra knew nothing of the exchange of letters. She had
told her grandfather about her experience in her own way.
His reply to her had been carefully penned.

"I am glad that you have discovered an answer that suits
you," he had written. "We all have the right to find an inner
peace in our own way."

Then he had gone on to speak of the sled dogs, the winter's catch, and the cold weather. Kendra knew that she hadn't been able to make him understand.

Now as Kendra excitedly packed a small valise for her trip home with Amy, she thought again of her grandfather. Oh, if she could only go home. If she could only sit and have a long chat with him. She was sure that he would be as excited as she was about discovering the Truth.

––––––––

Arrangements were made to travel with another student who was going to Amy's home community. It was a long drive by team. They had to make one stopover on the way. Amy and Kendra shared a small room over the kitchen of a farmer who took overnight paying guests.

"This works perfectly for me," said Amy. "It's a place to stop for the night and we'll be home by noon tomorrow."

Kendra was so excited, she could hardly sleep. Tomorrow she would discover for herself what a real family was. There had only been herself and her grandfather for as long as she could remember. She had a few scattered mental images of a laughing mother and a teasing father, but not enough for her to put together any kind of picture of a home life.

The two girls had a simple, early breakfast the next morning and started out again with their travel companion at the reins. The morning was bright, but the day still held the chill of early spring. Kendra was glad for the heavy coat that kept the brisk breeze from freezing her bones.

"We are almost there. Just over that next hill!" Amy exclaimed. "I can hardly wait."

Kendra felt the tingle go through her body.

––––––––

"I wish Reynard would hurry. I'm starved," said fourteen-year-old Thomas.

Amy laughed. "You're always starved," she teased him.

Kendra looked again at the young boy. He was tall and lanky, almost red-headed, but his eyes were much like Amy's. Carry, who was coming from the kitchen with a platter of fried chicken, looked much more like her mother, slight and much fairer, with a sprinkling of freckles across her upturned nose, and eyes more the color of blue cornflowers. Nell, the baby of the family at age eight, was brown-haired, her hair done in two long plaits much as Kendra had worn her own blond hair for many years. Except Nell's darker braids were enhanced by two large green velvet bows.

"You know that Reynard will be here just as soon as he can," said Mrs. Preston, entering the room with a bowl of vegetables in each hand.

Kendra had been informed that Reynard worked in the nearby town and rode horseback to and from his job each day. And that was all she knew. She was so busy studying the other members of the family that she had given very little thought to the one still missing.

Mr. Preston entered the room, his face shining from a recent wash at the kitchen basin. He was a big man, dark like his oldest daughter. His coloring was ruddy from working outside, and his hands reminded Kendra of her grandfather's. His face lighted easily into a teasing grin. He flashed one at Kendra now.

"Have you ever seen such an impatient brood?" he asked her. "Sort of reminds one of a nest of young magpies. Every one wants to be fed right now. I'm sure your family is much more civilized."

Kendra smiled. "I was the one and only," she admitted. "And for some time I've been the one *getting* the meal. Grandfather was most patient in waiting for it."

Then Kendra looked back at the table groaning with its burden of delicious-smelling dishes. "But I never fixed anything like this," she added. "Our meals were very simple."

They heard the kitchen door open and close again.

"Finally," breathed Thomas with a mock groan. "He's finally here."

Kendra could hear steps in the kitchen. Reynard had

stopped to wash at the corner basin.

"Let's be seated," said Mr. Preston, and the family moved in to claim the chairs around the table. One chair remained—directly across from Kendra.

She sat silently, her hands in her lap, her eyes on the vacant chair. Steps sounded behind her, and she sensed more than saw someone stop briefly and lean over to place a kiss on top of Mrs. Preston's head.

"Good evening, Mama," a low voice said.

"Reynard, I'd like you to meet Amy's guest from the university. This is Miss Marty. Kendra Marty."

Kendra turned slightly. She wasn't sure if she should stand or stay seated. She was about to rise, a smile tilting her lips, when her eyes met the eyes of Reynard.

She had expected a boy. She really didn't know why. All the Preston children had been just that—children. Kendra had thought Amy was the family's eldest. Now as she lifted her eyes she discovered, to her discomfort, that she was looking into the eyes of a young man. Dark, warm eyes, in a sensitive and pleasant face. Amy's eyes. But the resemblance stopped there. Reynard was fairer than his sister, slim of frame, and thoughtful in demeanor. Amy was rather sturdy like her father, full of enthusiasm for life.

Kendra did not rise after all. She sucked in her breath, lowered her gaze, and sank back into her chair. She had been so totally unprepared.

"Good evening, Miss Marty. I'm pleased to meet you," the same even voice was saying. There was warmth in his voice as well. Kendra looked up just long enough to see a hand extended toward her. She accepted it and was given a brief but sincere handshake.

"Let's eat," spoke up Thomas. Reynard chuckled and moved to take his seat.

All through the evening meal Kendra felt nervous and fidgety. She was afraid to lift her eyes for fear he might be looking her way. Yet she felt compelled to steal little glances at the man opposite her at the table. Why hadn't Amy warned her? She would have been much better prepared had she known that this brother was *not* one of the children.

But Kendra chided herself. What difference would it have made? And what could Amy have said? "I've got this older brother who is all grown up—and terribly good-looking?" No. Most certainly not. Besides, Kendra doubted that Amy even thought of her brother in that fashion.

"Stop it," she told herself. "You have rubbed shoulders with many young men in your classes, in the halls, in the cafeteria. You've even had an evening out with one of them. You've never acted like this before. Stop it."

And Kendra willed her wildly beating heart to slow its mad pace and allow her to enjoy the fellowship of the family supper table.

———

After the dishes had been washed and returned to the cupboard shelves, Amy took her seat at the piano in the family living room and invited Kendra to join her. They sang many of the songs from church. By now they were familiar to Kendra. She enjoyed singing and could join in wholeheartedly. One by one other family members joined them. Only Thomas, whose voice was changing, held back from the song fest.

Never had Kendra felt such joy. So this was what it was like to be a part of a big family. She had missed so much. She couldn't help but envy Amy.

After the singing they sat around the kitchen and drank hot cocoa and ate sugar cookies. The laughter and chatter rang through the room, and Kendra was reluctant to leave it, even though her eyes would hardly stay open.

"We need to get you two to bed," said Mr. Preston. "You'll never make it up for church in the morning."

Kendra smiled. She was tired. But she hated to break the spell of the evening.

"We'd better go," said Amy with a yawn. "We have lots more nights to be together. I guess we don't have to stay up all night on our first one."

Reluctantly Kendra rose to follow her friend. With a few changes in the family's usual sleeping arrangements, the girls would be sharing Amy's old bedroom. Kendra prepared to say good-night. Her eyes quickly traveled around the room to each family member. But when she got to Reynard, she found him looking at her. Her cheeks colored faintly, her words got all tripped up in her thinking, and she turned to follow Amy from the room.

Chapter Twenty-three

Back to the Wilderness

Kendra was deeply stirred by the Easter service. It was her first Easter as a new Christian, and as the pastor told the story of the Crucifixion and what it cost the Father to send the Son—and the Son to be obedient to His Father—tears filled her eyes. Wiping them away on her handkerchief, she never had felt such love.

On the ride back to the farm, Amy started singing and soon the others had joined in. Even Thomas dared to join them in spite of his voice cracking embarrassingly every now and then.

It was a glorious experience for Kendra. Already she felt a part of this wonderful family who had taken her in so quickly and completely.

The dinner was a simple but delicious meal. Kendra, used to a stew or Indian-style bannock, thought it a feast. She enjoyed every part of it right down to the apple pie.

After the dishes had been washed and put away, they played a family game together. Kendra had never played a game before and had to be taught the rules. She caught on quickly and soon proved to be a very competitive player.

When the menfolk prepared for evening chores, Kendra begged to go with them. She was anxious to see the farm and how it operated. She drew on a borrowed chore coat and set off with young Thomas, whose duty was to slop the pigs and feed the chickens.

"I'll gather the eggs," volunteered Kendra and began to move the day's "rent" from the boxed nests to her basket.

Kendra didn't care much for the pigs. They smelled awful to her sensitive nose and they pushed and shoved to get at the food in the trough, nearly knocking her off her feet.

"Now I know why it's an insult to call someone a hog," Kendra quipped as she removed herself to a safe distance and brushed at the dust on her coat.

They visited the barn where Reynard was milking a Jersey cow and laughed as he fed a barn cat with a long stream of frothy milk directly from the cow. Then they moved on to the horses, and Kendra patted each one in turn and fed them handfuls of hay. Mr. Preston was working with the horses. Kendra was especially taken with a big bay with a bold slash of white down the front of his face.

"That's Duke," said Thomas. "He's Reynard's horse. He rides him to work every day."

"Where does he work?" asked Kendra casually.

"In Stewart."

"Doing what?"

"He's a banker."

Kendra had expected a farm boy to be working at something quite different than banking. In fact, she didn't know much about banking at all. She and her grandfather had never had need of a bank. They bartered for their furs, trading them for needed supplies and accepting cash for the difference or leaving the funds for credit at the small post.

Kendra nodded and tucked the information away. Secretly she wished that Reynard was in some other occupation. A schoolteacher or keeper of books or even a clerk in a store. She had heard things about hard-hearted bankers who used their position to further their own ends.

But Kendra said nothing more, just continued to stroke the big bay and offer him handfuls of hay that he could easily have reached on his own.

When they returned to the house, Kendra spent a good deal of time at the kitchen basin. Even so, she couldn't wash all the smell of the barns away. It clung to her clothes and her hair, and she was embarrassed as she joined the family at the supper table.

No one seemed to notice. At least no one made comment. Kendra was glad for that and hoped her trip to the barn was not advertised by her very presence.

———

The week went too quickly. Kendra put every thought of returning to the city out of her mind. How could Amy stand to be away from her family? Kendra wondered. Why, if she herself had a family like that, she would never leave home. Then Kendra thought of her grandfather. He was just as dear. She loved him just as much—yet she had left. Left him alone to run the trapline when she knew he needed her help. Guilt clutched at Kendra. Again she resolved that just as soon as the term was over, she would return to her grandfather. And she would not leave him alone again.

———

"Would you like to go for a walk?"

Kendra was just wiping the last of the supper plates that Amy had washed in the large dishpan. She placed the dish on the stack in the cupboard and turned slowly. Reynard stood before her, her shawl in his hands, and a teasing smile playing about his lips.

Kendra managed a smile of her own.

"Does she really have any choice?" quipped Amy, looking on.

"Of course she does," replied Reynard good-naturedly. "I know where to hang this up again."

But Kendra wiped her hands on the flowered apron, hung the dish towel on its bar, and turned so Reynard could drape the shawl over her shoulders.

"It looks like a nice evening for a walk," she replied.

"That's exactly what I thought," said Reynard and winked at his sister.

They followed the worn path through the barnyard, down the lane, and beside the small stream. Kendra had never ventured very far from the farm buildings before and enjoyed the walk. She was not used to leisurely strolls after running behind the dog team or walking at a fast pace to and from her classes.

But this walk was totally unhurried.

"Thomas says you work in a bank," Kendra dared to comment. "What do bankers do?"

If he was surprised at her question, he did not show it. "Mostly books," he answered. "I started as a teller in the tell and—"

"The tell?" puzzled Kendra.

Reynard laughed. "Have you ever been in a bank?" he teased.

Kendra smiled and shook her head. She had to admit that she had never been in a bank.

"But I've heard stories about bankers," she added, her bantering tone not entirely covering her concern.

"Like—foreclosing mortgages and driving out widows and forcing beautiful young girls to marry them or be sent out penniless?"

Kendra had to laugh.

"I've heard those stories too," said Reynard.

"Are they true?" asked Kendra, still a hint of teasing in her voice but seriousness as well.

Reynard shook his head. "Would I still be single if they were?" he asked in mock innocence.

It was Kendra's turn to smile.

"What do you do?" she asked after a pause. "Seriously."

"Seriously? I'm pretty good at being serious. At least that's what Amy is always telling me. 'Oh, don't be so serious.' She says it often. Well, maybe I am serious—but there's always so much to think about—to ponder. Do you mind serious men?"

Kendra faltered. "Well—I—I don't know. I mean—I—I've never given it any thought. I—to tell you the truth, I've never thought too much about—about men at all."

"I like that," Reynard affirmed. "I've noticed that many girls your age seem to be thinking about men—or boys—all the time."

"But Amy doesn't—"

"Amy is too scattery to be thinking about any one thing for more than a minute at a time," laughed Reynard. Then with deep sincerity, "And I love her—just as she is."

Kendra nodded mutely.

"Now Carry. Carry is quite different. Already Carry does a good deal of thinking about boys." Again Reynard chuckled.

They walked in silence for a few more steps; then Reynard said, "But you asked about banking. Banking, for me, is mostly numbers. Good numbers. Bad numbers. People who have money in the bank and people who owe money to the bank. We are there to lend money if it is needed, but the big man at the top, whoever he is, he likes to be paid back. So far we have no bad debts. Oh, some people have struggled and had to have an extension on a loan. But we haven't had to foreclose on anyone or drive widows from their houses." He smiled again.

"And a teller?" prompted Kendra.

"A teller is at the cash drawer. Taking in deposits for accounts and cashing notes for customers," he explained.

"Oh," said Kendra. It really didn't sound complicated. "But you don't do that anymore?"

"Not anymore." Reynard stopped to pick up a flat stone and skip it across the small pond formed by a beaver dam in the stream.

"Ever watched beavers work?" he asked her.

"Yes," said Kendra softly.

"Kind of neat little fellows," Reynard remarked.

Kendra nodded. She did not say that she had not only watched them work, she had worked over them, skinning them out, stretching and tacking their hides on the forms, taking their pelts to the trading post. The thoughts racing through her mind made her shiver. Perhaps Reynard wouldn't think much of her occupation either.

"Are you cold?" asked Reynard and slipped out of his jacket and draped it over her shoulders before she could even answer.

They walked on together. It was easy to chat with Reynard. Kendra felt that she had gotten to know him quite well over the week she had spent at the Prestons. Although he was gone for work during the day, he seemed to slip so easily into the family circle at night when he returned. He always stopped to wash in fresh water at the family basin, then proceeded to the table where the family was usually waiting for him. Always he stopped on the way to his chair to bend over and press a kiss on his mother's brow or cheek or hair with an easy, "Good evening, Mama."

Kendra often wondered about this little ritual, but it seemed so sincere, so simple, that she couldn't question it. If she had a mother, she would want to do the very same thing.

"Are you enjoying university?" Reynard's question brought Kendra's attention back to the present.

"I—I guess so," began Kendra. Then she went on. "It hasn't been what I had expected—to be truthful. In fact, the answers that I was really looking for—about nature, creation, my inner longings, God—I wouldn't have even found them if I hadn't met Amy. University really doesn't give you the answers for all of that. There is so—so much taught about *things*. Knowledge. All for the head. Nothing for the heart."

Reynard nodded in understanding.

"But it's good—if one wants to be something—like a teacher—or a doctor—or . . ."

Kendra finished lamely, giving her shoulder a slight shrug.

"And you don't plan to be any of those things?"

"No. No, I just came because I wanted to learn. I'd never been to school—except for a few horrible months. Papa Mac—Grandfather—taught me, and then when I was old enough I studied on my own. And I had all of these—these unanswered questions. Nonie—the Indian woman who took care of me—tried to answer some of them with her Indian tales. I—I think I could have believed her, but Papa Mac said they were only myths. Totally untrue."

Kendra stopped. She still felt a sadness deep down inside. Sadness for all people who did not know or believe the truth.

"Nonie's close," she went on. "She really is. She just doesn't know who God really is—or that there's only one God—who made and controls everything."

Reynard nodded again. "You care deeply for Nonie, don't you?"

Kendra drew a breath. It was hard to put into words. She stood there, gazing out over the rippling pond water. Her thoughts traveled back to a very young, terrified child being held in comforting arms, breathing in the smell of woodsmoke from the bosom that cradled her. She thought of carefree days tramping through the woods, gathering herbs and roots and berries and learning how to use them.

She remembered an older Nonie, spending most of her time in her caned chair in front of her fire. But always, always when Kendra opened her door and called a greeting, the tired eyes lit up and a smile carved itself on the wrinkled face.

"Yes," she answered with a great deal of feeling. "Yes— I love Nonie. She—and Papa Mac have been all the family I've known."

"Do you—do you ever feel cheated—about the way you were raised?" asked Reynard.

Kendra turned to face him fully. The last light of twilight mixed with the first soft rays of the rising moon to caress cheeks and hair with a soft halo. Her green eyes deepened, sparkling with the intensity of her feelings. "Oh no," she said with sincere fervor. "I feel singularly blessed."

———

"Reynard is coming to the city."

Amy greeted Kendra with the news as soon as they joined together for their walk to class.

Kendra's eyes lifted. She couldn't explain the sudden little flutter she felt inside.

"What for?" She managed the simple question without her voice giving her away.

"He's on some bank business—a training session or something."

"When?" asked Kendra, her eyes focused on where she placed each step.

"He comes next Monday and stays until Friday," replied Amy. "Aunt Sophie is afraid he'll be terribly bored in the evenings with no farm chores to do, but I assured her that he'll likely be able to think of something."

Kendra looked at her friend. Amy was about to burst into a giggle. Kendra felt her face flush. Surely Amy wasn't implying that Reynard would be interested in spending some time with her. But she knew by Amy's face that she was indeed making such an inference. Kendra's flush deepened.

———

At the rap on the door, Kendra shifted in her seat at the book-strewn table. Mrs. Miller rose to answer the summons, casting a curious look Kendra's way. They did not often have visitors.

"Good evening," Kendra heard a deep, even voice say. "Is Miss Marty in, please?"

"And who shall I say is calling?" Mrs. Miller was asking, but Kendra was already crossing toward the door.

"Reynard?" she said.

"You weren't expecting me?"

"Well, I—I—"

"I should have written, but I didn't have your address. I wrote Amy. She was supposed to tell you."

"Well—she did—I mean she said you were coming to the city. She said . . ." Kendra faltered to a stop and held the door open.

"I do hope I'm not imposing—"

"Oh no. No, not at all. Come in. This is—I'd like you to meet Mrs. Miller. Mrs. Miller, Amy's brother Reynard. Reynard Preston."

Mrs. Miller smiled warmly and chatted easily for a few minutes, then turned and went back to the kitchen, leaving the two in the living room.

"I see you are studying," said Reynard, motioning toward the books on the table. "I'm afraid—"

"Oh no," quickly replied Kendra. "I've finished what needs to be done. I always work ahead."

"I thought—I wondered if you might like to go for a cup of coffee in that little shop up by Aunt Sophie's?"

Kendra smiled. She had never been in the little coffee shop and had always secretly longed to join the university crowd who sometimes gathered there, just to see what it was like.

"I'll get my shawl," she said with no hesitation.

———

They managed to spend much of the evening together each night of the week Reynard was in town. Kendra cautioned her heart over and over not to become involved, but she wasn't sure that it was paying much attention to her words.

On the last night before Reynard was to go home, they walked the river trail together. When they came to a bench, Reynard brushed it off and offered Kendra a seat.

"I've been hoping you'll be able to come out to the farm with Amy again. Guess it's getting too close to the end of the term now, but you could come as soon as classes are over."

He reached down and took her hand and Kendra did not resist.

"I'd—I'd like to," she managed, her voice little more than a whisper.

"Maybe we could even find a job for you—in town. The—"

"In town? A job?"

"Just for the summer. I know that when classes start again you'll—"

"I'm not coming back," said Kendra softly.

He looked surprised. Then his eyes began to shine.

"Well—if you're planning to get a job here," he said, "it might better be there. Then you'll be near—all the time."

Kendra lowered her gaze. "I'm not—not planning on a job—here either," she said.

He reached out and lifted her chin so he could look directly into her eyes. "What are you planning?" he asked seriously.

"I'm—I'm going back. Home. To my grandfather. He—he needs me. I never should have left him in the first place."

Kendra tried to pull away from the hand that held her prisoner so that she could turn her face from him. She didn't want to see the look that had flooded into his eyes. His fingers tightened around the hand he held.

"Do you have to?" he asked.

Kendra turned to him again and nodded slowly. "I have to," she replied, her voice deep with emotion. "I have to. He needs me. Nonie needs me. I have to—to tell them—about God. That I've found the answer."

His voice brightened. "Then you'll be back?"

Kendra looked up at him, then lowered her gaze. She shook her head slowly. "No. No, I'll not be back. Papa Mac needs me."

Silence hung heavily about them. Kendra felt chilled—isolated.

"Could—might we write?" asked Reynard, his voice husky with emotion.

Kendra raised her eyes to his. She shook her head slowly.

"I—I don't think it would be—wise," she managed in little more than a whisper as she pulled her hand out of his. "It—would only make it—harder."

———

Kendra had expected her trip back to the wilderness to be one that filled her heart with joy. It would be so good to see her grandfather. Wonderful to visit Nonie again. A treat to be welcomed by Oscar. But there was little joy in Kendra's heart as she packed her small cases, crated her acquired belongings, and boarded the boat for the first leg of the journey.

Had she done the right thing? Would she one day be sorry? Would it be purely selfish for her to stay?

She thought again of her grandfather—and of Nonie. Of their need to learn of the God Kendra had come to love. But couldn't she just tell them and then return to the city? Back to Reynard? Kendra longed with all of her being to come back.

"No. No," she told her weeping heart. "I can't. I just can't leave Papa Mac all alone again."

Chapter Twenty-four

Change of Plans

"It won't be long now, Oscar," said George. The dog team was gathered on the shore to wait for the incoming wagon bringing supplies to the post. And along with the supplies, Kendra was coming home. George had debated about bringing the canoe to transport Kendra back to their little cabin. It would have been much faster. But he had harnessed Kendra's dog team to the wagon-sled with Oscar in the lead and taken the overland trail. He knew the big dog would be almost as glad to see Kendra again as he himself.

So they stood together and waited, the dust in the distance announcing the coming of the supply wagon. She was almost home.

"It's been a long winter, hasn't it, boy?" George spoke further to the dog, his fingers curling in the long silky neck hair of the animal, then twining around and uncurling again. "Long—and miserable. But that's over now. She's almost home."

Oscar responded with a whine, his tail scattering dry leaves as it swept the ground and he looked up into the face of the tall bearded man who towered above him.

"You know—I think you sense that something is about to happen. Something out of the ordinary."

Oscar whined again.

The wagon drew closer. George squinted his eyes and

213

tried to pick out Kendra. There was a blur of color on the wagon. The freight hauler had more than one passenger.

"Sure hope she's on there," he mused more to himself than the dog.

But with a quick move, Oscar jerked from his hand and ran excitedly toward the approaching wagon.

"Oscar!" called George. "Oscar!" But the dog paid no attention.

George heard a frequent sharp yip as the dog closed the distance to the approaching team.

"Sure hope he don't go and spook those horses," George muttered as he followed absently after the dog. "Well—one thing's for sure. She's on there."

Just as George spoke the words a figure disengaged herself from the wagon and dropped to the ground, then fell to her knees. Kendra reached out her arms just as Oscar flung himself at her, nearly knocking her over. George watched as the two of them rocked back and forth, Kendra hugging and Oscar licking and wagging until he nearly exhausted both of them. George swallowed and reached up to wipe unwanted moisture from his eyes. Perhaps the brilliant summer sun was just too bright.

Kendra walked about the familiar cabin, letting her hand run over the rough boards that formed the sparse furniture. She had never realized before just how plain, how bare it was. But it was home, and she was glad to be there. She looked at the pile of crates and cases her grandfather had stacked in the corner of her bedroom, then lifted the topmost box.

"If I hurry I can get it all unpacked before I have to get supper," she told herself and started at the task. She nearly tripped over Oscar who refused to let her out of his sight. She reached down to give his head an affectionate pat.

"There's someone I sure would have liked you to meet," she murmured to the big dog, and then sighed. In spite of her joy at being home again, there was the shadow of leaving someone behind who might have become very important in her life.

———

Kendra did not wait to talk about her new faith. She brought up the subject with her grandfather that very night as they sat together after they had shared their simple meal.

"I found what I was looking for, Papa Mac," she said and noticed that he seemed to draw back.

"I'm glad," he responded carefully, and he sounded sincere.

"There really is a God," went on Kendra. "But He is so much more than just an—an unknown Someone out there someplace. He is real and He is personal and He gave us His Word, the Bible, so that we might understand all about Him."

Her grandfather nodded.

"But we—all of us—have cut ourselves off from Him. Because of sin—because of sinful, selfish choices we make.

George stirred in his chair.

"God said that if Adam and Eve, the first people, sinned they would die. But they chose to sin anyway." Kendra shook her head. It was almost beyond her comprehension that those two created beings could go ahead and do such a thing when it had been forbidden by God himself.

"The only way God could restore the relationship and have the penalty paid for people's sin was to send a substitute—a sacrifice. His Son, Jesus."

George shifted again. "Really, Kendra—" he began, but Kendra wasn't finished.

"He died for us—in our place. But that's not—not quite enough," Kendra hurried on. She wanted to be sure her grandfather had the complete picture before they stopped to discuss her newfound truth.

"We can—"

This time George did stop her. He held up his hand, his signal for silence. Even the dogs did not dare to bark or whine when George McMannus held up his hand in such a fashion.

Kendra silenced, but her eyes were pleading with the big man who sat before her.

"I think we need an understanding here," said George slowly. "I have let you speak your piece. I am glad you've found—what you were looking for. Some people—well, they seem to need—religion."

Kendra opened her mouth. The words wished to gush forth. She hadn't needed religion. She needed God. She needed a Savior. Everyone did. But George lifted his hand again and Kendra's mouth closed.

"Now—I grant you that right," went on George. "Heaven only knows you have had precious little to cling to in your short lifetime. I grant you that right. But—"

George stopped and ran his fingers through his graying beard. "I don't, Kendra. I'm—I'm just fine the way I am. I'm not *seeking*. I'm not restless. My soul isn't looking for answers."

He stopped again and looked at the young girl.

"Do you understand? Do I make myself clear?"

Kendra nodded, swallowed hard, and blinked back tears. Then she nodded again and lowered her gaze.

"Good," said the man, and he rose from the table to his full height. "Now, let's have no more of this serious talk. I want to hear all about your year of university. Come—leave the dishes. Pull your chair up to the fire and let's visit."

Kendra picked up her chair and crossed the short distance to the fireplace. George pulled his chair up beside her, and Oscar crowded in between the two.

George reached down a hand and stroked the big dog.

"We've missed you so much," he admitted. "Oscar and I— we been 'bout to drive each other crazy. It's good to have you back, girl. Mighty good to have you back."

When Kendra lay in her bed that night, her grandfather's soft snoring reaching her from the room beyond and Oscar curled up close beside her bed on the bearskin rug, she thought again of the earlier conversation. Large tears formed in her eyes and trickled down to her pillow. She had hoped so much that her grandfather would respond to her words. Had prayed for so many months that she would be able to say the right thing—in the right way. But it hadn't turned out that way. Not at all.

"Perhaps it will take time," she whispered to herself in the darkness. "I must be patient—and obedient—and show him—prove to him that it's real."

But Kendra still felt sorrow. She was concerned about her grandfather. What if something happened to him before she had a chance to live her new life before him, before he had opportunity to see that faith in God was real—and obtainable?

———

Early the next morning Kendra and Oscar headed out for the little settlement. She had to see Nonie. All the way along the trail that led through the tall pines and spruce, Kendra prayed.

"Help me to be wiser with Nonie, Father," she kept praying. "Help me to say things so she will understand. So she will accept."

When she reached Nonie's small cabin, she opened the door and called out as she always did. There was a stirring in the far corner where the furs were piled to form a bed.

"Amo-chika?" called Nonie in a weak voice.

"Yes—it's me," replied Kendra and hurried to the elderly woman.

Kendra fell on her knees beside the bed and wrapped her arms around Nonie's frail body.

Nonie reached with a trembling hand and felt the girl's face, her hair. Kendra realized with a painful wrench in her heart that the old woman no longer could see.

"Oh, Nonie," she cried, "I am so glad to see you."

Nonie answered with words of her own tongue—soft,

clucking, contented words that reminded Kendra of a hen gathering her chicks to the safety of her wings.

"You're back," Nonie said in English.

"I'm back," said Kendra.

"When you go again?" asked the old woman.

"No. I'm not going again," said Kendra firmly. "Papa Mac needs me here."

Nonie said nothing. The sightless eyes turned toward the smoked wooden ceiling. She uttered more words in her own tongue.

"Nonie," said Kendra, sitting back on her heels and taking the old familiar hands in her own, "I made the most amazing discovery when I was gone. All those stories you told me—about how the world was made—about the spirits—the good ones who help us and the evil ones that try to harm us—well, it's true. I mean—there really are good and evil spirits."

Nonie nodded silently. It was not news to her.

"But there is only *one* God," went on Kendra. "One God who made everything. And Mother Earth, she didn't make us. *God* did. He made the earth too. Everything. He is the one and only God. There aren't gods in the rocks or gods in the hills or gods in the bear or mountain lion."

Nonie looked frightened by Kendra's bold words. Would the girl call down the wrath of angry spirits?

But Kendra went on with confidence. "There is only *one* God—and He loves us. He is so filled with love for us that we never have to live in fear. We can love Him in return. You see, He made us."

"White man's god," said Nonie.

"No. No—*not* the white man's God. *Everyone's* God. He made all mankind. He placed them in a beautiful garden and told them not to eat of the tree that was planted there. But they did not listen. They deliberately—" Kendra stopped. What was a word that Nonie might understand? "They set their hearts to disobey," went on Kendra, her voice intense with emotion. "They would not listen to His voice. They shut their ears. Turned their faces."

Nonie stirred on her pallet.

"But God still loved them. He had said that the punishment for sin—for not obeying His word—would be death. Mankind would die—apart from God. They could not go to the new home—new forest He made for them. They would need to go to a terrible place—where all was pain and deep sorrow.

"God could not go back on His word. He had given His pledge—extended His hand. But because He still loved the people He had made—He had a plan. He sent His own Son—His only Son—and *He* died in place of the whole human race—white people *and* Indians. Took the—the curse on himself." She paused for a moment and took the old woman's face in her hands.

"It's true, Nonie. It's all in the Bible—the big Book. We can know this God. This *only* God. We never need to be afraid of all the evil spirits. God is greater. He is—His medicine is stronger. Much stronger. All we need to do is to believe in Him. To accept His great plan for us and ask Him to take away all the—the evil from our hearts. Oh, Nonie"—Kendra was in tears—"don't you see? A religion without a Savior is just not good enough. Jesus is the Savior—the only Savior—for us all. We can't do anything about our sinful hearts by ourselves—no matter how hard we try. But He can—and He will."

The woman had quietly listened to all that Kendra said. Her eyes gazed into emptiness. Kendra put one arm again around the frail body, the fingers of her other hand brushing lightly against Nonie's cheek.

"It's true, Nonie," Kendra said again, unmindful of the tears that ran down her cheeks.

Nonie shook her head slowly. Sadness seemed to pour from her very soul.

"White man's god," she said again.

"No, Nonie. *Your* God. *Everyone's* God," insisted Kendra.

"Too late," said Nonie, and she lifted weary and frail shoulders in a slight shrug.

"No. It's *not* too late. It's not. You can ask Him to forgive you right now. You can believe, right now. It's *not* too late."

Nonie shifted her slight weight. Kendra eased back gently and Nonie seemed to sink deeper into the furs that formed her bed.

"Too late," said Nonie again with resignation. "I live with Indian gods. I die with Indian gods. Too late."

"But, Nonie, you—"

"You go now," spoke the feeble lips. "Come tomorrow."

Kendra hated to leave. She knew the old woman had very little strength left. How much longer might she be with them? Would she listen to Kendra's plea on another day?

Kendra knelt in silence.

"You go now," Nonie repeated.

Tears again squeezed from Kendra's eyes and rolled slowly down her cheeks.

"You'll—you'll think about what I have said?" she asked the elderly woman, patting her hand.

Silence.

"Will you?" persisted Kendra.

"Make Amo-chika happy?"

"Yes—yes, it will make me *very* happy if you'll just think about it. Think carefully about what I have said."

Nonie nodded.

"Then, I think," she said solemnly.

It was the best Kendra could do. She slowly rose to her feet and left the cabin, Indian fashion, without a backward glance.

———

An Indian boy brought the news the next morning. Nonie had died sometime during the night.

George and Kendra would not be expected to attend the burial. The Indians would conduct the ceremony in their own way. Kendra mourned alone by her beloved stream. In the distance she could hear the beating of the funeral drums, too far away to hear the accompanying dirge that would be the death chant. Kendra wept bitterly. She had failed. She had come home too late. In the short time, she had not been able to make Nonie understand. She had been unable to effectively share her faith with the two people she loved the most. Nonie was gone. Her grandfather had forbidden her to speak. She might just as well have stayed in the city. She might just as well have encouraged the courtship of Reynard. For the first time since she had wept on the graves of her parents as a frightened and lonely child, she cried until she had no more tears.

———

George knew the death of Nonie was hard on his Kendra. He watched her as she moved about the cabin or tended the small vegetable garden or took her basket and headed for the woods, Oscar at her heels.

She was in deep mourning, and he did not know how to help her—what to say. He didn't know if he should draw out her feelings or let her deal with them in her own way, in her own time.

At last he could stand the sorrow-filled eyes no longer. She was sitting on the small bench at the front of the cabin where she often spent her evenings listening to the sounds of the closing day and drinking in the peace that seemed to seep from the twilight. George sat down beside her and spoke of Nonie's death for the first time.

"I know it has been terribly hard on you to lose Nonie," he began.

Kendra could not answer. Her tears were falling again.

"I'm—I'm sorry," he continued. "Truly sorry that you— that you have to face another sorrow. Another death."

"It wasn't just her death," Kendra said in a trembling voice.

"Not her death?"

"Not really. It was—it was just that she—she wasn't ready to die."

The words tore again at Kendra's heart.

"I—don't think I understand," said her grandfather.

"I—I went to see Nonie. To tell her about God. To tell her that she could—could have her sins forgiven—could know God as her—Savior," sobbed Kendra. She was sobbing openly now.

"You wanted to change her religion?" he asked softly, but there was a hint of accusation in his words.

Kendra's head came up. "I wanted to share with her the Truth," she said frankly, and he could see the fervor in her eyes. She really believed in what she had embraced.

There was silence. George shifted a bit. At last he spoke again.

"She didn't want to listen?"

"Oh—she listened. She let me say—say it all—but then she said—she said He is the white man's God. I couldn't make her—understand that He isn't. That He made all mankind. That He loves us all."

"I see," said George.

There was silence.

"Did she send you away?"

"She was very weak—and tired. She said for me to go and come again the next day."

"So she wasn't angry with you?"

"I—I don't think so. She called me—Amo-chika—just like she did when I was little. Remember? She said—she'd—she'd think about what I said if it would make me happy."

"She said that?"

Kendra nodded.

They sat in silence, each deep in thought. George spoke first.

"Then, she did that," he said simply.

Kendra looked up at her grandfather, not understanding his words.

"If Nonie gave her word, she also fulfilled it," said George.

"You mean—?"

George hesitated, then said, "If she was still able to—to think—straight—then Nonie pondered your words. Now I don't know if—if she believed them. But she thought about them."

"Oh, God." The words escaped from Kendra's lips without her being aware of them. It was a prayer. It was an earnest plea. It was a bit of heartfelt praise. Just two simple words, but her whole heart was wrapped up in them.

What if Nonie had thought on her words? What if she had actually understood them? *What if she had believed?* "Father, I leave Nonie's soul in your hands," she whispered.

At least in some measure, things returned to a normal summer routine. George went about his daily tasks and Kendra quickly seemed to slip back into the role she had left when she went away to university. But there was a difference somehow. Kendra's faith set her apart. She had a confidence, a peace, even as she moved about the cabin. George often heard her humming little snatches of song, and he had the feeling that she was in her room reading her Bible or praying in the early mornings or late evenings. He didn't know how he knew—he didn't actually see her—but he felt it.

Another fall came and went and soon winter was with them again, wrapping them in its chilling arms with falling snow. Kendra harnessed the dogs and put out her traps. She did not take pleasure in the death of the animals, but she and her grandfather were trappers and they had to make a living.

After the long winter, Kendra was glad to see another spring breathe through. As Easter drew near her thoughts were more and more on the wonder of it all—God's creation, His redemption for that creation. It was a joyous time. She recalled the previous Easter and her time spent with the Preston family. In spite of the happiness within her soul, she felt a tug of sorrow—of loneliness. Things might have been so different had she not been needed by her grandfather— by Nonie.

But Kendra breathed a little prayer, leaving her life and her future in the hands of the God she had learned to trust. He knew what was best. She could trust Him.

———

"Where is he?" Kendra said aloud for the umpteenth time.

She paced the floor again and looked out the window. It was already getting dark. Her grandfather should have been home from the woods long ago. He always came home long before sundown from logging out firewood.

Kendra went to the door and stood listening to the sounds of the approaching night. In the distance a wolf howled, and Kendra saw the hackles on Oscar's neck rise in response. She placed a hand on the dog's head without thinking, her eyes still hopefully straining to make out an approaching form in the darkness.

Then she returned to the kitchen, picked up a lantern, and drew a few matches from the can near the stove. She shrugged into her light jacket, slipped her knife into the side of her moccasin, and turned to Oscar.

"Let's go," she said to the dog. "We've got to find him."

She moved quickly through the forest with the lantern unlit until the darkness closed in around them. Then she stopped, drew a match from where she had tucked it in her sash and lit it.

Without a word to the dog at her side she hurried on. They both knew the trail to the fallen timber where her grandfather had been working. Oscar walked in step beside her, his ears forward, his eyes alert. Once or twice Kendra felt him tense and knew that some animal was near them in the heavy forest growth. With Oscar at her side, she didn't feel any concern.

By the time they reached the deadfall, it was completely dark. Kendra could only see within the brief circle of light cast by the lantern. She depended on Oscar's sharp nose and basic instincts to help find her grandfather.

"Find him, Oscar," she told the dog.

The dog moved forward, head up, nostrils pointed into the wind. Now and then he whined, but he did not stop nor look at Kendra, so she knew he had not yet picked up a scent.

"Papa Mac! Papa Mac!" she shouted every now and then as they wound their way through the fallen trees and discarded branches.

She was about to give up when Oscar stopped with his head turned, his whole body tensed.

"What is it?" Kendra asked, moving forward to place her hand on the dog's neck.

A whine escaped Oscar's throat. He turned and looked at her. Then whined again.

"Go ahead," she told him. "Find him."

The dog moved forward and Kendra followed closely. "Papa Mac!" she cried out again. "Papa Mac, where are you?"

A faint reply returned to her, borne on the sporadic breeze.

Both girl and dog surged forward.

They found him pinned by a log he had been working to cut free from a tangle of fallen trees. Kendra put the lantern on a nearby stump and quickly set to work with the handsaw, saying encouraging things to the man as she worked. "I'll have you out of here in no time," she told him. But the trunk was thick and Kendra was perspiring from hard work and nerves by the time she finished the task. She had to saw through the trunk again in order to get the log to a size she could move by herself. The minutes seemed to expand into hours before she was able to lay aside the saw and put all her remaining energy to moving the heavy section of log.

At last she managed to pull it off her grandfather and let it drop with a crash among other forest debris. She was panting heavily. George lay quietly, and Oscar's tongue reached now and then to lick the sweat from the man's brow.

When Kendra felt she could breathe again, she rose to her feet and picked up the lantern.

"You should be able to get up now," she gasped out. "Your leg is free."

Her grandfather did not move.

"Papa Mac," prompted Kendra, turning the lantern so she could she his face. It was white with pain. Kendra dropped on her knees beside him.

"I—I can't—get up," he managed to say. "The—leg—it's—" He could say no more.

Kendra crawled along his body until she reached the leg that had been under the log. She lifted the lantern and was relieved to see no blood. Then she noted the odd way the limb was lying. "I'll get the team," she said.

"You—you can't," groaned her grandfather.

"With the wagon-sled," went on Kendra. "I'll bring the wagon-sled."

He shook his head. "You'll never—get it anywhere near here—with all the tangle," he gasped through stiff lips.

Kendra looked around her. He was right. She'd never be able to bring anything into this part of the forest. Dead trees fell in every direction, mingling with others in a wild tangle of limbs and branches.

She felt panic. What was she to do?

Quickly she made herself think through her options. She couldn't leave him where he was. But she couldn't move him very far. She only had Oscar to help her, and he didn't even have a harness.

"I'll make you a bed—of spruce boughs," she began. She had to begin somewhere. She had to do something. "Then I'll—I'll start a fire. That will keep us until morning. Then—then I'll figure out a way to get you back to the cabin."

With the axe her grandfather had brought with him, she set to work cutting branches from the spruce and interwove them until she had formed a bed close beside him that was softer and warmer than the ground. Carefully she dragged and pushed her grandfather until she had him eased onto it. Then she began to clear and scrape away a spot to build a fire. She had to make it as close to her grandfather as she could, but she could not take a chance on setting ablaze any of the dry, tangled underbrush about them.

When she had all the loose boughs out of the way, she dug down with her knife until she reached cold, damp ground. This would make a safe base for the fire.

Carefully she gathered small sticks and dried grasses and drew another precious match from her sash.

In a few moments her little fire was blazing. Kendra noticed her grandfather extend his hand toward the flame, flexing his fingers. In spite of the fact that it was midsummer, the nights were cold.

"You make a good fire," he said calmly, as though they were camping out.

Kendra smiled. "I know," she replied. "My grandfather taught me. He said, 'Make a little fire. One that you can sit close to. White men make a big fire. Have to sit way back—and freeze. Indians make a little fire. Can cuddle up close—and keep warm.' My grandfather is a wise man."

In spite of his pain, George chuckled.

"Now I'm going to leave you—for a while," Kendra went on.

"What are you going to do?"

"I've piled up enough wood, right there to your left, so that you can keep the fire going. I'm going to the cabin. Get some supplies. I'll get some blankets and food and Oscar's harness and some hides and be back soon. Come morning we'll make a travois. We'll get you out of here. I'll be back as soon as I can. Oscar will stay with you."

"You're going alone?" asked George.

"I have my knife," replied Kendra with more confidence than she felt.

"Take Oscar. I'm fine. I have the fire."

"I'll feel better if you have Oscar too," Kendra insisted calmly. "I'll have the lantern."

Nearby an owl hooted.

"I heard that fellow before," George said, his voice low. "I thought—I thought for a while there he was calling my name."

Kendra's head came up sharply. "Nonsense," she said quickly. "You are going to be just fine. Once we get you home—get that leg patched up."

"Maybe," he answered softly. "Maybe."

"I'll hurry," said Kendra. "I'll be back just as quickly as I can."

She turned to go.

"Kendra."

His call stopped her. She turned to him, lifting high the lantern so she could see his face.

"I—I really did think that—that maybe this was *it*. Oh, not because of the—the Indian legend about the owl—but because—because of the pain—the fact I couldn't move."

Kendra felt horror wash all through her. She knew now his leg had been hurt badly. That it was likely broken in more than one place. But she didn't expect him to die. Surely, not—that.

"Kendra," he said again, and she heard his voice tremble.

"I—I didn't know if—if I'd make it—if you'd find me—in time—but—but I thought about what you said. I thought a lot about it. I did it. I—I prayed. I—asked for His help. His forgiveness. You were right. He really is there."

With a cry Kendra fell on her knees beside her grandfather and let the tears fall on his plaid woollen shirt.

He stroked her hair and whispered softly to her.

"It's all right. Even if—even if I don't make it. Even if— It's okay. I'm ready now. I'm ready. Honest."

Chapter Twenty-five

A Heart at Rest

"Do you mind—very much—leaving the wilderness?" George asked his granddaughter.

They were on the boat, all their belongings stacked around them. They both knew they had said a final goodbye to the little cabin they had called home for so many years. They had not brought much with them. There really hadn't been that much. Their personal items, Kendra's pile of books—and Oscar. Kendra could not bear to give up Oscar. All the other sled dogs had been sold—bartered off—to the trader at the post. The traps and skinning knives and snowshoes and sleds, the crude cabin furniture, garden tools and axes—it all had been sold to various trappers in the area, the canoe given to an Indian boy from the settlement. Gone. It was all gone now. A total way of living. A total life.

Kendra sighed deeply. She had loved the wilderness. She had loved it all. She had been happy there, communing with the God of nature. Her God—once she had discovered who He was. But she did not say the words. There was no turning back. She managed a smile.

"We need to get that leg of yours taken care of," she said simply.

She watched his hand stroke absentmindedly at his beard.

Both of them busy with their own thoughts, they sat in

silence, their eyes on the moving treeline along the riverbank.

George broke the spell. "I've really been a pesky nuisance, haven't I?"

"A nuisance? Of course not," Kendra was quick to declare.

Her mind went back to the time of the accident. How
frightened she had been when she knew how badly hurt he
was. She feared that she would never be able to get her
grandfather out of the tangled bush with only Oscar and the
makeshift travois to help her. But she had done it. She had
given him some of Nonie's special root medicine. It had killed
the pain some so he could endure the bumpy journey back to
the cabin. But the ride had been hard on the badly broken
leg. Kendra was afraid it might have been further damaged
in the transport.

It was healing now—to a measure. At least he was no
longer in constant pain. At least he could move about on it—
in a way. But they both soon had come to the realization that
he would never be able to run the trapline again. Kendra
offered to take over for him, but he refused to hear of it. There
seemed to be only one thing to do. To sell what they had and
move out.

A movement on the shore drew Kendra's attention. She
saw Oscar's head come up, his ears perk forward. She
reached for him and laughed softly.

"You see that moose? I suppose you'd just love to have a
merry chase," she teased her dog. She rubbed his ear and the
deep rumble in his chest subsided. It was going to be very
different for Oscar in the city. For a fleeting moment Kendra
wondered if she had done the right thing to bring the animal
from his wilderness home. All three of them were facing ma-
jor adjustments.

———

They moved into a small house just down the street from
Maggie. Even before they were settled, Kendra made arrangements for George to see a city physician. His prognosis

was not good. There might be a bit that could be done for George's leg, but it would never be restored to full use.

"You are lucky to have it at all. I'm surprised it healed as well as it did. Must have been five or six breaks there. You were lucky. Just plain lucky."

"I had a good nurse," said George. Then he added thoughtfully, "And a wonderful God."

The doctor just shook his head as though he still couldn't understand.

Kendra worried. Her grandfather was too young, too energetic, to be confined to a small house on a city lot. Would he be able to manage the enormous changes?

———

Kendra finally found a job doing housework for a wealthy family. It did not pay especially well, but it gave her a steady income and that was all they really needed.

George took over the household duties. Kendra was surprised at how easily he seemed to assume the role. But then he had been a bachelor for many years, she reasoned.

He also spent a good deal of time at Maggie's, puttering around her yard, working her garden, repairing anything that was broken.

The two old friends shared cups of coffee on the wide veranda and chatted over years that used to be. George took advantage of opportunities that arose to talk with Maggie about his newfound faith. Soon she was joining him and Kendra for the short walk to the little church each Sunday morning. The two prayed with more intensity, hoping that it would not be long until Maggie made her own commitment to the Lord.

———

"Kendra!"

At the sound of her name Kendra wheeled around. It sounded like—yes, it was!

"Amy!" she cried in return and the two friends ran to throw their arms excitedly around each other.

"What are you doing here?" they asked in unison. They both laughed.

"I think we need to sit down and have a good talk," Amy prompted. "Do you have time for a cup of tea?"

"I'd love to," replied Kendra, and they hastened to the nearby small cafe, chattering as they went.

"I'm teaching here in town," explained Amy. "Oh, so much has happened since I saw you last. I'm engaged. To a wonderful man. We're to be married in September."

"Wonderful!" exclaimed Kendra.

"Now that you're back—you can be my maid of honor. Oh, will you? Please—don't run off on me again."

Kendra laughed. "I'll not be running anywhere," she said. "Papa Mac broke his leg—badly. He won't be able to work the trapline anymore."

"Oh, I'm sorry. Where is he?"

"Here—in the city."

"Can't the doctors—?"

"No," said Kendra, shaking her head. "But—it's really not so bad. He's adjusted far better than I hoped. He has the house—and his puttering—and Aunt Maggie."

They found a table and sat down.

"Now," said Amy, "I want to hear all about what has happened since I saw you last. Then it's my turn."

They both laughed again. It was so good to be back together.

But what Kendra really wanted to know—what she could hardly wait to hear—was about Reynard. If Reynard was still single—or if he had found himself a girl—maybe even a wife.

———

"You look beautiful," said Kendra, and she leaned over to kiss her friend on the cheek.

Amy did look beautiful, absolutely glowing. Kendra had

never attended a wedding, and Amy was the first bride she had ever seen, and the sight nearly took her breath away.

Kendra seemed to fit right back into the Preston family when she went out to the farm for the wedding. She was amazed at how much the younger siblings had grown when she saw them all the evening before at the rehearsal. Thomas was as tall as his father. A big boy, sturdy and strong with an easy grin and an interest in anything that might qualify as a sport. Carry was slim and pretty and yes, very aware of male attention, just as Reynard had said. Nell was more subdued than she had been as a bouncy, energetic eight-year-old. But she was just as loving, and Kendra often felt the young girl close beside her, seeming to wordlessly ask for an arm to draw her close.

Reynard—was *not* married. Kendra's heart had skipped when she heard the news. Still, she knew that she had no claim on Reynard, even if she did have deep feelings for him. They had exchanged no promises, made no commitments. She did not know if Reynard still cared at all for her—in that fashion. In fact, she had no assurance that he had ever cared—in that way—unless his look, his manner were assurance. Or the pressure of his hand on hers. Kendra clung to a hope. A dream.

She turned her attention back to Amy, Amy the bride.

"Walt is a blessed man," she said with sincerity.

Amy smiled. "Oh, Kendra—I'm so happy—I could just burst."

She gave Kendra an impetuous squeeze.

"I—I just hope that you—that you will one day feel—just as I feel," enthused Amy. "In love. Blissfully happy. So—so loved and blessed."

Kendra blinked back tears. She wasn't sure why she suddenly felt like weeping. She was experiencing too many emotions, all wanting expression.

———

"Would you care to take a little walk?"

Reynard whispered the words very close to Kendra's ear. The wedding was over. The bride and groom had left in a flurry of goodbyes, beaming first at each other, then at the family and guests who were to be left behind. Now the guests, too, had departed and Kendra was helping gather the wedding gifts and pack them into boxes. She looked up at Reynard and nodded.

"I suppose—"

"Those will be looked after," he assured her.

Kendra smiled. "That's easy for you to say," she teased.

"Promise. I'll help you when we get back—if they aren't already boxed up."

It was a warm evening. There was no need for Kendra to get a shawl. They left the church together and strolled slowly down the lane that led them away from the small church building.

"You had me very worried," said Reynard softly.

Kendra looked up to meet his serious eyes.

"I was afraid I might never see you again."

Kendra lowered her glance. "I—I had—had thought the same," she admitted.

Reynard reached for her hand and Kendra interlaced her fingers with his.

"I've—thought about you, Kendra," he continued.

Kendra was unable to respond.

"And I've prayed." Silence followed. Then he chuckled softly. "How I've prayed." He laughed again. "Did you feel prayed for?" he asked her quietly.

Kendra lifted her eyes again. "I—I felt—at peace," she answered honestly. "Strangely at peace. I—I—"

Kendra wished to tell him how much she had missed him. How distraught she felt at the thought she would never see him again. But she wasn't able to say the words. Instead, she answered quietly, "In spite of my circumstances—I felt that—that God would work it all out—in the right way for—for all of us."

His fingers tightened on hers.

"So He brought you back."

Kendra nodded. "He—He brought me back. Not—not in the way I had—had hoped. I mean, I certainly would not have asked that Papa Mac be—be—"

"Of course not. But his accident *did* make him think about God—about his salvation," Reynard reminded her.

Kendra nodded. She still could not think about that without tears of joy.

"So—I guess lots of good came of that accident—for many of us," he continued.

He stopped and turned to her.

"Kendra," he said softly. "You must know how—how I feel about you. Would it—would it be presumptuous of me to ask if—if I might call. I know that it won't be—quite as I would like—me being here and you in the city. But I could come as often as possible on weekends—and we could write. It would be okay now—wouldn't it?"

He went on before Kendra could give her answer. "I know that—that it isn't the way a young lady might wish to be courted—but—but—"

Kendra lifted a hand and rested it against his chest. He seemed so apologetic—so troubled by their situation. She did not wish him to think she felt cheated by their awkward arrangement.

But she didn't know quite what to say—or how to say it.

The silence seemed to stretch out between them.

"That is—if you feel the way I do," Reynard said at last.

Kendra could not look up into those intense brown eyes. She was afraid they would look into her very soul and discover the love that filled her being.

He reached for the hand and drew her a bit closer.

"Do you, Kendra?" he asked softly, placing a finger under her chin, lifting her face so she had to meet his eyes. She remembered the other time, long ago, when he had done the same thing. She had been enamored with him then. She loved him deeply now.

"Kendra—I've prayed so much—about us. About what God might have in mind—for our future. All I ask—all I dare to ask is that you—grant me the opportunity to—to try to show you—how much I care."

Kendra nodded mutely.

He smiled then, one of relief. "I'll come to see you as often as I can. I promise. I'll try to make it next weekend."

Kendra still could not speak. She was too overcome with emotion. She had prayed too. When things had looked so—so impossible. When she could only place her life in the hands of God and ask that His will be done. When it seemed that she might never see Reynard Preston again. But now— But she couldn't bring herself to tell him all that. Not now. Not yet.

———

He did come. That very next weekend. And as often as he could over the months that followed. George McMannus soon came to recognize the sound of Reynard's eager steps on the broad sidewalk. Even Oscar would lift his head from the mat where he rested and cock his ears forward. Then he would turn to look for Kendra, who always seemed in such a hurry to get to the door.

———

"Kendra's in the house."

George McMannus straightened up from the rose he was pruning and looked at the young man who stood before him, his hat held in nervous hands.

"I—I know, sir. At least—that's what I was counting on."

Surprise showed in the older man's eyes.

"I—I wished to see you, sir," went on Reynard, his eyes lifting from his hat.

"Me?" Oscar moved from the shade of the tree where he had been watching the proceedings and pushed against the younger man for a bit of attention. Reynard reached a hand down absentmindedly and rumpled the dog's ear. Oscar pressed more closely against him.

"Well," said George, "let's get in out of the sun."

He turned to lead the way to the back door.

"I—I would like to talk to you here—first," Reynard said. Then added quickly. "If you don't mind."

George stopped and turned, eyes narrowed, as though trying hard to see through the young man before him to study his very thoughts.

He waved a hand at the bench that stood beneath a large poplar and Reynard moved toward it.

Reynard did not make George wait. He lifted his head, took a deep breath, and hurriedly began. "I'm—sure you must know how I feel about Kendra."

George nodded.

"I—I wish to marry her, sir."

He stopped and toyed with his hat. George watched him, sensing his nervousness and feeling empathy, yet at the same time aware of some discomfort of his own. He had known this would come. He couldn't possibly keep her forever. Yet— He wished there were some way to put it off. To hold on to her for just a bit longer.

He drew in a big sigh, turning his gaze off somewhere in the distance, his left hand stroking his graying beard. He wasn't ready to answer—yet.

"I'm asking you, sir, for her hand in marriage."

At last George stirred himself. He turned to look at the eager, nervous young man. There was no one to whom he would sooner entrust his little girl.

"What does Kendra say?" he asked.

Reynard looked surprised. "Oh, I wouldn't ask Kendra before asking you, sir. I need your permission—for that."

George looked steadily at the young man. He nodded silently. "Then perhaps you should ask her—now—with my permission," he said, fighting to keep his voice even and controlled.

Without rising from his seat, he turned toward the house.

"Kendra," he called, and Kendra answered through the open window.

"Can you join us?"

When she came from the house, Kendra was surprised to see Reynard. She hesitated, reaching down to nervously toy with the hem of her apron.

Reynard stood to his feet, his eyes on Kendra's face. George waited a moment, then said, "This young man has just asked for your hand in marriage." Both men heard the sharp intake of Kendra's breath.

Silence followed while Kendra cast a glance toward Reynard. He looked at her pleadingly as he shifted nervously from one foot to the other.

"How do you feel about it?" asked George. "Do you wish to marry him?"

It seemed too blunt. So—so sudden. Kendra lowered her gaze, her hands still twisting in the apron.

"Well—?"

Kendra lifted her eyes and looked directly into those of the young man.

"Yes," she said, and her voice was strong. "Yes—I wish to marry him."

Reynard stepped quickly forward and reached for Kendra's shoulders.

"I guess it's settled then," said George. But no one seemed to be listening.

The two stood close to each other, their eyes exchanging promises of love. George knew he had been forgotten. He cleared his throat loudly and Reynard stirred, his cheeks coloring slightly.

"You'd better get that girl out of here and let her know how special she is," suggested George. "There are too many nosy neighbors for you to be saying it here in the garden."

"Thank you, sir," Reynard said, and his voice was filled with excitement. Confidence.

George watched them go. One hand reached down to stroke Oscar, who had moved to press up against his knee, the other reached toward his beard.

Though he fought against the tears, they could not be held in check. His little girl had left childhood behind and entered womanhood. He had known it would come. Should have been prepared, but it all seemed to have happened so quickly. Wasn't it only yesterday that he had stood in the garden of the Home, bracing himself for the meeting with a nearly four-year-old. Now—now—

He wiped carelessly at the tears with his flannel sleeve. If only—if only Mary could see her now. A beautiful young woman—vibrant—in love.

He had to let her go—with his blessing.

People Making A Difference

Family Bookshelf offers the finest in good wholesome Christian literature, written by best-selling authors. All books are recommended by an Advisory Board of distinguished writers and editors.

We are also a vital part of a compassionate outreach called **Bowery Mission Ministries**. Our evangelical mission is devoted to helping the destitute of the inner city.

Our ministries date back more than a century and began by aiding homeless men lost in alcoholism. Now we also offer hope and Gospel strength to homeless, inner-city women and children. Our goal, in fact, is to end homelessness by teaching these deprived people how to be independent with the Lord by their side.

Downtrodden, homeless men are fed and clothed and may enter a discipleship program of one-on-one professional counseling, nutrition therapy and Bible study. This same Christian care is provided at our women and children's shelter.

We also welcome nearly 1,000 underprivileged children each summer at our Mont Lawn Camp located in Pennsylvania's beautiful Poconos. Here, impoverished youngsters enjoy the serenity of nature and an opportunity to receive the teachings of Jesus Christ. We also provide year-round assistance through teen activities, tutoring in reading and writing, Bible study, family counseling, college scholarships and vocational training.

During the spring, fall and winter months, our children's camp becomes a lovely retreat for religious gatherings of up to 200. Excellent accommodations include heated cabins, chapel, country-style meals and recreational facilities. Write to Paradise Lake Retreat Center, Box 252, Bushkill, PA 18324 or call: (717) 588-6067.

Bowery Mission Ministries are supported by voluntary contributions of individuals and bequests. Contributions are tax deductible. Checks should be made payable to Bowery Mission.

 **Fully accredited Member
of the Evangelical Council
for Financial Accountability**

Every Monday morning, our ministries staff joins together in prayer. If you have a prayer request for yourself or a loved one, simply write to us.

 **Administrative Office:
40 Overlook Drive, Chappaqua,
New York 10514 Telephone: (914) 769-9000**